CAKE

The Newlyweds

J. BENGTSSON

CAKE: The Newlyweds

Published in the United States.
Edited by Dorothy Zemach
Book design by DJ Rogers Design

Printed in the United States.

ISBN-13: 978-1984924957
ISBN-10: 1984924958

DEDICATION

Dedicated to my wonderfully patient husband, Ben.

CHAPTER ONE

CASEY - PRESENT DAY

Don't Give Up On Me

"Jake! In the bedroom – now! I'm ovulating."

One Mississippi, two Mississippi… good lord, what was taking him so long? There was no way he hadn't heard me calling for his stud services. It's not like I expected him to be Michael Phelps fast, but a little hustle wouldn't have killed him. *Five Mississippi, six Mississippi*... This was getting ridiculous. A few months ago, had my husband gotten the call for sex, he'd have come running with a smile on his face and his pants already bunched around his ankles. Now, we were already on eight Mississippis and his naked butt still wasn't in my bed. I suppose now that lovemaking was on a timetable and colorful flow charts had become our only foreplay, his lack of enthusiasm was not without reason.

Finally, Jake's fine-looking frame filled the doorway. What was that – fifteen Mississippis? Definitely not his best effort.

Impatiently, I held up my ovulation journal and tapped on the cover. "You. Me. Sex. Baby."

He didn't take a step forward, nor did he look particularly eager to begin checking things off my list. Crossing his arms in front of him, Jake leaned his body lazily against the doorframe and humored me with one of his lop-sided grins. "Ooh, baby, talk dirty to me."

"Oh, you want dirty?" I asked seductively, walking across the bed on my knees. "I'll give you dirty. Menstrual cycle, fallopian tube, egg, sperm," I whispered in my sexiest voice. "Fertilization."

"Yeah…" Jake groaned, amusement playing out over his face. "Say the word… I know you want to."

"Vagiiiina." I made sure to elongate the word, all while adopting the sexiest lip pout known to man.

"There it is!" Jake clapped his approval. "Nothing like clinical baby making terms to get me going."

"Well, I know what you like. Now get over here, Hotstuff, and procreate with me. According to the ovulation chart, the optimal time for impregnation is now."

"Like *now*, now?"

"Yes, now." Hadn't I made my intentions perfectly clear when I'd hollered for his semen moments earlier? "Like *yesterday*, now."

"I thought you were kidding. You realize I'm taking the stage in an hour, right?"

"That's not a problem. I can have you out of here in a couple of minutes."

"A couple of minutes? Wow, that sounds really hot, babe."

The smile faded from my face. Fun and games were over. It was time to get down to business. "I'm serious, Jake. This is important to me… and I thought it was to you too."

Pushing off the door, Jake straightened his back, and I could almost see the process by which his body coiled into a tight ball of tension. "It is."

No, actually, it wasn't. Having a baby was the last thing he wanted. I'd known that all along but, due to recent circumstances, what he wanted and what I needed had become two wildly different things. In the end, he'd simply bowed to the pressure.

Jake, sensing the sudden change in mood, walked toward the bed with his arms reaching for me. I flung myself onto my back and rolled away.

"Don't be like that," he said.

"Like what?" I feigned ignorance. Of course, I knew what he was referring to, and that I was the unreasonable one, but that didn't make it any easier.

Jake watched me, no doubt uncertain where our conversation was headed, but worried enough to take it slow. "You know as well as I do that waiting three hours isn't going to make a difference."

"Maybe, maybe not; but what I do know is if we don't get pregnant this month, then I'm going to remember that you didn't want to do it at my exact moment of fertility, and it will be on your head."

Jake's eyes narrowed as irritation washed across his face. "Seriously? You're blackmailing me?"

"It's not blackmail…just a friendly warning."

"Huh, 'cuz there was nothing friendly about it."

It was as if the words he spoke slapped the sense back into me. Jake was right: there was nothing friendly about my behavior at all. I was nothing more than a baby-making bully. What the hell was I doing? Was my judgment so clouded that I would risk losing my husband to fill the gaping, bleeding hole that had once been my heart? *Don't give up on me.* Tears swelled in my eyes. I didn't want to cry, but it was a process that couldn't be stopped. Crying had become part of who I was; and, I feared, who I'd always be.

As I did multiple times a day, I mourned for old Casey, the fun-loving girl who found joy in the simplest of things, the girl who would never consider blackmailing her husband into sex because, back then, all it would have taken to get his attention was a sexy, sideways glance. Oh, how I missed her!

Sorrow, I'd discovered, had a way of sapping the sexy clean out of a person. Now, on a daily basis, I felt like a blubbery, soggy slug slithering my way through life as I left a trail of slurpy tears in my wake.

Without my even realizing it, heavy droplets had begun falling from my eyes, making way for what was sure to be a spectacular water show. Not wanting to give Jake yet another front row seat to the festivities, I shakily rose from the bed and slunk from the room.

"Casey?" Jake called out, his own body slumped under the weight of my sadness. "Come on. Come back."

"No. Never mind." I blinked away the emotion that blurred my vision and headed for the exit of the tour bus.

Jake jogged up from behind and pried my fingers from the door handle. Gripping my shoulders, he turned me around slowly, pulling me into a hug so tight that I knew I couldn't fight my way out. Still, my body was unwilling, or perhaps it was just unable, to accept the comfort he was offering. *Don't give up on me.* I wanted his love but felt numb to it all. Unsurprisingly, Jake didn't back down, keeping me cocooned in safety until my shoulders finally wilted in response to his unyielding devotion and the dam gates opened. Wave after wave of sorrow poured from the core of my fractured heart.

"Shhh, I'm here. You're going to be okay. Just let it out." Jake carefully stroked the tangled strands of my hair as if I were a precious possession he was safeguarding. His loving touch only made me feel worse. My suffering affected him just as much as his earlier struggles had affected me.

Gripping his hand, I searched out his eyes and spoke with as much strength as I could muster. "I'm sorry. I'm trying to pull it together, I really am. I thought as time passed it would get easier, but it hasn't."

Jake tightened his hold on me. "It's been only a few months. No one is expecting you to suddenly feel better. This isn't something you get over, Casey, it's something you deal with in the long term. You've got to take it one day at a time."

Even though the day-by-day approach he was suggesting had, so far, gotten me nowhere, I nonetheless nodded my head. Of course I should pay more heed to Jake's advice, as he certainly knew a thing or two about coping; yet even his ability to survive unimaginable trauma was doing nothing to help my own handling of the situation. When it came right down to it, I wasn't Jake. I didn't have his inner strength, nor did I have his off-the-charts survival skills. I was inherently an emotional being, feeling everything to uncomfortable extremes. When I was happy and in love, the radiance shimmered off me like a disco ball at an 80's prom. But in my current state of disarray, it felt as if a light had been turned off somewhere inside, and I was casting shadows so wide that anyone in a hundred-mile radius was blanketed by my gloom.

As with all my crying marathons, the tears eventually dried up, but there was no need to worry about a drought. Within a few hours, the coffers would refill and once again be locked and loaded and ready to flow. When my stuttered breaths died down to hollowed hiccups, Jake broke from our hug and led me back into the bedroom. He gently lowered me onto the bed, and I sank onto its soft sheets, drained and disheartened. Taking his place beside me, Jake grasped my hand and placed it over his heart, a gesture that always calmed me.

Don't give up on me.

"Maybe you should stay in the bus for the show," he offered. "Get some sleep."

"No, I can't be in here alone. It's too quiet. I'll just start thinking."

"Lassen will be here."

"Lassen's a worthless lug," I said, my insult making me sound like an overindulged toddler.

"What's going on with the two of you lately? Yesterday he said you threw a plastic plate at him like a Frisbee."

"Yes, that's right. I almost got him, too."

A smile broke out over Jake's face. "Was there a specific reason, or were you just working on your target practice?"

"He acts like I've got the bubonic plague. Every time he sees me coming – tears or not – he gets all bug-eyed and pasty-faced. The other day he covered his nose and mouth with his shirt… hence the flying plastic disc."

"Okay, I get your frustration, but give the poor guy a break. You know he hates feelings, and right now, you're just a giant swirling hotpot of them. Just try to be nicer to him."

Placing the palms of my hands over my eyes, I groaned in a long, drawn out manner. The last thing I wanted was to give Lassen a break, but I also didn't want to put Jake between us. "Fine. I'll be nicer, but only for you."

"Thank you," Jake said, amused by the effort I was making on his behalf. "Oh, and while we're on the subject of Lassen, he has requested that you stop dumping your used Kleenex in his wastebasket. He wants me to tell you that it's disgusting and that it makes him want to vomit."

A wicked little smile chased away the frown. That was just the reaction I'd been going for.

Jake studied me a second before playfully poking me in the side. "I know you're doing it on purpose, Case, so you'd better wipe that smile off your face when Lassen's around."

He knew me too well. Messing with Lassen had become a full time job for me lately. He was always such a grump, and pushing his buttons took little to no effort at all. Sure, I could be nicer to Lassen, but plotting against him was really the only thing that kept me going these days. I laughed, allowing the lightness to ease my sadness.

"You're a brat," he said, grinning. "But at least you haven't lost that sense of humor of yours."

A lump formed in the back of my throat when I thought of the reason for its suppression. I burrowed in closer to his warm body feeling sudden remorse. "Jake?"

"Yeah?"

"I'm sorry for sexually harassing you."

He squeezed my hand. "It's okay. I didn't take it personally."

"You never do. How can you be so forgiving? I don't deserve it."

He turned to his side and propped himself up on one elbow. Jake's fingers caressed my cheek as those grayish-green eyes of his, brimming with affection, gazed into mine. "Yeah, you do."

His devotion heartened me. Our love was real. That much I was certain of. I felt its force every day, with every touch. It terrified me to think if I didn't pull myself together soon, Jake's love for me might fade.

"I'm trying, Jake. Don't give up on me."

He flinched at my words. Of course, I understood that he wasn't being given the credit he deserved, and that he was prepared to fight alongside me in this battle, but we were still in the early stages of my decline. Would he have the strength to stick by me for the long haul?

"I will find a way, I promise."

Jake leaned in, his face inches from mine, and his hair tickling my forehead. "I know you will. I have faith in you."

"Why? What makes you think I can make it through this?"

"Because I know you. The way you've pushed me through one crisis after another, there's nothing you cannot do. You are, and always will be, a force to be reckoned with."

I could almost hear the inspirational music playing in the background and brightened at the memory of the woman I used to be – strong, fierce, and committed to the cause. We'd always scraped through every obstacle placed before us and emerged stronger for it. There was no reason to believe we couldn't do it again.

I felt the tiniest ray of hope lifting my dour spirits; yet fear still nagged at me. "The thing is, I'd fight to the death for you, Jake; but for myself, I don't know how far I'd go."

"And that's why you have me."

"Until you get tired of my bedroom bullying and replace me with a shiny, new Casey."

"Not gonna happen."

"You don't know that for sure."

"Trust me, I do. You've ruined me for anyone else."

"Ahh. Really?" I asked, pretending to be ridiculously flattered by his backward compliment. "I've ruined you?"

"Only you would find a positive message in that," he said, amused and clearly relieved by the change in mood.

I pulled up to plant a kiss on my man. "I love you, Jake McKallister."

Emboldened, he rose to his knees, straddling me, his eyes tempered by warmth. "I love you too, Casey McKallister. And on those days where you feel like you're dangling off the ledge, I'll be there to pull you back up. I'm never going to let you fall. Do you hear me? I've got you."

It had only been eight months since we'd stood in front of a crowd of our loved ones and vowed to love and cherish one another until death did us part. I'd meant every word then, and I meant every word now. And even if this great loss managed to tear us apart in the end, Jake would always and forever be the man I loved.

In one swift movement, he sat up, pulling me with him. As we both shifted on the bed, I caught sight of the seriousness of his expression, and my stomach turned over. Whatever he was about to say, I felt certain I wasn't going to like it.

"Please don't take this the wrong way, Casey, but I have to get this out. I know you want a baby, but I really think this isn't the right time. For everyone's sake, you need to get to a better place before we have a child of our own."

I felt a little stab to my heart. He'd never wanted a baby in the first place, so I had to wonder if he was just taking the opportunity to reiterate his position. But then, he'd had ample time to back out before today and had not, so I had to believe he was being sincere – that he truly believed it was a bad idea to bear a child in this current toxic environment.

Problem was, I didn't agree. Maybe he was right, and yeah, he probably was, but my brain was not leading the charge on this one. "I hear what you're saying, and I agree with you… to an extent… but I don't see a way forward without a baby. I'll just linger indefinitely in this weird kind of limbo. I know it's not an ideal mindset to have when bringing a baby into the world, but haven't you ever had that feeling that something has to change or you just can't move forward?"

Jake kept his eyes focused on mine, and I could see the recognition in them as he nodded. There was no doubt he understood my dilemma, whether he currently agreed with my solution or not.

"I need something to fill the hole in my heart. I can't really explain it but… but… I just feel…I don't know…I just feel like having a baby to love would take away the sadness. That precious little life could fill the void left by…." A sob caught in my throat. Just saying the name that finished the sentence made the nightmare all too real. "Anyway, I know you probably think it's selfish, and that making a baby on a timetable is not the way it's supposed to be, but…"

Jake abruptly stood, pulling his shirt up and over his head. Tossing it aside, he then began the arduous task of wiggling his way out of his overly tight concert jeans. I observed his actions with surprise. This current turn of events had definitely not been anticipated. The humor of the moment was not lost on me, and even though my spirit was shrouded in sorrow, laughter still came. Jake stopped undressing, appearing both concerned and confused by my flip-flopping mood swings. Perhaps he thought I'd finally lost my mind, and maybe I had, but that dumbfounded expression on his face only served to escalate my antics further as I dissolved into full-blown hysterics. It was an odd combination of guttural sobs and gut-busting laughter and it went on for a full, very uncomfortable minute before I finally calmed down enough to breathe normally once again.

His mouth slightly askew, Jake just stood there with his hands on the waistband of his jeans, which had impressively been worked halfway down his thighs. Steeped in disbelief, he asked, "What the fuck is happening right now?"

Feeling nothing but overwhelming affection for this man who would stop at nothing to put a smile on my face, or a baby in my arms, I reached out and lightly tapped his naked chest. "Nothing. Put your clothes back on, dork. We're not having sex. You have a concert in forty-five minutes. Our baby can wait three more hours."

Eight Months Earlier

CHAPTER TWO

CASEY

That Face

I leaned against Jake, struggling to keep my droopy lids open. By the way he tilted his head against mine, weighing me down like a heavy blanket, it was clear his exhaustion mirrored my own. Although the evening was still young, the early hour belied the work we'd put into the day. An endless parade of activities and chores had kept us moving non-stop in preparation of the event we'd both been waiting for since Jake had dropped to one knee and proposed a little over a year ago. And now, snuggled in a worn loveseat in my parents' hotel room, we were ticking off the last hours of our single lives. By tomorrow at this time, we'd be wed.

Giddy didn't even come close to describing how I was feeling about my pending nuptials. The animated racing of my heart kept me in a perpetual state of euphoria. I'd even been caught, on multiple occasions today, humming a happy tune. And you know what? I didn't care who heard me. The fact of the matter was, in the arena of love, I'd scored. As a young girl dreaming up my fantasy guy, I couldn't have conjured a more perfect mate for myself. Jake was my heart and soul. Ours was the type of love that could, and would, last the trials of a lifetime together.

The dreamy smile returned to my face, pushing aside the fatigue. I only had a few more minutes with Jake before his brothers figured out where he was hiding and dragged him off kicking and screaming to the bachelor party he adamantly professed he didn't want. And once that happened, our next meeting would be at the church, as I walked down the aisle into his waiting arms.

My heart began thumping faster as a happy song spontaneously sprang to my lips. But before the melody could take flight, I caught sight of a disturbing reflection in the mirror. Not my reflection, mind you. As previously stated, mine was Disney princess perfect. But Jake's? What the hell? Let's just say his expression conveyed less 'You complete me' and more 'I just swallowed a bottle of Drano.'

I blinked back my surprise. When had that face started? The downward turn of his lips was in stark contrast to the day we'd spent together. Jake had been dialed in from the beginning, gamely keeping pace with me as he posed for pictures with all of my relatives, most of whom he hadn't met until today. He'd been nothing but charming and gracious. So where was that grimace coming from? Had Jake just been acting the doting fiancé for my family? God knows, he was an expert at playing to the crowd. Being congenial was part of his job; yet even outside of it, in his everyday life, Jake had an uncanny ability to turn it on and off at a moment's notice; and now, it appeared, he'd been twisting the faucet when he thought I wasn't looking. Suddenly, I had a bad feeling about tomorrow. Was he second-guessing us? Would he back out at the last minute? No. I knew Jake. He'd never do such a heartless thing to me. So then why the hell did he appear to be fighting back the gag reflex?

Thinking back on the past few months, it occurred to me that I'd seen this same 'clogged drain' look on his face before, but it hadn't seemed as significant back then as it did now… mere hours before exchanging our vows. He should be feeling ecstatic, like me, not mentally preparing himself for a stomach pumping. What were the chances that his anxiety-ridden face was just a result of everyday, run-of-the-mill, pre-wedding jitters?

I mean, please, there couldn't have been a less stressed groom. Jake had hired a top wedding planner, Boris, and handed the reins over to him. Because of the secret nature of the nuptials, Boris, who had quickly become my very best friend in the entire universe, named the wedding *Operation Pretzel.* Get it? Tying the knot? I know it might sound totally cheesy, but Boris and I found it wildly funny at the time. We'd laughed and laughed and had even come up with a pretzel-shaped hand signal.

As for Jake, he seemed thrilled to have pawned me off on Boris. With my new bestie in the picture, it gave Jake the excuse to take a totally hands-off approach to all things wedding-related. He'd even gone so far as comparing himself to a backup singer, saying he was happy to just harmonize in the background as Boris and I took the lead. We all knew it was a cop-out, but who was I to argue? I'd been handed a blank check and full rights to the wedding of my dreams. I mean, as long as the groom showed up with a smile on his face on the day, what did I care if he partook in the planning stages or not?

Besides, just between us, Jake's ideas were basically crap. Don't get me wrong – he was a brilliant musician and an amazing man – but he was sorely lacking in the area of personal taste… except, of course, when it came to his choice in brides. If it were up to him, the wedding guests would be dining on hotdogs from 7-Eleven while sucking down their own personal 44 ounce Slurpees. Just to give you an example of what we were dealing with, when Boris sought out Jake's opinion on his preferred cake flavor, my fiancé replied, 'Funfetti.'

Sure, I hadn't needed his opinion during the planning stages, but perhaps I should have at least paid better attention to his moods. Maybe then this change in his demeanor wouldn't have come as such a shock to me.

Perhaps sensing me analyzing him, Jake instantly turned the frown around and his eyes softened as they connected with mine in the mirror. In response to my questioning look, he dipped his head and gently brushed his lips against my forehead.

"You okay?" I asked, loud enough only for him to hear.

"Yeah, sorry. I was just zoning out."

I didn't believe him. Not for a second. This was Jake we were talking about, and if he were feeling anxious, there was a whole array of issues it could be.

"Are you sure? Do you want to go somewhere and talk?"

His hand felt for mine and upon first contact, our fingers entwined like a braided knot. He squeezed. "I'm fine, Case."

I looked away from the mirror, but now I was the one frowning. Something didn't feel quite right; but what was I going to do, accuse him of having second thoughts about marrying me? If he truly was just zoning out, then I'd be putting thoughts into his head. But what if he wasn't?

What if he had changed his mind? Oh, god. He was going to leave me at the altar, wasn't he?

"Casey?"

I'd surely turned several shades of gray in the time it took to totally overreact.

"You all right?" Jake questioned.

No doubt my expression now matched his from moments earlier.

"Uh-huh. Yeah. Sure."

Breathe, psycho. Jake would never leave you high and dry like that. Would he? I checked the digital clock on the phone in my parents' hotel room. 8:53 PM. Fourteen hours. Jake just needed to hang in there for fourteen more freakin' hours. Then he could wig out all he wanted because we'd be married and there'd be nothing he could do about it. *That's the spirit, Casey!*

"Not that I don't love your stimulating company, but when can I expect to get my sofa back?" My mother's question thankfully silenced the irrational voice in my head. "I want to watch a little TV before bed."

"I'm still hiding from Keith," Jake answered.

"Well, could you do it in the hallway?" Her flippant question was followed by a sly smile, and Jake ran with it.

"I could, Linda, but that would sort of defeat the purpose of hiding, now, wouldn't it?"

They exchanged conspiratorial smiles. He no longer received the special treatment from my mother. That had disappeared along with the gushing and cooing. Jake was now just a part of the family, and he and my mother had developed a very comfortable camaraderie.

"Mom," I said, feeling the need to defend my fiancé, "what happens if you throw him out and then he gets attacked by the strippers Keith hired for the bachelor party? How are you going to feel then? Use your brain."

"Fine," she said, sighing loudly. "If it'll make you feel better, I'll provide him with a handful of dollar bills before kicking him to the curb."

A familiar rhythmic knock rapped on the door. It could be no other than my brother Luke.

"Oh, great, more company." Mom groaned, then winked and let him in.

Luke's eyes immediately settled on Jake. "Seriously, dude? You're such a wuss."

"If you rat me out to Keith," Jake replied. "You no longer get backstage access to my concerts, and there goes your love life."

"Okay, first, you underestimate me; and second, you give me way too much credit," Luke said, totally contradicting himself. "Keith already figured you'd be hiding in here. Man up! You're living on borrowed time, bro. And as far as my love life goes, I haven't been able to close even one deal at your concerts, so that's an empty threat to me."

Jake sat up, an expression of disbelief on his face. "If you can't get laid at a rock concert, you're beyond any help I can give you."

"I agree with Jake on this," Mom said, her eyes twinkling in amusement. There was nothing she liked more than to wedge herself into discussions about her children's love lives. "There's really no excuse."

"Mom. Please," Luke said, struggling to ignore her completely before continuing his conversation with Jake. "If you had more variety backstage, maybe I'd have a chance."

"Are you suggesting it's my fault you can't score?"

"In a roundabout way, yeah, I am. You set me up to fail from the get go. It's not like I'm going to have a chance with the type of ladies who get backstage at your concerts. They're all rock solid tens. I need some females who are marginally flawed to have even the slightest chance."

"Sooo… you want me to ask security to look for eights, is that what you're saying?"

Luke considered the question, even going so far as to tap a finger to his chin. "I think that's still too high a number. Let's shoot for fives to sevens."

"Okay, sure. Any other requests I can pass along?"

"Well, since you're asking, I do like brunettes… or wait… even darker. Yeah, I like the silky black hair color. But, then again, I have a thing for blondes too. And red-haired women... ooh, yes indeed. You know what they say about redheads, right?"

"I'm not sure I do."

"They're blondes from hell."

Jake reacted by wincing. "I wouldn't lead with that line."

"Of course not. Anyway, I'll tell you what, man, just surprise me. I'll take whatever, as long as they're, you know..."

"...not too hot." Jake finished his sentence.

"Exactly." Luke gave him a thumbs up before settling his gaze on me, seemingly surprised I was in the room at all.

"Well, hey there, Spacey Casey."

"Hello yourself, Pukey Lukey."

"Alrighty," Mom said, clapping her hands to get our attention. "Now that everyone's reacquainted... and knows what to look for in a soul mate for Luke... what do you say we wrap this thing up? And by that, I mean, this sanctuary city is closing down, so please leave immediately."

"Wow, Mom. What's your hurry? Your only daughter is getting married tomorrow. You should be thankful I want to spend my last moments of freedom with you and Dad."

"Wait, Dad's here?" Luke asked, looking around. "I thought he'd already gone down to the bachelor party."

"He's not going. Jake gave him a pass, so he's spending his free time on the toilet."

"Still?" my brother asked, with a tilt of his eyebrow. "He was in there when I stopped by earlier."

"Not still. *Again*." Mom answered, unfazed. "He's in and out of the crapper all day. Old guys poop a lot."

"I'm not pooping," Dad's frustrated voice called from the bathroom. "I'm reading. It's the only place I can go where I get a little peace and quiet from your mother."

"He says it like it bothers me." She directed her comment toward us from behind her hand. "I only wish he'd stay in there longer, but unfortunately his legs fall asleep at about the twenty-minute mark."

We all snickered at her comment.

"Such an amateur," Luke commented, shaking his head. "I can make it at least thirty before the tingling sets in. And Mom, I know you're itching to boot us from the nest, but can you at least grant us a five-minute reprieve? If Miles is coming, he'll be here by nine."

"If? Why wouldn't he be coming?" Jake asked. "He was all excited earlier."

"Yes, but that was before he got in trouble, and now he's trying to talk Darcy into letting him come."

Miles was our oldest brother and had been married for nearly twelve years to his high school girlfriend, Darcy. Together they had two children, Sydney and Riley.

"See, this is the part of wedded bliss that I don't get," Jake said, the slightest hint of a whine lifting the words. "Why does Darcy get to decide if he goes out or not? That's bullshit. I'm just letting you know now, Casey, you're not going to be the boss of me."

Mom and I exchanged amused eyebrow arches, as my father laughed hysterically from behind the locked bathroom door.

"Good luck with that, Jake," his hollowed voice called out. "Perhaps you're unfamiliar with that old adage – the apple doesn't fall far from the tree?"

"No, I've heard it," Jake answered, loud enough for him to hear.

"Uh-huh, well, Casey didn't even hit the ground. Good luck, my man."

Palming my man's face and drawing him toward me, I said, "Don't listen to my dad, sweetie. As long as everything is exactly the way I want it, I'm totally flexible."

Mom snorted out her approval and stepped over Jake's outstretched legs to give me a high five.

"You disappoint me, Linda," Jake said, shaking his head. "There was a time I was your favorite person."

"That was when you were all fresh and new, like a shiny penny," Mom mused. "Now you're like one of those corroded coins from the 70's. You still have value, but you're not going in the coin collection anytime soon, you know what I mean?"

Jake gaped at her a moment before dipping his head into his hands. "Oh, god, Casey is exactly *you*!"

"What did I tell you?" Dad yelled from his throne.

"It's better you found out now." Mom patted him sympathetically. "So you said 9:00 PM, right?"

"Yes, Mom. What's your hurry?"

"If you must know, I need to put on a mud mask so my skin looks revitalized in the morning."

"In that case, you might not want to rinse it off," Dad chuckled, continuing to butt into the conversation from afar.

Mom didn't even blink an eye at his insult. Instead she asked Luke, "How did Miles get in trouble?"

"Well, somehow Riley got his arm stuck in the vending machine down the hall."

"The candy or the soda machine?" she asked.

"Does it really matter?"

"Not really, but I was kind of thirsty. If he's stuck in the soda machine, that puts a damper on my plans."

"Lucky for all of us, it was the candy machine." Luke pulled out a bag of M&M's from his pocket. "Miles greased up his arm, and on its way out, Riley managed to grab four bags of these babies. Cool, huh?"

Jake nodded in agreement, and Luke poured some into his open palm. Only those two would find my nephew's descent into a life of petty crime a positive thing.

"Anyway, the candy heist happened on Miles's watch, while Darcy was showering, and now she's pissed."

"Understandably," Mom agreed.

"Yeah, well, anyway, he's trying to escape now, but I don't know if it will be possible. I mean those kids are…"

"Wild?" she said, interrupting Luke.

"No, evil. I was going to say evil."

"Luke. They're children. Be nice."

"Me? Riley keeps repeating everything I say and not in a friendly way. He's making me feel insecure. And Syd, she's got the makings of a true sociopath. First she crawled under the bed and tied my laces together, then when I went down flat on my back, she tried to smother me with a pillow."

"I'm sure Sydney wasn't trying to *actually* smother you," our mother said, attempting to explain away the behavior of her adored granddaughter.

"Oh, I'm, pretty sure she was. She had a back-up pillow and everything. Anyway, Spacey Casey, my advice to you would be to keep your corroded penny as far away from our little niece and nephew as possible; that is, if you ever desire to have children of your own."

"Speaking of that," Mom said, drawing the words out longer than need be as she scanned Luke with her eyes, "when can I be expecting some from you?"

"Children?!" he asked, as if it were the stupidest thing she'd said all year.

"Yes. What did you think I meant?"

"Well, I don't know. Were you not listening to the earlier conversation I was having with Jake about my lady problems?"

"Oh, I thought it was just a problem at his concerts."

"No, no. It's a problem pretty much across the board. Here's the thing, Mom," Luke settled in for a teaching moment. "And, believe me, I do understand it's been a while for you, but having kids requires the organs of both sexes, and since mine hasn't seen anything but the inside of a white tube sock for some time now, the closest I'm going to get to making your dream come true is a pair of baby booties."

"Oh, god!" Dad groaned. He always did hate our frank sex talks. "Get out. All of you!"

"Don't listen to him," Mom said, waving off his demands. Her face was already aglow with the promise of juicy gossip. "Why don't you just go out and find yourself a nice woman, then? Instead of dirtying up perfectly good socks?"

"Well, dammit, Mom. Why didn't I think of that?" Luke pretended to write her advice down on an imaginary piece of paper. "Have sex with *actual* woman."

"You cannot tell me that no one is interested. You're the full package."

"The great thing about moms," he said in mock admiration, "is how truly delusional they are when it comes to their own offspring."

"Oh, please. She's right," I said. "You're handsome…"

"Uh-huh," Luke agreed.

"Funny…"

"Uh-huh."

"Tall…"

"Uh-huh."

"And employed."

"Uh-huh. All valid points except you forgot about the elephant in the room." Luke grabbed his belly to emphasize that he was the oversized mammal in question.

He'd always been a bigger kid, his whole life. While Miles and I were on the shorter, scrawnier side, Luke had been not only awkwardly tall from a young age, but also impossibly wide. It wasn't like his size had ever stopped him; in fact, by the time he was eight or nine, Luke had football coaches dropping to their knees in gratitude. Not only was he a big boy, but he also had a fighting spirit that propelled him to sports stardom in high school and beyond. But without the daily practice that had defined his school years, Luke had added some extra weight and had been struggling to lose it ever since.

"If you can't find a good woman because you're carrying a few extra pounds," Mom said, "then clearly you're looking in all the wrong places."

"It's not a *few* extra, but thanks for the understatement," Luke said, sighing. "I've got to get my ass moving and not just to the refrigerator. Too bad I can't afford a personal trainer, like some people I know."

Jake looked up as if he'd just realized the 'some people' Luke was referring to happened to be him. "If you're talking about me, I don't have a trainer."

My brother grimaced. "Of course you don't."

"I hear the gym is a great place to meet women," Mom piped in, never one to give up on a challenge.

"Oh, I'm sure it is… if you look like him." Luke aggressively singled out my husband-to-be. "Or any one of his goddamn brothers. You guys suck."

"You're deflecting. Stay focused on the task at hand. What about a Starbucks, or a park? Or hell, Luke, just head for the corner bar. I'm okay with your betrothed being able to pound them down as long as she has the will power to lay off the liquid while she's pregnant." Mom was digging deep now.

"Interesting. And would you also accept a drug addict, as long as she halts her heroin intake while my child is in utero?"

Mom's eyes were lit with amusement. "I mean, if that's all I can get, I guess."

"Why don't you just meet your baby mama online, like everyone else?" I suggested.

"You don't think I've tried? Trust me, that's not the solution. A few weeks ago, they suggested my cousin."

"What?" I gaped, unable to control the snickering. "Wait – first or second cousin?"

"Again, does it really matter? What is it with you and Mom and your weird questions?"

No one was listening to his objections as we were all holding our breath in anticipation of the answer. Even

Dad yelled from the bathroom, demanding to know which cousin.

"Fine – it was Brooke."

"Brooke?" Mom blurted out at the exact moment her brows hit the ceiling. "Harvard grad Brooke?"

"That would be the one. And let me just say, tomorrow's going to be exceedingly awkward."

"Good lord, whatever did the two of you have in common?"

"Apparently we both like dogs – and shared genetics."

"Well, that's just... wow, just awesome, Luke," Mom cooed. "I'm sure the two of you will make a lovely couple."

"Uh-huh, have a good laugh, but unless you're okay with your grandchildren sporting an extra nostril and a smattering of belly buttons, then Brooke's probably not an ideal choice."

"So you're telling me you haven't found one interesting woman on those dating sites?" I asked. "Three quarters of the population under forty are signed up."

"Oh, I've found interesting women, but the only ones interested in me are... how should I put this nicely... cuckoo for Cocoa Puffs."

"How about you try to revise your shallow points system?" Mom proposed.

"Are you suggesting I go below a four?" Luke blurted out, clearly offended. "Jesus, Mom. Thanks for the support. I'm not a bad-looking guy. If I got rid of a spare tire or two, I'm fairly confident I could rank higher than I currently do, but until then, I'll have to settle for the Heathers of the world."

"Do I even want to know?"

"I think you *need* to know what I'm dealing with here. I came across this woman on Tinder, totally within my range, and she looked sweet. Nice smile. But then I scrolled down."

"No, dude!" Jake said, clearly enjoying Luke's misadventures. "Never scroll down."

"Well, I did!" he spat back, trying to maintain his livid exterior, although the smile threatening to break free gave him away. "Nothing I can do about it now. Anyway, I read her tagline, and it's all in third person. Heather likes brisk walks in the park. Heather likes candlelight dinners by the water. Heather likes microwaving small, defenseless animals. Uh, yeah, Heather, I'm no relationship expert, but I think I know why you're still single."

"Okay," Dad said, finally exiting the bathroom with a newspaper wadded under his arm. "So meet a woman the old-fashioned way… at work."

"I sell generators, Dad. My job is not sexually friendly. Most of my clients are doomsday survivalists, and let's just say their daughters don't shower as often as they probably should."

"But on the plus side," Jake added, "you might survive the apocalypse."

"Yes, this is true, but the question is... would I want to?"

"I give up," Dad said, throwing his hands up in defeat before turning to my mother. "We can't even get him a basement dweller, Linda. I think we can both agree that this one's a lost cause. Let's focus our hopes and dreams on Casey and Jake."

"I'm with you," Mom agreed.

Miles made it with a minute to spare. He stepped into the room munching on a bag of peanut M&Ms.

"You were paroled." Luke brightened up. "Good for you."

"Only after taking Riley to the lobby and making him apologize for what he'd done. The kid was bawling. Hopefully he's learned a valuable lesson."

"I should say the same for his daddy," Mom reprimanded.

"I already got reamed by Darcy," Miles grumbled. "I don't need your input."

"I see you're eating the stolen contraband."

Miles smiled sheepishly before throwing a few more chocolates in his mouth. "Someone has to. Darcy wouldn't let him touch the candy after what he did. It would send the wrong message."

"Oh, right. Right." Mom nodded.

"Anyway, I have to be back by midnight, so let's get this party started. I just got the text from Keith. It's in the recreation room downstairs."

Jake reluctantly unraveled his body from mine and stood up. He hadn't wanted a bachelor party – insisted against one, even – but, after lengthy negotiations with Keith, he'd relented. In exchange for his cooperation, Jake had been promised a low-key affair. It wasn't that he was opposed to having a good time with the guys, but when you're a world famous musician trying to pull off a secret wedding, getting photographed stuffing dollar bills into a G-string is probably not the best way to stay under the radar.

Even though Jake had taken a hands-off approach to the wedding preparation, there was one thing he had asked for – and that was a private, laidback ceremony, away from the prying eyes of a curious world. But keeping our wedding a secret proved well beyond my skill set, so in addition to hiring Boris, Jake had assembled a team of players to coordinate the entire production, complete with a security detail that rivaled the Secret Service.

Once they took over the specifics, my job had basically become picking out color swatches… and lying. Oh, so much lying. See, for security and privacy reasons, no one could know where the wedding would be taking place. Our guests were simply given a 'save-the-date' and nothing more. The actual venue would be revealed the day before the ceremony, and travel arrangements would be prearranged for those coming from out of town.

My friends, my extended family, and even curious onlookers on the street pestered me endlessly for wedding details, but every word out of my mouth was a bald-faced lie. I had us marrying all over the west coast, had grossly overestimated the size of the venue, and had greatly embellished our guest list to include not only celebrities of the A-list variety but also kings and queens… of smaller countries, of course. The point was to throw everyone off our tail, especially the press, whom my lies always seemed to trickle down to. No one, and I mean no one, would predict our wedding would take place in a quaint little church in Arizona with seating for no more than one hundred and fifty of our nearest and dearest.

Jake lived his life in the spotlight, and as his significant other, so now did I. And although I'd come to accept that for the rest of my life, I'd share my man with millions of others, this ceremony – our wedding – was ours alone. We'd both agreed we wanted to take it back to where it all began because, well, Jake and I were sentimental that way. The place that had brought us together would also be the one to wed us in holy matrimony.

"Dave, last chance," Jake said, addressing my father. "Bachelor party with the guys or mud mask with the wife? What'll it be?"

"Neither… it's earplugs and a pillow for me. But here's a dollar. Please stuff it somewhere for me tonight."

"Not happening." Jake grinned, giving it right back. "My hands will remain firmly on my lap."

"Um, I'm thinking all our hands will be on our laps," Luke said, winking. "To avoid, you know, embarrassment."

"Keith wouldn't dare hire entertainment. He knows better."

"Does he, though?" Luke's voice went up an octave. "I don't know your brother very well, but he strikes me as a slow learner."

Jake laughed, and then reached for my hands and pulled me to my feet.

"Give us a second," he said to my brothers, before leading me out into the hallway and shutting the door.

Still holding my hands, Jake quirked his lips into a mischievous grin and took a few steps back, guiding me along with a spicy swivel of his hips. My body moved in unison, matching him step for step in a suggestive little salsa. The flirtatious flickering of his eyes effortlessly reeled me in and kept me dangling helplessly on his line. What was he up to? This seductive show he was putting on would lead us nowhere, and we both knew it.

"What are you doing?" I asked, the slightest quivering of my lips the only giveaway of how his animal magnetism was getting to me in the most sensual of ways.

Jake jerked me forward, enveloping my body in his arms as his hands gripped my buttocks, and his heated breath prickled the skin of my sensitive neck. "Wishing," he murmured.

"Wishing what?" My words came out more like a moan as I pressed into the erection straining beneath the rough fabric of his jeans.

"Wishing I was spending tonight with you and not a bunch of dudes."

His fingers dipped lower, sending twinges of heat throughout my body and forcing a shuddering gasp from my lips.

"Stop," I protested, pushing him back, and feeling the immediate cooling of the air between us. My body still inflamed, I quaked a little at the lack of physical contact and slapped his shoulder in frustration. "Don't promise me a service you can't provide."

He reached for me again, but I shied away. Attempting to ward him off, I held my hands out in front of me, but Jake performed some wickedly cool crossover move, hooking his arm around my waist and pulling me in again. Our eyes met in a fiery display just as our lips made contact and his mouth crushed into mine. We stayed in the tight embrace for longer than was appropriate in a public place, and when we finally broke apart, I was a quivering mass of sexual energy.

"Just something to remember me by tonight," he whispered.

"Me? I won't be the one with a naked stripper's ass gyrating in my lap."

"Nor will I, I assure you."

"You say that now, but what happens when they get a little alcohol into you?"

"Casey," he said, playfully mocking my words. "I promise, you are the only woman I'll ever allow to rub her ass all over me."

I couldn't stop the smile that traveled across my lips. He was just so damn hot with that confident swagger of his. And truthfully, I wasn't concerned. Jake had never given me a reason to doubt him, so I didn't. Taking his long, agile fingers gently in mine, I led him to the end of the hall and stopped in front of a large picture window.

Jake, his carnal bravado tempered, placed his hands on my hips. "So, this is it, huh?"

"I guess it is," I answered, staring into his eyes and falling for him all over again. "I really am going to miss you tonight."

"Tell me again why we can't spend it together?"

"You know why, Jake. The groom can't see the bride before the wedding because… well, I actually don't know why, but it's tradition, and you *will* cooperate."

"I'm not saying I won't. I'm just saying it's stupid."

"Your objection is duly noted."

Jake playfully dipped his head into my neck, the scratchy stubble of his unshaven face tickling my skin and sending shivers racing down my spine. I leaned back, touching the sides of his face and setting a gentle kiss to his lips. "If you're a good boy at your bachelor party, I promise you a wedding night to remember."

"I'm always good."

"Says the rock star." I grinned. "Okay, so here's a thought. Just because we can't see each other doesn't mean we can't talk on the phone, you know?"

"For phone sex?" he asked, perking up.

"No, Jake. No more sex until we're married. Surely you can wait one day."

Jake's brows angled as if he were perplexed by something. "Why would we be talking on the phone, then? I don't get it."

"Um... just to talk, duh."

Opening his eyes wide, Jake laughed and pulled away. "Oh, hell no. You can't have it both ways. If we're not sharing a bed, I sure as hell don't want you yapping in my ear all night."

Gasping in mock annoyance, I smacked him in the chest. "I can't believe I'm marrying such a heathen."

"Your choice," Jake stated matter-of-factly. "Say the word and we'll call it off."

His words rang in my ears as I tried to make sense of their meaning. After the expression I'd seen in the mirror earlier, even teasing about such things played into my fears. "Why would you say that?"

Jake instantly backtracked. "I was just kidding."

"Well, it wasn't funny."

We locked eyes, and I swear I saw a flash of that damn Drano face again before he corrected himself.

"I'm sorry. That was a stupid thing to say."

We stood there staring at each other uncomfortably before Jake shifted his gaze out the window. Something was definitely off with him, and the anxiety was eating me up inside. This was a conversation that couldn't wait fourteen hours.

"Jake?"

Reluctantly he turned back to me. "What?"

"I'm catching a strange vibe from you, and it's freaking me out a little bit."

"I'm fine, Casey. I just made a stupid joke, and you're overanalyzing it like you do everything. Maybe I'm a little nervous, is all. I don't get married every day."

"I feel like you're having second thoughts… like maybe you don't want to marry me anymore."

Jake's body visibly stiffened. "It was a *joke*, Casey. Trust me, I want to be with you. I love you. That's the one thing I am sure of."

The way he said it, filled with uncertainty and strife, sent a chill through me. "What other things aren't you sure of?"

A prolonged silence stilted the conversation. Jake leaned back against the windowpane, struggling to find the words, or maybe trying to come up with a plausible lie.

"Is it about the therapy sessions? Are the nightmares back? You know you can trust me. Whatever you have to say, I'll listen and I won't judge. You know that, right?"

"Yeah. I know," he said, with a hint of irritation. "And if I have anything to say, you'll be the first to know."

"Will I be? I mean you were pretty secretive with me about why you ended the sessions. I just want to be there for you, but I can't if you keep secrets from me."

"An unhealthy chunk of my life has been kept a secret from you, Casey. You knew that about me before accepting my proposal. You can't change the rules now, not on the eve of our wedding."

"If you want to get technical, Jake, you're the one who changed the rules. One of the things you promised was that you'd get therapy. That lasted three months."

"You never said how long it needed to last."

"Me? I wasn't the one who suggested it in the first place. Please get your story straight."

Jake didn't have a response to that. He knew as well as I did that what I was saying was true. I'd never pushed him into therapy; it was after a conversation with Kyle that he'd come to the conclusion he needed it.

We stood there without words, looking out over the Arizona night sky. Unable to handle the silence another second, I grabbed his arm and wrapped it around me as I leaned into him. Jake squeezed tightly and then reached out, took my hand, and raised it to his lips before saying, "I love you. I want to marry you. Why can't that be enough?"

I didn't care about the damn therapy. I just wanted him happy. Sometimes I wondered, given his background, if that would ever truly be possible, although there was no turning back now. I was fully vested in this man, and the way I saw it, neither one of us could survive alone. Our strength had always been together. Casey and Jake. Cake.

"It's enough."

CHAPTER THREE

JAKE

The Honeybee

Stepping into the hotel rec room with Casey's brothers, I was shocked by the scene that greeted me. A smile stretched across my face as I took in the theme of tonight's party. Instead of flowing liquor and women dancing on poles, there were balloons, facemasks, and cupcakes topped with action figures. Keith had turned my bachelor party into a little kid's superhero-themed shindig.

"You like?" Keith asked, straight-faced, as he flung back his Batman cape in a dramatic display.

"I… wow… it's…"

"Totally KAPOW! Right?" He nodded, using his first of many superhero words of the evening. "You wanted something tame tonight and I aim to please, so one dry, super-boring bachelor party for my little bro! You're welcome."

I scanned the group of about twenty guys. All were wearing costumes or capes and sipping punch from cups with explosive words like BOOM! And ZAP! Shaking my head at all the idiots I called family and friends, I narrowed in on one very special one: Lassen. My driver had somehow managed to squeeze himself into a Superman costume that was about twelve sizes too small for him. Every nook and cranny of that big, beautiful belly of his was outlined by the fabric. The flimsy material wasn't intended for over-stretching, and Lassen looked about ready to detonate all over the vinyl flooring. A wig of black slicked-back hair sat on top of his long, gray mountain man tresses like a dead animal pelt. He hadn't even tried to tuck his hair up under it. It truly was a treat for the eyes, and I took him in like an ice cream sundae.

"Lassen, you went all out, my man. I'm blown away by your commitment."

"Yeah, well, it's because your asshole brother didn't buy any costumes larger than an XXL."

"How would I know you needed extra X's?" Keith defended himself.

"Um… by looking at me." Lassen somehow made himself appear even larger as he loomed over Keith with a snarl on his face.

In an attempt to tame the beast, I laid my hand on his shoulder. "Don't worry what anyone else thinks. I think it fits you like a glove. An O.J. Simpson glove, but still a glove."

"I don't get paid enough for this shit," he grumbled.

After helping Casey's brothers find the perfect costumes – the Hulk for Luke and Ironman for Miles – the group of us spent the evening playing arcade games and sipping on virgin cocktails, a.k.a fruit punch. It was probably the most fun I'd had at a party since I was… well, a kid. Turns out, laughter was what I needed to settle my rattled nerves. Keith had found a way to send me off into the adult world in the most juvenile of ways… and I'd expected nothing less of him.

My father, dressed as Thor, pulled me off the foosball table after another crushing loss to my drummer, Chet. We'd gone three in a row, and there was no beating the guy. I thought I was quick with my hands, but he was at a whole other level of hand-eye coordination.

"That was just embarrassing," Dad said, shaking his head in disappointment. "You need to know when to concede defeat."

"Says the guy who cheats at *every* board game."

"Only because when you kids were little, you would punch, scream, and pout over who the winner was. But, you see, if I won every time, no fighting. It was genius, really."

"So then why are you still winning?"

"Tonight's not about me, Jake." He expertly deflected the question. "Let's talk about you."

"No, thanks," I scoffed. "That's one subject you know I hate talking about."

"Well, then, this will be a short conversation."

"Very." I nodded. "Where's your hammer, Thor?"

"Kyle took it. Said something about playing whack-a-mole with Quinn's head."

"Oh, that's…" I stopped to ponder the vision of that in my mind. "Disturbing."

My father didn't seem the least bit concerned about his youngest son, although that probably had something to do with the fact that Thor's hammer was made of flimsy plastic.

"Where's *your* costume?" he asked.

"Keith granted me an exemption."

"Makes sense."

"Why's that?"

"Because you're already a hero."

I bristled at his words. "I really hate when you say shit like that."

"Why? It's true."

My father always gave me way more credit than I deserved. I didn't have superpowers or a desire to protect the world from ruin. Really, all I'd done for humankind was save my sorry ass. "In whose world?"

"In a lot of people's worlds…" He stopped talking for a moment, struggling to control the unexpected emotion breaking up his words. "…but mostly mine."

I shifted in place, uncomfortable with my father's sudden sentiment. "Where did that come from?" I asked.

"I have no idea. I've been feeling a bit nostalgic today."

"Or maybe you're just getting weepy with old age." I spoke with bravado but, truth be told, I'd also been walking a very thin emotional line today.

"That's entirely possible. But you know, I think about where you were, that broken kid, and who you are now… it makes me proud to know you." Again Dad broke down as he forced the remaining words out of his trembling throat. "You may not consider yourself one, but you're my hero, kid."

Dammit, now I was swallowing back the noticeable lump in my throat. What the hell was wrong with me? This whole day – actually, the past few weeks – had felt like an ending of sorts, like life was about to change forever, and the uncertainty of it all was messing with my head.

Struggling to preserve my cool, I averted my eyes to the cup in his hand, printed with the word 'WHAM.' It was so stupidly random I had to smile. My dad had a way of sidetracking me with his wackiness. And I'd counted on his lightheartedness during the darkest days of my life. Without his positive attitude and penchant for off-color jokes at all the wrong times, I was sure I wouldn't be the man I was today. Crap, here came the feelings. "Thanks for always being there for me, Dad. I know I don't say it often, but… I love you."

His fingers pressed together like lobster claws, my dad clumsily wiped the tears away. I couldn't tell if he was trying to be funny or not, until his words made clear he wasn't. "You don't need to say it. I already know."

Unaccustomed to sharing such personal truths, we stared awkwardly at his superhero cup, struggling to find words… any words. Mercifully, my father pulled it together in time to turn our raw honesty into a joke. "Well, this sucks."

"I know, right?" I loved the guy, but he was not someone I wanted to dive into a deep conversation with. "Can I ask you something without you breaking down like a baby?"

"Probably not, but you can give it a shot."

"Before you married Mom, did you ever have any doubts that you'd be a good husband and father?"

He eyed me with interest. "Why? Are you having doubts?"

"Me? No. I'm asking for a friend."

"Oh, right." Dad laughed. "Here's the thing about me. I married your mother when I was twenty-three. I was so damn immature, I doubt I gave it a moment's thought. It wasn't until after we were husband and wife that I was like… oh, snap, this shit is real."

"Please don't use that word."

"*Shit*?" His face twisted in surprise at the thought that I took offense to swear words, when I myself used them on a very regular basis.

"No. *Snap*. That word's not for your age group."

"For reals? I'm fly."

"Ooh… no." I cringed. "Just stop."

"Pffft." He waved off my recoil. "I don't think you realize how totally awesome I am. My son's a rock star, you know?"

"So I've heard. Can you please finish your story?"

"Oh, right. So, I had to grow up on the job. Marriage is not easy. You've got to work at it, but the rewards are great. And I'm not just talking about sex, which is..."

I jumped in to stop him. The last thing I wanted when I was already stressed was to hear a story about him and my mother getting it on. "Dad, seriously… no."

"Sorry. Anyway, if you're feeling this way now, it's because you're a more introspective person than I ever was – which is code for 'You overthink things.' My advice to you is to just relax and enjoy the ride. It's unpredictable, but damn, is it ever worth it."

"So then why do you always make Mom sound like your parole officer?"

"Because it's funny. And true. She owns my ass… just like Casey will own yours in just a few short hours."

"Dammit, why does everyone keep saying that? I'm not going to wuss out like the rest of you."

"Oh, no?" Dad's grin transformed his entire face. "Talk to me again in twenty years."

"Casey's not like that."

"Neither was your Mom… until we got hitched. And then it was…"

Dad made his hand into a fist and squeezed. His face took on the look of a man being clocked in the nuts. I laughed despite myself. He was always good at dispensing unhelpful advice, similar to those ladies who circled around a first-time pregnant woman in order to pepper her with tales of their own unbearable childbirth suffering.

"Whatever, Dad."

"You don't believe me? Fine. Let me share with you my theory on the similarities between marriage and honeybee sex."

I didn't give him the benefit of a reply, as I knew more was coming and I didn't want to delay what I was sure would be an entertaining explanation.

"See, the virgin queen takes a mating flight with a dozen or so male drones. Now, I know what you're thinking… those are some lucky bees, right?"

"No, I really wasn't thinking anything at all."

"I mean out of the hundreds of eligible bachelors in the colony, she picked those winged studs. Except there's nothing lucky about it because while the two are having tiny little honeybee intercourse in the sky, at the very moment of reckoning, the drone's genitals explode, and all his bloody miniaturized parts seal off the queen like a microscopic butt plug!"

My eyebrows shot to the sky as I jerked my head up in alarm. This definitely wasn't where I thought the story was going. "Jesus."

"Exactly." He nodded, like it all made perfect sense. "After the queen got what she wanted from the poor hapless dude, he became totally useless to her."

I waited for my father to offer up any more words of wisdom, but nothing followed. That couldn't be it. "And?"

"There's no *and*, son," he said shaking his head. "That's marriage."

Still a little shell-shocked from Dad's rather unpleasant portrait of holy matrimony, I made my way over to my younger brother, Kyle, lounging on the couch. His eyes were closed, and one leg hung over the armrest as if he hadn't a care in the world. I envied his relaxed state of being. If I had just a tiny bit of his slacker mentality, I was convinced I'd be a happier person. Taking in his costume of choice, I had to smile. Of all the superheroes he had to choose from, Kyle had settled on Ant-Man. Of course he had. My brother could never just be normal and select a run-of-the-mill crusader. Oh no, he had to pick a 'hero' who, in conjunction with millions of his closest ant friends, had brought villains to justice by hoisting them over their heads and marching the bad guys off to prison.

A swift kick to the side of the sofa didn't produce the instantaneous effect I'd hoped for. Instead of being jarred to a vertical position, Kyle casually opened his eyes, yawned, and stretched an arm out in front of him, reminiscent of a cat waking from a daylong slumber. Was he really napping during my bachelor party? What a dick. I pushed his leg off the armrest. "I'm not sure if you're aware, but when you lie like that, it totally shows your junk."

Kyle sat up and rubbed the sleep from his eyes. "I think the word you were searching for was 'Hello.'"

"Shouldn't you be out there saving the world from crumbs?"

"Ooh, good one." Kyle faked a laugh. "Perhaps you're uninformed, but Ant-Man is a very complex guy with unique powers."

"Yeah? Like what?"

"He can reduce in size."

"That's self-explanatory." I said, pretending to yawn. "What else?"

"Well, he can command an ant army with his special helmet."

"To do what?"

"I don't know." He shrugged, putting little to no effort into selling himself. "Ant stuff."

"You can do better than that."

"Okay, how about this?" The glint in Kyle's eye was unmistakable. "He has inferiority issues when it comes to the stronger, more powerful, and more handsome heroes who always outshine and underestimate him. Sound familiar?"

A grin spread across my face. "I love your costume, man."

"That's more like it," he said, matching my expression. "What can I do for you?"

"Nothing. I'm trying to escape Dad."

Kyle nodded as if he completely understood my reasoning. "Ah, yes, the infected, ingrown hair on his butt cheek."

"What? No." Damn, that man needed supervision when he ventured into public spaces. "Why would he be advertising that?"

"I mean as far as abscesses go, it is fairly impressive."

"I don't care if it's the size of a small country, I don't want that thing anywhere near me. I'm already traumatized enough."

"Do you want to tell Ant-Man about it?"

"Why not? It involves your insect brothers, so you might have a unique perspective. Dad just managed to connect marriage to the most disturbing *Animal Planet* fact ever. Did you know the male honeybee's testicles explode after he mates with the queen bee?"

"Whoa, dude, that's brutal. I need to watch *Animal Planet* more often."

"Yeah, me too. Anyway, his point was that marriage is similarly terrifying. Apparently, once I get married, Casey will transform into a queen bee, absorb my genitals, and keep me at her mercy forever."

"Yikes," Kyle said with a dopey grin on his face. "Good luck with that."

"Right? Anyway, the part I don't get is what would the incentive be to knock up the queen?"

"Are we talking about you or the honeybee right now?"

I smiled. "The honeybee."

"I think we both know the incentive," Ant-Man theorized. "At least he dies happy, right?"

"But does he, Kyle? Really? I mean, his nards detonate into a bloody mess and then he drops dead. I can't imagine that being a satisfying climax."

Kyle studied me as if he actually had something profound to say, but then he opened his mouth and ruined the moment. "I think you're making a big deal out of nothing. Everyone knows when you get married, you don't use your balls all that often anyway."

I took in that smug expression on his face but consoled myself with the knowledge that he didn't have all that much wiggle room either. The way his relationship with Kenzie was going, he didn't seem too far off from walking down the aisle himself. Maybe when it was his nutsack on the front lines, he'd have more compassion for my situation.

I nearly smacked Quinn with the door on the way into the bathroom.

"Oh, shit. What were you doing behind the door?" I complained.

"Um, exiting," he said, appearing amused by his comeback.

"Well, don't do that around me. It's creepy."

"Sorry, next time I'll send you a text when I'm finished pissing."

Quinn made a grand gesture of stepping back to allow me entrance. I took a quick pass at him with my eyes. He was also dressed up as Superman but, unlike Lassen, he filled out his costume like it was an actual fitted glove. I was still having trouble grasping the fact that my youngest brother was all grown up and standing a couple of inches taller than me. I'd always viewed Quinn as a little kid, but now, at eighteen years of age, he was anything but. Packing a solid twenty pounds of muscle and rockin' the disheveled hairstyle, baby Quinn was putting the rest of us McKallister boys to shame.

"I hear Kyle's looking to kick your ass."

"Yeah. I told him my theory, and he freaked out and tried to hit me with the hammer."

"What's your theory?"

"Just that he picked his costume to complement his ant-sized package."

"Ah. Now I'm getting a clearer picture."

"Anyway, no way could he beat my ass. I can take him down in an instant."

"I don't know, Quinn, Kyle's scrappy."

"And you think I'm not?"

It was hard to ignore the challenge in his voice, but I forced myself not to take the bait. Quinn and I hadn't been getting along all that well lately, and the last thing I wanted tonight was confrontation. He followed me back into the bathroom… okay, it looked like I was getting company. Thankfully, Quinn honored the bro code by averting his eyes so I could relieve myself. Too bad he didn't think to keep the chitchat down to a minimum.

"Sooo," he said, elongating the word, "I'm still waiting on the songwriting session you've been promising me for over a year now. Any idea when that might happen?"

Oh, crap. Not this again… and certainly not at this very moment. "I'm pissing, Quinn."

"Sorry. Please continue."

Now that he'd graduated high school and was no longer under the iron rule of our mother, Quinn was focused solely on his music career and rallying for a spot as an opening band for *the* opening band on my next tour. We weren't exactly seeing eye-to-eye on the issue. By using good old-fashioned nepotism, he and his band wanted to sidestep the process of actually earning a spot on a successful tour. There was something to be said for hard work, though, and if Quinn's only route to fame was by piggybacking off mine, he wouldn't have a lasting career.

I hadn't even finished buttoning up my jeans before he was back on the same line of questioning.

"So?"

A heavy sigh was my only reply.

"Come on, Jake. Just give me thirty minutes of your time. That's all I'm asking."

No. He was asking for a lot more than that. "I'm getting married in a couple of hours. Can we postpone your future for another day?"

"You've been postponing for as long as I've been asking," my brother said, kicking around a paper towel on the floor with the toe of his shoe. "Pretty soon you'll run out of excuses. I mean, it's a yes or no question. How hard can it be?"

"In that case, no."

My brother's eyes narrowed into angry slits. "You're such an asshole sometimes, Jake. You act so high and mighty, but you're not all that."

I didn't like the accusation in his words. For the first time, I realized there was more to his resentful attitude than just being a surly teen. "What's up with you?"

"You want to know what's up? I'm tired of you treating me like I don't matter. Anytime I bring up music, you brush me off like I'm some kid with delusional dreams. Well, I've got news for you, dickhead, I'm going to be a musician whether you like it or not."

"Be my guest. It's not like I'm trying to stand in your way."

"It's not? Because from where I'm standing, it sure looks that way. All I'm asking for is a little of your time, and that's too much for you to spare."

"You don't want time, Quinn. You want a handout. There's a difference. I did it on my own. Why can't you?"

"Because I'm not you, Jake! I don't have a built-in tragedy to impress the judges." Immediately Quinn's face creased as he winced at his own words. "That… I didn't mean that."

But his piercing words had already hit their mark, and through bared teeth, I snarled back at my brother. "Fuck you! I know what you meant."

"That's not… I didn't."

"Save it, Quinn. Find yourself another sugar daddy. I quit!"

"You can't quit something you never were." Quinn pushed off the basin and brushed past me on his way to the door; then stopped abruptly and walked back. "No. You know what? I'm tired of you acting like you're the only one who suffered. Did you forget that I grew up in the eye of your fucking hurricane?"

"Oh, well, shit, Quinn, I'm sorry if my suffering offended you. I should have been more sensitive to your delicate needs."

Looking about ready to explode, my little brother stood there clamping his hands into fists. I waited for his screaming reply, but somehow he held onto his temper. In an even tone of voice, he said, "Actually, I changed my mind. I don't need or want your help anymore. I'm done begging for your time."

A sudden draw of air turned our attention toward the door just as Finn, my sister's fiancé, strode in. Upon eyeing the two of us in our impromptu pissing match, Finn didn't skip a beat. "Hey, guys. I hear this is where all the dicks hang out."

His comment was unexpected enough to draw a snort of laughter from me. I glanced at Quinn in hopes the joke had evoked a comparable reaction and our argument would be over, but there was no levity in his terse stance. In fact, my sudden amusement set him in motion. Quinn headed for the exit, kicking the garbage can into the wall on his way to the door.

"That's just the attitude I want on my tour," I said to his exiting back, succeeding in doing nothing more than pouring fuel on the fire.

He spun around, his jaw tense and twitching, and I waited for a volley of grenades to be lobbied in my direction; but again, Quinn refrained from comment, choosing only to flip me off as he disappeared from view.

"Whoa," Finn said, his eyes twice their normal size. "What's gotten into him?"

"Apparently, I'm not making him famous fast enough."

"Ah, like you did for me?"

"Right."

After introducing Finn to my agent, his career as an actor had taken off, and he'd just wrapped up a supporting role in a major studio movie. But the difference between him and my baby brother was that Finn had put in the work. He'd struggled for years and paid his dues and now, finally, things were happening for him. There was no better way to appreciate success than to fight for it.

Quinn didn't get that. He saw my early success and pointed to it as reason enough for him to get moving. But my experiences as a young musician had scarred me, and I didn't want that for him. My brother needed more than just talent and looks to make it in the business… he needed grit, and from what I could see of his coddled existence, he had none.

I settled my attention back on Finn, who was appropriately dressed in a Spiderman costume, seeing as he *was* the human version of that specific hero. A former stuntman who specialized in jumps and wall-climbing, he could scale any surface with ease. Although after the arrival of his four-month-old daughter, he'd been spending a lot more time with his feet planted firmly on the ground.

Finn was a hands-on dad and had taken to fatherhood with ease. He adored his little girl like nothing I'd ever seen. His devotion as a father was one of the things that scared me about taking the next step with Casey. As soon as we were married, she'd want to start a family, and as much as I wanted that myself, I was genuinely concerned over the type of father I'd be. Most men went through life without ever knowing what they were made of. I, unfortunately, couldn't say the same.

Shaking off the uncomfortable thoughts, I asked Finn, "Where's your sidekick?"

For the past hour he'd been on daddy duty with a picture-perfect Gerber baby strapped to his chest. I suppose if you had to wear an infant around, my niece Indiana wasn't a bad one to put on. In fact, I'd argue she was the cutest baby ever to rock a superhero bachelor party. Clad in a Supergirl onesie, with a head full of wispy, light brown curls, Indy was as cherubic a little champion as they came.

"Your dad's got her. He knew I was about to bring Indiana back to Emma, so he talked me into taking a piss just so he could delay her departure time a few more minutes."

"Sounds about right. He's actually scaring me with all that impromptu singing he's been doing. I mean the minute she's in his arms, it's like he turns into Barney the Dinosaur."

"Finally! Thank you. I've been trying to figure out who he reminds me of." Finn laughed. "Anyway, I've got to wrap things up because Emma's expecting the baby back, and if I don't deliver the goods, it's on my head."

"You too?"

"Huh?"

"Nothing, it just seems everyone I know is totally whipped by their woman. I expected more from you."

"Really? Have you *met* your sister?"

"That's true. Lucky for me, I picked a less complicated girl than you."

Finn scoffed at that. "Every girl is complicated, some are just more skilled at hiding it than others. False advertising, if you ask me… like those damn erectile dysfunction commercials."

Oh god, I felt a honeybee story coming on.

"They give men a false hope of what a long-term relationship looks like. You know how they go – the pretty, smiling trophy wife doting on her man while serving up hors d'oeuvres and rubbing his back… all while he watches the big game on TV. And she's *happy* to do it. I mean, perfection, right? WRONG. That shit's not real. What human male has ever lived that fantasy? Not one… ever in the existence of human males. We're talking not even cavemen, okay?"

"Well, cavemen didn't have televisions… or, you know, hors d'oeuvres."

"Focus, man!"

As he said that, Finn started stripping at the urinal. His costume was essentially an adult-sized onesie, and required a partial undress just to empty his bladder. We were friends, but not that good of ones. I turned away.

"You see," Finn continued the discussion as he peed, "the commercials aren't going to show real life scenarios. Where are the tampon wrappers in the trash? Or the home-cooked meal she makes that's so nasty you wouldn't even feed it to the neighbor's dog, who barks all night while the baby's sleeping?"

"I feel like you're talking about yourself now."

"I'm talking about all of us, Jake. We need to drop these lofty expectations of marriage. Sometimes she's going to be a bitch and sometimes you're going to be an ass, and *all of the time* the neighbor's dog will bark, but you make it work because you love each other and she's the only woman you want."

Finn shook it off and redressed. "My point is, if she makes you happy, who cares if you're whipped?"

"You're missing my point, man. I'm *not* whipped, nor will I ever be."

"Oh, okay," Finn said, eyebrows arched high in amusement. "I thought I saw the movie *La La Land* on your phone the other day. Maybe I was wrong."

"That," I mumbled, looking away in shame, "wasn't mine."

"Right. Of course. And the ruffled, powder blue comforter with all those flowery pillows on your bed was your idea, then?"

"I..."

"Uh-huh. And the potpourri in the bathroom that smells like an Abercrombie model took a shit... also your brilliant mind at work?"

I hesitated. He was right. Casey was firmly in control of my masculinity. She'd taken over my whole damn house even though she didn't even officially live there. I was already a goddamn honeybee drone, and we weren't even married yet. "Well, fuck."

We left the bathroom, and the minute we turned the corner, my father was there, flying Supergirl down the narrow hallway. Indiana's eyes, wide as saucers, conveyed her pleasure with the activity by flailing her arms wildly. In the few short months Indiana had been on this earth, the two had formed an unbreakable bond. It was as sweet as it was irritating.

"Is she not the cutest baby you ever saw?" he asked, but didn't bother to wait for a reply as he took off with her back down the hallway. Finn gave chase, much to the baby, and my father's, delight.

I grimaced in annoyance, but nonetheless followed after them, having no other direction to go.

"Does she have to go?" Dad complained, pressing his lips to Indiana's rounded cheeks.

"Yep, it's her bedtime," Finn confirmed. "Time to say goodnight."

Dad took his time baby talking to Indiana before finally returning her to her father. Still unable to keep his hands off her, he ran his fingers through her soft hair before catching Finn's eye and musing, "You know, Finn, I'm not sure if I say this often enough, but thank you for having unprotected sex with my daughter."

Clearly taken off guard, Finn blinked back his amusement and answered in question form. "You're welcome?"

After seeing off Finn and Indiana, I was intercepted by my brother from another mother, Mitch. Had it not been for him switching up the wedding party and pairing me with Casey two years ago, I probably wouldn't be standing here today awaiting my own nuptials.

"The Green Hornet, huh?"

"Yeah." Mitch reddened. "I got to the costume table last."

"Really, even behind Ant-Man?"

"Yes, surprisingly, Kyle had one of the first picks."

"Of course he did."

"He scares me a bit, that one," Mitch said, amused.

I laughed. "You and me both. I mean look at him right now. What the hell's wrong with him?"

We both looked over at our younger brother, who had taken Lassen's black wig and tied it around his waist to give the appearance of a giant, hairy bush. Mitch and I laughed at his antics. A lot could be said about Kyle's questionable decision-making, but even with all the accolades I'd earned over the years, there were times I wished I were him, gliding through life in an easy, fun-loving way.

"Although I have to say…" Mitch broke into my thoughts. "Kenzie seems like a good fit for him. They're both sort of nutty in a very functional way."

"That's the most accurate description of them I've ever heard," I agreed. "They definitely bring the fun."

"Speaking of fun, I'm really looking forward to his best man speech tomorrow."

"Oh, god, don't remind me. He has one directive… don't embarrass me."

"Well." Mitch gripped my shoulder. "Good luck with that, man."

I nodded, adding a pout for a touch of humor.

"Anyway, Jake, I just wanted to tell you how happy I am for you and Casey. She's a great girl. I know you guys will be really happy together, just like Kate and me."

Finally, someone who wasn't regaling me with anxiety-inducing pep talks! He and Kate seemed to have an equal, and wuss-free, relationship. Maybe I needed to hang more with manly Mitch just to even out all the other questionable males in my life... although I doubted I could spend enough time with him for any of his awesomeness to rub off on me.

After his wedding, I'd aimed to be more involved in Mitch's life, but the reality was, I'd only seen him three times since then. It didn't seem like a lot, but it was three times more than I'd seen him in the ten years before that. It's not that we didn't want to get together, but he lived in another state, and, well, life got in the way.

"How's Max?"

"As cute as ever. He's at a really fun age now. Talking up a storm. And you'll be happy to know, my son can actually carry a tune, sort of like his namesake."

I was taken aback by the last piece of information. Mitch and Kate had chosen to name their first son Maxwell Jacob, and although I'd thought it was just a coincidence they'd used my name, Dad claimed it had been deliberate. Mitch, however, had never confirmed it until just now. Why he'd chosen me was a bit of a mystery, as the two of us had never been close.

"You want to know why we named him after you, right?" Mitch said, as if reading my mind.

"I'm a little surprised, is all. Don't get me wrong, I'm honored, but you and I… you know."

"Yeah, I know. It's not about us, or the friendship I hope to one day have with you. It's about your resilience and strength. Kate and I want our son to know you don't give up when the going gets tough. Who better to look to for example than his uncle?"

Why his explanation bothered me I couldn't say, but I lashed out accordingly. "Um… I can think of a lot of better people to look up to than me. What exactly do you plan on telling him about his uncle's *resilience*? Are you going to leave out the part where I stabbed a guy to death?"

Mitch jolted at my graphic reply. See, I wasn't the best role model, now was I? Maybe he should rethink the kid's name. I mean it's not like I asked for the responsibility of being a moral compass for his son. God knows I had no fucking clue what I was going to tell my own kids someday when the topic would inevitably come up, but I sure as shit wasn't going to portray myself as some resilient protagonist.

Unfortunately, my sudden outburst altered our easygoing conversation, and now Mitch looked justifiably uncomfortable. Dammit, how much more socially awkward could I get? That's why I needed Casey. She balanced me out and covered for me when my behavior lacked the required tact.

"Sorry. That was…" I shook my head, unable to come up with a fitting excuse. "Just sorry."

Appearing genuinely concerned, Mitch waved off my apology while zeroing in on me and asking, "Everything okay with you?"

"Yeah. I'm just off today. I didn't mean to lash out at you. It's cool you named him after me, it's just… I think you might be confusing my resilience with dumb luck."

"Or maybe you're confusing dumb luck with resilience. You know what they say about luck, right?"

I shook my head, not realizing it had its own saying in the first place.

"Luck is not about getting what you want, but surviving what you don't want."

I had no response to his words. I'd never thought of it in those terms before. If that were the case, I was the luckiest guy alive.

"Anyway…" Mitch shifted uncomfortably. We'd never had the type of relationship where heart-to-heart conversations were the norm. "Enough about that. I don't want to upset you before your wedding. I remember being in your shoes. God, I was so nervous."

"That's me. All day, I've felt dangerously close to losing my shit."

"In that case, if I were you, I'd keep my distance from Dad. The night before my wedding, he told me some horrifying story about..."

"The honeybee?" I shouted out, slapping my hand against the wall.

"Yes. He told you that one too?"

"Like an hour ago. I think I'm scarred for life, and that's saying something."

"Yeah, well, I barely slept that night because I was having nightmares of my nards exploding every time I closed my eyes."

We both laughed, bonding over our shared trauma.

"Someone needs to keep him on a leash during weddings," I said. "Or at least warn the others."

"Nah, I think we should keep that information to ourselves. Why should the rest of them get a free pass?"

How could I argue with that?

"Anyway, I've got to head to bed. Now that I have a kid, I can barely keep my eyes open past eleven o'clock." He gripped my shoulder. "Try not to get too nervous. Go into tomorrow feeling confident, knowing that what you and Casey have together is something special."

"Thanks, Mitch. That's the best advice I've heard all day."

The party ended shortly after, and I was escorted to my room by no fewer than a dozen superheroes. With capes flying and ridiculous kung fu moves by out-of-shape pretenders, no one was able to see past all the masked crusaders into the center of the crowd where I was conveniently ducking to keep from being seen. It seemed for now at least that Operation Pretzel was still a closely guarded secret. I'd had doubts earlier in the evening as I worried the bachelor party would be my undoing. The last thing I needed was to be photographed in a drunken stupor the night before the ceremony. Casey and I and a team of specialists had worked tirelessly to keep the specific date and location of our wedding a secret from the press. After extensive searches in the Los Angeles area, an exasperated and overwhelmed Casey off-handedly suggested having the wedding back where it all began, sort of like a retracing of the steps that led us to each other.

I'd jumped all over the idea, not only because I had a soft spot for Arizona, but also because it would force Casey to radically trim the guest list, something I'd been pushing for all along. I didn't want or need a big star-studded event. Marrying in a quaint little church with just Casey, me, and a small group of our family and friends was the way I'd always pictured our wedding day to be.

The Avengers left me at my room with a promise to be dressed exactly the same for my wedding. Yeah, not only would that not fly with Casey but Boris would surely drop dead on the spot.

Keith stayed back after everyone had gone. I grabbed his hand and gave him a quick back-slap hug as a gesture of thanks.

"Did I do good?" he asked, even though he already knew the answer. "Were you sufficiently underwhelmed?"

"I was, thank you. It was perfect. Just what I didn't know I wanted."

"Awesome. It's the least I can do. You've always been there for me."

A response didn't seem necessary. We both understood his reference. Keith had, on occasion, required some special assistance that only a sum of excess money could provide, and I'd given it freely. Keith had always been my favorite charity.

"So there's something I've been meaning to talk to you about," I said, hesitating as I searched for the right words.

"I know Sam will be there tomorrow. It'll be fine."

Samantha was Keith's ex-girlfriend. They'd broken it off a while back, and as far as I knew, tomorrow would be the first time the two had seen each other since.

"Damn, you're good," I said.

"Not really. I've already heard from Mom and Emma, and I promised them the same thing… I won't cause a scene," Keith said, shaking his head. "You guys have no faith in me."

"I wasn't going to ask for your cooperation. I actually wanted to apologize."

"Well, that's new. I'm listening."

"Just so you know, I was against inviting her. I like Sam, but you're my brother, so my loyalty is to you. That being said, Casey and Sam are still friends, and she didn't want to leave her out."

"I got it, Jake. Casey called me a while back. She explained everything. It's not a problem. I promise there will be no fireworks."

Acknowledging him with a nod, I figured I'd try my luck and dig a little deeper. "I know it's none of my business, but what happened between you two?"

"Apparently women get tired of waiting for their men to get their shit together. Who knew?"

Keith gave off the impression he was fine with the whole thing, but I could hear the frustration in his voice.

"What shit are you talking about?"

"*What shit?*" he asked, high-pitched and disbelieving. "Look at me. I'm a screw up… always have been."

"No. That's not the way I remember it."

"Oh, yeah? How do you remember it?"

"You had it all, Keith. We all worshipped you. Hell, I wanted to *be* you."

"I bet you're happy that didn't pan out."

Keith smiled, but there was no humor behind the pleasantries.

"What's going on with you?"

"According to 'what's-wrong-with-me.com,' I'm an insecure person who abuses alcohol and drugs as a way to both fit in and self-soothe."

"What do you have to be insecure about?"

"That's a secret," he said, putting his finger to his lips. "And I know you're accustomed to bailing me out of tight spots, but this is beyond your reach."

Crossing my arms in front of me and keeping my eyes locked on him, I let it be known that very little was outside my scope, and not only that, but secrets were my goddamn specialty. Keith faltered, clearly uncomfortable with my silent ultimatum.

"Fine," he grumbled. "If you really want to know, it all started with Mitch."

"Mitch?" My voice did one of those weird upturns, twisting the name into something cartoonish.

"Yeah, you know, Dad's other son?"

"I know who he is. I'm just confused what your problems have to do with him. He lived in another state. We barely saw him growing up."

"*You* barely saw him. But when we were all really young, he and his mom lived down the street. Dad had shared custody of him at the time."

"Really? I had no idea."

"I'm not surprised. You were pretty young, maybe four or five, when they moved to Arizona. Anyway, Mitch and

I had a rivalry from the start. I'm not sure how much of it was my own jealousy, but he didn't help matters either. Everything was a goddamn competition to him, and you know me, I'm not much of a fighter. Anyway, the two of us were always jockeying for Dad's attention. Nine out of ten times, Mitch got it. He excelled at every damn thing he tried, especially sports. Dad loved watching him play, and bragged about him to his friends. He never talked about me like that. I mean, Dad loved me and always showed it, but it never felt like he was proud of me. Then you come along with all your fucking musical prodigy perfection, and I was doomed. You see where I'm going here?"

"Yeah, I'm getting a pretty good picture."

"All I can say is thank god for Kyle. He's as unremarkable as I am. You know, the more I think of it, the more convinced I am that Kyle and I were pre-cum babies."

I replied to his observation with a hearty laugh. Keith's theory of their placement in the ejaculation cycle really would explain a few things.

"You and Mitch and all the other siblings got a full load of genetic material, but not Kyle and me, oh no. We were false starts, the opening band…"

"The appetizers before the main dish," I added helpfully.

"Exactly."

"The fart before the shit."

Keith laughed and pushed me into the wall. "Okay, now you're just being mean."

CHAPTER FOUR

JAKE

The Uninvited

After promising Keith I'd keep my mouth shut about his personal issues with Mitch, we said our good-byes. Although I could see where he was coming from, I also didn't feel Mitch had done anything wrong. Was it his fault he was a good athlete? Or mine, because I could play a few instruments? Keith's issues with Mitch were the same ones Kyle had with me. If we had certain talents, was it wrong of us to cultivate them if it overpowered the accomplishments of others? I didn't have an answer to that, but one thing was clear: Mitch and I were a lot more alike than I'd ever realized.

Alone for the first time all day, I leaned against the door. As fun as the bachelor party had been, I felt like shit. Casey had given me the opportunity to come clean early in the evening, and I'd turned all predictable, denying that a problem existed and freezing her out. At the same time, would it even matter if I told her? Would it change the outcome of tomorrow? I knew she'd marry me no matter what confessions I made, but this one would surely hurt more than the others. This one involved our future and all she'd imagined it would be.

"Nothing you can do now," I said out loud, pushing off the door and brushing off the nagging guilt. My stomach growled. Keith had filled the party with candy, chips, and sweet stuff, but nothing of any substance really. I picked up the phone and called room service. A steaming plate of steak fajitas was delivered to my door a mere thirty minutes later. That had to be some record. I enjoyed my dinner, stripped to my boxers as I watched an entire episode of *Hoarders* because, quite frankly, I couldn't look away.

Turning it off before I could get sucked into another episode, I retreated to the bathroom to complete the shit, shower, and shave portion of the evening. And, using our hallway encounter as inspiration, I jerked off without ever having to cover my tracks.

Yep, all in all, it was a good last night as a free man. The peace and quiet alone should have been enough to buoy my spirits. Not to imply that Casey talks a lot… although she does have a lot to say… about everything… at all times…

Okay, she talks a lot.

But that was part of her charm. Since meeting Casey, my stress levels had plummeted. There were times even when we were apart that we'd text or Facetime and I could feel her with me. We could be in separate countries and still be connected. So why was it tonight seemed so different? Even though we were in the same hotel, the distance between us felt wide as if we were on two edges of a fault line, and my side was crumbling fast. Dammit! I'd squandered my chance to enter our marriage with a clean conscience… or as least as clean as it ever could be, given my sordid past. Maybe it wasn't too late. I picked up my phone to text her and see if we could meet, but then I caught sight of the time – 1:48 in the morning. She'd be sleeping by now, and if I woke her, it would only be cause for alarm. I put the phone back down and stood in place, feeling strangely disoriented. A sudden eeriness displaced the stillness in the room, and I was struck by the sensation that I wasn't alone. I drew in a sharp breath as chills prickled my skin. Oh, god, not tonight. On high alert, I paced the room, checking the windows and walls as if that might ward off an unwanted visit.

Yet I knew better. If they wanted me, they'd come at night, while I slept. That was when I was most vulnerable and unable to fend them off. Why now? It had been over a year since the last ambush, and nothing had changed in that period of time. They knew damn well I couldn't give them what they wanted. Hell, they couldn't demand such things from me in the first place because they weren't even real! At least that's what I told myself, because if I really was having nocturnal visits from dead people, then I had bigger problems than I cared to admit.

I had to assume the anxiety over keeping secrets from Casey the night before our wedding was what brought them to my doorstep at this late hour. They'd always fed off my stress, but since meeting Casey, there hadn't been as much of it to go around. But tonight, alone and susceptible, it would be a virtual feeding ground. I needed to shut them down before they could ever get started because, if there was one thing I was certain of, the ghosts of horrors past were here to ruin my wedding, and a trip down Ray Davis's memory lane was sure to do just that.

Staying alert was key. I couldn't risk closing my eyes. Not tonight. Not on the cusp of having everything I'd ever wanted. Precautions needed to be taken. Without haste, I flipped the in-room coffee maker on and began brewing the first of many cups. The hope was that a heavy influx of caffeine might help me outwit and outlast my tormentors. If I could just make it to morning, the light flooding through the windows would drive out their darkness.

With the remote in one hand and a cup of coffee in the other, I watched another episode of *Hoarders* and had begun on the third when an unexpected development drew a startled gasp from my throat. I'm no expert, but once you start finding petrified cats under piles of trash, don't you think maybe your hoarding problems have exceeded the skillset of a Hollywood television host? Changing channels in rapid succession, I didn't stop until I found one that was off air. I stared at the blank screen, mesmerized by the soft hum. The white noise was working in much the same way Casey's relaxing buzz did.

I stayed strong for a couple of hours, keeping the unwanted visitors at bay, but as my drowsy eyes began to droop, even the endless cups of coffee were not enough to save me. Slowly I drifted off into oblivion and into the nightmare world, which now only existed in my dreams. Whether I liked it or not, another night would be laid to waste in Ray's handcrafted hell. Only tonight I wouldn't be suffering alone, as I'd been joined by a handful of angry spirits hell-bent on making me pay.

My unwelcome companions had first appeared to me at one of the lowest points of my life, during a time when hallucinations had become my new reality. Talking bugs, bleeding walls, and spiteful spooks had all become a part of my uninvited extended family. Emerging through the cracks in the rickety floorboards, each apparition was more ghastly than the next. Even as a thirteen-year-old kid banging his fist on death's door, I knew instantly who they were… the alumni, if you will, of Ray's former victims…

but what they wanted from me had yet to be revealed. In all their deathly decay, the ghosts had materialized after the injury to my knee and stayed with me throughout that last excruciating week of captivity.

At first I'd cowered in their presence, begging for mercy, as I assumed their presence was an ominous sign, a signal of my impending demise. However, the only pain they ever inflicted was on my impaired mind; which, at the time, could no longer be trusted. It soon became clear that these were no murderous ghouls, but tortured young souls fighting, just as I was, to free themselves from a killer's hold. They were not my adversaries, but my brothers-in-arms – the band of bloody misfits I'd been destined to share the afterlife with; or at least, that had been the plan until I made my harrowing escape and left them to their misery for all of eternity.

It was with these doomed spirits that I spent the final night of my pre-wedded life, tossing and turning, covered in a cold sweat as I battled the ghosts of nightmares past. I think it goes without saying that when morning mercifully rolled around, I was far from the confident, enthusiastic groom Casey expected me to be. Hell, at this point, she'd be lucky if I wasn't babbling incoherently in a corner after the nocturnal torture session I'd just survived. How was I supposed to get my head right before the ceremony with the memory of a half a dozen souls screaming in my ear?

This was exactly why I'd fought to keep awake. Now I was a mess, and I had no one to blame but myself. It was too late to contact Casey. Besides, what could she do, anyway? I just had to pull it together on my own and get through the day. All I needed was a little self-soothing. What had I read again on that topic? Ingest hard drugs. Uh, yeah, probably not the best idea. Talk about swapping one problem for another.

Maybe I could take a cue from toddlers and get into the habit of thumb sucking. That seemed to calm them right down, but… oh, hell, who was I kidding? I'd tried it before and it didn't fucking work!

The only other thing I could think of on such short notice was deep breathing. Yes, that one seemed reasonable. I mean, how hard could breathing be? I did it all day long. We had a winner. Focusing on taking long, soothing inhales while blowing out the air in loud, exaggerated grunts, I soon discovered it did nothing but make me focus on inhaling and exhaling, and in no time at all, I was hyperventilating and breathing into a paper laundry bag I found in the closet.

Okay, so this was definitely not working. Soothing myself had been an epic fail, and now I only had three more hours left to get my shit together. I needed Casey. Picking up my phone, I called her number but was disappointed when it went to voicemail. I didn't bother leaving a message. She was getting married today. There was no way she had time for me.

My thoughts were interrupted by a hasty series of knocks on my door. Because I'd awakened so late, I'd slept through the meeting time with my groomsmen. I opened the door to Kyle, who immediately startled at my appearance.

"Oh, shit. Are you okay?" he asked. "Why aren't you ready?"

"Rough night."

His eyes rolled over me. "I should say so."

"Why? Do I look that bad?"

"Well, remember that time you got the stomach flu and it was coming out of both ends for two days straight?"

"Yeah."

"Right, so, you look only slightly better than that."

"Dammit. Okay. I'm going to jump in the shower. Can you stall for me?"

"Please. You know that's my specialty."

Talking to Casey was going to have to wait. I'd just have to get ready and meet her at the church. I'd be cutting it close, but what was the alternative?

Peaking out the door, I eyed the building across the courtyard. The last time I was here, I'd been forced to run across the patio area to avoid getting caught by a group of teens, but this time I didn't see anyone but a security guard patrolling the area. Nice. Operation Pretzel was in full swing. It appeared Casey and I had pulled off the impossible. I'd arrived at the church a while back, and after meeting with the minister and dressing in my tux, I was ready to go with an hour and a half to spare. This was the time I'd slip over to the other building and pull Casey aside. It would be a quick trip, long enough for me to come clean and get back to my side if she still wanted to marry me after my confession.

Just as I was pushing the door open, a hand reached out and slammed it shut in my face.

"I wouldn't do that, Jake."

Winded and flushed, Kyle stood beside me panting as his hand gripped the door handle, preventing my exit.

"I need to see her real quick."

He raised one brow. "Before the wedding? Bad choice, dude."

"Look, I know all about the wedding rules, but this can't wait."

"Actually, it might have to," he said. "We've got a minor security issue."

"I just checked. Everything looks good… right?"

"Um…." Kyle hesitated. "It depends on what your definition of 'good' is."

"Probably the same as most people's. Why? What happened?"

"It appears we've had a leak, but there's no reason for alarm. It's really not a big deal. Security is handling it."

"Does that mean the media is here?"

"They are," he affirmed. "And a few fans, too, but they've been pushed back."

"Pushed back? That doesn't sound like a few."

"It depends on your definition of 'a few.'"

"Three or four… a few."

"Right, so our definitions are a bit different. When I say 'a few,' I'm talking in the hundreds."

"Agh, Kyle! Just spit it out! You're starting to piss me off."

"We've got a few hundred fans and paparazzi gathered outside the church. But the local police are on it, and so there's nothing to worry about."

"The local police, now? Are we going to have a problem getting to the reception?"

"Um…," he hesitated again. "You know."

I glared at Kyle.

"It might be best to take the pictures in the church, is all I'm saying."

"Why?"

"We've got an overhead issue."

"Overhead? As in a helicopter?"

"… -ers," Kyle corrected, wincing. "As in plural."

I could feel the frustration bubbling over. "So let me get this straight. We've got a militarized operation going on right outside the church doors, is that what you're telling me?"

"Hey," Kyle said, throwing his hands up. "Don't bust my balls. I'm just the delivery boy, here to escort you to those on the security team that actually matter."

I glanced back over to the other building, trying to decide what to do, but in the end, the approaching thump of rotary blades made the decision for me.

"Shit! Take me to Vadim."

The long hallway curved around the back of the church, connecting the bride's room with the groom's. I'd been here before; had taken this exact passageway to sneak back to Mitch and the guys after the secret rendezvous with Casey a little over two years ago. Arriving at the end of the corridor, I shifted nervously outside the door where Casey was waiting for the ceremony to begin. Chances were pretty damn high she wasn't going to appreciate my last-minute intrusion. The meeting with Vadim, the head of my security team, had taken longer than I'd expected, and now I was cutting it way too close.

I'd hoped my self-preservation instincts would kick in and I'd be able to just push the entire discussion until after we were married, but that approach had me feeling like a fraud. She needed to hear this before we were wed. This was no little white lie I'd been withholding from her. No;

this was a life-altering truth, one big enough to put an industrial-sized damper on all our lofty hopes and dreams. How could I, in good conscience, bind myself in holy matrimony to Casey, knowing I might not be able to give her what she wanted most in the world? Dating her was one thing – she still had an out – but strapping myself to her side till death did us part, under false pretenses, well... someone needed to warn the poor girl, and that someone, unfortunately, had to be me.

Opening the door to the bride's waiting area, I was assailed by the surging backdraft of cheap hairspray and high-end perfume. Unprepared for the onslaught of noxious chemicals, my reaction time was too slow, and before I had time to take cover, I'd already snorted up the poisonous vapor like a line of coke. The unwelcome olfactory stimulation drew an almost instantaneous pounding in my head, and a steady stream of toxic tears dripped from my eyes.

Still determined to find my bride, I stumbled my way through the plume only to find myself blocked once again, this time by a barrier of wall-to-wall green. I'd almost forgotten Casey had chosen this specific accent color until it assaulted my senses. Green ... oh, wait, sorry: *mint.* She'd been very specific about that distinction, as if mint were not even a distant relative of the green family. In hindsight, I should have put my foot down on her color choice. And maybe I would have had I not lost my veto power after casually throwing out the idea of dressing the bridesmaids in black. Casey's highly sarcastic response had been, "Ooh, yes, great idea. We could dress up the flower girls in some black lace, smoky eyeliner… maybe add an eyebrow piercing or two … or better yet, Jake, a neck tattoo."

It took a moment to realize the excited buzz that had greeted me upon entering the room had now been replaced by hushed whispering, and every female in the place was staring back at me in horror. I usually got a better reception from women. Wiping the tears from my burning eyes, I took a step back, surprised by the adverse reaction I was receiving. Okay, so maybe I'd underestimated the breaking of the 'Do not see the bride before the ceremony' wedding ritual, but did Casey's nearest and dearest really have to act like I'd broken one of the Ten Commandments?

"Jake!" My mother swiftly crossed the room, appearing suddenly nauseous. "What are you doing? You can't be here."

"I need to talk to Casey."

"The wedding is about to start. Does your father know you left?"

"I don't know. I don't run everything by him. I really need to talk to Casey."

Her eyes darted around nervously. "You'd better not be doing what I think you're doing," she whispered, gripping my arm and trying to steer me from the room.

"Mom!" I dug my feet in and pulled my arm from her hold.

Casey's voice sounded from somewhere beyond. "It's okay, Michelle."

The bridesmaids parted the sea of green, and at the end stood my bride, radiating beauty in a strapless white wedding gown. I'd always thought Casey was pretty, but today, in that plunging neckline sprinkled in crystals … and the soft veil and the white flowers … the sight of her nearly brought me to my knees. I swallowed hard, trying to remember the reason for my intrusion until I caught sight of Casey's eyes, flooded with tears. It was only then that it dawned on me why everyone was gaping at me now: they thought I was breaking off the wedding. Certainly the chemically induced tears I was shedding had done nothing but drive home the misperception that I was here for nefarious reasons.

"Casey, I…"

"Don't even think about it," she said, putting a hand up to stop me. Our eyes met, and hers were blazing. With her head held high, Casey grabbed her dress and stomped toward the door. "Not here. At least give me that one courtesy."

Chapter Five

Casey

The Wedding

Don't kill him. Just hear him out. Maybe he has a valid reason. No, you know what? He's leaving you at the altar. Kill the bastard.

As I walked out of the bridal room and into the hallway, I could feel him lapping at my heels. I spun on the pointed toe of my beautiful Jimmy Choo glitter pumps only to have him nearly crash into me. Without waiting for an explanation, I placed my hand on his chest and shoved him away with every last bit of strength I had in me.

"Casey...please let me..."

Oh, no. If he thought he was getting the first word in this altar-dumping, he was sadly mistaken. Not only would I be taking the first word but also the third, and very last one to boot.

"I asked you last night if you wanted to talk!" Each word in the sentence became progressively louder until I was shouting the final bit. At this point, I wasn't even trying to spare the ladies on the other side of the wall. If I was going down, everyone would be going along for the ride.

Mimicking Jake, I began ticking off memorized lines straight from his lying mouth. "'*I'm fine, Casey,*' '*I'm just nervous, Casey,*' '*I want to marry you, Casey.*' That's what you said!" For good measure, I shoved him again.

Although my throat burned a bit from the shrieking, I was pleased with how successful I'd been in impersonating his voice. Maybe I'd added a touch too much 'whiny bitch' to my impression of him; but then, the dream crusher deserved every tiny little thing coming his way.

My ex-fiancé seemed uncertain of how to calm the wild banshee in me, so he attempted the old 'Talk the jumper off the roof' strategy by lifting both arms up in a calming gesture and slowly walking toward me in soothing strides. Surprisingly the approach seemed to be having the desired effect on me, and I was contemplating hearing him out, but then he recklessly miscalculated by placing his pointer finger to his lips and saying, "Casey, shhh."

"Do not 'shush' me!" I snarled through gritted teeth. "You have some nerve! I just can't believe you! You're leaving me? Is that what this is? You're leaving me AT THE ALTAR?!? Do you have any idea what a diabolical douchebag that makes you?!"

"I'm not..."

Perhaps Jake was trying to answer my question, but I was in no mood to give him that chance. Waving my irate hand in his face, I continued my tirade. "Listen, sparky! I'm not interested in your half-witted excuses. How dare you? I'm just... I can't even look at you right now, turd-bucket!"

Holy hell! That expression on his face had better not be amusement.

"Casey, can you let me talk?"

"No. I think we're past explanations, you...you... polynomial pissant!" Oh, crap... had I just insulted him with a math term? Yes. Yes, I had. Dammit, I needed to focus. "We're at the point now where I kick your ass across state lines."

Oh, my god! Was he laughing at me? Unable to control the rage, I opened my fingers and let my palm fly straight for Jake's face. Impressively, he caught my wrist mid-slap.

"Whoa, okay, right to the violence," he said, looking more entertained than anything else.

"Oh, you're going to get worse than that, dipwad! You realize my whole family is out there... aunts, uncles, cousins. I've even got second cousins once removed waiting for me to walk down the aisle. And my poor Aunt Betty – they wheeled her here from the hospital, Jake. The hospital!"

"It's not like she was dying," he said, releasing my wrist. "She had bunion surgery."

"I don't care!" I shouted. How dare he downgrade her very real medical condition! "She's here, her toe doubled in size, and now, like all the others, she will get to witness my complete and utter disgrace!"

"I didn't come here to break it off with you."

I tried to focus on his face, but the furor had me seeing double. Please tell me he wasn't proposing what I thought he was proposing? Did he seriously think I'd even consider continuing to date him after he callously dumped my ass at the altar?

"Oh, huh," I tapped my finger to my lips trying to pretend like I was actually giving his outrageous proposal some merit. "So what you're saying is – you just want to go back to where we were BEFORE you humiliated me in front of everyone. Wow. How convenient for you. Yeah, I don't think so, assbutt."

Dammit. I really needed to cool it with the insults. Now I was just grabbing any two off-colored words and hooking them together.

"The wedding's still on," he said, rushing the words out before I could stop him again. "If you'll still have me after you hear me out."

"What? I don't... why would you pull me out here just before the ceremony?"

"We need to talk. There's something I've been trying to tell you all morning, but one thing after another has been getting in the way. And then when I finally did make it to you...well... obviously, I miscalculated what your reaction would be."

I could hear him talking, but he might as well have been speaking an alien dialect for all the words meant to me. I opened and closed my mouth numerous times without any sound until Jake came to the rescue, sort of, by transforming his hand into a talking puppet to illustrate his point. Finally I understood.

"Hold on there. Are you telling me that you scared the living baby squirrels out of me so we could have a nice little pre-wedding chat? Have you ever heard of the talking device called a phone, genius?"

The sheepish grin gave me the first bit of relief since his teary-eyed invasion set me on a collision course with crazy town. Maybe the wedding really was still on; but if that were the case, it made Jake the stupidest groom to have ever roamed this earth. I slapped his chest with my perfectly manicured hand.

"Would you please stop hitting me? You really need anger management classes. And assbutt? Where do you come up with that shit? I mean how awesomely redundant was that?"

All the tension dropped from my body as I felt the tiniest of smiles grace my face. “Well, you know, I do have a gift for the spoken word.”

He nodded in amusement.

“So, what are you saying?” I asked, still shaken. “Are we still getting married?”

“It depends. Are you going to continue hitting me?”

Jutting my chin out, I answered defiantly, “It depends. Are you going to marry me?”

We stared at one another a moment before dissolving into laughter. Once we’d quieted down, I slapped his chest again just because I needed to.

“What were you thinking, Jake? Do you have any idea how bad that looked back there? And why were you crying?”

“I wasn’t crying. When I walked into that room, it felt like someone squirted a napalm bomb in my eyes. The tears just started pouring. You know how sensitive my eyes are.”

Tears pooled in my own eyes as I struggled to keep the disappointment at bay.

“Hey, are you okay?” Jake pulled me into his arms, guilt evident in his remorseful face. “I’m so sorry I scared you.”

“It’s not that… it’s just, we can’t ever have that moment now.”

“What moment?”

"When you see me for the first time as I walk down the aisle. And your eyes fill with love and you think to yourself that I'm the most beautiful bride ever. That moment is ruined. I just don't understand. I mean, I thought Boris and I were pretty clear with you about all the rules. Your only job was to follow them."

He dipped his head into my shoulder. "I'm so sorry. But if it's any consolation, I had that moment when I saw you at the end of the bridesmaid tunnel. You took my breath away, and I promise, you were, and are, the most gorgeous bride I've ever laid eyes on. In fact, I would have taken more time to marvel had you not turned into bridezilla and started calling me the world's greatest insults. Sparky? Babe, that was epic."

I nodded, returning his smile. "I don't think I can stress enough how much you deserved it."

"No, I got the gist of it."

"So what did you come to say to me that was so important it couldn't wait until after we got married?"

The mood shifted, and Jake's relaxed demeanor turned troubled. "You asked me a question last night. I came here to answer it."

I knew instantly this wouldn't be something I wanted to hear. "Okay," I answered, hesitantly.

"I should have told you last night, I know that. I just have so much trouble opening up. And then I had a bad night… didn't sleep much… I felt terrible about lying, and I just really needed to see you."

Regardless of the stunt he'd just pulled, my heart ached. I knew what rough nights were like for him, and I wouldn't wish those on my worst enemy. "You want to tell me about your bad night?"

"Just… nightmares."

"Ray?"

He didn't answer, but his sudden rigidness answered my question.

"Don't let him take this day away from you, Jake," I whispered, lifting my hand to stroke his strong jawline.

"It's not just that, Casey. I should have come clean with you yesterday. I've been worried about getting married, not because I don't want to be your husband, but because I don't want to let you down. You have all these ideas about what you want our life to be like, and I just… I don't know if I can do it."

"Do what?"

"Give you what you want. I don't know if I can be the husband you expect, or deserve, and I sure as shit don't think I can be the type of father you want for your kids."

What the hell was he saying? And where the hell was this all coming from? Trying to regain my composure, I smoothed down my dress and cleared my throat before asking the question I feared the answer to: "Are you saying you don't want children?"

"It's not that I don't want them, but I see Finn and how natural he is with Indiana, and I feel like… no, I *know*… I can't be like that."

The revelation rocked me to my core. I'd just taken for granted that he was into the whole fatherhood thing. We'd talked enough about it, and he'd never voiced concern in the past… or had he? Suddenly, it occurred to me that every time I brought it up, Jake humored me before changing the subject. This had been in front of me all along, but I hadn't seen it because I didn't want to. How many other things had he been hiding from me in plain sight?

"You can't possibly know how you'll be as a father until you are one."

"I know, it's just…I've thought a lot about this recently, and I'm just not sure."

"You're breaking my heart right now, Jake."

"That's why I didn't want to tell you. I didn't want you to leave me, but I can't let you go into this marriage under false pretenses."

"I'm going to ask you again – do you want to have kids with me?"

"I do… but at the same time, I don't."

"That's not an answer, and I need to know this, Jake, because that's something we've always agreed on wanting – or at least I thought we did, and now if you're changing your mind…" I stopped talking and looked away. What exactly was I saying? Was I really willing to give him up if he didn't want to make babies with me?

"I want them, Casey. I do. But the thing is, someday the kid is going to grow up and hear stuff about me. How can I explain what happened in a way that won't scar our kid for life? Is it really right to bring a kid into the world who's going to have to live under my umbrella with all the crap it covers? I just… if I had kids, I'd want them to be proud of me."

"Of course they'd be proud of you. You're so much more than just one horrific act perpetrated against you twelve years ago. You can't base your future on what happened in the past."

"You don't understand. My past will never go away, and our kid will be the one to pay the price one day."

Tears were slipping down my cheeks now. It felt like my world was imploding. The two things I wanted most didn't want each other. "Your kid will be proud of you no matter what, Jake," I said, feebly.

"Sure, but he'll also be embarrassed by me. I deal with enough shame, Case. I can't feel that way with a child."

"But these are all things you can work on. You should never have to feel shame."

Jake looked away, not meeting my eye, and I knew then that he was telling me the truth. This was something that was eating him up inside.

"Okay, look. If you're not ready to start a family, then I'm willing to wait… as long as you promise me that you will work through the issues."

"You mean more therapy."

"Yes, that's what I mean."

Jake dropped his head to study the floor as his hands clenched in frustration. "Therapy makes me feel worse."

"Then we find someone else. You just have to try harder. I've seen you when you truly want something. You don't back down. So don't give up on our kids. Bartholomew and Enid need you."

"Who are Bartholomew and Enid?"

"Our future nerdy, rocker babies."

"Wait, what?" His stunned reaction was tempered only by the amusement playing out over his face. "Those are the names you've picked out? They're all nerd and no rock. You might as well put a *Kick me* sign on their backs. Now I really don't want to have kids with you."

I laughed. He was back to his good-natured self, and my anxiety melted away. "Well, do you have a better idea?"

"Um…yeah… like any other names in the entire universe!"

"Can you be more specific?"

"You need to think more 'Kick-ass' and less 'Kick my ass'. Something like Axl or Cash, or for a girl, Stevie."

"Oh, Jake." I sighed heavily. "You know I'm not cool enough to raise a Stevie."

"You just have to try harder," he said, playfully mocking my words. "Find a new therapist who can talk the nerd right out of you."

I grabbed him by the tux collar and pulled him into a kiss. "I love you, Jake McKallister. Thank you for warning me, but I think I'll take my chances."

Since meeting Jake, I'd known he was the one for me, so I had no choice but to put every last bit of my faith in him. I held out my hand. 'What do you say? You ready to get this show on the road?"

He grabbed it, flashing me his most gorgeous smile. "Let's do this."

Just to be on the safe side, I delivered Jake to the groom's room and instructed the men not to let him out of their sight until we were safely married. The wedding was now officially late, and I had a roomful of bridesmaids who probably assumed it had been called off entirely.

The moment I re-entered the bride's room, all chatter ceased as every head turned in my direction. It was clear by the look of utter pity on all of their faces that the whole lot of them expected the worst. Who could blame them? Neither Jake, with his teary-eyed interruption, nor I, with my loud declarations of hatred, had given them much hope.

Boris came rushing to me. "Oh, honey, I'm so sorry." He ran his hands over my face. "What did he do to you? You just look awful."

"I do?" Touching my fingers to my own face, I wondered exactly what had happened to change my appearance so drastically in the fifteen minutes I'd been gone. Two soggy, colossal plunging tears, that's all I'd allowed myself. Surely Boris could work with that.

"He's an idiot and you're better off without him. I never trusted him in the first place. You're a strong, fabulous woman, and you will get through this."

My bridesmaids fanned out around me, making a protective circle. Their misinformed concern warmed my heart. At least I knew who my friends were. In quick succession, the questions came flying.

Jake's oldest sister, Emma, asked, "What can we do?"

"Do you need to sit down?" Kenzie, Kyle's girlfriend, grasped my arm and prepared to lead me to a chair.

Her lips thin with anger, Jake's mother, Michelle said, "Let me go talk to him. I'm sure he's just nervous."

Okay, this needed to end now, before someone said something they would regret – like Boris, who was seconds away from eating his offensively supportive words. "Um… hello, ladies," I said, clapping my hands. "What is this, a funeral?"

A blanket of confusion percolated through the room, and everyone looked to each other for answers. Perhaps they all thought I was in denial… but not my mother. If there was one person in this world who knew me inside and out, it was she. Instantly picking up on my mood, and without skipping a beat, Mom slyly asked, "That depends – is Jake's body in the hallway?"

"No." I laughed. "He's alive and breathing, people. And, I don't know what all these long faces are for, but I'm getting married in a few minutes, so is it too much to ask for some smiles?"

The shift in the room was immediate, and relief dripped off every surface. Except for Boris. Poor, poor Boris. He was now gagging on his words, and by the nauseous look on his face, they weren't tasting real good coming back up.

"I… I didn't mean anything bad when I called Jake an idiot. I don't think that at all. He's very smart. I…just…"

"Boris, relax. He *was* an idiot. How many times did we have to tell him he couldn't see the bride before the ceremony? I mean, use your brain, dude, am I right?"

He let out a long, deep breath, using one hand to place over his heart and the other to fan his bright red face. "Please don't tell him I said that."

Closing my mouth, I turned the imaginary key and flung it over his shoulder. He mouthed *thank you*, and all was forgotten.

"Do I really look that awful?"

"Not at all," he said, smiling with his mouth but not with his eyes. "We're just going to…" Boris abruptly stopped with the pep talk once he'd examined my face and fluffed my hair. Perhaps coming to the realization that my beauty issues were well beyond his vast capabilities, he screamed over his shoulder, "Hair. Makeup. Now!"

His minions came running, and while I was undergoing the transformation from hideously dumped Casey to radiantly wedded bride, the others were ushered to the lobby of the church. I looked around. Had my maid of honor also left? Her level head would do me well now. It had taken a lot of thought about who I wanted in that position in my wedding procession. I had so many amazing girlfriends who all supported me in their own unique ways. In the end, the woman I chose had always been there for me and was a constant reminder of how blessed a life I led.

"Yes. We're a go," I heard Boris say into his phone.

Suddenly nerves attacked my calm and my hands began to shake. "It's starting?"

"As soon as the bride arrives, it is." He beamed, holding his hand out to me. "Shall we?"

I stood on my shaking legs, suddenly self-conscious. The church was packed full, and in a few minutes' time, all eyes would be on me. "Do I look okay?"

"I say this to all my brides, but this time I mean it. You're the most beautiful of them all." Boris' eyes shone with affection as he took me in from head to toe and, I have to say, I almost believed him.

"Thank you for everything, Boris. It's been a pleasure."

"That, my lovely lady, it most certainly has."

Anxious flutters tickled my chest. "Whew. I'm nervous all of a sudden."

"No need. You're marrying the man of your dreams. Never stop smiling."

He was right. I was lucky beyond belief. Hooking my hand through his folded arm, I smiled radiantly. "I'm ready, Boris. Take me to my man."

The click of my heels was the only sound we made on our way to the front lobby. This was the exact path I'd walked at Kate and Mitch's wedding, and I had a moment of déjà vu. I remembered the racing heart and the fluttery exhilaration of seeing him again. He'd rocked my world from the first time I'd met him, and he was still doing that now. In all honesty, I shouldn't have been surprised by that interruption before the ceremony. There was an air of unpredictability with Jake that had always intrigued and challenged me. He was complicated and tough, possessing just the right amount of mystery to keep things interesting. But at the same time, he had a wit and charm to him that I could only have dreamed of in a mate. This was the amazing man I was marrying. And if I had to postpone holding his baby in my arms, it would be worth the wait.

The lobby was filled with a hushed excitement. All the people I loved had gathered here to celebrate the beginning of a new chapter in my life. I scanned the room, seeking to capture the extraordinary moment in my mind. This was it. My future was about to begin.

The music started playing in the church before flowing down the aisle and out into the lobby where we stood. My father walked to my side and kissed my cheek.

"Dad."

"My sweet little girl. Look at you now. I'm not sure I'm ready to give you away just yet." His misty eyes threatened to break me down, but I swallowed back the lump and smiled at the man who'd treated me with love and respect my whole life and who had taught me to demand the same treatment from my own mate one day.

"You've done your job," I whispered. "It's time to let me go."

He nodded, wiping the tears away, and then offered his arm to me.

Jake's younger sister, Grace, began the processional, followed by Emma and Darcy, then my good friends Kate and Kenzie. The final bridesmaid was Wilhelmina, or Willa for short, my best friend since third grade. The flower girl and ring bearer, my niece and nephew, Sydney and Riley, followed them down the aisle.

My matron of honor came to me then, her eyes glowing with love as she tenderly touched both my cheeks with her capable hands.

"This is your moment, Casey. Go out there and shine."

"I will, Mom."

She hugged me tightly before fitting the veil over my face. Her trembling lip was the only giveaway to the emotion of the moment. My mother, my best friend, my confidante, and the woman I loved most in the world. She gave me my personality, my zest for life, and my loving heart. I would not be who I was without her and was forever grateful to call her Mom. For all those reasons and more, it was only natural that she would take that place of honor in the procession.

I stood close to my father as my mother began her walk down the aisle. When the music briefly stopped, I took a deep breath and looked to my father for guidance as I had my whole life. He squeezed my hand, saying, "You got this."

And then the music began to play for me; the moment I'd been waiting for since Jake dropped to one knee and proposed fourteen months ago. But really, I'd waited longer than that. This was a milestone most girls dreamed of, and I was no exception. The fact that I was about to walk down that aisle into the arms of my one, true great love… well, that was beyond humbling.

I stepped into the doorway and watched as every person in the church turned to stare as I came into view in my billowy white gown with an armful of my very favorite flowers, the same varieties Jake had decorated the wooden arch on the beach with when he'd asked me to marry him. Jake! My eyes moved off the guests and traveled down the aisle. On the stairs, smack dab in the middle, stood my betrothed waiting for me. Even as far apart as we were, our eyes connected, and nothing had ever felt so right. I would have run to him had I not thought Boris would beat me over the head with a party favor.

Goosebumps prickled my skin as I began the walk, never taking my eyes off the prize. And oh, lord, what a prize he was. It wasn't just that he was a gorgeous man or that he was beloved by millions or that he could buy me whatever I desired; no, it was something far less material... simply put, Jake had given me his heart. And that might seem standard protocol for all grooms, but with Jake, it wasn't just a matter of falling in love. He'd had to battle demons, survive battles, and hand himself over for healing. So yes, it was a big deal that he was standing up here today wearing his mended heart on his sleeve. It was a damn big deal, and with my vows, I would promise to make it my duty to always keep it beating strong.

I didn't even remember getting to the end of the aisle, but when I did, Jake was waiting for me, strong and proud. He and my father exchanged a handshake before Jake broke wedding protocol, again, and hugged me.

Bending his head, he whispered, "The moment wasn't ruined. I've never, in my life, seen anyone as beautiful as you."

Climbing the stairs together, we met the minister, who began the proceedings. "Ladies and gentlemen, we are gathered here today…"

Jake and I stared into each other's eyes as the man regaled us with his words of wedded wisdom. We were not the first lovebirds to stand before him, and would certainly not be the last, but we were unique in our own way… two opposites, who together made perfect sense.

Somehow five minutes passed, and I barely heard a word. My mind was flooded with memories, from our first meeting to our whirlwind courtship through the hardships we'd faced. All of that had come together for this flawless moment in time. Thankfully there was a recording of the proceedings because I'd need to watch it back just to know what had happened during the ceremony.

"Casey?"

I looked up to find the minister staring at me expectantly.

"Your vows?" he prompted.

"Oh, yeah. Oops."

One job. I had one job: pay attention during the wedding; and I couldn't even do that. Unable to trust my memory at such an important moment in my life, I unfolded the crumbled paper in my hand.

"Jake, in writing these vows, I was consumed by finding the perfect word to best describe how I feel when I'm with you. There were many contenders. *Loved*, of course, because you show me every day in both your actions and your words that I'm cherished. *Respected*, no doubt, because you want me to always shine in my own right. And let's not forget *happy*, because, with you, I'm never without a bright smile on my face. But, Jake, the word that best describes how you make me feel is *lucky*.

Lucky that Mitch and Kate had the sense to pair us up for their wedding. Lucky that you didn't get a restraining order against me when I pulled that dancing prank on you during our first meeting. Lucky that I get to look at your handsome face every day for the rest of my life. But most of all, I feel lucky to have found you – my love, my best friend, my dream come true. I love you, Jake McKallister, and I always will."

Throughout my vows, Jake kept his focus on me, reacting to each of my words with varying displays of emotion. It was clear my sentiments hit him in the core, and it took him a moment to gather himself in order to give his own vows. And when he began, no visual cues were needed.

"Before you, Casey, I'd seen love… even thought I knew what it was all about. I've created songs dedicated to it and watched others parade their happiness before me. Yet, realistically, I had no faith in the concept of love, and I never imagined finding it for myself. Then you came along, with that ridiculous banana binder of yours, and turned everything I thought I knew upside down. Casey, I love that, in the middle of a kiss, I can feel you smiling. I love that when you ask for directions, you request that words like *east* and *west* not be used. And I love that you hold up sappy signs for me as I'm getting off airplanes. Because of you, I now get to flaunt my own happiness in everyone else's faces. So thank you for that."

Jake paused, not only to allow the giggles in the church to fade away, but also to change the vibe of his speech from playful to sentimental. Taking my hands in his, he continued. "You're my changing storyline. My favorite dream. My redemption. I can now say with confidence, I finally get it… I know what love is. It's you, Casey, from beginning to end."

Maybe I should have been bawling after Jake finished his heartfelt speech, but all I felt was joy. There wasn't anything more he needed to say. No matter where this world took us, I had made a difference in it. I had changed this man for the better… made him feel again, and love – and if that were the last gift I ever received in life, I would die a happy woman.

The minister placed his hands over our joined ones and had us repeat after him the traditional wedding vows: 'To have and to hold from this day forward, for better or worse, for richer and for poorer, in sickness and in health, to love and to cherish; from this day forward until death do us part.'

Looking out over the group gathered to witness our union, I was suddenly grateful for the smaller crowd. These were the people who loved us, who wanted us to succeed.

There were no hangers-on in this group. No people here for a photo op. These were just friends and family, eager to witness our love and the beginning of our life together. So as Jake slipped the ring over my finger, it was our beginning, but also in my heart and mind...an ending. The search was over. I'd found my other half, the man I would grow old with. In that moment I pictured us timeworn and gray, sitting shoulder to shoulder in a diner booth, not because there was no room to sit on the other side, but because we just liked being close to one another. I'd make sure he stayed interested in me by keeping him on his toes at all times. A little kiss here, a butt grab there, and of course, the paper from my straw blown straight into his face when he least expected it. That's what the ring meant to me... a lifelong friendship with the man I loved.

And with one final, heart-thumping sentence, the minister smiled and proclaimed, "I now pronounce you husband and wife."

CHAPTER SIX

JAKE

The Reception

Was there a certain protocol to kissing the bride? I wasn't sure. Maybe that was something I should have checked on before standing up in front of everyone, clutching her face, and planting a solid lip lock on her… with tongue. Based on Casey's zealous reaction – and that of her female relatives, whom I'd caught fanning themselves after the steamy kiss – I'd scored solid tens across the board. However, I hadn't taken into consideration the rest of the judging panel; namely her father and brothers, who seemed not nearly as impressed as the females. If I had to guess, my combined scores would have come in somewhere in the average range.

All in all, though, a solid showing, given the way I'd been feeling after seeing Casey walking down the aisle at the beginning of the ceremony. If anything, the kiss was a reflection of her splendor. I'm not trying to be overdramatic here, but it really was like an out-of-body experience… as if I were looking down on the proceedings wondering who the hell the lucky bastard was who got her. The fact that *the bastard* was me became clearer and clearer the closer she got. If human eyes could bulge like those of cartoon characters, mine would have been a few inches outside their sockets. Casey was beyond all expectation… my tailor-made princess. Her purity and grace were magnified by the beautiful face under the veil. Her expression was serene, like a woman who was sure of her choice in soul mate. It struck me then that Casey was so much more than I deserved. Had she not met me, her life would have been a whole hell of a lot easier. But I'd fought hard for my bride, and selfish or not, I wasn't going anywhere until I made her mine.

And making it official was just what I'd done. Casey and I stood facing the guests, soaking in the applause and well wishes. I couldn't remember a moment I'd felt as happy as now. We were husband and wife. Life, from here on out, would be lived together. I'd promised her to try harder…

and I would. Giving her everything she wanted was my priority even if it meant facing the ghosts of my past.

I glanced at my bride only to find her peering up at me with a glint in her eye and a conspiratorial grin on her face. Maybe she was remembering the searing kiss. I know I was still fevered from it. But when the music started, I realized that smile of hers had nothing to do with the kiss at all… Casey had something more sinister up her sleeve. She was taunting me with weddings past.

"Don't look at me like that, babe," she said, laughing. "You know exactly what's happening here."

My eyes left her in order to stare down the wedding party. Surely they weren't a part of this shakedown – but one look at all those expectant faces and I knew Casey had turned them against me. I made eye contact with Keith, but he shrugged. My brothers, even? Dammit. Defectors! All of them.

"We are *not* doing the wedding dance!" I protested. I'd managed to dodge it once before at Mitch and Kate's wedding, but like a case of aggressive crabs, it was back to haunt me. I really had no choice. Either I looked like a douche for not finding Casey's joke whimsically fun, or I looked like a total idiot for pretending to be a happy participant in one of the stupidest ideas any bride or groom had ever come up with to entertain their guests.

Casey nudged me forward, her eyes pleading for my cooperation. Well, shit. This was happening. I was doing the dance. Mentally preparing myself for the humiliation, I looked to Casey for guidance just as the music suddenly stopped, and the entire church erupted in laughter.

I looked around, not sure what was happening, but certain I was the butt of the hysterical joke.

Casey grabbed my shoulders. "I'm just kidding," she said, laughing. "I'd never do that to you."

"So we're not…"

"No dancing, Jake… just your standard wedding fare."

What the hell? Twice! She'd gotten me twice with the same damn joke. How could I not have known? I bent over and grabbed my knees, exhaling audibly. When the shock passed, I looked up at my new bride and said, "You suck."

"I love you too. Now walk me down the aisle."

Because of the helicopters overhead, the outdoor portion of our wedding pictures was canceled and everything was taken inside the church after the ceremony. It was just as well since the temperature had already hit triple digits. I'd planned my tour schedule around an August wedding, giving myself four weeks off between the end of the European leg of the tour and the beginning of the Asian shows. Since the decision to move the wedding from Southern California to Arizona happened after the tour had already been set and tickets had been sold, there was no option but to marry in August… when it was hot as balls outside.

Because of security issues, those of us from the wedding party were given a police escort to the reception where our other guests were waiting. Originally the plan had been for Casey and me to leave the church in our own limo, but we didn't want the police to make a separate trip just for us, so we hitched a ride with Kyle, Kenzie, and Keith.

The crowd of well-wishers who'd been pushed back earlier in the day were now crowding on the small two-lane road leading out from the church. Some people held signs or flowers, but one committed woman stood on the curb in a wedding dress and veil.

"Ahh she's pretty," Casey cooed. "And look, we're twinning."

"Uh-huh, and by the looks of it," Kyle said, "You're both marrying the same guy. I'm honestly surprised she's not splattered with pig's blood."

"She doesn't have to be a creepy stalker, Kyle. Be more sensitive. What if she was just jilted by her fiancé? Those things happen," she said, elbowing me in the ribs. "Right, Jake?"

Before I could respond, the woman on the curb answered Casey's question by lifting up the top of her two-piece wedding gown to reveal 'marry me' written across her bare breasts.

"Whoa!" we all screamed in unison, not having expected such a bold proposal. Casey playfully tried shielding my eyes.

"Damn, that was so unexpected," I said, my vision still trained on the words written on her bosom. It's not like I hadn't been flashed before, but this was the first time by a woman wrapped in white satin.

"What did I tell you?" Kyle said, a smug look of satisfaction on his face. "Stalker."

"You know, Jake." Keith smirked. "If you'd just held out a day longer, you and the flasher could have been so happy together."

Kyle was peering out the window with a puzzled expression on his face. "You know what I wonder? How did she write that on herself? Wouldn't that be upside down when you look in a mirror?"

"Try backwards, dumbshit," Keith insulted, slapping him on the backside of his head. "Kenzie, I thought he was getting smarter dating you."

"Look, bud." Kenzie addressed him directly. "I do the best I can, but I only have so much to work with here."

Kyle grabbed for her as she squirmed away. "You don't diss me and get away with it," he said, throwing himself over her as she squealed in laughter.

"Oh, Jesus. Happy couples everywhere," Keith complained. "Why didn't I ride in the kids' car?"

"I thought you had a girlfriend," Casey said. "You asked to bring her to the wedding, anyway."

"I never said I was bringing her. I just wondered if I could invite someone on such short notice. But she wasn't my girlfriend. We went out twice. I didn't bring her because I didn't want to introduce her to the family and get her hopes up."

"*Her* hopes up?" Kyle grinned. "Yeah, Keith, you're the catch of a century."

"Well, I'm no Uncle Paul, but…"

Kenzie looked around, confused. "Who's Uncle Paul?"

"Only the hunkiest old guy alive today. And did anyone happen to catch a glimpse of his date?" Keith asked.

I thought back to the guests in the church but had no memory of even seeing my dad's older brother… and a fifty-five-year-old man with One Direction hair and a dark, leathery tan was not easy to miss. Nor were the types of women he normally dated. Knowing Uncle Paul, his date would be ravishing. When we were younger, the women he brought around had always starred in our wet dreams. "I did not. She was that good, huh?"

"Dude. She was bangin'… and our age. I mean, I totally bow down to the man. How does he do it?"

"It's the surfer thing," said Kyle, in all his infinite wisdom. "Doesn't matter how old you are, girls just dig it. Right, Kenzie?"

"Oh, yes. I love it. Kyle's super sexy when he arrives home smelling like seaweed and trailing sand through the apartment. I especially enjoy when he comes to me crying about chafing and wants me to rub soothing ointment in places I don't want to talk about."

"Um, FYI Kenzie, I don't cry. I simply articulate, in a very manly way, that I have sand collecting in areas of my body that terrify me."

"I told you, Kyle, you can't get kidney stones if sand collects in the tip of your penis."

"And you know this how? Do you have a medical degree that you forgot to mention?"

"If it bothers you that much, go see a doctor," Kenzie said. "Or better yet, Google it."

"Right, because the Internet is *the* place for sound medical advice."

Casey put a stop to their bickering by pressing Keith for more information on the mystery woman he had been thinking of bringing to the wedding but didn't. "You're talking about the woman you met at the studio, right? I thought you said she was perfect for you."

"Yeah, I thought she was, but turns out I was wrong." Keith shrugged, seemingly indifferent to the conversation. "There were red flags from the beginning."

Both Kyle and I groaned in unison.

"What? You guys are assholes. You didn't meet her so don't go hating on me."

Keith always found some excuse for why he couldn't get serious with a woman, and usually it was the pettiest excuse you could imagine. He dumped one for wearing red toenail polish and another because he didn't like the way she ran her tongue over her teeth.

"What horrible disorder did this one have?" I asked. "A hangnail?"

"I'm not sure I know what you're referring to." Keith knew full well where this line of questioning was going but was playing coy for laughs.

"You don't think it's just slightly weird that you won't call a girl back because you don't like the way she pronounces 'caramel'?"

"Okay, I stand by that one. Caramel is not three syllables and you know it!"

I groaned. "You're the nit-pickiest person I've ever met."

"I like what I like." Keith slid down in his seat, hooking his hands behind his head. "Big deal."

"You never told us what this one did," Casey asked, clearly excited for the answer.

"She probably blinks too much," Kyle said.

Keith's lips curved in delight as he caught our amused expressions and matched it with his own. "Well, now I don't want to say."

"Did she have a crooked toe?" Kenzie suggested.

"Or bad breath?" Casey guessed.

"You make me sound so shallow." Keith beamed. "If you must know, she parts her hair in the middle."

The four of us traded puzzled expressions.

"You know, like smack dab in the middle. I'm telling you, it's a total deal-breaker."

Laughter swept through the ranks. Even for Keith, hair parts were stretching it. He hadn't always been this way, but since breaking up with his ex, his focus was all off. Keith needed to just let her go and move on. I couldn't tell yet if being in the same room with Sam after so many months apart would be good for him or not, but at least we didn't have to contend with either of them bringing a date.

"Damn, that girl with the middle part must've been hideous." Kyle shuddered, fixing his stare on Kenzie with a mischievous grin wide across his face.

"Hey." She jabbed him with her thumb. Her hair was currently being worn with a part smack dab down the middle.

"No offense." Keith said, offhandedly. "It looks good on you."

"Oh, right. Thanks."

I watched her run her fingers through her straight hair, flipping a few strands here or there to lessen the stark appearance.

Trying to be nonchalant with a question she really wanted an answer to, Casey asked, "Did you see Sam at the church?"

"She was in the back, but yeah, I saw her."

We all watched him.

"What?"

The stare down continued.

"I'm not sure what you think is going to happen, but I can assure you, we aren't getting back together. Samantha made that perfectly clear."

We arrived to fanfare. Boris had made certain of that. Because we were robbed of the church exit we'd been hoping for, a cascade of white feathers floated down on us as we entered the reception hall.

"Please tell me Boris didn't pluck the feathers off live doves for this," I whispered in Casey's ear, while keeping the obligatory smile on my face.

Casey leaned into me. "Maybe if you were a little more involved in the planning process of our wedding, you would know that there are a thousand naked birds convalescing in the avian hospital as we speak."

"Did we at least send them get well cards?"

"We did. They should be up and flying in a few years' time."

I blew a feather out of my face and smiled at my wife before giving her a kiss on the cheek. Seconds later we were surrounded.

Casey's parents were standing at the end of the welcoming committee, and Linda immediately embraced me. "I'm so happy you're officially part of the family. Now I don't have to pretend to be nice to you anymore."

"Oh, were you being nice before?" I asked, meeting her mischievous grin with my own. "I couldn't tell."

Linda grabbed my face and kissed my cheek. "You know I love you. And I especially adore how much you love my daughter."

I leaned in to give my new mother-in-law a hug. "I'll make her happy, I promise."

"You already do."

Linda and I had hit it off on our very first meeting, and our friendship had only grown from there. And now that bond extended to the rest of Casey's family. Just as I would for my own flesh and blood, I'd do anything for the Caldwell clan. Such an attachment might seem natural to most people, but for me it was a somewhat surprising development. I'd spent so many years cut off from others, believing I didn't have the capacity to develop feelings of love toward anyone who hadn't been in my life from the very start.

Casey had proved that theory wrong when she charmed her way into my life overnight. Still, that could be explained away as romantic love. Caring for a whole group of people – that was a different story. Yet that's what happened when I was first introduced to the Caldwells. They'd welcomed me in with open arms, accepting me despite my unusual profession… and highly checkered past. Spending time with them never felt forced and I found myself easily bonding. It just went to show that there was no chokehold on my heart and there never had been. The limitations I'd placed upon myself were entirely of my own doing, and once I let go of them and opened up to the possibilities, I was able to blend them into my world. When I exchanged my vows this afternoon, I hadn't just gained a wife, but an entire family.

Dave placed his hand on my shoulder and, maybe it was just me, but it felt like his fingers were digging into my flesh a little more aggressively than they should have been. One look in his direction told me he wasn't feeling the love like his wife was.

"Really?" he asked, shaking his head at me. "Was that really necessary?"

I knew exactly what he was referring to – the kiss – and I smiled sheepishly. "Sorry. It wasn't planned, if that helps."

Dave made a show of swallowing an invisible lump before saying, "No, it doesn't go down any easier. Here's the deal, Jake. I know my daughter's an adult… it's just… I'd rather not have her romantic life, for lack of a better term, shoved down my throat. You know what I'm saying?"

"I definitely do."

"Good. Nice chat."

His fingers disengaged as he walked away, and I followed after him with my stunned eyes. That was badass! When had Dave, the mild-mannered office manager, become an ex-CIA shakedown artist? One thing was for certain, in the future, it would be wise to keep the steam level in the 'dad-pleasing' mild range with Casey for the rest of our lives.

Luke came galloping up, shaking my hand and slapping my back in unison. "Welcome to the family, bro. Is this a good time to ask for a loan?"

The smile on his face was contagious. Luke was just a good-natured person, who shared so many admirable traits with his sister. It really was impossible not to like him. Over the past two years, Luke had taught me a thing or two about not taking life so seriously. He really could teach a class in positivity. After all, this was a guy who, when told to 'have a good day,' always responded with, 'Have a better one.'

"Don't do it, Jake," Miles said, coming up behind him and putting his brother in a choke hold. "I loaned him money in the second grade and he never paid it back."

"It was a gumball machine," Luke said, performing an awkward pirouette to extract himself from Miles's grasp. "I cannot believe you still bring that up. Would you like me to pay you back? Would that make you happy?"

Luke made of show of checking his pockets for change, and when he couldn't find any, he asked, "Jake, do you have twenty-five cents on you?"

He'd been asking for loans since the beginning of our relationship – not for the money, mind you, but for the laugh he got by pointing out my income. "Not for you," I responded.

"Eh, that's okay. I wasn't going to pay Miles back anyway, the tightwad."

My mother, her arm hooked in Casey's, arrived to give me a hug, but we ended up doing a weird three-person one instead. "That was such a beautiful wedding," she said, her eyes filling with tears.

"Are you crying?" I asked, smiling my amusement by her predictable display of emotion.

"What?" she said, slapping my shoulder as a smile spread across her face. "Why is it that you and your brothers insist on finding enjoyment in my tears?"

"They just come at such random times, is all."

"There's nothing random about it, Jake," Casey said, pushing me. "They're wedding tears."

"Exactly." Mom dabbed hers dry with a far-off, dreamy look. "There's just something about being on the cusp of life with your whole world waiting for you that slays me every time. It's going to be a beautiful ride."

Her normally stoic posture sagged under the emotions of the moment. There was more to her words than just standard sentiment. The life she spoke of, the one waiting for me, had only been made possible by my mother's undying devotion. I gathered her into my arms and whispered in her ear, "Thanks to you, Mom."

With the ceremony behind us, it was time to focus on fun, and that's just what I intended to do. After last night's challenges, I needed to relax and just let loose. The free flowing alcohol helped with that. If there was ever a time to celebrate, it was now. I'd just married the woman I loved and was surrounded by a group of people who wanted only the best for us. The steady stream of well-wishers kept Casey and me busy nearly the entire reception. There would be no sneaking off to a hidden balcony tonight or a trip to some corner table to rest our weary feet. Tonight we took center stage, and it was our happiness that was on display.

Well, that and all the amazing touches Casey and Boris had put into making this an unforgettable night. The two had outdone themselves. The way they paired and blended items to capture both our personalities made the reception seem almost homey to me. From the hanging floral centerpieces, each featuring floating glass balls resembling bubbles, to the single most unique party favor I'd ever seen – a crystal-encrusted guitar-shaped calculator – it was clear that every detail had been planned and executed with care. The best part of all, not having been an active participant in the planning process, were the surprises that awaited me at every turn. I had to hand it to Boris. He was well worth the exorbitant amount of money I'd paid him.

Perhaps my favorite part of the evening's touches was the menu, which Casey had handpicked to feature everything I loved to eat. It wasn't a fancy dinner meant to impress, but a downhome meal of tri-tip and baked potatoes. While I chowed down, Casey was busy holding court and looking effortlessly ravishing in her wedding gown. Not able to help myself, I frequently leaned over to give her kisses, just because she was so incredibly beautiful and I loved her so damn much.

Midway through dinner, Casey and I were surprised by a performance by Quinn, accompanied by Emma on the piano. He'd stepped up to the microphone, appearing not only confident but also older and wiser than I'd ever seen him. He caught my eye, almost defiantly, as if he thought maybe I'd shoo him off the stage or something. Suddenly I felt bad for the interaction we'd had last night. He'd probably been working on this song for weeks in order to surprise me, and I'd been a total dick to him.

Quinn gripped the microphone. "I have a confession to make. I was Jake's youngest and first fan. When I was a little boy, I used to hide in the family room to listen to him play. It wasn't just that I loved his music, which I did, but I actually imagined myself being him. I swore I'd be as good as that someday. Well, I'm still trying, but the thing with Jake is that catching up to him is a losing battle because the better I get, the better he gets. Still, it's a challenge I take on every single day of my life. I'm committed to making him proud no matter how long it takes. Jake, you're my brother, my mentor, and my inspiration. And Casey – I liked you from the very start. You're a great addition to the family. Congratulations to both of you."

And with those heart-felt words, Emma led the way on the piano and then Quinn began to sing. For the first time in my life, I really listened. The subtle nuances in his voice, the tonality, and his superior guitar playing skills shocked me. Quinn was no hanger-on. He was the real goddamn deal. How had I not seen this before? He wasn't looking for a handout. Quinn just wanted my approval. I swallowed hard, feeling like a total jerk for the way I'd been treating him.

Casey gripped my hand, no doubt sensing my inner turmoil. Leaning in, she whispered in my ear, "It's never too late to work things out."

No, she got that right. I had a whole lot of groveling to do.

Kyle's best man speech followed a number of heartfelt toasts, and without even knowing what was on his notecards, I suspected he would bring the fun… and, of course, I wasn't disappointed.

"Hi, everyone. Can I have your attention please? My name's Kyle, and I'll be your best man for the evening."

After pausing for the applause, as well as a few chuckles, Kyle continued. "I'd like to start by saying thank you to whoever's bright idea it was to have a wedding in August... in Arizona. I'm sweating in places I never knew I could sweat. Now, I'm not pointing fingers at anyone, *Jake and Casey...*" Kyle dropped his voice to boom our names out over the microphone. "...but I'd really like to know the thought process behind *that* selection. I mean, I'll be the first to admit, I don't always make the smartest choices. In fact, some might say my decision-making skills closely resemble those of a squirrel when crossing a busy road, yet even I would have thought twice about having a wedding in the desert at the exact time of year when birds are forced to use potholders to pull worms out of the ground."

The reception guests laughed, and I settled into my seat. Kyle was off to a good start, a few jokes to lighten the mood. There was no need for concern.

"Let's move on to why I'm here... to deliver a mildly funny, heartwarming best man speech to honor my brother and his beautiful new wife." Kyle stopped to look down at his notecards before throwing them up in the air and watching them cascade to the ground. "Nah, we don't need these. I've always been more of a seat of the pants kind of guy. What do you say? Should I wing it?"

No. No winging it. Anything but winging it. By the amused smirk on Kyle's face, I knew it was already too late. He was improvising, and there was nothing I could do to stop it. Buckling in, I held on for the ride.

"First off, I'd like to acknowledge my brother for picking me. Dude, I know you had options, and, honestly, you probably should have taken them. This could very well become the second very bad decision of your wedding."

The crowd applauded his cocky warning, seemingly bloodthirsty for some good old fashioned dirt. But although Kyle certainly had the mud to sling, I had faith that he'd never bury me under a pile of sludge. Kyle was nothing if not loyal. He had my back even when I gave him no reason to and had never, in all the years, waivered in his devotion to me. So even though he was clearly planning on embarrassing me, I was certain his ribbing would be all in good fun. After all, Kyle knew the boundaries and had never been one to toe the line.

"So where to start? I met Jake in the 90's and, to be honest, when we were first introduced, I wasn't all that impressed. He's not a bad-looking guy now, but back then, ladies, he was bald, chubby around the middle, and he had these short, stubby little legs."

"I was a baby," I called out.

"Jake, please don't interrupt. See, this is the type of thing I have to deal with on a daily basis. Anyway, as I was saying, our dashing groom wasn't what we'd consider classically handsome back then; and to make matters worse, he wobbled around when he walked, stumbling into walls…

and, you know, the way he carried that bottle around, I'll admit I thought he had a drinking problem. But thankfully our little sumo wrestler grew out of the awkward stage and became a pretty cool toddler – then an even more impressive kid. I took to following him around just so I wouldn't miss anything. And that, in a nutshell, is our relationship today. The end."

I pushed back my seat and abruptly stood, clapping for him, as if it truly were the end of his speech.

Kyle acknowledged my presence, grinning, before saying, "Sit down. I'm not finished with you yet."

And that's when I got to hear his retelling of the time when I was eleven years old, at a waterpark with my friends, and they dared me to go down the slide both headfirst and backward. The string on my swim trunks had broken earlier in the day, and I'd tied it loosely together to keep them up. Well, the minute I hit the rushing water my shorts ripped clean off and I rode the whole way down naked.

And, of course, he couldn't forget to tell the story of the flock of geese that flew over the stage during an outdoor concert and began dropping shit-bombs on those of us performing below. Yes, I looked up at the most inopportune time and took a direct hit. The creamy white concoction splattered all over my face, invading my eyes, mouth, and nostrils. The concert was postponed fifteen minutes so I could go backstage to take a shower… and throw up.

He then retold the story of his first meeting with Casey and how he knew the two of us were meant to be when I refrained from murdering Quinn after he made me eat the booger bean in the Bean Boozled jellybean game we were playing.

"Casey, on behalf of our family, I want to officially welcome you. And now that you're a McKallister, you've got to start behaving like one. So just to make things easier for you, I've compiled a list of the family rules that we'd like you to follow.

Number One: Refrain from laughing at our father's jokes. They aren't funny, and by doing so, you're only encouraging the behavior to continue.

Number Two: Whoever sees the cat puke on the floor has to pick it up. Playing ignorant and pretending not to see it only works when no one else is home.

Number Three: When you get up from your seat to move about the room, do not expect your spot to be there when you get back. The McKallister household honors the rule of 'Move your feet/lose your seat,' and those who fail to comply will be senselessly beaten. Please note... calling 'slaps' will not, in any way, protect your spot. However, carrying the chair with you throughout the house is not only acceptable, but also encouraged.

And finally, Number Four: Life is short. Break the rules and have fun doing it. But for the love of god, don't let Mom catch you doing it. Oh, wait, that one was for me.

Anyway, on a serious note, Casey – I think I speak for all of us when I say we're proud to call you family."

Kyle paused once more, before clearing his throat and addressing me directly. "And to my big brother who I've loved and admired all my life: I couldn't be happier for you. I know you weren't looking for love the day it came pounding on your door, but you never faltered, and now look what you have to show for it – a woman who loves you unconditionally. You've been blessed, man. Never forget it. And just remember, Jake, as you embark on this journey of love and marriage, that the very last person you think about right before you fall asleep is the one your heart belongs to. So, with that in mind, I'll make sure to text you every night before bed. Love you, brother."

Kyle's speech earned him a standing ovation and my undying respect. It also ended the dinner festivities, and Casey and I headed to the center of the stage to share our first dance. The song was one I'd written for her soon after we'd fallen in love, and it had become one of my greatest hits. Titled *Shades of Blue*, it was more than just a song about falling in love; it was also a song about falling back into life. I hadn't realized how dark and monotonous my day-to-day existence had been until Casey came along and painted a bright swath across my normal path, and suddenly the sky was bluer, the grass was greener, and my world exploded into a kaleidoscope of color.

Casey, her eyes glimmering, stepped into my arms and I gently took her face in my hands and kissed her. Unlike last night in the hallway, this kiss was tender and loving, mirroring the incredible love I was feeling for her in the moment. Dropping my hands to her waist, Casey glided effortlessly in my arms as we swayed to the music. I tucked my head into her shoulder and softly sang the words of our song for her ears only.

After sharing our first dance, we began the mingling portion of the evening. And that's how I found myself here, trapped in an impossible conversation with a pair of sisters I'd been told were Casey's second cousins.

"So is this your first trip to Arizona?" I asked the wide-eyed females.

Giggles, then more unintelligible words erupted. I hastily looked away, fighting to hold off the laughter that was threatening to override my good manners.

I had spent the last seven minutes of my life trying to have a conversation with these women, and although they were able to speak in full and complete sentences for Casey, neither one of them had been physically capable of communicating with me. So far I'd only been able to decipher nine actual words. Figuring it was a nervous habit these sisters had, I didn't want to appear to be making fun of them, but with every garbled word they spoke I could feel my resolve fading.

Casey lightly brushed her finger against my hand, and we glanced at one another. The slightest tip of a smile on her lips forced me to bite down on my tongue. She was just goading me now. I gave her the 'Can I go now?' look that a small child might give his mommy, but she wasn't letting me off the hook so easily.

With a sly smile on her face, Casey said, "Louisa, why don't you tell Jake about the trip you took to Mexico recently?"

And when Louisa launched into her giggle chatter story, I had to stop her.

"I'm sorry. I need to catch my brother real quick before he leaves. When we see each other later, I'd love to hear the end of it." *Or even a couple words of it,* for that matter.

And without meeting Casey's traitorous eye, I kissed her cheek and hurried away.

"Quinn," I called to him. He saw me coming and abruptly turned to leave. Great. Was this the state of our relationship?

"Hey, hold up."

Quinn stopped and slowly rotated until we were facing one another. His body had taken on a rigid stance and that jaw of his was, once again, tightly clenched.

"I'm sorry, okay?" he said, immediately defending himself. "I shouldn't have said those things to you last night. And I definitely shouldn't have flipped you off. I lost my cool and I regret it. But I meant what I said about not bothering you anymore. You're right. I need to do this on my own."

"No, you don't. I was being a jerk. You're my brother, and I should be helping you out."

"That's the thing, Jake. I don't want you to feel like it's an obligation."

"Look, even if I wanted to help your band get a spot on my tour, I can't. The opening bands aren't my decision. My label picks them. Even if I went to bat for you, it wouldn't matter."

Quinn put his hand up to stop me. "There's no band. Not anymore."

My eyes widened. This was news to me. "You quit?"

"Something like that. When I asked you to help me with my songs, it's just me. I'm going solo, and I'm nowhere near tour ready, so relax."

We both stood there silently. I could feel the chill between us and wasn't sure how to remedy the situation without making things worse.

"That song you wrote…"

Quinn's cheeks flushed as he looked down. "I know I messed up the second chorus."

"Did you? I didn't hear anything."

"Don't lie. I know you did."

He was right. I had heard it. But the song had been performed with such heart that it hadn't mattered. "I was going to say – it was great."

You would have thought I'd told him I was sporting a third nipple by the way he reacted with such shock.

"Are you being serious? Or is this just your way of trying to smooth things over?"

Every word that came out of Quinn's mouth was riddled with skepticism. He either had no faith in himself or no faith in me. Somehow I suspected it was somewhere in between.

"I'm dead serious. You were incredible."

Quinn just stood there staring at me, a mix of emotions playing out over his face. I swear his eyes misted over before he cleared his voice and said, "Thanks."

"Hey." I nudged him. "I'm proud of you."

He met my eye again, only this time the only emotion to be found was anger. "Now I know you're lying. You're never proud of me. You don't even like me, Jake."

"What?" How could he think that? "You're my brother. Of course I like you."

"No. You like Kyle and Keith. You just tolerate me. Don't deny it. Every time I talk to you or ask you anything, you brush me off."

Did I? It was true I didn't spend much time with Quinn, and yeah, I flaked on him on a regular basis, but it shocked me that he would think I didn't like him.

"Quinn." I reached for him, but he backed away, and now I could clearly see the hurt in his eyes.

"Forget I said anything," he hissed through clenched teeth.

"No. I want to talk about this. I'm sorry if I made you feel that way. I promise you, it wasn't intentional."

"It's always been this way. Ever since you came home. You never wanted anything to do with me. I try so hard to get your attention. I mean…" Quinn laughed bitterly. "I try to be *you* every goddamn day. It's just never enough. Ever!"

It hit me then, like a baseball bat to the head, why our relationship was what it was. Quinn was dead right. I did treat him differently, and now I knew why. He was me… had I not been kidnapped all those years ago. Quinn represented everything I could have been. He had the childhood, the girlfriends, the sports, the garage band with his friends, the prom, the graduation. And now, without having to go through any of the trials I'd faced, Quinn was going to have my career. Holy fuck! I was jealous of him.

"Are you okay?" he asked, forgetting his own hurt feelings to tend to me. "You look like you've seen a ghost."

No, not a ghost… just a giant dose of reality. I blinked in rapid succession, trying to make sense of what my mind was telling me. My behavior was responsible for this rift between us. I did resent him without even knowing it. He hadn't deserved the scorn I'd heaped on him over the years. It wasn't his fault that he'd been safe at home with his baby blanket while I was being tortured within an inch of my life. It wasn't his fault that he'd lived the life I'd always wanted while I'd floundered for years in a sort of hellish purgatory. Feeling suddenly off, I steadied myself against the wall.

"I'm fine," I answered, covering for my weakness. "I think I had too much liquor."

"Oh. Okay."

He didn't believe me, but he also understood I wouldn't be elaborating.

"I'm guilty of everything you just accused me of. I haven't been listening to you but, Quinn, I heard you tonight. And trust me when I say – you are good enough."

"You don't have to say that."

"I know I don't. I'm speaking the truth. I admit I've been nearly non-existent in your life, but from now on, I'm going to do right by you, okay?"

Clearly emotional from our exchange, Quinn dropped his head and nodded. I stepped forward and embraced him. At first shocked by my gesture, he tensed at my touch, but as I held on, my baby brother slowly relaxed. When I felt his arms go around my back, I knew I'd been forgiven. That's how it was with family. The ties were always there;

you just needed to remember to tighten them every once in a while.

We broke apart and I slapped him on the shoulder. "I've got to get back to Casey. Are we good?"

"Yeah," he smiled, looking more relaxed than I'd seen him in a long time. "We're good."

"And Quinn?"

"Yeah?"

"That was a killer song. You're the real deal, man."

I'd just rejoined Casey, who was deep into a conversation with her Uncle Alan about his spotty bowel movements, when Sam, Keith's ex, wandered up to give me a hug.

Sam was the gold standard girlfriend. *Earthy* was the best way to describe her. With long, sun-streaked hair, tan skin, and minimal make-up, she didn't need much more than her natural self to be attractive. But it wasn't her beauty that was the most remarkable thing about her. Whether for humans, animals, or environmental causes, Sam's compassion was continually on full display. It was probably what had attracted her to Keith in the first place. He was a wounded soul in need of saving, and that was Sam's specialty.

The first time I met her, I knew she was different. I'd just returned home from my first tour and was trying to readjust to family life again when Keith introduced us.

Interactions with strangers were awkward for me back then. Either the person was regarding me with pity or was promising me their undying love. Sam did neither. She treated me like any other teenage boy; she was the first person after the kidnapping, and outside the family, to make me feel normal.

"Congratulations," she said. "I couldn't be happier for you and Casey. You're hands down my favorite couple."

"Mine too," I joked. "Damn, Samantha, it feels like I haven't seen you in forever."

"I know," she replied, dropping her head just a smidge and appearing genuinely sad. "I miss you guys so much. When Keith and I broke up, it was like losing half my family. I had a hard time of it. Thank god for Casey, so I can keep tabs on all of you."

"Yeah. Sorry about that." I shifted uncomfortably, feeling strangely guilty. I had dropped her like a hot potato at the first mention of their break up. She'd been like family, but Keith was my flesh and blood, and my loyalty would always be to him. "It sucks you two didn't work out."

There was no denying the look of pain that accompanied her solemn head nod. "Yes, it does."

"Samantha Anderson!" Casey squealed, enveloping her in a hug and saving me from trying to come up with something else to say to my brother's ex. "You came, girl."

"Of course. Like I'd miss this for the world. Jake, you should have seen your face when Casey punked you in the church."

The three of us laughed. I still hadn't quite gotten over it and couldn't wait to return the favor.

I felt a sudden movement. Keith had appeared by my side out of nowhere, giving me a tight squeeze on the shoulder to let me know what a douche I had been for conversing with the enemy. "What did I miss?"

"Nothing. We were just making fun of Jake," Casey said. "Like always."

Keith nodded and then turned to look at his ex for the first time. "Sam," he said, tipping his head to her in greeting.

"Keith," she replied, mimicking his exact acknowledgement.

"You look good."

"So do you."

Then silence. The four of us stood there awkwardly.

"Well, this isn't uncomfortable at all," Casey said. "I just had a conversation about poop that was more stimulating than this."

"Well, here's something that might be more pleasing to your ears." Keith perked up. "Guess who showed up at the reception demanding to see her husband?"

"Who?"

"A certain bride, all dressed in crazy."

"No way!" I blurted out. "Jesus. Kyle was right."

"Sorry," Sam interrupted. "But I feel that I'm missing a crucial element of this story."

"Jake has a second wife, of the horror movie variety," Keith explained. "We passed her on the street on the way here, and she flashed us some serious tit."

"Only in the McKallister family," Sam said, shaking her head as a huge smile appeared on her face. "See, this is what I miss about not hanging out with you guys."

"Breasts?" Keith asked, feigning ignorance.

Sam laughed, spontaneously touching his arm, probably more out of habit than anything else. Realizing her mistake, she immediately pulled away, but not before locking eyes with Keith. The two stood there staring at one another for an uncomfortably long time. Casey poked me in the back, perhaps to initiate some sort of action on my part.

"Casey and I need to go talk to her Aunt Betty about... um... her bunions."

That broke the spell between them, and Sam hugged us both before we left.

"Bunions?" Casey said incredulously, whispering as we walked away.

"I panicked. It was the only thing I could think of on short notice."

We both turned back toward Keith. He'd taken Sam to a corner, and they were in deep conversation.

"So, is your heart set on a little bunion banter, or would you like a special surprise?"

"What kind of surprise?"

"Let's just say it's a blast from the past."

"Hopefully not from my past, Jesus," I said, only half joking.

"*Our* past, Jake. I'm not a sadist, geez."

She led me to a table with a woman and her teenage daughter. The mother seemed familiar, but I couldn't place her until she nudged her daughter and the girl turned around. Casey was smiling like a loon when realization hit me who these two were: the mother and daughter from London. They were the ones who'd kept Casey occupied while I performed and even saved her from being chucked out of the venue for 'pretending' to be my girlfriend. It had been a crucial weekend for us as a couple, and by the end of those three days, I'd fallen hard for the girl. So hard, in fact, that our lives would never be the same. In a roundabout way, this mother and daughter pair were a part of our love story, and it was a cool touch to add them to the guest list.

"Do you remember us?" the mother asked, standing up to greet me. The daughter followed her lead.

"I do. From London, right?" I reached my hand out to shake theirs. "I'm terrible with names, sorry."

"I'm Angela and this is my daughter…"

Suddenly her name came to me, and I confidently blurted it out: "Lauren."

Both nodded enthusiastically, and Lauren, once a shy, introverted girl, caught my eye and I immediately noticed the difference in her. Not only was she wearing makeup and sporting a stylish haircut, but Lauren had also ditched the thick glasses and downward gaze that had given her the appearance of an insecure young teen.

"You remembered!" she answered, a crimson blush coloring her cheeks. I smiled. There was the girl I remembered.

"Thanks for coming all this way," I said, attempting to reassure her that she was welcome.

"We wouldn't have missed it. After Casey invited us, I didn't sleep for weeks."

"Not only that, but it was a long time to keep a secret from her friends."

"Girl, I feel you." Casey exhaled, blowing out a stream of relief. "I haven't spoken a word of truth in months."

"Says the bride moments after exchanging her vows."

Casey gaped at me as if she were offended. "You're the one who told me to lie."

"Not to me," I said, protesting her faulty accusation. "I thought that was self-explanatory."

Mother and daughter watched our squabble with grins on their faces.

"You two are exactly as I remember you," Angela said.

"For better or worse," Casey replied, hugging Lauren to her. "I'm so glad you're here. It's great to finally see you again in person."

Casey had periodically kept in touch with the girl over the years as a way to help bolster her self-esteem, but seeing Lauren now, so confident and outspoken, I wondered if she might have had more influence on Lauren than even she could have anticipated.

"Well, when you get back home, you'll need a picture to show around," I said, standing on one side of Lauren as Casey got on the other.

And as we hammed it up for the camera, I smiled in Casey's direction. She had such a good heart. Inviting Lauren and Angela hadn't been for our sake at all; it was to give Lauren another moment to shine. I grabbed Casey's hand and squeezed.

***

Boris ushered Casey and me to the side of the reception hall where the towering cake glimmered in white frosting. Although I'd seen the masterpiece from a distance, it wasn't until I gotten closer that I saw the personalized touch that seemed to adorn every single thing at our wedding.

Our initials, C + J, were carefully placed inside hearts that were formed by candy crystals. The hearts were scattered over the different layers. It was a simple image but the meaning for us was huge, symbolizing our unity.

A 'Cake' cake. I hugged Casey to me. She beamed, and we kissed for the crowd.

From the corner of my eye, I saw Boris walk up with a smaller cake, and when I took a closer look at the clearly homemade confection, I laughed. It was one of my mom's Betty Crocker cakes. I raised my brow to Casey. Could it be?

She nodded. "Funfetti."

Chapter Seven

Casey

Super-Sized

Guests spilled out of the reception hall as we ducked into the limo and pulled away. I'd planned for nearly a year for the perfect wedding, and although there had been a few blips along the way, I couldn't have been happier with the outcome. With Jake's arm resting securely over my shoulder, we waved goodbye to all our family and friends, and I tilted my head toward my new husband and ran my finger over his handsome face.

"Thank you for marrying me, Jake McKallister."

"It was my pleasure." He tipped his head in return and gently brushed his lips past mine. That sparkle in his eyes was something I hoped to see every day for the rest of my life.

"What was going through your mind while I was walking down the aisle? You looked so emotional."

Jake glanced at me and then quickly looked away, his face rife with the same sentiment as earlier. "This might sound weird, but once I got over the shock of seeing you walking toward me in that dress and looking so incredibly beautiful, I thought about the kid I used to be, sitting in the dark, alone and scared for my life. I couldn't even have imagined having someone like you back then, but if I'd known you were in my future, maybe it would have been easier to get through all that."

The honesty of his words sent a lump to my throat and tears to my eyes. I wasn't sure what sort of answer I'd been expecting, but it certainly wasn't that. Although a generic answer wouldn't have been Jake, either.

"I wish I could have been there for you back then."

He squeezed my hand tighter. "You're here now, and that's all that matters."

The way he shifted uncomfortably and the grimace, which appeared out of nowhere, was indication enough that we were done discussing his time with Ray for now. He'd poured his soul out to me once, but that was a long time ago, and now I rarely, if ever, got anything more that these tiny snippets of truth. I'd given up pushing for details, as it usually just ended up in an argument about him dropping out of therapy. My greatest wish would be for him to be able to work through his issues completely, but I understood that it might be too much to ask of him. It was very possible that I would never know the full story, nor did I particularly want that information. Some things, I reasoned, were better left unsaid. It was hard enough hearing about this stuff happening to a stranger on the news, but when that person was someone you loved, it took on a whole new meaning. That being said, I was always willing to snatch up any piece of information he was willing to offer, no matter how tiny or insignificant.

"What were you thinking walking down the aisle?" he asked, moving the focus away from him.

My face immediately reddened, thinking about those moments. "Well, now I don't want to say, because it's a little shallow compared to your answer."

"I'm sure it wasn't shallow."

"Okay, well, when you were standing up there at the altar, looking smokin' hot, I was thinking that all my friends and family would be totally jealous, and that made me happy."

"Ooh, yeah," he winced. "That was super shallow."

"I told you," I said, pushing against him in retaliation for making me reveal my superficiality. "Wait, no, I change my mind. I was actually thinking about how lucky I was to have found you."

"Uh-huh, right."

"You don't believe me?" I snubbed my nose up at him playfully. "I'm hurt."

At that moment, my stomach rumbled so loudly that it startled us both.

"See, even your stomach doesn't believe you."

"My stomach's no traitor. It's just hungry because I haven't fed it much in the past day or so."

"Why the hell not?"

"To look good in my wedding dress, duh."

"Okay, now we're back to the whole shallow thing, Casey."

"Fine, if you must know, my shallowness was something I was hiding from you until we got married. Surprise!" I splayed my fingers out like an explosion while adopting crazy eyes. "Have fun dealing with my shit for the rest of your life."

"Right back at ya!" he said, with perfect timing. We enjoyed a hearty laugh. One thing was for sure – we were quite the pair.

"Why didn't you eat at the reception, then?" he asked, laying his hand on my stomach.

"I didn't want to drop anything on my dress! Or, god forbid, smile and have parsley in my teeth. Now it doesn't matter what I look like because I'm not trying to impress anyone anymore."

"Except me, your husband."

"Exactly, except you."

Jake shook his head at me, smiling. "You're all Miss Snarky tonight, aren't you?"

"Mrs."

"Oh, right."

I turned excitedly in my seat, nearly jumping up and down on my designer clad bottom. "McDonald's!" I screamed. And as I watched it pass by on the left hand side of the street, I placed both hands on the window and whispered with a sad little pout, "Big Mac. Fries."

Jake found that wildly funny, and when he stopped laughing, said, "Maybe I'm reading you all wrong, but did you want to stop at McDonald's?"

"Wow, Jake, you're like a mind reader."

"Did someone have a little too much champagne tonight?"

I shrugged, but in reality, I was barely drunk. It was more just that I was giddy with life.

Jake called out to the driver and his security guy in the front seat. "Can you please get this woman to the nearest golden arches?"

After completing an illegal U-turn, the driver pulled into the parking lot, and I cheered. I was one step closer to the first solid food I'd eaten in about a week. Our limousine pulled into the drive-thru, and I rolled down my window, eager to give my order, but the narrow drive-up lane made navigation difficult. Jake and I exchanged an amused glance as the driver backed up and pulled forward multiple times in an embarrassing effort to make my fast food dream a reality. It soon became clear that we'd gotten horribly wedged between a concrete retaining wall and the ordering screen. More and more cars lined up behind us. Now there was no way out but forward, and that seemed impossible, given the circumstances.

"Oh, my god," I whispered, in an attempt to quell the giggles that were fast approaching. "Tell me this is not happening right now. Are we seriously stuck in the drive-thru at McDonald's?"

"It definitely appears that way," Jake said. "And you want to hear something even better? See that car right there?"

I looked over at the wine-colored sedan he was pointing at and nodded.

"That's paparazzi."

"No!"

"Yep." He nodded. "And so is the blue one over there. I can see the flash bulbs going. This will be on TMZ by morning."

That's when the laughing began. Mine, that is. I felt the rise of hysteria slowly creeping up, and soon I'd dissolved into a fit of uncontrollable giggles. I could picture the memorable headline: *Jake McKallister Trapped in Drive-through on Wedding Night*. The thought only made me laugh harder, setting off an intense urge to pee.

Jake didn't seem nearly as amused by the jam we found ourselves in, peering intently out the windows while the rescue efforts took place. His security guard had already hopped out of the limo to offer help, as did a man from the car behind ours. Still, we were making very little progress. For every forward movement, the limo had to take a similar backward one. After several minutes, we were no closer to freedom.

By now, three photographers were out of their cars, snapping pictures of our predicament.

"At least they can't see inside," Jake said, bravely looking on the bright side.

"Um, yeah, about that. I have to tinkle."

He glanced over. "You have to what?"

"Tinkle," I repeated.

He stared back at me with a blank face.

"Piddle?" I tried.

Still nothing from him.

I sighed. "I'm about to piss myself."

His brows raised. Finally! It took him long enough. "You've got to be kidding."

"Do I look like I'm kidding?" I groped myself just a little bit to drive home my point.

"You can't wait until we get to the hotel?"

"I mean, I guess if I knew which century we'd be arriving, sure, I might be able to hold out, but as it appears now, we'll be stuck here a good long time. So, no, I can't wait."

Jake sighed as if I'd been planning this inconvenience all along. "All right, I'll have Pete escort you in. Just ignore the paparazzi. Don't answer any questions."

"Uh, Pete?" I asked, scrunching my face to show my displeasure with his suggestion. "Yeah, I don't think that will work."

"Why not?"

"The dress. I need help lifting it."

Jake studied me a moment before realization dawned on him. "Wait… are you… you want me to go into the women's bathroom with you?"

"I mean, I guess I could ask Pete."

Jake didn't hesitate a second longer as he opened the limo door, stepped out, and offered up his hand to me. "Oh, and Casey, don't forget to smile for the cameras."

Luckily for us, two more of Jake's security guys had been following behind our limousine and ran up as we exited the vehicle, and they held back the paparazzi as we crossed the grass. We almost made it to the restaurant when the heel of my expensive shoe caught in the crevice between the grass and the concrete, snapping clean off. Jake, who'd been holding my hand, jerked back and gaped at me in surprise.

"My heel broke."

"No, it didn't," he said, grinning.

"I'm afraid so."

"This is like a scene out of some warped Cinderella movie."

I laughed and was about to remove the other shoe when Jake swooped me up in his arms and carried me across the threshold of the McDonald's. Oh, the romance of it all!

"Excuse me. Coming through, people," Jake called out, now clearly enjoying himself, as he weaved past diners. For this late at night, the restaurant was impressively busy. Good for them. Jake used his foot to push open the women's restroom, and we came face to face with two women washing their hands at the sinks. They both jerked their heads in our direction and seemed ready to pounce on Jake for illegally crossing into their sanctuary when they took a closer look and their mouths dropped to the floor.

"Ladies, I'm really sorry about this, but my bride is about to..." Jake stopped mid-sentence to address me. "What did you call it in the limo?"

"Tinkle," I answered.

"Yeah, she's about to tinkle all over me if I don't get her into a stall and help her with her dress. Please don't call the cops on me."

Jumping into action, the women pushed open the handicapped stall and directed him in. My dress barely cleared the entrance.

"What can we do for you, honey?" one woman asked. Not to me, mind you, but to Jake. I had become invisible in this scenario.

"Make sure you get all the tulle under the dress," the other added helpfully.

"I will," he said, setting me on my feet and closing the stall door.

"If you need anything, hon, we'll be right out here."

I rolled my eyes and Jake held back a laugh as he helped me lift my strapless, A-line sweetheart wedding dress up around my waist and held the layers of fabric out of the way. I barely made it over the seat before I was relieving myself.

Interestingly enough, I'd never noticed how loud urine could be until I was listening to mine cascade into the bowl below me while my brand-new husband was hovering above me, pretending not to hear. As my cheeks blushed in embarrassment, my mouth went into overdrive.

"I don't know if I ever told you this," I began in a conversational tone, "but my college boyfriend once recorded himself peeing for a full minute fifty-eight seconds."

"No, I don't think you've ever mentioned that before," Jake said, his voice monotone, not seeming the least bit impressed.

"I mean, maybe it doesn't *sound* amazing, but I'm telling you, that video went on and on. I was able to totally dry my hair in the time it took for him to empty his bladder. How do you guys hold so much pee?"

"Casey," Jake interrupted. "I don't mean to rush you along, but I'm in a girls' bathroom with my hands up your dress. Can we talk about your ex-boyfriend some other time?"

"Oh, yeah, sure. I'm almost done, actually. I was just making small talk to ease the awkwardness."

"Uh-huh, because it's not at all awkward for you to be fondly remembering another guy on our wedding night."

"I'm not remembering him, per se… just his nether regions."

The ladies on the other side of the stall began to giggle something fierce. Shit. I'd forgotten they were there.

"I was just kidding," I called out to them. "I never think about any other guy's privates." Oh, no. That came out all wrong, too.

"Casey." Jake abruptly stopped me from any more unnecessary babbling. "You're done. No more chatter."

"Right. Sorry." I finished the clean-up and flushed. Jake's face came into view as the layers of my dress began to fall down around me. Thankfully, he appeared rather amused.

"You're a piece of work, you know that?" he said, shaking his head.

"If that was meant as a compliment, then thank you."

"Are we done here, or do you have any further interesting facts about past hookups you'd like to share with me?"

"No. None as interesting as the last."

"Thank god. Hey, what happened to the other dress you were planning to wear for the reception?" he asked, pushing open the stall. "That would have come in handy tonight."

The women had pressed themselves against the wall as they awaited Jake's exit. He flashed them his megawatt rock star smile, and I thought both might slide to the floor in a puddle of glee.

I stared at him in the mirror as I washed my hands. "I changed my mind at the last minute. I figured, when will I ever wear a more beautiful gown, or look as pretty as I do tonight?"

"You don't need a fancy dress. You always look beautiful to me."

It was a lovely sentiment ruined by the sharp intake of air from one of the women, followed by a chorus of contented sighs. We exchanged a knowing glance in the mirror. They were going to need tending to before we could leave. Jake nodded at me before wedging himself into the middle of his restroom groupies and smiling for a selfie.

The security guys were waiting for us when we stepped out; and so, unfortunately, were the paparazzi. They were quick to snap shots of Jake and the three of us women with a clear view of the women's bathroom sign in the background.

"That's not what it looks like," he said gamely to the photographers before addressing his own staff. "What's the limo situation?"

"They're removing a wooden post, and then we should be good to go. Probably five more minutes, I'd guess."

"Well, then, we've got time to get my wife some food."

Ignoring the clicks of the cameras, Jake took my hand and headed to the counter. Every person in the building was gawking at the scene we were making. A barefoot woman in a wedding gown at a fast food restaurant was unique enough, but when you paired her with a world-famous musician, the interest level more than quadrupled.

His bodyguards followed close behind, ready to take down any overzealous hamburglars, but we needn't have worried, as everyone was on their best behavior. Again, I couldn't get over the turn-out at such a late hour. I mean, who knew this many people got the munchies at one in the morning?

Our turn arrived, and Jake ordered for us.

"Small, medium, or large?" the cashier asked.

Jake glanced at me for guidance.

"The bigger the better," I said, getting dangerously close to gnawing on the countertop if this ordering business got any slower.

The young male cashier actually looked between the two of us before settling his stare on Jake as if to confirm he was okay with his new bride taking on such a demanding challenge at this late hour.

I snorted in irritation.

Jake smiled in amusement at my reaction before wisely backing me up. "You heard the lady. It's her wedding day. Supersize her."

Our hotel was only a few blocks away. Our driver pulled into the valet section of the parking garage and let us be so Jake and I could remain in the back of the limo, eating our late night meal and enjoying being alone together for the first time as husband and wife.

"Okay, here's another one," I said, lazily running my finger over the veins on the back of his hand. "When I'm stressed or anxious, I do math in my head to calm myself down."

"Why are all your confessions so damn nerdy?"

Nudging him playfully with my bare foot, I said, "Oh, I'm so sorry I don't have a more socially relevant catalog of phobias."

"Do not," Jake warned, forcibly pushing my toes off his tuxedo pants, "touch me with those! You know I can't stomach your feet without protection."

That only prompted more foot worship, in the form of me rubbing mine all over him. Jake screamed his displeasure before relocating to the other side of the limo and defending himself with a pair of appetizer forks he'd found on the bar.

"Really, Jake? Do you honestly think those tiny forks will protect you? Perhaps you forget I come from a hearty stock of women with podiatry issues. Bunions are the least of our problems."

"Ooh, yeah, I'm so scared. It's not like there's a multitude of foot conditions in the world."

"You're joking, right?" I employed the use of my fingers to aid in the countdown of the painful conditions I'd probably inherit one day. "There's corns, calluses, plantar fasciitis, ingrown toenails, plantar warts, and let's not forget my personal favorite, hammertoe."

"Stop!" He grimaced, covering his ears. "Please make it stop."

I felt no sympathy for the plight he now found himself in. "Hey, buddy, you had two full years to ask the pertinent questions. Now we're married, and there are no give-backs."

"See, I feel like you were hiding this particular issue from me."

"It would seem that way, wouldn't it? Anyway, enough about me. It's your turn. Hit me with another confession."

He sighed, straining hard to come up with another entry into our 'Who's weirder?' game. "Okay, I never drink the last gulp of anything."

I pondered what he'd said a moment before scrunching up my nose and asking, "Really? Why?"

He shrugged. "I don't know. It grosses me out."

"So you just leave a little bit in every cup?"

He nodded.

"Wow, Jake, that's just so incredibly weird."

"Oh, and your habit of arranging food into happy little family units isn't?"

"Says the guy who won't adopt a male dog because he doesn't want the canine's genitalia on his car seats."

"Nobody wants that!"

Jake's voice peaked in amusement, and we both laughed with the comfortable camaraderie of two people who truly understood each other. It was difficult to fully describe the wonders of loving your best friend… of having someone you trusted with your life to walk you through the good times and bad. Jake was that person for me, and despite the conversation we'd had before the wedding, I was certain that he and I still shared all the same aspirations, even if his might need a little fine-tuning. I had no doubt children would be part of our future, and that there would come a time when Jake would hold our baby in his loving arms and not even remember the doubts he'd once harbored.

My eyes caught on his sculpted face, and a knot formed in my throat. Damn! What man looked that good in a tux? It really was criminal. Suddenly, I had an overwhelming desire to consummate our marriage in the most primitive of ways. Okay, making love inside a luxury limo was probably not considered primeval, but it was hot and dangerous, and that was how I wanted us to remember our first time together as husband and wife.

I must have been staring at him for too long because he cocked his brow and asked, "What?"

I ran my tongue seductively over my lips, giving Jake his first indication of things to come. Gesturing with my finger, I made it known I wanted him by my side. He didn't need to be told twice. Setting down the forks on the way, he slid into the spot next to me, looking every bit as randy as I felt.

"You are about to be a very happy husband," I whispered seductively, flicking my tongue over his lips. Jake ran his fingers down my throat, tracing a line to the dip between my breasts. His hand slid under the silk and into the white lacey brassiere, which had miraculously provided my breasts with the oomph they so deserved. With a single-minded focus, his warm hand circled my nipple, and I groaned on contact. Jake lifted his lust-filled eyes to mine; then, catching my jaw, he tilted my head and we stared at one another with a hunger neither of us could deny. I dipped in closer as his lips pushed into mine, rough and wanting. Our mouths drew open, sealed by the bond of our lips, and my tongue pushed against his.

Jake's hands gripped the sides of my face, his fingers resting in the tangles of my hair, the sheer force of the kiss bruising my lips. My body pulsed with desire, aching for something more. Wrapping my arms tightly around his neck, I kept our lips moving as I lifted my leg up and over, straddling his lap as I pushed against him. A hollow groan released from his throat but was stifled by the barrier our lips had made.

Jake broke roughly from the kiss, panting. "Jesus, Casey. You're making me crazy." With no reprieve for him in sight, I continued rotating my hips, no more able to control my lust than he. "If we are doing this" – he gasped out the words as my tongue slithered into his ear, my hot breath sending shivers through him – "Then I…um… I… oh fuck… um… I need to text… um Pete. Keep him… others… away."

As my nails raked jaggedly over the back of his neck, Jake arched his back, wedging me in tighter onto his package. He was slowly losing his cool, and even though texting was probably not the sexiest thing he could be doing at the moment, I agreed with the principle behind it.

"Send the text," I murmured in a low and heated tone. Jake, flushed with desire, pulled out his phone, typed something out, and tossed it on the seat beside us. As I leaned in closer, my tongue traced lightly along the edge of his ear, giving the lobe a tantalizing little flick. Jake's body trembled in a muted, restrained quiver. Our eyes locked and his softened with the unmistakable look of love. Leaning in, I dangled my lips over his until he lifted his up and our lips slowly came together. I melted slowly, deliciously into his arms, our mouths locked on one another, and I savored this moment with him as if it were our first.

The confines of the limo and the steamy heat inside only served to heighten the senses. Pulling apart from him, I flicked his lip with my tongue playfully then pushed him back against the seat. I removed Jake's expensive Armani coat and flung it to the other side of the limo before tackling the shirt and tie. My fingers deftly went to work unbuttoning, but after the eighth one, I got impatient with the tedious process and just pulled the dress shirt out of his tuxedo pants and up over his head. With the buttons on his sleeves still attached, the shirt hung in front of him, binding his wrists like handcuffs. Whatever Houdini moves he'd have to make to free himself was none of my concern, as I'd already moved on to his well-muscled stomach, delighting in the feel of his sculpted abs. An animalistic little growl accompanied my mouth as I dipped my tongue into the deep ridges. Jake's body shook as he laid his head against the cool leather interior of the limo.

Pulling me off his lap, Jake made quick work of his pants. He'd only managed to free the dress shirt from his left wrist so it was dangling off the right. After wriggling out of my panties, I was trying to figure out how I was going to get out of my wedding gown when a thought occurred to me.

"Babe, would you mind if I kept my dress on?"

A deep, sensual chuckle vibrated through the vehicle before he nodded his approval and said, "I'd expect nothing less."

I straddled his lap, dress billowing out on all sides. White fabric was everywhere, but we'd have to make it work; I was determined to get one more spectacular use out of my beautiful gown before it went into storage forever. Suddenly I was aware of Jake's mouth tugging gently at my ear as he waded his way through the fabric of my wedding gown to get to the good parts beneath. Once his long, agile fingers found their way under my dress, he immediately used them to stroke the inside of my thigh. Dampness formed between my legs, sending a blistering shiver rattling my body that spread out evenly to all my extremities.

With only the dull glow of the overhead car light to illuminate our faces now, I felt a staggering sense of reckless desire and unrestrained anticipation. I arched in pleasure as his fingers traveled along the dips and curves of my body before wandering up between my legs and teasing me in that most desired of places. Everything pulsed as my body adjusted to its yearnings and intensified hunger. I pressed against his hand, taking what my body desired while balancing myself by pushing down on his thighs for support.

The windows had sealed in our steam, protecting us from gawkers while cloaking us in a sheet of sticky, humid spice. We moved together in unison as waves of sensation threatened to overtake me before I even had my husband inside me.

Jake gripped my waist and rubbed himself against my entrance before positioning me over him. I moaned as he slowly lowered me down. My hair, once styled so beautifully, was now cascading over my shoulders in a tangled mess. I stared intently into his eyes as we moved together in perfect rhythm. His open mouth hovered below mine as he took shallow breaths and I could do nothing but attack them lustfully. My tongue pushed into his mouth only to find his ready and waiting.

Breaking our kiss, Jake traveled down my neck, that tongue of his tracing wet lines across my skin and making me shiver. All the while he moved in me, growing harder and more intense with each passing minute. I dropped my head back as Jake's tongue formed snail trails along my sensitive neck. Wrapping my arms tighter around Jake's neck, I bucked into him, panting as I encouraged his participation. But Jake was making me wait, and in turn, taking away the very last remnant of my self-control. With my body in a heightened state of desire, I swept my fingers through his hair.

Jake said nothing as he clamped his lips against the side of my neck and began pumping, thrusting steadily in and out, supporting me. As he controlled my movements with his powerful grip on my backside, I felt myself rapidly heating toward the boiling point, and my thoughts became clouded, my consciousness submerging in a rising sea of liquid passion. My legs clamped tighter around him, and suddenly Jake's hips bucked hard against me, and I felt him release in long, jetting bursts deep inside me. The sensation triggered my own climax, and my head jerked forward, bumping against the limo window as my entire body clenched with a powerful shudder, legs locked, nails violently raking Jake's neck and shoulders. I made no sound other than a tiny, choking gasp, and time seemed to stop. When I, at last, managed to draw another breath, I realized I had scratched Jake's skin hard enough to draw blood; and he looked at me with mild surprise before devouring my lips with a deep, long kiss.

Giddy from our lovemaking session in the limo, I skipped my way down the hallway to our honeymoon suite. Jake trailed behind, refusing to partake in such childish antics, yet there was no doubt he found my mood infectious. The wide smile on his face was proof positive.

I stopped at the door to our room. "You're planning to carry me over the threshold, right?"

"I feel like there's been a whole lot more carrying today than in the average wedding."

"Well, you know, if your limo hadn't gotten stuck and my heel hadn't snapped off, you could have cut the carrying in half."

"Although I feel it important to add that the limo never would have gotten stuck had you been able to wait the five minutes it would have taken to get to the hotel and order room service."

"True, but if I hadn't demanded fast food, then we wouldn't have been eating it in the backseat of the limo, and…well… you know what happened after that."

He nodded, smiling. "You win."

Scooping me into his arms, Jake carried me into our room and dumped me unceremoniously onto the bed. His face was flushed with the effort as he collapsed beside me.

"I wasn't too heavy, was I?"

"No. God no," he said, through ragged breaths.

"Maybe I shouldn't have eaten all the fries."

"If you recall, I did try to help you out with those, but you actually bared your teeth at me."

"I was smiling."

"No. You made a snarling noise, too."

"Fine. So I was territorial. Everyone knows there's no 'we' in 'fries.'"

Jake rolled his eyes then sat up on the bed to look around. "This is nice."

I sat up too. Damn. The dark distressed-wood four-poster bed was draped in white cloth, and the high-ceilinged room was decorated in homey yellows and browns. A huge spa tub sat off to the side. Too bad we were only spending the one night here before jetting off to Cabo in the morning.

"You know what I want to do right now?"

"What?"

I stopped myself, realizing how stupid a request it would be. "Never mind. You'll think it's stupid."

"I'm usually down for pretty much any ridiculous thing you ask for."

I dipped my head to the side and smiled slyly. "Okay, you asked for it."

I stood up on the bed and started jumping in my wedding gown. I'd watched it once in a movie, and thought it was the cutest, most romantic thing I'd ever seen. Of course, I was sixteen at the time, so maybe some of its charm was due to my youthful fantasies.

"Oh, god," Jake said, not budging. "I take it all back. This I won't do."

" Come on, babe, you know you want to." Holding my dress up as high as possible, I joyfully kicked my feet up behind me.

"No. I really don't want to."

"But you will because you love me, right?"

"No." He laughed. "I married you. I think I've proven my love."

"All right. That's fine. Don't worry about it." I sighed, feigning disappointment. "This was just a childhood dream of mine, but no biggie."

I really didn't care one way or another. I just liked giving him a hard time for fun. "But whatever, Jake. You do you."

He watched me jump, an amused smile on his face.

"Are you coming, or what?" I finally asked.

"Yeah. I'm coming," he said, with zero enthusiasm as he dragged his butt off the bed. Jake climbed up and stood there as I bobbed up and down. I grabbed his hands and forced him to jump with me. The way our heads bobbed up and down and the bed creaked below, we both started laughing. Soon we were in full-blown hysterics and completely out of breath. Jake and I collapsed in a heap, panting like we'd run a marathon.

After catching my breath, I rolled over, propped myself up on one elbow, and planted a big, smoochy kiss on him. "You're already an awesome husband."

"Why, because I do what you want?"

"No, because you do what I want just to make me happy."

He smiled, grabbed my cheeks, and squished my lips together to give me a kiss. "I do like you happy."

"Yes, you do." I had no doubt my eyes were shining with the love they felt. He was just so damn amazing. "I love you so much, Jake McKallister. It actually hurts sometimes."

He wrapped his hand around the back of my neck and drew me in, locking our mouths in a lingering kiss. When he finally broke away, he said, "I hurt for you all the time."

Chapter Eight

Jake

Honeymoon

Walking with purpose, I rounded the aged barn with the metal shingles, sliding my hand along the rough wooden surface. It seemed so harmless, so old and worn, but it wasn't. There was nothing innocent about this place or the land it stood on. My heart rate began to rise and my breathing shallowed. I wasn't alone. I knew they were following me, and I wanted to scream at them to back off. What did they think I was here for in the first place?

I glanced down at my list, but it wasn't like I really needed it. Each tiny detail had been etched in my brain like a twisted poem. Still I clutched the worn paper in my hand, more for comfort than anything else. "#6 Due South. A single boulder in the meadow with five marks carved in the base of the stone."

I could see it, that boulder… it was there in my dreams… always that same damn boulder. "Five marks carved in the base of the stone." I hated knowing these things. They were his secrets, not mine.

"Jake, wake up."

I opened my eyes slowly, disoriented, as the boulder disappeared from my vision. Casey, my beautiful new wife, was sitting beside me wearing my t-shirt and gently rousing me by patting her hand on my stomach. Over the past two years, we'd devised the least invasive wake-up call. When I was deep in a dream, an abrupt awakening could affect me for hours. But allowing me to wallow in a nightmare was no better a solution. I sat up, rubbing my eyes, and actually looked down at my clutched hands, searching for the list, though it wasn't there.

Casey placed her hands over mine. "You okay?"

"What was I doing?"

"You were breathing really heavy. I got scared, so I woke you up."

"It's okay. I was just having a nightmare."

"Who was following you?"

"What?"

"You kept telling someone to back off."

Running my hands through my hair, I wondered how much I should tell Casey about this dream. We had a deal: every time my nightmare was bad enough that she needed to wake me, I had to share one detail with her. Although my first instinct was always to lie to her, I'd made a concerted effort not to.

"Ghosts."

"Ghosts?" she asked, her skin erupting in goosebumps. There were times she seemed so innocent. Was that how a person reacted who'd never seen the dark side of life? I'd been so young when my world imploded that I didn't remember what it was like before I was jaded.

"It's a dream," I said, trying to justify my answer. "You asked."

"What did they want, these ghosts?"

The answer to that question had haunted me for years, and even though I knew the answer to it, I would never admit it to her. Against all odds, I'd built a life for myself, one that included this amazing woman beside me. I wouldn't allow *them* to take that from me, no matter how selfish it might seem.

"I don't know," I said, trying hard to sound unfazed. "You woke me up before I could ask them."

She smiled even though she didn't seem at all happy with my response. "I'm serious."

"So am I. Can we please stop talking about ghosts? They're such a turn off."

I yanked her down onto the bed and rolled over her. Although still appearing troubled, she didn't protest when I removed her t-shirt or when I began running circles around her nipples with my tongue, but her worried mind was not yet ready to concede; her body wasn't giving in to my touch. Casey wasn't convinced. She wanted more from me, but we both knew that wasn't happening. So the question was, would she allow me to change the subject through distraction, as I was doing now, or would she shut me down entirely? It had gone both ways in the past, and recently she'd been getting harder to redirect.

Teasing a trail down her stomach, my fingers and tongue worked in unison until, slowly but surely, Casey's body relaxed under my caress. Once I moved between her thighs, all was forgotten. At least for her.

The ultra-exclusive resort where we were spending our honeymoon sat on a secluded stretch of pristine coastline and offered sweeping ocean views as well as luxury amenities. Casey and I had some excursions planned later in the week, but the first few days were spent entirely in the villa. There was no need to go elsewhere. We had everything we could possibly want and more. The private pool and spa aside, we were steps away from the sandy beach where we sat multiple times a day watching the waves roll in. It was relaxation at its finest, and we were taking full advantage of our time together – like now, lounging on inflatable mattresses in our pool with a drink in hand and the ocean as our scenic backdrop.

"Ooh, hon, you're starting to burn."

"No. It's called a tan. I think you forget that I have a superior skin tone, which doesn't require the application of suntan lotion every twenty minutes, unlike some people I know."

"Oh, okay," Casey said, feigning indifference despite the fact that my insolence drove her insane. "Suit yourself, but don't come crying to me tonight when you're the shade of a solo cup."

"When have I ever come crying to you?" I asked, all bravado, no bite.

"True. You're more of a whiner."

"I prefer brooding."

"Brooding suggests a level of cool that you just seem to lack," Casey teased.

"Excuse me. I'm pretty sure if you looked up the meaning of the word *brooding* in the dictionary, they'd skip the definition altogether and just place a picture of me there."

"Yeah, I guess," she said, pulling her sunglasses off to look at me. "What word would be next to my picture?"

"Hmm... that's a tough one. Let me think," I said, pretending to waffle on the answer before blurting out, "Loquacious."

"That's a big word, sweetie. Good for you."

"I know. The only reason I know what it means is because when I was writing my vows, I looked up synonyms for talkative, and just like that, I had a new word."

She laughed, but it died off more quickly than expected. I glanced over. Her eyes were closed, but she wore a frown on her face. *Shit, did I offend her?* Using my hands as paddles, I splashed my way over to her and grabbed her mattress to pull us together.

Taking her hand, I said, "Hey, I was just kidding. I love that you're loquacious."

"No, it's not that." She hesitated. "Can I ask you something?"

Figuring it had something to do with my dream from earlier, I steeled myself for her question.

"Do you think I should quit my job?"

I couldn't have been more surprised if she'd told me she wanted to quit math… if you could even do such a thing. I attempted to sit up on my inflatable, but miscalculated and tumbled into the water.

"I'm not sure how to interpret that answer," she said, after I'd resurfaced and shaken out my sodden hair. I pulled her mattress into the shallow end and stood next to her.

"That's because I didn't give one. I didn't know you were considering it."

"I love my job, and when you were still in LA, it was great, but now that you're gone all the time, I don't like missing you. I go home to an empty house, and I wish I were with you. Sometimes I wonder why I'm even doing it, you know. It's not like we need the money. But then, I also feel this need to get some use out of my degree. I just don't know what to do."

"That's not a question I can answer for you, Casey. I don't want you to resent me later if I give you the wrong advice."

"But if you had a choice, would you prefer I be with you?"

"You're my wife. Of course I'd prefer that, but I don't require it."

"Wow, look at you, all politically correct."

Swinging her mattress toward me, I bent down and kissed her. "I know, I'm dying a little inside right now. I want to tell you to drop everything and come with me, but if I make that decision for you, I have a feeling it'll come back and bite me in the ass. So my answer is, whatever you want, honey."

"Blah!" She pretended to vomit. "Terrible answer. You're lucky you're hot."

"I know, right?"

Wincing, I stepped out of the shower and checked my sunburn in the mirror. Dammit. How was I going to hide this from Casey? After boasting of my superior skin tone, I had some explaining to do. Nursing the ache, I didn't have a chance to cover up before she walked into the bathroom and smirked as she ran her eyes over my charred skin.

"Wow, such a beautiful tan. You were right, Jake, no lotion needed," she said, grinning, then slapped my naked butt. "And hurry up. Gabriel will be here in a few minutes, and we don't want him to mistake you for a lobster."

The knock came on schedule. Gabriel was nothing if not punctual. My stomach growled at just the sound of his knuckle hitting wood. Gabriel was our personal chef, and today would be the third night he'd come to our room to whip us up a tasty meal.

"How are my favorite newlyweds?" he asked jovially, using that same line every night before serving us the dinners I'd prearranged with the resort. There would be no culinary surprises for me. The problem with personal chefs, I'd found, was they always wanted to get creative with their food selections, and I was anything but an adventurous eater. Give me the basics. I was a meat and potatoes kind of guy. The last thing I wanted was experimentation in my mouth.

Gabriel, ever the professional, abided by my wishes for dinner, but appetizers and between-course samplers were fair game in his book, and before I knew it, bite-sized nasties began showing up on my plate. I mean, was it so hard for him to grasp that not everyone enjoyed octopus tentacles sliding down their throats? Normally such behavior would rub me the wrong way, but not with Gabriel. He was too damn nice, like a friendly grandpa who spent his days doting over his grandchildren just because he could. When it came right down to it, I didn't have the heart to offend him by not eating what he set on my plate. That's not to say I *actually* ate the stuff, I just pretended to. While Casey gamely sampled his offerings, I was busy stuffing mine into napkins, as so many dogless children the world over had done before me.

Regrettably, my silence on the issue only encouraged Gabriel's creativity, as he believed I was actually enjoying his creations. Each day he brought forth bolder, more *Fear Factor*-worthy selections for me to try. We'd only been here three days and the dinner thing was already starting to stress me out. In desperation, I'd taken to stashing paper towels in my pants pockets. Since I never knew what was coming my way, I went into every meal prepared for the worst. As for Casey, she found my efforts insanely entertaining, as if I wasn't doing it for my very survival but for her unbridled amusement.

So it was with great apprehension on my part when Gabriel presented Casey and me with a covered platter after dinner. I pictured the severed head of some exotic beast drizzled in apricot sauce, which was sure to be a delicacy somewhere in the world. I glanced down at my measly stash of paper towels. No way would they be enough to cover whatever monstrosity lay beneath.

"So first," Gabriel began, moisture pooling in his eyes as he fanned his face. "Oh, gosh, I told myself I wouldn't get emotional. You just mean so much to me."

I fidgeted with my paper towels. Oh, fuck, this was going to be bad.

"You two made this old man believe in love again." Full-on tears were now squirting from his eye sockets.

"Ahh, Gabe," Casey said, exiting her chair and flinging her arms over his burly shoulders. I wanted to remind them both that we'd only collectively known each other for three days, certainly not enough time to warrant sobbing. Nor was it enough time for Casey to have given him a nickname.

"And…and I…" More weeping. "I made a cake…"

Oh, thank god! Just a cake. No maggot cheese in a bread bowl or embryo eggs dipped in blood pudding.

"It's okay," Casey said, rubbing Gabriel's back. "Nice easy breaths."

Although I wasn't a fan of sweets, I didn't fear them either. So while Gabriel bawled, I shoved the paper napkins in my pocket and leaned back in my seat, feeling as though I'd just dodged a rather slimy bullet.

"It was my mother's favorite cake and became my signature dessert. Everybody just adores it, but my mother, you know, she… she passed away a while back."

Gabriel broke down again, forcing Casey to continue practicing her nurturing skills. Anticipating this might take a while, I pulled out my phone to check my messages when I sensed resentment focused at me. I glanced up to find Casey, her lips perched in a thin, terse line, motioning me over to their circle of love. My eyes widened. What the hell? Was I also expected to comfort him? Look, I felt for the man, I really did. Losing a parent, at any age, had to be devastating, but – I don't think I can stress this enough – I'd known the man for *three days*! I barely hugged my own father, and I was fully vested in him.

Like an ornery child, I shook my head. Casey's eyes narrowed as she scowled in my direction. Not a good look on her, I might add. Meanwhile, Gabriel seemed totally oblivious to our non-verbal squabble as he continued with his heartbreaking tale. Apparently, this was no ordinary baked confection. Gabriel's cake was a masterpiece of sorts, served to celebrities and politicians alike, and he rattled off a long list of famous names to prove it. Somehow I just knew that mine would be added to the roll call the next time he told this tale.

Anyway, the story went something like this – or at least the condensed version did: the cake had been a special family recipe from his mother who, sadly, passed away two years ago. He hadn't been able to bake it since her death, but seeing Casey and me so in love had inspired him to plug in the old mixing bowl again. Casey held his trembling body as a new wave of emotion played out. I hated to be cynical, but when I counted back how many hours, in total, we'd spent with the guy, I came up with eight.

And when the big reveal finally arrived, Gabriel proudly opened the lid to his baked marvel, a German chocolate cake, and although I was no baking expert, the brown creation topped with nuts and coconut was underwhelming even by my standards. It looked more like a hedgehog dipped in dirt than an edible dessert. When I looked to Casey to judge her reaction, she appeared as let down as I felt.

"Oh, Gabriel, this looks fantastic," she said, lying through her teeth. "We are so full right now, but I for one can't wait to give it a try a little later tonight."

"Nonsense! Surely you have room for one more bite to make an old man happy." He was already cutting into the cake and extracting a slice. Resigned, I pulled the paper towels out of my pocket. I was going to need them after all.

"Thanks so much," Casey said at the door with Gabriel, as she tried to get him out of our suite. "It was just heavenly."

"Oh, honey, you are an angel. My mama is smiling down on you tonight. I know it might be tough, but don't fill up on too much cake because I'll be back in the morning to prepare you both a wonderful brunch."

"Yay!" Casey said, clapping her hands. From my seated position I mouthed 'Yay' and silently clapped, mocking her fake joy. Once the door shut, she flattened her back against it and covered her mouth with her hands. Our eyes met from across the room and smiles broke across our faces.

"Oh, my god! That was" – Casey said, as she walked back to me – "painful."

"I blame you and your whole Dr. Phil act."

"What was I supposed to do? He was close to a breakdown, and it's not like I could count on you and your ice-cold heart."

"This is our honeymoon, Casey. I feel like we're letting an emotionally disturbed chef get between us… and he carries knives. I'm just saying."

"Stop being dramatic. So, what did you think of the cake?"

I shrugged. "I don't know. It's in my pocket."

"What? I saw you put it in your mouth," Casey said, laughing.

"No. You *thought* you saw me put it in my mouth. You know I don't trust any cake that doesn't come out of a Betty Crocker box."

"Jake, we really need to cultivate you. That will be my pet project in our coming life."

"Good luck with that. Anyway, you'd better get started. Gabriel is expecting a half-eaten cake by first thing tomorrow morning."

"Me? I hate German chocolate cake," Casey said, wrinkling her nose.

No way had I heard her correctly. "You don't hate *any* kind of cake. You've made that very clear over the years."

"I make an exception for this one. You know I despise coconut unless I'm spreading its lotion over my skin."

"Why didn't you tell Gabriel that, then?"

"For the same reason you've been shoving food into napkins for days," she answered, her voice raised in amusement.

"Well, what are we going to do?" I asked. "You saw him – if we don't eat this cake, he'll need a forty-eight hour hold in the nearest psychiatric facility."

"We'll tell him we were just too full."

"Great idea. And then a new one will show up tomorrow night, and the night after that. At some point, you're going to have to eat the cake."

"When did this become *me* and not *we*?"

"When you became emotionally involved. You called him Gabe, Casey. Now he thinks he's part of the family."

"Well, no way am I eating it, so what do you suggest we do – wrap it in paper towels and stuff it down your pants?"

"Sadly, there's just not enough room in there," I answered, pleasing myself with the big dick reference yet slightly offended when it garnered no response.

"All right, so we throw it away."

"I tried that on night one, but Gabriel took out the trash and I swear he took a quick look at the contents and saw the snail I tossed in there. No, unless we take it to a dumpster ourselves, he'll find it."

"Yeah, you're probably right. Okay, I have an idea. Why don't we flush a couple of slices down the toilet? There will be no trace of it, and he'll still think we ate some of it. Problem solved."

I thought about her suggestion for a moment then nodded. That wasn't a half-bad solution. Reaching over, I tousled her hair. "Look at you using that fancy degree of yours."

"I knew it would come in handy one day."

Casey and I cut realistic pieces from the body of the cake and fed a small, sample-sized chunk into the toilet to test her theory and, just as predicted, the chocolaty mass broke apart in a vile display before swirling and whirling and disappearing completely from sight.

"Yes!" I exclaimed as we high-fived our good decision-making abilities. We were totally going to rock the communication part of a solid marriage. "Next."

She dumped a similar-sized piece into the water and flushed. Once again it spun aggressively in the bowl before vanishing. This was the smartest idea we'd ever come up with as a cohesive unit. We cheered our good fortune.

But with success came a feeling of invincibility, and simply put, we got cocky. The following slice, bulkier in size, seemed to go down without problem at first, but a hollow burping sound emanating from the innards of the toilet soon put a damper on the fun, and before we knew it, the toilet was hemorrhaging German chocolate cake. Casey and I watched in horror as our good idea became anything but.

The thing about flushing food down the toilet, I have since learned, is that it doesn't look the same going down as it does coming up. Going down it still looked strangely like a hedgehog; but coming back from the bowels of hell, Gabriel's dead mother's cake was nothing more than a pleasant smelling pile of excrement… and it was rising.

"It's gonna blow!" I shouted, jumping back as I looked for the nearest exit.

"Can you plunge it?" Casey screamed, in a swirl of panic.

"With what?" I yelled back. "*My hands*?"

So much for our communication skills. As it became evident that we were going to have more on our hands than just a depressed chef, Casey and I clung to each other as we helplessly watched the poo-nami of German chocolate cake crest in the rapidly shrinking toilet bowl. Just as the first bits and pieces began to drain over the sides, the water miraculously stopped flowing. Holding my breath throughout the entire ordeal, I allowed myself to breathe only when I felt our situation had stabilized.

"What do we do?" Casey whispered, as if she instinctively knew we weren't in the clear just yet. The rising waters might not have breached the levee, but that didn't mean we weren't still in imminent threat of flooding.

"Would sneaking out of the hotel in the middle of the night be too extreme?"

"For the average human, no. But with your name on the guest registry, we are screwed. You're just going to have to call for maintenance to come and plunge it."

"Why me?"

"No way am I going to stand there and have them thinking that mess came out of my butthole. You're a guy. They'd expect shit like that from you. So to speak."

"I feel like this is a good time to remind you that flushing the cake down the toilet was your college-educated idea."

"Yes. And clearly it was a poor one, but now you're going to have to cover up my crime and dispose of the body. That's what good husbands do."

Before tonight, the luxury suite we'd booked for our honeymoon had been all it was promised to be. Casey and I had been so pleased with the accommodations we hadn't found a reason to leave the room... until this very moment. Now, I'd rather be anywhere in the world but here.

"This way," I said, opening the door wider and letting the maintenance guy in. I followed behind in a solemn procession, knowing that what I had to show him would be uncomfortable for the both of us. Scanning the room, I searched for Casey, already knowing what I'd find – nothing. She was gone... abandoning me in my time of need.

We'd only been married three days, and she'd already shown her true colors.

Standing in the doorway as the man entered the bathroom, I braced myself for the reaction. There was no explanation that would make sense so, when he turned toward me with question in his eyes, I just kept my mouth shut. Embarrassment colored my cheeks as I shrugged my shoulders and averted my eyes. Really, no clarification was needed, and he knew it. As horrible as it might be, this was his job, and I comforted myself with the possibility that perhaps this experience might inspire him to go back to school and get an education.

Seeing no reason to prolong the inevitable, I stepped back, leaving him alone to clean up the mess we'd made. My ears were assaulted by deep gurgling sounds that resonated through the walls. Again, embarrassment seeped through. Whatever was happening in there, I didn't want to know. From the corner of my eye, I saw movement behind the drapes. Casey! The coward. Oh, no, she wasn't getting out of this one.

Like a cheetah, I sprang from the bed and lunged for her. She screamed, making a run for it, but I was too quick and grabbed her. Casey swung her legs up in an impressive attempt to escape me. Her screams were loud enough to bring the maintenance man rushing from the bathroom, plunger in hand. Sweat and confusion dripping down his horrified face.

"It's okay. Sorry. Sorry." Casey held her hands up to calm the man before breaking into a chorus of giggles so impressive that it made her McDonald's fit seem tame. "We're just joking around," she said hiccupping through the hysterics. "Sorry."

Not appearing the least bit amused, the disgruntled hotel worker turned away and bravely returned to the task at hand, mumbling something in Spanish under his breath. Oh, yeah, his silence was going to cost me.

There were two things wrong with our sunset snorkeling adventure. One, it was at sunset; and two, it involved snorkeling. The name itself should have tipped Casey off that she wasn't going to like this particular adventure, yet not once during the planning process had she voiced any objections. It wasn't until we were on the boat headed for Chileno Bay that my bride shared with me her traumatic snorkeling experience as a child. Apparently an unruly clownfish had tried to French kiss her off the coast of Mexico when she was ten, causing Casey to gasp in shock and suck a gallon of water down her tube, nearly drowning her in the process.

Or so she says. If you asked me, there seemed to be a lot of embellishing going on in her version of events. Casey had never been known for her factual storytelling. For example, her clownfish was named Pennywise and had long razor-like teeth as well as a propensity for head-butting unsuspected snorkelers. One thing was for certain: I'd be fact checking her story with Linda as soon as we came home. But for now, I had bigger issues at hand – namely that I was in the ocean at sunset with my newly minted wife strapped to my back like a tortoise shell. With her arms wrapped tightly around my neck and legs around my waist, I was struggling to stay afloat in this lop-sided embrace.

How we'd gotten into this predicament was easy to pinpoint. Moments earlier, our well-meaning tour guide had tossed some food in the ocean directly in front of us, causing an aquatic flash mob to form around us. School was in session, and its tens of thousands of pupils were swirling around us at a dizzying speed. Casey jolted her head out of the water, and I could hear her screaming before I'd had a chance to resurface myself. Even with the goggles covering the vast majority of her face, I could see the terror playing out in her eyes.

"They're sucking me into their vortex," Casey shouted before lapping up a healthy mouthful of sloshing waves. As she gagged and flailed, her grip on my neck tightened and she proceeded to choke the life out of me.

"They're just fish," I wheezed. "They can't hurt you."

"Tell that to the victims in *Jaws*."

"Well, that wasn't real, so…"

"And what about the fatalities in *Sharknado*?"

"Okay, really not real."

"Look, I just hate fish, okay?" she said, with the whiniest of pouts. "They think they run the ocean."

"Yeah." I agreed. "Who do they think they are?"

"Exactly. I'm not even going to eat them anymore. That's how much I hate them."

"Shellfish too?" I asked, knowing full well that anything with shrimp in it was her very favorite meal *ever*.

"Let's not go crazy here," Casey replied, clearly amused by the conversation while remaining sufficiently terrified. "Look, I realize we've only been out here three minutes, but I want to go back to the boat." A gurgle sounded from her throat after all the water she'd consumed. "I'm totally cool with waiting for you to swim but, babe, I'm done snorkeling for this lifetime."

Seemingly determined to put the nail in the coffin of our snorkeling trip, the guide ignorantly dipped his hand back into a bucket and tossed yet another handful of food into the whirlpool. The grip around my neck tightened into a noose as Casey, not waiting around for me to rescue her, tipped us both backward and swam out of harms way.

"Casey," I gasped, "You're sort of strangling me right now."

I felt her grip suddenly detach as she scrambled onto the boat, not even looking back. It was then that I realized she hadn't been trying to save me. Casey had been using me as a human shield against the fishy hooligans who ruled the sea. The thought occurred to me that I was lucky this wasn't a real life *Jaws* situation because I'd most definitely be dead by now.

The following day, we tried our luck at another water sport, this one above the water line. Renting jet skis, Casey and I quickly acclimated ourselves to the machines and were thrashing through the waves at breakneck speeds having a frolicking good time until something behind me caught my attention.

"I think we're being followed," I shouted to Casey. She immediately looked back to see a man trailing us. He was a big guy, with a shiny bald top and a GoPro camera strapped to his forehead. It hadn't occurred to me that I might get recognized out on the water, so my bodyguard had stayed on shore. Maybe the best approach would be to let this guy take his picture so he would then leave me be; however, such an outcome was never guaranteed. Sometimes the photo chasers graciously disappeared after getting their shot, but other times, they morphed into flesh-eating bacteria. There was never any way to gauge the direction of any particular encounter until the gangrene set in.

I turned to Casey to get her opinion, only to find her standing up on her jetski looking like a goddess in her yellow bikini top and jeans shorts combo.

"Let's dust him," she said, flashing me her most mischievous smile. Oh, hot damn! That's what I liked to hear. I had my very own personal Charlie's Angel. She took off like a bolt of lightning and I whooped my approval of her can-do attitude. Pushing down on the throttle, I took off after her. In a life filled with uncertainty, Casey was the one path I always followed.

We rode through the choppy waters, leaving the shutterbug in our wake. My sexy wife suddenly turned into the fiercest of competitors as the two of us hit the choppy waters at top speeds, sending our jetskis airborne on multiple occasions. No way was that follicly-challenged hanger-on with the geek headgear going to keep up with my girl.

It wasn't until we'd circled back around that we saw the unmanned jetski bobbing on the surface, and its passenger flailing in the water. Casey and I exchanged glances. I could already tell what was going through her mind before she even opened her mouth.

"He's wearing a life vest." I shrugged, as if that might get me out of having to rescue my water-stalker at sea.

"We can't just leave him out here. There's nobody around."

"Sure we can. We'll go get help."

"And what if we can't remember where we left him and he drowns? We'll never forgive ourselves."

"Actually, I might not be all that heartbroken," I said. Casey raised a brow at me as she fixed an angry scowl on her face. Strangely enough, she appeared more amused than anything else, probably because she knew I wasn't going to let the dude drown.

"Oh, fine!" I huffed. "We'll rescue him. But I get to be Pamela Anderson."

We sped toward the thrashing photographer as I assessed the situation. His jetski had drifted away from him and he was now floating on his back.

Pulling up next to him, I asked, "Can you swim to your jet ski?"

"Can't swim." The man was panting something fierce. "Too fat."

I fought the urge to laugh at his straightforward comment. He was a big guy, no doubt, but all of his weight was carried smack dab in the middle of the most magnificent beer belly I'd ever laid eyes on. He could have been carrying septuplets in there. I had to give the guy some credit – that kind of extended gut required a lifelong commitment.

"Okay, hang on. I'll go get your jetski."

Trying to maneuver one machine while riding another wasn't easy, and by the time I returned, the guy had propped himself up onto the footboard of Casey's jetski and the two were having a full-on, lighthearted conversation complete with unbridled laughter. Did she have to make friends with everyone?

"...and with all those girls," she said, shaking her head at her new buddy. "That's impressive."

You know what else was impressive? Me... dragging a 600-pound jetski through the water with one hand!

Casey finally acknowledged my presence, her eyes sparkling with enthusiastic wonder. "Jake, Tony's on his twenty-fifth anniversary. He and his wife have four daughters. He was hoping to get a picture with you to show his girls. Isn't that sweet?"

I wiped the sweat off my forehead with the back of my hand, struggling to find the joy in Tony's awesome home life. What the hell did I care how many years he'd been married or how many children he'd sired? The fact remained he was cock-blocking me on my honeymoon.

"Yeah, awesome. Can you pull yourself up onto the seat?"

"Man, I can barely get off the toilet."

Casey laughed like he was some top-rated stand-up comic before looking back at me to confirm my reaction was similar to hers. It wasn't. Not even close. This guy was wasting my time. I could be back at the hotel getting it on with my new wife; but no, I had to save his sorry ass first.

"You can at least try to lift yourself up, right?"

"I guess I could try. If it'll make you happy."

Tony acted like he was doing me a huge favor, when in reality, he was the one in imminent danger of sinking to the ocean floor like the anchor of a fishing vessel. Although

I had to admit, that belly of his was floating nicely. Tony heaved and grunted, his plumber's crack on full display. And, like passing by a car accident with bodies littering the road, I couldn't look away. That hairy line of fur, which presumably had started somewhere up his back, disappeared between the whitest butt cheeks I'd ever seen.

It wasn't until he'd extracted about two inches of his body out of the water, that my eyes diverted back to the task at hand. It had been a gallant effort, but after twenty seconds of trying, Tony sank back down into the water like a seal sliding off a buoy. "Yeah, sorry, Jake. It's not happening. I need a damn forklift."

Was he using my name like we were old buds? Minutes earlier he'd been chasing after me like some creeper. Tony swiped his hand over his polished head. Still sporting tufts of hair on the sides, he was the type of bald that wasn't fully committed to the cause.

"You're going to be fine, Tony," Casey said soothingly, before turning to me and lowering her voice. "He's going to drown, isn't he?"

"No, he's not going to drown. If I have to, I'll drag him through the water."

"Why don't you just wait with him and get the pictures out of the way, and I'll go get help?"

"Pictures?" My voice raised a pitch. I was saving his life. Wasn't that enough?

"For his daughters. Geez, Jake. It's his anniversary. Just wait here. I'll be back soon."

"No way. What if you fall in? There are fish in the water, remember?"

"Fine. Then I'll wait and you get help."

"I'm not leaving you with some stranger."

"He's not a stranger," she protested. "It's Tony."

"No. He's definitely a stranger. Jesus, Casey. How have you survived this long?"

She rolled her eyes at me as if I were the unreasonable one.

"Anyway, we stick together or let him drown. Your choice."

"Um…hello… hi," Tony waved from his sunken position. "I can actually hear you."

"Relax," I said. "She picks you."

After a comedy of errors, which included me jumping into the ocean and attempting to forcibly shove his ass up and out of the water, I devised a new plan. With Casey holding onto my jetski, I transferred over to Tony's. Standing up for better leverage and height, I leaned down and offered him my hand. "On the count of three, lift yourself up."

By the time I said three, I'd yanked him up, but instead of getting his leg over the seat, the man face-planted directly into my dick and balls, forcing a wail from my mouth as loud as a mating whale.

His muffled voice was blocked by my package as he asked, "Would this be a bad time to ask for your autograph?"

Tony's wife Teresa was waiting for us on the dock. She was all hair and makeup and loud exaggerated talk. When we brought her water-logged husband back to dry land, you'd think, given they were celebrating their twenty-fifth wedding anniversary, that her concern for his safety would be paramount. Think again. After Casey explained to her what had happened, not only was Teresa *not* the least bit concerned over his predicament but she smacked Tony upside the head and chastised him for eating the chimichanga platter the night before. As if an extra pound here or there would have made such a huge difference when it came to hauling his ass out of the water.

Not to be outdone by her nagging, Tony went to town in an attempt to embarrass her by making an off-colored joke about the incredible amount of biking, hiking, and fornication the two had been doing since arriving in Cabo. Teresa pursed her lips and circled her finger by her ear in the universal signal for 'He's cuckoo.'

Casey and I were spellbound; our eyes swiveled back and forth between the bickering lovebirds as if we were watching a heavyweight prizefight. It took less than a minute for us to become fully vested in the relationship of these two outspoken strangers. So amused were we by them that I was even reluctantly persuaded to accept their offer of a thank you drink. Well, one drink turned to plenty, but it was only after Teresa offered up a nightcap back in their hotel room that I motioned for my bodyguard to take us away before we got drunk enough that a night of swinger sex with Tony and Teresa began looking like a good thing.

While I was okay with never seeing our drinking buddies again, Casey was drunkenly exchanging phone numbers with Teresa. Had I not been so wasted myself, I would have warned her against being so damn friendly all the time. Okay, I'll admit, they were a fun couple, and yes, Tony turned out to be a cool dude when he wasn't bobbing for my dick, but couldn't she meet someone and just for once not become lifelong friends with them? I'd need to talk to her about that… just as soon as I found a toilet to throw up in.

It wasn't until I woke up in the morning with a massive hangover and saw the anxious text from my mother that I understood the extent of Tony's gratitude. He'd gone straight to social media to tell his amazing rescue at sea story. In his version of events, Casey and I came off as modern day saints… heroes who'd risked life and limb to save a stranger from a murky death. I was finding his storytelling quite entertaining until I clicked on the accompanying video Tony had apparently taken of us without our knowledge or consent. It was all over the Internet.

"I still can't believe he was taking video the whole time we were out there with him," I complained, pointing at my phone's screen. "I blame you for this. I wanted to let him drown, but nooo… you just *had* to go pluck him out of the water."

"Tony's only trying to make you a star." Casey lifted her head off the table to groan.

"I'm already a star," I answered, wiping a dollop of drool from my lip. "I don't need Tony's help."

"Okay, whiny boy. You've had enough googling for one day." Casey plucked the phone from my hand. "Besides, there's worse press you could be getting. Just be happy that the video is of you saving Tony and not of you jetskiing away. You can thank me now."

Unable to keep her head up, Casey laid it in her outstretched arm. I dropped my head next to hers. We were a pathetic pair.

"Thank you," I whispered.

"You're welcome." She reached up and rubbed my temples.

Casey's phone went off with a rapid succession of buzzes. "Who keeps texting me?"

"Um, I'm thinking Teresa."

"How did she get my number?"

"I'll give you one guess," I said, pointing my finger at her in accusation.

"Well, you should have stopped me," she said, burping up a party favor. Her face turned green, and she sat for a brief moment, no doubt trying to establish which direction the contents were going. Once the determination was made, she sprinted off to the bathroom.

The last couple days of our honeymoon were spent sequestered in our suite. We'd had enough adventure for the week and were content just to float in the water and enjoy the time we had left alone together. On our last day in paradise, I swam while Casey lay by the pool's edge and soaked up the rays. Diving down under the water line, I kicked off the side of the wall and torpedoed myself underwater, surfacing just above Casey.

"Well, hey there, hunk," she said, recovering nicely from my sudden, watery intrusion into her peaceful nap.

"Hey there, girl in the yellow bikini. You wanna get naked with me?"

"I might be able to be persuaded... with the right foreplay."

"How about an upside down soggy kiss? Will that do it?"

"I don't know. Why don't you give it your best shot?"

I leaned in, dangling over her, my hair fanning out and tickling her face as I held my lips just above hers, not yet touching. Her eyes met mine and I could see the desire already flowing through them. I knew her body well, and making her crazy with lust was currently my only mission. Lightly trailing my tongue over her bottom lip, Casey parted her sexy pout to allow me in, but I didn't plan on taking the easy way. Keeping her wanting… that was me giving her my best shot, and judging by her tiny little moans of pleasure, I was succeeding.

Her body trembled as I reached down to her bikini line and traced my wet fingers up her tan stomach, between her springy breasts, over her angled collarbone, and up to her sleek neck. Casey wriggled in place as my hand made its way back down and disappeared under her bikini bottom. Arching her back, Casey groaned as she reached up and grabbed both sides of my face and pulled me down until our lips met and her tongue invaded my mouth.

We were in the strangely erotic upside down kiss long enough for her to break away and say, "Stop. Not yet."

I pulled my hand out from between her legs and slid her body along the sunbathing mat she was lying on. Her skin was like silk as the warm water mixed with her lotion, creating the most sensual feel for my wandering hands. Resting her head on my shoulder, Casey floated on her back as I slid my fingers over her slippery flesh. I left no part of her untouched, and just as I'd been challenged to do, I had my wife naked and wanting.

"Jake, please." There was no need for her to finish her sentence, as I was already taking care of her need. Turning her around, I held her up against the side of the pool. Casey wrapped her legs around me as I entered her. Our eyes locked and we stared at each other in lust. It wasn't possible to want her more. She was it for me, my final stop on a long and harrowing journey. We held each other tightly, consummating our marriage for the last time in our honeymoon paradise.

CHAPTER NINE

JAKE

Takes One to Know One

My first order of business upon returning from the honeymoon was Quinn. I'd flaked on that kid more times than I cared to admit, so there was no way I wasn't keeping my word to him this time around. We made plans to meet at our parents' house the following day. Not only could I work with Quinn on his songs, but a visit would satisfy my parents, who were eager to hear about the honeymoon.

Casey and I had been on the road for only fifteen minutes when she said, "Can we stop for a cup of coffee?"

"Like in the store?" I asked. Was she crazy?

"Yeah, Jake, like normal people do. Sit inside and sip some coffee. Is that so weird?"

I didn't immediately respond because, yeah, it was a tad weird. I was a goddamn rock star. I didn't just go into coffee shops and sip coffee. Not anymore, at least. Not since my popularity exploded last year and I had to have a bodyguard with me just about everywhere I went nowadays. Not that he was with us today. I hadn't thought I needed him. We were just going to my parents' house, where the only person I needed protection from was my father and his exploding nutsack stories.

"Never mind," she sighed. "I'll just hop out and get it for us."

The disappointment in her voice surprised me. We males weren't always good at picking up on such social cues, and I was no exception, but Casey definitely appeared let down by the fact that I didn't want to get mauled at the coffee shop.

"Am I missing something here? If you wanted to go for coffee, why didn't you tell me before you left? I would have had Vadim come with us."

A tempered laugh escaped her, but again, I sensed something was off. My gut was telling me she didn't find any of this funny.

"Sometimes…" she began, before abruptly stopping herself.

I waited for the rest of her sentence but it never came. "Sometimes what? Talk to me, Case."

"Sometimes I wish we could be like other couples and take a walk through the park or sit down for a cup of coffee, is all… and not with Vadim tagging along. He's like the Terminator, Jake. He scares people."

"That's the point of a bodyguard."

"Well, I don't like it. And I don't like him being a third wheel. Having a homicidal cyborg along everywhere we go kills the romantic vibe. Why can't it be like our honeymoon all the time? No one bothered us at the resort."

"Because everyone paid handsomely *not* to. When you're rich, you have to pretend you don't care about famous people. It's in the handbook. Look it up."

Casey glanced over at me and her face softened, the stress lines gone. She responded coyly. "Coffee shop patrons are a sophisticated bunch. My bet is they won't care either."

"That's highly doubtful, but I'll tell you what, if you don't mind standing around for an hour while I sign autographs and take pictures, then why the hell not?"

"Really?" she perked up.

No. The last thing I wanted to do was fake happiness for a bunch of strangers. But if it made Casey happy, and proved my point in the process, then I supposed it was a win-win. "Sure. Okay. Let's get coffee."

Casey sat back in her seat, her arms crossed in front of her, a smug smile suddenly appearing on her face. Wait a minute! Had I just been conned?

"Casey?" I asked, still not believing that my beloved was so shrewd.

"Yes?" she answered in the sweetest, most affecting voice.

"You just played me like a deck of cards, didn't you?"

"Yes, sweetie, I sure did."

I parked the Jeep out in front of a Starbucks and turned to my wife. Her eyes sparkled in amusement. I shook my head. If she wanted to play – well, then, game on.

I jumped out and waited for her on the curb. Instead of trying to cover up with a cap or sunglasses, I decided to go au natural. I typically hated being gaped and gawked at, but today I welcomed it. Let's just see how sophisticated her coffee crusaders were. There was no doubt in my mind that in a matter of seconds, my line would be longer than the one for a cup of joe. That would teach her.

Offering up my hand, Casey playfully slapped hers into mine and began to swing it like we were two six-year-old girls. Oh, she was good. She thought she could shame me into a second-place finish. But that's not how this little coffee break was going to play out. I would not allow her to get the upper hand in this game of ours… at least not without a fight.

The door opened with a swoosh of air, carrying the backdraft of the flavorful scent of coffee out onto the sidewalk, beckoning others to the holy land. I kept my head held high, making eye contact with other patrons as we took our place in line. Jaws began to drop all over the coffee shop. It was only a matter of time now.

Throwing my arm over Casey's shoulder, I dipped into her neck, giving it a little nibble for the fun of it. Teaching her a lesson didn't have to be boring. If done properly, learning could be beneficial for all. Casey reveled in the show I was putting on for her benefit.

Whispering in my ear, she said, "You're absolutely delectable right now, aren't you?"

I shook my head at her in disappointment. She wasn't supposed to be liking this. And where the hell were my selfie takers? No one was bothering us. This was ridiculous. Who was I going to have to screw in order to get a little fan girl gushing?

When we arrived at the cashier after several minutes, the middle-aged woman behind the counter stared at me, her face flushed and her eyes all aglow. Here we go. She was about to blow. Finally. Jesus.

"What can I get for you two?" she asked, looking between Casey and me. "And, just so you know, your drinks were already paid for."

"What? No, that's not necessary," I replied, looking around at all the patrons waiting on their drinks. Every single person in the place was staring in our direction. "Who paid for us?"

"Well, you had multiple offers, but the gentleman over there was first in line when you came in, so he got the honors."

The honors? It's not that people didn't offer to buy me stuff all the time, but this was different. This wasn't the typical celebrity stuff. No, there was definitely something more taking place here

"What you two did for that poor man, wow, so brave," the cashier said, nearly misting up as she spoke. "There just aren't enough good people like you in the world."

Casey and I blinked back our surprise. Tony and his exaggerated rescue video, the one he'd spliced together to feature only the good parts, was certainly making the rounds on the Internet. My bar buddy had been nowhere near drowning when we'd come upon him in the water that day. The life vest clinging to his bulky curves was holding up nicely in the waves and would have kept him afloat long enough for someone else to find him, yet Tony had modified the truth to make us look like heroes.

"Just own it," Casey said, behind her smiling teeth.

And then they came, flocking to us from all directions, offering up handshakes and good wishes on our wedding. Typically when fans rushed me, Casey was cast aside like an afterthought, but not today. This time she was front and center and loving every second of it. Thanks to Tony's video, I wasn't the only famous one in our relationship. Not when the girl in the yellow bikini was in the house.

As we waited for the security gates to open into my parents' house, Emma pulled up beside us.

"Well, if it isn't our very own superheroes," she said. "Very cool rescue at sea."

"It was nowhere near that cool in person," I answered.

"Deny all you want, but Casey's bikini has its own Instagram account."

"HA!" Casey blurted out, high-fiving me. "That's what I'm talking about!"

"You were looking good, girl," my sister complimented Casey.

"Are you guys just getting here? I though we were going to be late."

I glanced into her car for Finn but found only an empty passenger seat. Maybe she was referring to her and the baby, but then she rolled down the window to reveal Finn sitting in the backseat with Indiana.

"Emma?" I chastised her. "You don't even allow him in the front seat?"

"What?" My sister shrugged. "The baby was crying."

"Dude, I swear," I said, eyeing Finn in the back. "She might as well strap you in to your very own big boy seat."

Finn flipped me off with a smirk stamped on his face.

The gate opened, and we drove up to the house. Emma honked to let our parents know we were all there. They came out, followed by Grace and a tall, spiky-haired kid I'd never seen before. Glancing over at Emma, she read my mind and whispered, "Boyfriend."

"No," I gasped. Not Grace! "She's too young for a boyfriend."

"She's seventeen."

"Seriously?" I asked in surprise, as I started doing the math in my head. Damn. Emma was right. Grace was actually seventeen. Who knew? I scanned the boyfriend. I didn't like him on principle alone. "What's with the blue hair?"

"I don't know. I assume he dyed it."

"Really?" I asked, all sarcasm. "He didn't come out of the womb that way?"

Emma turned off her engine. "Since when are you an overprotective brother?"

"Since she started dating *that*. Why would he want to spike his hair all over his head? He looks like a sea urchin."

My sister rolled her eyes. "He looks worse than he actually is."

"Oh, really? Would you let him hold your baby?"

Emma recoiled. "Are you crazy?"

"Yeah, that's what I thought."

Finn opened her door and offered his hand. Climbing out, she pulled him to her and kissed him. Emma wasn't one to openly flaunt her relationship, but there had definitely been a change in her since meeting Finn and giving birth to Indiana. She smiled with her eyes now, something I hadn't seen her do since she was a child. I wondered if the difference was only due to Finn and the baby or if she'd been seeking professional help. She'd mentioned the idea to me once, but we'd never discussed it since. Now I was left wondering if therapy had helped lift the weight off her shoulders.

Damn, I was jealous. Why hadn't therapy had the same affect on me? Probably because I'd never really given it the chance to work. At the first sign of strife, I couldn't get out of there fast enough. And now I was being tormented by my demons while she was moving forward with the sunniest of dispositions. If Emma, the most inflexible person I knew, could find peace and a renewed sense of calm, maybe I needed to reevaluate my own progress. The nightmares were getting more intense, and I was left trying to stay a step ahead of something that was so much bigger than I was. Eventually I'd be swallowed up.

"They're adorable, aren't they?" Casey asked, following my gaze. She too was watching Emma and Finn's public display of affection, and it was making her swoon.

"Sure, if you like that sort of thing. Are you ready to meet the other adorable couple?" I asked looking in the direction of Grace and her blue-haired boyfriend. "This ought to be fun."

"Be nice," Casey warned.

"Aren't I always?"

"Um… might I remind you that you wanted to let Tony drown? So no, not always."

We joined Emma and Finn and walked to the porch. There was no need for either of them to get Indiana out of the back of their car as my dad had already extracted his favorite human from her car seat, and the two disappeared through the front door.

"I guess we'll see Dad later." I nodded my head in his direction.

"Oh, you'll see him again," Emma confirmed. "As soon as Indiana poops, throws up, or cries, he's outta there."

After exchanging niceties with my mother, I grabbed my little sister and wrapped her in a protective embrace.

"Someone's been holding out," I whispered in her ear.

"Someone hasn't been home in months," she fired back, before pulling her boyfriend closer and saying, "This is Rory."

He stepped up to Casey and me, looking terrified. Good. That's just how I wanted him.

"Hi," Rory said, his voice cracking.

Was he still going through puberty? Jesus, if that were the case, this kid was on track to be seven feet tall.

"It's really nice to meet you both. Congratulations on your wedding."

When I didn't make an immediate move to take his outstretched hand, Casey stepped in and took it, but not before giving me a warning glare. "It's nice to meet you too, Rory. If Grace had told me she had a boyfriend I would have added you to the guest list."

"Oh, well, we haven't been dating long, so it would've felt weird to impose on a family event."

At least he had that much sense. "So, Rory, is it?" I spoke up for the first time. "It's weird that Grace has never mentioned you."

"Yeah, well, she didn't mention you to me either. At least not until a couple of weeks ago."

Really? Huh. Now this was interesting information. Gracie stood between us looking about ready to die. How did this kid not know she was my sister? Everyone at her school knew. Unless… "Wait, you two don't go the same school?"

Mom shifted uncomfortably, and Grace looked out over the horizon.

"No," Rory hesitated. "We don't."

What exactly was happening here? It was obvious there was something they weren't telling me. In fact, there was something about this kid that didn't make sense at all. He wasn't the typical Southern California teen that filled Grace's wealthy suburban high school. Where had she met this guy?

Almost like he could read my thoughts, Rory tipped his head up, making eye contact with me for the first time, and what I saw in his gave me pause. The average person might miss it but I knew that look well. I saw it everyday in my own reflection in the mirror. Shame.

Taken aback, I averted my eyes and cleared my throat. "Well, it's good meeting you, Rory," I said, offering my hand to him. I no longer wanted to bust his balls, as I was certain someone else had already beaten me to the punch.

Quinn and I spent the next two hours working on his songs. It didn't take much to point him in the right direction and fix some of the issues he'd been having. I felt bad that it had taken me this long when it was so little effort on my part to help him out. Most surprisingly about the time I spent with him was that we worked so well together. There was no animosity between us at all. When it came to music, Quinn and I spoke the same language.

The talent was there, yet Quinn had somehow stalled and was just spinning around in place. What was he waiting for? God, I hoped it wasn't me.

"So, do you want to tell me what happened with that band? They seemed legit."

"They were." Quinn nodded, studying his hands and looking conflicted. "But it wasn't me they wanted. It was my… uh, how should I put this … my connections."

And by 'connections,' he meant me. I wasn't sure what had gone down, but it was pretty clear he'd been used, and that was never a good feeling. "That's shitty. Sorry."

Quinn watched me for a moment, almost like he was sizing me up to see if he could trust me. I must have passed because he started talking. "I came into it thinking they wanted a lead singer and that I was going to be, you know, a part of the group, but they weren't interested in my songs and I mostly just sang backup and played guitar. Then they started badgering me about your tour and were pressuring me to ask you. Anyway, when I couldn't deliver…" Quinn's voice trailed off.

"Oh," I shifted, uncomfortably. These were the stories I never heard from my siblings, but it couldn't have been easy for them to navigate their way through life under my very invasive fame. "I'm sorry. That sucks."

He shrugged. "I'm used to it."

"That kind of thing happens to you a lot?"

Quinn looked away, but not before I saw the pained expression on his face. "Enough that I should have been smarter. I'm usually pretty good at knowing when people are using me, but I guess I just wanted it too bad to really trust my gut."

It occurred to me then that Grace and Quinn had lived a totally different childhood than the rest of us. Their paths had been dictated by tragedy. There were no early morning trips to the beach with Dad, no playing outside until the light of day faded to dusk, and no real track they could travel on that didn't have my train rolling over it.

"I've never really thought much about how my fame affects you and Grace."

"It's not that, Jake. I love that you're my brother. I'm so proud of you. It's just…" Quinn cleared his voice, his brows furrowed in frustration. "People ask me questions about you all the time, and I have to make stuff up because I don't know the answers. I don't know you at all. Not one little thing."

I sat there quietly, letting his words sink in. Quinn was right. We knew nothing at all about each other. I couldn't tell you what he liked or didn't like. I didn't know if he had a girlfriend, what his favorite sports team was, or even if he'd been a good student while still in high school. Damn, how had we drifted so far apart that we weren't even connected as brothers at all? And the worst part was I knew it was my fault. I had done this to us.

"Ask me something. Anything," I blurted out without thinking about the consequences. Would I even be able to deliver? Did I have a choice? I was ground zero in this scenario, so our relationship needed to start with me.

"Okay," he said, blinking back his surprise by my offer. "What's your favorite movie?"

I tipped my head back, brows raised in surprise. "You can ask me anything and that's your question?"

"Well, I have thousands of questions, but I figured I'd better start small."

"*21 Jump Street*. You?"

"Same." He nodded.

"I've got one," I said. "If you can eat one food for the rest of your life, what would it be?"

"Potatoes."

"Whoa." I kicked back in my chair. "You didn't even hesitate."

"Nope," he said, laughing. "Think about it. Potatoes are the most versatile food there is. Breakfast? Hash browns. Lunch? French fries. Dinner? Baked or scalloped. Snack? Potato chips. Getting shit-faced with friends? Vodka. See, unlimited possibilities."

"Good god. That was better than a persuasive essay. Now I'm reevaluating my choice."

"I know what your answer would be," Quinn said, predicting my favorite food. "Tri-tip."

"Yep." I nodded. "What's with the vodka?"

"You mean how it relates to potatoes, or if I'm drinking it with friends?"

"Both."

"Vodka's made from potatoes, and no, I don't get shit-faced with friends on a regular basis. I don't have time for that crap. I have a plan for my future."

"I see that," I said.

The grit I hadn't given him credit for during my bachelor party was on full display today. This kid had drive and talent… a deadly combination.

"Okay, Jake, I have another question. If you could take one thing to a deserted island, what would you take?"

"That's easy. Casey. What about you?"

"My guitar."

"Obviously you don't have a girlfriend, then."

"No," he laughed. "But, honestly, I haven't met a girl I like more than my guitar anyway."

"Someday," I said.

"Yeah, someday," he replied, but he didn't seem all that convinced. He was silent a moment before looking up at me cautiously. "Okay, so you said anything, right?"

"I did. Are you going to make me regret it?"

"Maybe. There's something I've wondered about for a long time."

Yeah. I was definitely going to regret it, whatever the question was.

"After you came home, you never talked to any of us, but sometimes I'd hear you whispering when you didn't think anyone was around. One time I snuck in and listened. You were saying the same five names over and over. Jack, Anton, Rex, Wilson, and Felix. Who are they? And why were you saying their names?"

I sat there dumbfounded. Never in a million years was I expecting that question. I actually had no memory of repeating their names; but then, that time after arriving home from the hospital had been pretty torturous. My mind wasn't right at all.

"Is that too personal?" he asked.

"No, it's just… I've never told anyone about them before. Do you promise to keep this between us?"

Quinn leaned in, his voice a breathy whisper of intrigue. "I promise."

"Do you know how many victims Ray had, how many they dug up?"

"Twelve, right?"

"That's the official count. Yes. But that's not how many victims there were."

"Really?" His eyes had doubled in size at this piece of information.

"There were more… five, to be exact."

"Jack, Anton, Rex, Wilson, and Felix," Quinn said.

I nodded.

"How do you know their names?"

I didn't answer for the longest time because I wasn't sure how. Finally I tapped my finger to my temple and answered. "They live in my head, and no matter how hard I try to get them out, they never leave."

That turned out to be the end of our anything-goes question game. I'd revealed more than I wanted to and had given him more than he'd bargained for.

I stood up abruptly. "I've got to get back to Casey."

Quinn, still staring at me wide-eyed and open-mouthed, finally got his wits about him and said, "Yeah, okay,"

Heading for the door, I turned when Quinn called my name. "Jake?"

"What?"

He fidgeted with his guitar. "I shouldn't have asked that."

I stared at him a moment before replying, "And I could have lied."

Why hadn't I lied? It would have been so easy to tell him I couldn't remember, but instead I admitted to Quinn my deepest and darkest secret. Not only did I divulge they existed but also that these wayward ghosts lived inside my head. Crazy much? I could only imagine what was going through Quinn's mind. No doubt the poor kid hadn't expected such honesty from me. He probably thought I was insane because that's how it sounded to my own ears. At least maybe now he understood why I was emotionally unavailable to him. There were just too many damn people competing for my time.

Indiana must have taken a giant doo-doo in her pants, because when I came out of the music room, my father was baby-free and waiting for me.

"Hey, can I talk to you for a minute?" my father asked. The wrinkles in his forehead and the serious tone of his voice instantly put me on edge. Were he and mom getting a divorce? Had he gone bankrupt from a previously undetected gambling problem?

"Everything okay?"

My father nodded, but it was a solemn gesture. Oh, no. What was wrong? Could it be a death in the family? Cancer?

"I think I owe you an apology," he finally said.

An apology? I almost had a panic attack for an apology?

"What do you have to be sorry for?"

"Your pre-wedding freak out. I can't help but think it was because of the honeybee story."

"It had nothing to do with the damn honeybee. And, it wasn't a freak out. I just wanted to talk to Casey."

"I hope you know I was just joking around. Marriage is not like honeybee sex at all. At least not mine. I mean sex with your mom is…"

"Okay!" I interrupted before my ears heard something that couldn't be reversed. If I thought I had nightmares now… "Move on."

"Right. Anyway, all I'm saying is, your mom and I have a great relationship. In fact, you and Casey remind me of us when we were younger. That passion and chemistry you have for each other… that was what it was like for us, and still is to a lesser extent. I mean, we're not as young and nubile as we once were, but we can still work up a sweat, if you know what I mean."

I nodded grimly. Yes, I got the meaning loud and clear. I motioned with my hands for him to speed up.

"Anyway, we've been through so much together over the years, and at times, it would have been easier to just call it quits – but then I'd remember that twenty-year-old girl I met at the beach, all legs and breasts. Oh, man, Jake, your mom was… whoa… sexy as all hell."

"Dad, I'm serious. I'm going to leave unless you can get to your point without further references to my mother's body parts. You do have a point, don't you?"

"Relax. I do. See, I joke around about your mom being a drill sergeant and all, but the truth is, I want her to take control. The less I have to think about at home, the better. If she's running the show, where am I? Relaxing. I'm not sure if you realize this, but we McKallister men come from a long and proud line of marital wimps. We do what we're told and we're happier for it. When your mom is happy, I'm happy. Get it?"

"Okay, so, then why can't she be happy when you're happy?"

"Oh, no," he said, appearing completely shocked by my ignorance. "It doesn't work in reverse."

I laughed. "You're so full of shit."

"Am I? In three generations, not one McKallister man has divorced. You tell me who's crazy."

I found my way to the kitchen, where Mom was pulling condiments out of the refrigerator. I'd been hoping to catch her alone so I could get the scoop on Grace's boyfriend.

"So what's with this Rory kid?" I asked, plopping myself down into a counter stool.

Like earlier on the front porch, my mother stiffened. Now I was more curious than ever. She walked around the counter and took a seat beside me.

"You know last year when I asked you to donate to an organization that helps foster kids who've aged out of the system?"

I wrote a lot of checks. Remembering specifics wasn't normally a requirement. "Not really, but go on."

"Well, it was used to help purchase a 26-unit apartment complex that we then turned into a living facility for young adults who've bounced around the system for years until they hit the age of eighteen and were forced out on the street. Most of these kids don't have any survival skills because they've never had anyone to teach them. Anyway, I volunteer there, and it's where I met Rory. I know he looks a little edgy, but he's really a wonderful kid."

Remembering that look in his eyes, I said, "That may be true, but something bad has happened to him."

Mom's forehead furrowed. She seemed genuinely surprised by my assessment. "Why would you say that?"

"I can spot an abused kid a mile away."

"Really? I didn't know that. What are the signs?"

"It's nothing you can outwardly spot. It's just a feeling. It comes down to his body language and that look in his eye."

"Huh. That's interesting."

"So, what happened to him?"

"I don't know. They don't tell me anything about the kids' histories. I'm just a volunteer and not privy to their files. I help them learn life skills, help them with their studies if they're going for their GED or are in community college."

"I didn't know you did that."

"Well, I just wanted to give back a little. I have some experience dealing with kids who have been through traumatic experiences, and most of these foster youth have had rough experiences, even if it's just being bounced around all their lives."

"How old is Rory?"

"Quinn's age. Eighteen, almost nineteen. Rory and I actually became friends a while back. He's a drummer; quite talented, actually. That's what caught my eye about him in the first place. Somehow he reminded me of you."

"I'm still not understanding how Grace fits into this picture."

"She's been volunteering with me too. At first it was just to bolster her college application, but then she became very invested in the lives of these young adults and was making friends with them. One in particular stood out."

"He's the total opposite of what I'd picture for her. I mean, he looks like a punk rocker, and Grace is more a preppy, frat-boy type of girl."

"No, actually she's not. Grace has changed quite a bit over the past year. She has a compassion for others that makes me so proud. Maybe they are an odd pairing looks-wise, but Rory's actually very similar to her in personality. I can see why she likes him."

"And it doesn't worry you – them being together?"

"I'll admit, at first I tried to dissuade her, but then I realized how hypocritical I was being. Here I am volunteering to help improve these kids' lives, and I'm telling them they can do anything, be anything – but at the same time, thinking they aren't good enough for my daughter? What kind of message am I sending to Grace if I don't allow her to see Rory when his only visible fault is the messed up childhood that he had no control over? And besides, compared to the other two boys that your sister dated, Rory is a dream come true."

I understood what she was saying, but something about Rory still troubled me. "All I'm saying is, be cautious. You don't know what he's been through. He might be more screwed up than you think."

"Thankfully, Linda and Dave didn't think the same way about you."

I jerked my head up, gaping at my mother. Damn, that was brutal… but so undeniably true.

"Sorry… that was… not nice," she said, hesitating between words. "I feel a little protective of him, I guess."

"And I was being a hypocrite, so we're even."

The two of us sat there quietly for a few moments before she changed the subject. "Did Dad find you?"

"He did."

"Everything good?"

"Mom, it wasn't his story that caused the freak out, if that's what you think. You know me well enough to know there's a whole array of issues that could have been bothering me."

"But you worked it out with Casey, right?" she asked, sounding hopeful but resigned that I rarely, if ever, worked things out.

"I mean, yeah. Sort of. We're married."

She nodded, examining the ketchup bottle. I knew she wanted to press for more information but decided against it. "Well, you and Casey look blissfully happy."

"We are."

The tension drained from her face and a twinkle shone in her eye. "I love seeing you like this."

As if she'd heard her name being called, Casey entered from the backyard and slid into my arms so effortlessly that she felt like an extension of me.

"Speak of the devil…" Mom grinned.

"Uh-oh, what were you two discussing about me?"

"I only have good things to say about you, always."

"Right back at you," Casey said, smiling warmly at my mother. She then turned to me. "How was the session with Quinn?"

"Well, other than the fact that I learned what a douche I've been for the past twelve years, we had a very productive session."

"Did he tell you that?" Mom asked.

"No, I came to that conclusion all on my own."

She laid her hand on my shoulder. "I'm glad you finally talked to him. Quinn looks up to you so much. All he really wants is your approval."

"So then, why didn't you tell me I was acting like a chump?"

"Would you have listened?"

The lie would be *yes*, but we both knew the truth to be *no*. I shook my head smiling.

She laughed. "That's why."

A lingering side-effect of the loss of power I felt with Ray was that I needed to be in control of every situation. I never wanted to feel the way I did with him, helpless and afraid, so I sealed myself off to all but a trusted few. Somehow Quinn found himself outside of the bubble. That was going to change from this day forward.

"I don't know what you are talking about," Casey said, grabbing my jaw and kissing my lips. "Jake? Hardheaded? I find him to be very obedient."

Mom laughed hard at that, as well she should. God knows she'd come face to face with my disobedience more times than she could ever count.

"I'm telling you," my dad said, padding through the kitchen just in time to catch the tail end of our discussion. "It's the McKallister man's curse. Wimps, I tell you. The whole lot of us."

Chapter Ten

Casey

Married Life

Time flies when you're having fun! And for four blissful weeks, I was having fun. Of course, most of the time was spent on my back with my brand spanking new husband right where he was supposed to be, but then I blinked and it was over. One minute I was preparing for the wedding of my dreams, and the next I was standing in the airport terminal hugging Jake goodbye. Those four weeks we'd spent together post-wedding were the happiest of my life, and that was saying something because on a regular basis, I was pretty damn happy.

But then he left, and all I had to keep me warm and comforted were the incredible memories… well, that and bowls of ice cream, a furry creature, and a blue knitted mermaid blanket. In the month and a half that Jake had been gone, I hadn't accomplished a whole hell of a lot on the personal front… unless you counted the multiple television series I'd binge-watched on Netflix. My productivity at work was another story altogether. I was killing it there, even bringing my work home with me because, in all honesty, I didn't have anything better to do. Sure, I hung out with friends, and Kenzie had become a staple in my life since Kyle had also taken off on tour with Jake. But girlfriends were no substitute for my hot hunk of a husband.

Every day, I thought of running away and joining the circus – Jake's circus, that is – but then sensible Casey would pipe up and chastise me for wanting to throw away the opportunity of a lifetime. The opportunity I'm referring to was an entry-level position at a respected public accounting firm in downtown Los Angeles, offered to me soon after my engagement. It couldn't have come at a better time, as Jake was still recovering from his medical crisis, so work and travel for him had been limited. He spent the break from touring working on a new album while I was learning the ropes in a new job. For months, the two of us enjoyed evenings out after work and lazy weekends just being together. That's how I wanted my workdays to start and end every day of my life – with me in his arms.

But it was never meant to last. By March, Jake had started a world tour, and I stayed home playing the nerdy numbers detective by day and the bored housewife at night. Even though we were apart for the months leading up to wedding, it hadn't seemed as bad as now. Maybe it was because I had something to look forward to, and the planning took up all my spare time. But now that the wedding and honeymoon were over, the days apart seemed long and labored, and I was finding it more and more difficult to justify staying in Los Angeles while he was off touring the world.

So I ate more ice cream, watched more television, and went to bed at old people hours. It was in this vulnerable state of mind that I met Lieutenant Dan. I hadn't been looking for a man to fill Jake's shoes, but sometimes fate just forced your hand. In my defense, I had been left unsupervised. You certainly couldn't leave me alone for extended periods of time without risking me doing something stupid – like, say, bringing home a stray tomcat and naming him after my favorite character in *Forrest Gump*.

I literally stumbled upon Lt. Dan while out on a jog. Running wasn't my thing, but neither was the little ice cream pouch settling on my lower belly. I needed something more to offset the enormous amount of calories I was scooping into my mouth on a nightly basis, so I supplemented my exercise routine with a light evening jog. And that's where I found him, dark and mysterious, a man of few words. He was the answer to my lonely prayers. And before I knew it, that surly tomcat had meowed his way into my heart. We could have been something beautiful.

Too bad Lt. Dan turned out to be a grade A feline asshole!

Believe me when I say I wasn't looking for trouble when Lt. Dan wandered into my life. I'm sure when he first laid eyes on me he was probably thinking I was an easy score – a little extra kibble on the side. He wasn't looking for a long-term commitment; but too bad for him, I wasn't a one-night stand type of girl, and the moment I caught sight of that scrawny green-eyed boy, I was on a mission to save his furry little soul. Plucking up my new man, I took him to my nice warm house and fed him a wonderful three-course meal. You would have thought I was an award-winning chef the way Lt. Dan went on and on about the cuisine. If only Jake were that appreciative.

Once I'd filled his tummy full, it seemed silly not to invite him to stay for a nightcap, so we settled in for the evening, watching a little TV, eating a little ice cream, and, because no one was around to judge me, retreating to the bedroom where we snuggled all night. So content was he with his new digs that Lt. Dan hung around all weekend. I could just feel the connection, it was so real – and dare I say, I was falling in love. But come Monday morning, the kitty Casanova couldn't get away from me fast enough, bolting between my legs and out the door the first chance he got.

I'd met these love 'em and leave 'em types before, so I really wasn't that surprised when he abandoned me, nor was I expecting to ever see him again. But as it turned out, Lt. Dan's belly had fond memories of our time together, and he was back a few days later, ready for a fill up. I know. I know. I was totally getting played. But I was lonely enough to welcome him back each and every time. And there were a lot of times.

So went our one-sided relationship. Lt. Dan would disappear for days on end, no doubt sowing his feline oats to a steady stream of furry floozies, only to find his way back to me when he needed a good solid meal and a little heartfelt cuddling. And I, like the needy mistress I was, would wait patiently for his triumphant return.

After a few weeks of this questionable behavior, I'd decided I no longer wanted to share him with other pussycats, so I made a commitment to adopt him and reform his wandering ways. First up, supplies. I bought them all, silently praying Jake wouldn't come home for a surprise visit to find a four-story cat mansion in his living room. I needed to ease him into this ménage à trois.

Second up was the vet. For being a stray, Lt. Dan was surprisingly healthy. He was given a thorough exam, followed by shots and a microchip embedded in his neck.

During the visit, the vet strongly encouraged me to neuter him. I hated to do it, but with his Lothario ways, Lt. Dan really had forced my hand. And so, that's how my poor tomcat left the pet hospital without his testicles.

Wracked with guilt over my part in his decimated love life, I showered my guy with gifts, and I think he might just have forgiven me when I slipped the black studded collar around his neck. If he couldn't be a stud in real life, at least he could be wrapped in them. But like the little traitor he was, Lt. Dan hid behind the couch, and when I opened the door one day, he bolted.

Maybe we just weren't meant to be. I comforted myself by reasoning that you could take a stray off the street, but you couldn't take the street out of the stray. Bad boys could never be reformed. So the next time he turned up on my doorstep, I had half a mind to send him packing myself until I caught sight of a note tied to his collar… *from his actual owners!* Apparently my kitty gigolo was actually named Skittles, and he was no promiscuous alley cat – instead he lived in the lap of luxury in a two-story home down the street. And, as you might imagine, the people who lived there were understandably baffled as to what had happened to their cat's balls.

So that was the end of our unhealthy relationship. Skittles went home to his family, and I went back to my ice cream. It never would have lasted anyway because I needed a feline who put me first... and clearly that was not Lt. Dan.

Jake returned the last week of October for a scheduled break before the North American leg of his tour kicked off. We fell right back into our comfortable love affair, and having him in my arms again sealed the deal for me. The decision was made. I was quitting my job. Life was too short not to live it to the fullest, and for me, a full life meant being by Jake's side. I'd found a freelance job and planned to work on the side while touring in order to keep up my skills, but that would be the extent of it. Jake, of course, was ecstatic, and immediately made plans to move my things onto the bus so they'd be waiting for me when I arrived.

As I'd already given my boss two weeks' notice, the only thing left to do was tell my co-workers. Dragging my feet something fierce, I decided to divulge that information after the Halloween office party. That way my friends could still meet Jake before I was gone. I owed them that much, considering my marriage had been the running joke in the office for an entire year. You see, according to my co-workers, I was but a delusional fan conjuring up a fake relationship with a famous rock star because, well, I was bat-shit crazy. After every office party Jake missed – four in all since I'd begun there – the conviction had only grown stronger.

Finally I had the chance to prove my sanity, but only if he made a showing. I checked my watch again. He was forty minutes late and counting. I could almost hear the cackling come Monday morning. For the love of god, where was he?

Jake's absence might not have been so noticeable had I not made the ill-conceived decision for us to dress up in a couple's costume. Jake hadn't been too keen on the idea, but as always, had caved under pressure. Yet now, in hindsight, it might have been too ambitious for our first Halloween outing as a married couple. Perhaps I should have eased Jake into the whole new world of playing dress up by allowing him something simple and noncommittal to start out with, like a ghost or a whoopee cushion. Either that or I could have stressed the importance of commitment when it came to a couple's costume. There was just no wiggle room. If you were dressing as a duo, both sides needed to show up. I mean, when was the last time you saw a Fred without his Wilma or a slice of bacon without his eggs? I'll tell you when: never. Because these things didn't exist as separate entities, and when one half of such an iconic pairing wanders into a party without the other… well, that'll just result in prolonged moments of awkward silence.

Currently, I was living in one of those moments, dressed as one side of a peanut butter and jelly sandwich. I'd chosen this costume for two reasons. The first was because of its convenience – it slipped right over the head, thus making it much less likely Jake would balk at the idea of wearing it, and in turn, keep my dream of complete couple cohesion alive and kicking. And the second reason was because, well, it was just frickin' hilarious. Or at least it would have been had the peanut butter shown up on time. Sadly he had not, so now here I was just a sad slice of toast smeared with a healthy dollop of deep red jelly. It wouldn't be so bad, I suppose, if my coworkers weren't mistaking me for a soiled sanitary napkin.

Catching sight of more snickering in the corner, I called Jake again. "Where are you now?"

"Two minutes away from the place I was when you called me last. I'm doing the best I can, Casey. The 10 freeway was shut down, and I've been taking side streets ever since. It's not like I'm enjoying this urban jigsaw puzzle."

"Okay, I'm sorry. It's just, if you don't show up soon, I'm going to need to change my pad."

"What?"

"Never mind, inside joke. Just get here when you can."

I hung up and checked the time. I should probably wait five minutes before calling him next time. It sounded like he was getting testy, and the last thing I needed was a grumpy guy in a peanut butter costume getting mouthy during my time of the month. Plus, it went without saying: I wanted Jake to make a good impression. Not that it would be too challenging to impress my coworkers. He was famous, so short of acting like a giant douchebag, he'd rock their world. Still, it was important to me that Jake be on top of his game, if only just so I could properly show him off.

Without looking up from the phone screen, I could hear my two giddy coworkers making their way over. I didn't have to see their faces to know who was coming. I smiled before they even opened their mouths. Nat and Sandra, my best buds. Both worked in the back office with me. Nat was in her forties and was never without a smile on her face. Her hair was streaks of blond down to her shoulders, impeccably curled in big, bouncy twirls. She wore blue-rimmed glasses and colorful tops every day to work. Just seeing her in the mornings made me want to breathe in her fresh air. I was attracted to her like a flower to the sun. Not surprisingly, we hit it off instantly, and by my first afternoon in the office, we'd already planned our weekend outing together, even going so far as to pick the chick flick we'd be enjoying.

Sandra had taken longer to win over: twenty-eight floors, to be exact. Actually, it was more like fifteen, but who was counting? Yes, I was one of those people – the type who made friends in elevators. We'd started out chatting about the weather, which, let's be honest people, it's Los Angeles – ninety-five percent of the time the sun was shining. Not much to report there. Then we moved on to the restaurants in the area, both professing our love of Mexican food. By the time we'd reached the twenty-eighth floor, we were just finishing up an enthralling conversation about intelligent life on other planets.

Sandra flicked her fingers in front of my face to jolt my mind back into the present. "When we vote on costumes, my money's on you. Sure, it's a little nauseating, but you get extra points for originality."

"Again, I'm jelly… blackberry jelly."

"Right. You know, hon, if you took birth control pills, there'd be no need for such bulky protection," Nat said, joining in the heckling.

Sandra dropped her voice as she carried a devilish grin on her face. "I have a tampon in my purse, if you prefer something more discreet."

Unable to keep the amusement off my shamed face, I threw what I knew they wanted most, my husband, into their faces. "Sure, keep cackling, ladies, but when my creamy peanut butter shows up, we'll just see who's laughing."

"*If* he shows up. My money's still on you Photoshopping yourself into those wedding photos," Nat said.

"Or," Sandra added, speaking directly to Nat, "at the very least she should be providing proof in the form of a pair of his signed underwear – but nooo, that's too much for the little princess here to share with us less fortunate souls."

"You want proof? Look who's walking through the door right as we speak!"

Both my coworkers spun around, tongues already dangling from their mouths like overheated dogs, but instead of feasting on my rocker hubby, they got an eyeful of Darrell, our version of Dwight from *The Office.* He was currently dressed like… well, himself… because there was no time for fun in his dismal world. The only reason he showed up at all was for the free food.

"Yuck, Casey," Sandra groaned. "I can't unsee that. Jake's not coming, is he?"

"If you stick around long enough, maybe. He's stuck in traffic."

"Of course he is." Nat grinned.

My phone rang, and I held my hand up to my friends. *Please be him.*

"Can you come to the lobby?" Jake asked, the frustration in his voice unmistakable. "They won't let me up."

"They won't let you up? Why?"

"I don't know, Casey. They just said you had to come down here."

"Weird. Okay, I'm coming."

I hurried to the elevator, wondering who would prevent him from coming up. It wasn't like we had tight security or anything. Hearing a swishing sound, I looked up to find a dinosaur bounding down the hallway. It was one of those blow-up kinds that swayed and bounced as it moved. So randomly ridiculous, I couldn't help but laugh. The dinosaur stopped directly beside me, apparently never having received the company memo on sexual harassment and personal space. Neither one of us spoke as I focused on the lit up button on the elevator. I could feel him staring at me. Great, I had to get in the elevator with this thing.

"How's it going, sweet stuff?" T-Rex finally spoke, and damned if he didn't have just the right amount of prehistoric swagger.

"I'm good. Nice costume."

He nodded, and his whole body moved with him. I shook my head, but there was no hiding my amusement. Dino took that as his cue to up his game by taking another side step toward me and trying to touch me with those stubby arms of his.

"Okay, let me stop you there, bud," I said, moving away. "I'm a single species kind of girl."

T-Rex laughed, and I jerked my head up, recognizing it instantly.

"Jake?"

Dino swamped me like he was in the middle of a mosh pit, those ridiculous stumps for arms everywhere as I squealed and dipped away. Loud kissing sounds accompanied the bobbing head against my neck and I was nearly screaming in laughter when several of my coworkers flooded into the hallway.

One guy looked ready to attack, so I pushed Jake off, still giggling, and said, "It's okay. We're married."

There were all sorts of different reactions coming from my would-be saviors. First and foremost, relief. These were accountants, after all. The last thing any of them wanted was a chance to prove their manhood. Relief, however, was quickly replaced with surprise when those in the hallway realized just who was under the dinosaur costume.

"Sorry about the noise. He just surprised me. We'll be in soon."

As the crowd dispersed, I pulled Jake around the corner.

"Let me at them," he joked, swinging his arms around helplessly.

"I can't believe you," I said, zipping him out of the costume. "You weren't stuck in traffic at all, were you?"

"This is LA – of course I was stuck in traffic, just not for as long as I led you to believe," Jake said, then stopped to look at my costume.

"What are you, anyway?"

"I'm the jelly to your peanut butter, remember?"

"Oh, Jesus, you look like a homicide victim who totally bled out."

"I like that better than the other suggestions making the rounds."

I pulled his peanut butter costume out of my bag and slipped it over his head. Still half in his dinosaur suit, Jake was a hilarious sight. He swiveled his hips in a strip tease move until the rest of the T-Rex fell to the ground.

"You know if you wanted to go as a dinosaur, Jake, you could've just asked."

"Since when do I have to ask my wife's permission to dress in prehistoric garb? I don't remember that being in our vows."

That face. His smirk. I grabbed him and planted a kiss on those delectable lips.

"It was in the fine print," I said. "You might have missed it."

"Uh-huh," he said into the hollows of my open mouth as he kicked the kiss up a notch. Catching sight of the unmistakable fire in his eyes, I wrapped my arm around the back of his neck at the exact moment his tongue dipped between my lips. This was the way he'd been since arriving home a few days ago… randy as all hell. And despite what my costume suggested about my time of the month, I was clearly in heat. It took nothing but a sexy tilt of his head to turn me on; or in this case, a slice of bread slathered in peanut butter. There was just something about the way he wanted me, with such intensity and steam, that turned me into a quivering mess at the flip of a switch.

I tightened my grip on him as our mouths worked in unison. If I hadn't already quit, this unprofessional bit of hallway PDA would certainly get me fired. Regaining my wits, I placed my hand on his chest and stepped back.

"Behave," I reprimanded him, but in all honesty, I needed a scolding too. The fact that we couldn't keep our hands off each other was proof enough that I'd made the right decision to join him on tour. "Let's go. And, Jake, it goes without saying that you'll be on top of your game tonight. Remember, we're going for 'Wow.'"

And that's just what he did. When it came to wowing, Jake was a natural. He didn't have to do much more than open those luscious eyes of his to get the approval of the females, and a little chat about classic 80's pop bands did the trick for the males. He'd even stolen a math joke off the Internet for the occasion: 'Dear Math, I'm not a therapist, solve your own problems' - which really slayed the crowd. We were a room full of accountants, after all.

By the time the party had wound down, Jake and I were arguably the most popular peanut butter and jelly sandwich this side of the San Andreas Fault. We were also the gauge by which the party ended. I'd noticed the phenomenon before at parties. No one ever left before Jake. It must have been a fame thing, like people were afraid of missing something cool. So as we moved toward the exit, so did everyone else.

Waiting for the elevator with Sandra and Nat and her husband, I embraced my friends and shared with them my news. It hadn't come as a huge shock to them, since we'd talked about the possibility many times, but there were still sad faces to contend with.

"It's all right, Casey. I get it. I'd do the same thing," Nat said, encouragingly.

That was followed by Sandra's stamp of approval. "Hell, I don't know what took you so long."

Then Darrell, the office asshole, pushed passed me and smugly tossed in his two cents. "You'll never work in this town again."

CHAPTER ELEVEN

CASEY

Heavy Heart

I stood on the sidelines, content to just be in the midst of the controlled chaos. A steady stream of people bustled around, each with a specific job to do. Occasionally a greeting or two was thrown my way, but typically I wasn't paid more attention than any other person on Jake's team. They'd long ago accepted me as one of them, and that's what I loved about this blended family.

It had been a couple of months since I'd quit my job and joined Jake on the road, and truly it had been the right decision for me. Although the plan had been to work part-time doing freelance work for small companies, the jobs just kept coming in, and I found myself working nearly as many hours as I had been before. But at least now I wasn't stealing and castrating small animals to satisfy my loneliness.

Being on the road with Jake and his crew felt like home, and it was just where I wanted to be.

Conrad, one of the equipment guys, passed by me, formed a pistol with his hand, and crudely pointed it at me.

"Two more days and you're toast," he said, smirking.

Oh, hell no. If he wanted to trash talk, I was prepared to fling it right back in his face. "That's it, cupcake. You're going down."

"Ooh, big talker. I've seen you play video games, Casey. I'm not worried."

"Right, but you forget I have your boss to hide behind."

Conrad shook his head, good-naturedly dismissing me as he went on with the task at hand.

I might not have had an official job on the team, but I still served a purpose. On Jake's Outlast World Tour, I was the self-ordained Fun Time Leader. And as such, I made it a point to find fun and exciting things along the way to engage the band and crew. Next up – Laser tag!

Turning my attention back toward the stage, I was surprised to see Jake strolling in my direction. Dang, he was a hunk. He was covered in a slick sheen, and I watched him swipe a towel off one of the speakers and mop his face with it. I nodded my approval, mesmerized, as always, by his glow. Catching me ogling him, Jake smiled his most seductive smile before beckoning me forward. Yeah, he was sexy, I'd give him that, but it wasn't enough to persuade me to step foot out on that stage with him in front of thousands of his fans. I shook my head. Jake nodded his. Oh, lord, he was coming my way.

Um, hello, dude! You have a concert going on, with paying customers, I wanted to say, but Jake didn't seem the least bit concerned that while he was seducing me, an unattended and unruly mob might break free from the barriers at any moment and storm the stage. No, his translucent eyes were fixed on one thing only: me. He sauntered over to me, playing up the sexy singer fantasy. It was an act that had starred in every woman's dirty dreams since Elvis first stormed the stage all those years ago.

And when he arrived at me in all his glory and planted a wet, slippery kiss on my lips, I knew I would follow him anywhere... and Jake was taking me for a ride. His hands cradling my face and lips still locked on mine, he walked the two of us backward onto the stage and in clear view of the roaring crowd. I should have been mortified by this very public display of affection, but that would have required full control over my highly aroused body and soul, and such control was not possible while Jake was tempting me with his wildly sexy self.

In fact, I'd nearly forgotten we had an audience until every red-blooded woman in the crowd screamed her approval as I wrapped my legs around Jake's waist in response to him lifting me off the ground. I dipped my head forward onto his shoulder as his lips caressed the prickled skin of my neck. We needed to stop this before being slapped with a misdemeanor charge for lewd conduct in public. As it was, our impromptu make-out session was probably already trending on Twitter.

Jake seemed to come to his senses at the exact time I did, and he carried me back to the side of the stage, keeping his mouth on me the entire way. How he kept from tripping on all the ground wiring was a testament to his exceptional skills of seduction. Arriving back into the shadows, Jake set me down on my shaking legs. We stared feverishly at one another, soaking in the raw chemistry we produced by just being in the vicinity of each other. Neither of us had any excuse for our sizzling sideshow other than that we were newlyweds and couldn't keep our hands off each other. I had no doubt if Jake weren't in the middle of working he would have carried me off like a caveman and ravished me in some rocky grotto… or in this case, his high-end luxury bus. Same principle.

"You're crazy." I laughed, immensely enjoying the absurdity of him interrupting his entire set just to make out with me. It was moments like this that I applauded my decision to join my very sexy husband on tour. "Go!"

Thankfully, Jake was a seasoned professional and managed to jump right back into his set with ease. I was still a bit of an amateur myself, so it took a little hand fanning to cool my jets. Of course, I was counting on getting some action later tonight, so I didn't want the flames to go out entirely.

A few songs later, Malik, one of Jake's crew, nudged me. His lips moved, but I couldn't make out what he was saying. Holding up my finger, I removed the special earplugs that canceled out some of the harshest sounds on stage.

"You need to call your brother," he said.

"My brother?" I repeated, not understanding how he would know this.

"He's been trying to get in touch with you."

I instantly pulled out my phone and saw numerous missed calls and messages from Luke. Fear cycled through me. It was not normal for him to call me in the first place, but this many messages? Something wasn't right. Hurrying away from the side stage to Jake's dressing room, I dialed Luke's number with shaking hands.

"Casey?" he said, his voice cracking with emotion.

My bones chilled, and instantly I feared the worst. "Yes. It's me. Is Mom okay? Dad?"

Luke broke down, and that in turn upped my terror.

"Luke," I screamed into the receiver. "What happened?"

"It's Miles and Darcy. There was an accident." Luke broke off his sentence and unintelligible sobs came from the other line.

"Luke! What happened?" I repeated.

"They didn't make it."

"What do you mean, they didn't make it?" My voice was shrill with anger. How dare he play such a horrible trick on me?

"Their car was hit head on. Darcy died on impact and… and Miles… he… he made it to the hospital, but… Casey… he just passed away."

A chill barreled through my body, blanketing my insides with ice. My teeth began to chatter as I tried to make sense of the words Luke was speaking. There had to be some mistake. Why was it so cold?

"Casey, are you still there? I'm so sorry. I… I didn't want to be the one to tell you, but neither Mom nor Dad could do it."

Luke broke down again, and while I listened to his heavy sorrow, the reality began to seep in. My fingers had frozen over, and the grip they had on my phone was crushing. Gone. No. It couldn't be. And then the most horrible realization hit me.

"Sydney and Riley?" I screamed out, now shaking so violently that nausea was taking hold.

"They're safe. It was Miles and Darcy's anniversary. They went out to dinner. The kids were safe with Mom and Dad when it happened."

Too many emotions… too cold… the ice had numbed my brain, and very soon the hypothermia would set in, and I'd be a frozen corpse. Only then would I be exempt from facing the pain that reality had just forced upon me. Not Miles. Not the big brother I'd adored my whole life. Not Darcy, as much a sister to me as I'd ever known. And their kids. What was going to happen to their kids?

"Do they know?" I asked, beginning to understand the implications of what was now happening to my family.

"Sydney does. She was still awake when Mom and Dad found out."

"Is she? I don't know. Is she okay?"

"She hasn't said a word. She's just… numb, like the rest of us. They're going to let Riley sleep and tell him tomorrow. None of this feels real. Miles can't be gone. He just can't."

"Where are Mom and Dad? Can I talk to Mom?"

"I don't think she can talk, Casey. You just need to come home. Right now. We need you."

After hanging up with Luke, I scanned the barren room, unsure how to feel or even what to do. Jake was in the middle of a performance. I didn't have the time to wait for him to finish. If he knew, he'd cancel the rest of the show, but that would still take too long. I needed to get to the airport. I needed to book a flight. I needed help.

Sean, Jake's manager. He would handle it. He could handle anything. I shot off a text, and minutes later he was in the room, scooping me off the floor. I hadn't even realized I was down there.

"I'm so sorry, Casey. I don't know what to say. I texted my assistant, and she's securing you and Jake a private jet."

"I can't wait for him."

"You won't need to. I'm going to call off the rest of the show."

"He's only halfway through it. I don't want to disappoint his fans. You can't tell him until it's over."

"That's not going to work. Jake will want to be by your side. He needs to know."

"No," I blurted out forcefully. I had no time to argue my point. I only wanted to be obeyed. "I'm telling you to let him finish. Please get me a driver so I can stop at the hotel to grab my bag. Then I want to go straight to the airport. My family needs me now."

Sean grabbed me by the shoulders and forced me to meet his eye. "Listen to me, Casey. Your family will want Jake there supporting you. Either let me call off the show or wait the forty-five minutes for it to be over, but please don't leave without him. He's your family too."

His words hit where they were intended, and I gulped back the giant sob sitting in the crook of my throat. Sean kept his eyes trained on me, and it was clear he had no motivation other than concern for Jake and me.

"What do you want me to do?" he asked, looking strangely helpless for a guy who could do anything.

The first tears began to fall. This was real. My brother was dead. I couldn't do this alone.

"Cancel the show. I need my husband."

I was packing my bag at the hotel with the help of Sean's assistant when Jake burst through the door. Even from across the room I could see the worry lines crossing his forehead. His eyes swamped with sadness, Jake hurried to my side and swallowed me up into his safe, loving arms. He represented safety, and I welcomed his strong presence. Neither one of us spoke. There was no need. We both understood the crippling loss and the unimaginable challenge ahead.

The sob I'd been suppressing bobbed up and down in my throat like a buoy waiting for a wave of emotion to knock it over. But right now was not the time to let it go. I needed to be strong. There was a little girl and a little boy who were worse off than I was right now. There was a father and a mother who were feeling the grief of losing their oldest child, and they needed my level head.

"I don't know what to say," Jake whispered.

"Why did this happen? Two kids are left without their parents." The first prickling of rage began to rise up inside. "I'm just sick. Why? It's not fair. None of this is fair."

"No. It's not."

Jake didn't try to reason with me, as he knew better than most how unfair life could be, and nothing he could say or do would make any of this right.

"My mom, Jake. What am I going to say to her?"

"I…I don't know, Casey. Maybe there's just nothing to say."

No, there really were no words. Life had just changed forever, and I had no experience dealing with such grief. Even when Jake had fallen into a coma, I hadn't succumbed to sorrow because I'd still had hope. This was different. All hope was lost. Miles and Darcy were gone, and no bedside vigil would bring them back. I was stepping into a whole new world. Burying my head into Jake's chest, I cried.

We arrived in Arizona just past midnight and sat in somber silence on the drive to my parents' home. It seemed no words could accurately express the mood, so none were spoken. Jake's hand was firmly in mine, a reminder that I wasn't alone even though the emptiness I felt inside could fill a stadium. It seemed I'd cried all the tears I had to cry, and my bloodshot eyes stung from the strain. Jake had been texting Luke during the trip and was tasked with passing on the grim information to me. There was apparently no point left in going to the hospital, as my parents had already identified both Miles' and Darcy's bodies.

Their bodies? That's all that was left. I gulped back the shock of those words and of my parents having to say goodbye in such a manner. I wished they had waited for Luke or me, so we could have shouldered some of the pain for them, but at the same time, I was relieved not to have had to do that myself. If all I had left of my brother and his wife were memories, I wanted them to be good ones. But what of my parents? They'd brought Miles into this world and had been the last to see him go. I couldn't even begin to imagine what that was like. I didn't want to.

I hadn't even known the tears had started up again until Jake pulled me tighter to him. Laying my weary head against his shoulder, I grabbed the arm he'd laid over my shoulder and drew it toward my chest, hanging onto him for dear life. His lips brushed past my forehead as his body settled against mine. It would be the last moment of peace for a very long time.

People were milling about as we walked through the front doors of my childhood home. It was a solemn affair that greeted us. Heads were hung in despair as we moved between grievers, adding our own sorrow into the mix. Miles and Darcy's kids had both fallen asleep in exhaustion, propped up on either side of my father. I'd been told that Riley had awoken to the sounds of sobbing and had to be told of his parents' death. Any later attempts to move the exhausted children into beds had failed miserably, so they were allowed to remain where they felt most comfortable.

Leaving Jake with my father and brother, I found my mother in the living room. She was sitting in the center of our sectional couch, staring at the wall adorned with family pictures, her own mother nestled by her side. As I came around the room and took the other spot beside her, my mother didn't acknowledge my presence. In fact, I wondered if she knew I was there at all. She seemed to be in a sort of trance as her eyes moved back and forth over the pictures.

Meeting my grandma's eyes, she lightly shook her head as if to warn me to keep silent. She then looked down at her hand, which was tenderly stroking my mother's. Understanding the meaning, I nodded before folding my fingers into my mother's and wrapping my arm around her back. Together the three of us sat like that for a long while. No words were spoken between us. Even when the kids woke and the sounds of their crying filled the space around us, my mother remained dazed.

I considered leaving her side to tend to my niece and nephew, but decided against it. My mother's devotion to her children had been absolute, and now, in her time of need, I was determined to give it back. Suddenly, the sweet sound of music wafted through the air. I swallowed the lump in my throat as I imagined my husband sitting quietly at the piano, gently pressing down on the keys in a desperate attempt to soothe not only his own sorrow but that of those around him. My mother turned her head toward the sound, blinking a few times in rapid succession before focusing her gaze back on me. I could see the fog clearing. Jake's music seemed to awaken her.

"Casey? You're here," she said, squeezing my hand.

"I am, Mama. I'm here."

The lines in her face deepened as she cupped my cheeks in her shaking hands. It was then that we both succumbed to the sadness.

Chapter Twelve

Jake

Bereavement

Miles and Darcy were laid to rest five days after the fiery crash that took their lives. According to witnesses at the scene, the young woman who hit their car head on had been texting when she ran a red light. Three lives gone, just like that. Most of the last few days, I'd wandered around aimlessly, offering support where needed and just being there for Casey as she and her family grieved. I was unaccustomed to being the supporter, as my whole life had always been about people rallying around me. I'd never really considered the toll my tragedy had taken on those around me until the tables were turned and it was I who stood by helplessly, struggling to ease another's pain.

My family had turned out in force for the funeral. In the over two and a half years Casey and I had been together, a bond had formed, especially between our mothers. Last year had been my mother's time of need, while I lay near death in the hospital, and it had been Linda who'd been there to offer her support; and now my mother was sadly returning the favor. Whatever bond they'd formed over the years was serving its purpose today, as Linda seemed to draw strength from my mother, who certainly knew a thing or two about grief.

My eyes settled on Casey. She was showing the enormous strain of the past few days, and I struggled to comfort her in her time of need. At this point, I was taking my cues from my wife and allowing her the time she needed to cope with the overwhelming situation. Her main concern now was her niece and nephew, and Casey had channeled her grief into supporting them.

As I watched her now, Riley was curled up in her arms. Only seven years old, his hourly cries for his mother tore at all our hearts. In contrast, his sister, Sydney, remained silent and stoic beside Luke. Although she'd shed a few tears during the service, Sydney was clearly holding back. Her body stood rigid, a slow simmering fury bubbling just below the surface. I wondered when we could expect the explosion I was sure would come. I recognized that look of utter devastation on her face. I could feel it in my bones. Her heaviness weighed me down in a way I hadn't experienced in years. I'd gladly have borne the pain she was now carrying, as my shoulders were used to the burden, but Sydney… she was so small and fragile, a girl mere weeks away from celebrating her tenth birthday, forced to confront death and all its unsatisfying consequences.

Luke, focused on a conversation with his cousin, didn't see Sydney slip away and exit through the back door of the church. Through the window, I followed her path to the large fishpond on the edge of the grounds. She appeared so tiny as she sat on her knees by the water's edge. Not wanting her to be alone, I walked down the trail toward her. Sydney blocked the sun with her hand as she turned to acknowledge me.

"What are you up to?" I asked, kneeling down to her level.

"Finding rocks."

There was a pile of them sitting beside her. I nodded, picking up one of my own and turning it in my hand. "Do you collect them?"

She didn't answer right away, and I stayed silent. Finally Sydney tilted her head to the side and said, "No, I'm going to throw them at the fish. See if I can knock them out."

I was a bit startled by her nonchalant admission. What was it with the Caldwells and their fish hate? "Why are you going to do that?"

Sydney looked back down at her rocks. "I just want to."

Okay. That was disturbing. "What'd the fish ever do to you?"

She thought about that for a minute. "Nothing."

"So is it nice to take your anger out on them?"

"Probably not," she said, shrugging. "But nobody's nice to me, so I'm not going to be nice to anyone else, and I'm going to start with the fish."

"Ah, I see. You plan on starting with something small and defenseless and then working your way up."

"Exactly." Sydney peered up at me, the tiniest of smiles transforming her strained face. "I guess I could hit you with the rocks instead if you want?"

Her precocious comment caught me off guard, and I couldn't help but laugh. With her humor and quick wit, I'd always thought of Sydney as a mini Casey. It was almost like watching her grow up gave me insight into what my wife had been like at the same age.

"How about this? We spare the fish… and my head… and use that shed back there."

Sydney gave what I said some thought before asking, "Can I break the window on the side?"

"No." I laughed. "Not the window. Geez, kid, work with me here."

"Fine, but if we get busted, I'm making you take the fall."

Sydney and I gathered as many rocks as we could carry and went around the side of the church to the old shed. All the guests were heading into the large reception room across the parking lot, and Casey caught my eye as we passed by, glancing apprehensively between the two of us, clearly seeking reassurance that her niece was all right. I nodded in reply. Yes, she was okay… a little malicious at the moment, but okay.

So as the others gathered for refreshments, Sydney and I spent the next ten minutes unloading on the shed. The hollow thwack of the rusting metal was strangely satisfying. Neither one of us held back, and we pelted the wall with ferocity. She seemed to gather strength with each punishing blow, and when our ration of rocks was depleted, Sydney improvised. With tears streaming down her cheeks, she continued the assault by kicking and beating the shed with every last bit of strength she had left. Whatever turmoil she was suffering in her head and heart needed this noisy release. I wasn't concerned by the damage she was causing because it would only be temporary. I'd already decided the corroded hazard had to go. By the end of the week a nice, shiny new shed would take its place.

Sydney's exhaustion stamped out her fury, and she slid to the ground, her back against the siding. She rested her head on her bended knees, the energy it took to cry zapping her of all earlier bravado. I skimmed down the shed myself and settled in beside her. Together we sat silently for a long while. I understood the benefit of quiet reflection. Not every situation required words. Eventually, she stood up and solemnly walked back to the reception room. I followed a few steps behind.

Re-entering the room, I sought out Casey, and when I found her in a tearful embrace with her mother, I decided to let them be. Filling a small plate with food, I took a seat next to Luke, who was staring out the window.

"Hey, you okay?" I asked. It was a stupid question, as his swollen, puffy eyes and crimson face indicated he was anything but.

"Yeah, I don't…I don't know how I am. I saw you out there with Syd. Thanks for watching her. I didn't even realize she'd left."

"She's angry."

"I know. She's been taking it out on Riley."

"Yeah, well, she just beat the snot out of the shed out back, so I think Riley will be safe for the next few hours. In the future, though, a punching bag might be a smart buy."

"This is going to be really hard, Jake. I mean, how are we going to get these kids through this? I don't know how I can do it myself. It's just unbelievable, you know. One minute he's here, and the next…"

Luke struggled for control, but it was a losing battle. "How do you go on when your world has crumbled around you?"

His brows furrowed as he tipped his head in my direction. It was as if Luke had just realized he'd inadvertently personalized the question towards my own formerly crushed past.

"I didn't mean, like, I was trying to get advice from you because you know what it's like to…." He stopped himself, looking miserable. "Anyway, it was a rhetorical question."

"Yeah, I got that."

"You know the thing I keep thinking about over and over? It's not Sydney and Riley being orphans or my parents having to bear the loss of their son. All I can think about is that I don't have anyone to call a brother anymore. Brothers are like… well, you know… it's just different. You're connected in ways that are hard to explain. I always took for granted Miles would be there for me… that I could call him up if I was having a bad day or needed advice, but now he's gone and I… I just don't have a brother anymore." Luke's body shook from the force of the realization and I felt the pain right alongside him. There was a time in my life where I thought I'd lost everyone I loved. The despair was raw, and I was filled with so much regret for what could have been. As luck would have it, I was given a second chance, but sadly Luke never would. I reached out and gripped his shoulder.

"I know I'm not Miles, but I'll be your brother whenever you need one."

CHAPTER THIRTEEN

CASEY

Runaway Train

The weird thing about life was that it just kept moving on. I watched the days pass by with little interest. It was times like this that I was grateful I was an accountant. There were no emotions in numbers. You could always count on them to be there when you needed them. When it came to work productivity, I'd never been quicker or more efficient than I was now, in the throes of grief. The faster I worked, the more files flooded my inbox, and I attacked them with vigor, feeling nothing but gratitude for their sterile distraction.

After spending four weeks with my family, I returned to Jake and the tour. Although he'd been ready to call it off altogether, my mother made him promise to continue on like nothing had happened. But something *had* happened and now everything was different. The joy was gone. I stopped going to Jake's concerts. The excitement of the crowd, once the source of much enjoyment, now rang hallow to me. How could anyone be happy in a world where my brother no longer existed?

I cried a lot now. Sometimes it was as little as a swelling of tears in my eyes, but other times it went all the way up to gargantuan crying marathons that lasted hours and involved anyone unlucky enough to cross my path. Usually that person was Jake.

Although he was outwardly supportive, I could feel him pulling away… or maybe it was me pushing him in that direction. I wasn't sure if there was a difference, really. Either way, I felt the distance between us as if we were separated by oceans. Intimacy was a thing of the past, as I couldn't seem to coax my body into feeling anything but numbness. The last time we'd tried, I was more like a limp rag doll than a vibrant young newlywed wife. It wasn't like I wanted it to be that way, I just couldn't come up with any way around the pain that stabbed into my heart on an hourly basis.

The 'Fun Time Leader' that the crew had counted on to brighten up their stops along the way was no more. The magic was gone, and each city blended into the next in a haze of monotony. I began wandering, sometimes for hours on end, just going wherever my feet would take me. The first time I wandered, it caused a panic between Jake and his security crew, so now I was assigned a bodyguard at every stop.

Today's trek had led me to a quaint Main Street in the old part of town where I found a comfortable Deli and Bakery with an outdoor seating area. Glancing around my surroundings, I took in the sight and smells; young and old alike were milling around, waiting for their thinly sliced meat on fresh baked bread. I'd found myself here after a good four-mile walk. At least it was good for me. Poor Dom, today's reluctant bodyguard, was currently resting his weary feet at a table off in the corner.

His bald head was flushed crimson, and droplets of sweat raced down his face like rain on a windshield. It was clear he wasn't used to getting this type of cardio workout. Or maybe it was just the duration of walk that had done him in. After this hike, he was sure to ask for reassignment. What did I care? If Jake insisted on having me followed, then his cronies had damn well better be able to keep up.

A screaming toddler pulled my focus off Dom. Good lord, the kid had a set of lungs on him. I watched the young mother with interest as she tried to get her offspring in line.

But he wasn't having any of it, and threw his body onto the floor in a display of unmatched fury. Instead of inspiring me to move away from the tantrum, the boy's rage actually brought a smile to my face. What could possibly be so terrible in his little world to warrant such a reaction?

With her baby girl in one arm, the mother attempted to right her small charge, but he'd taken to arching his back in protest. The woman glanced at me, blowing a strand of hair out of her eyes. I smiled at her sympathetically.

"You like babies?" she asked, ready to hand hers off to me. *I don't know.* Did I? I used to love children, but now even they held no joy for me. "This looks like it'll be a two-hand job."

I held out my arms for her. Why not? What else did I have to do? Besides, Dom needed a breather before I led him back to the stadium. The moment the warm little bundle was placed in my arms, I felt an instant thawing of my steely heart. The baby peered up at me, her eyes so filled with wonder at the world around her. Her innocence captivated me. I ran my finger along the top of her nose and the baby reached up to grab it. I beamed at the sweet thing. The mother looked up from the deep negotiation she was having with her toddler to check on us. Again we exchanged smiles, and she resumed the task at hand.

Returning my attention to the baby, I was surprised to see she was still watching me intently, and I wondered what she saw. I could only imagine how unimpressed she must be. But then again, maybe babies had superpowers that we adults just overlooked. Maybe this baby girl could see past the sadness. Maybe old Casey was in there smiling back at her. The thought gave me a surprising measure of peace. I was still me; wounded, but me.

Feeling lighter than I had in weeks, I made a fish face, mugging for my infant audience until she let loose the most adorable giggle I think I'd ever heard in my life. It was music to my ears, and for the first time in a long while, I laughed. Holding this treasure gave me a feeling of pure, unbridled happiness.

Suddenly I understood what needed to be done to turn this out of control train around: I needed a baby. Jake and I needed a baby. It was the only answer that made sense to me and it had been right in front of me all along. So what if Jake hadn't worked out his issues with being a father? He could always just learn on the job. We could do this. I could come out of this tragedy intact. All I needed was one of these.

I hadn't even realized I was crying until the baby's mother stared at me in alarm.

"Oh," I smiled, wiping the tears away. "Sorry. She's just so beautiful."

The tension eased off her face as I handed the baby back.

"Are you all right?" she asked, her forehead furrowed in worry.

"I will be, in about nine months."

Giving Dom a break, I allowed him to call for a ride. I needed to get back to Jake as quickly as possible. If all went as planned, I'd be on my back within the hour. Jake was in the bus with Sean going over the night's playlist when I burst through the door. His eyes widened in surprise at the sight before him. I was smiling.

Sean looked between the two of us and excused himself. Once he left, I flung myself on Jake, kissing him all over. And instead of asking me a series of questions, he just accepted the sudden change for what it was: a welcome relief.

"You're a breath of fresh air," he said, working his lips around the back of my neck where he knew it drove me wild.

"I feel good, babe. I finally figured it out."

"Figured what out?"

"How to recover from the loss."

Jake extracted his lips from my skin and appeared every bit as interested in my magical cure as I had been at the deli. "How?"

"A baby," I said, nearly clapping out my excitement.

"A baby?" he queried, with none of my glee.

"Yes. A baby," I confirmed, grabbing his hands and pulling him onto the sofa with me. "Hear me out."

I went on to explain what happened at the deli and the reasoning behind the decision, and although he didn't seem entirely convinced, Jake didn't veto the plan either. Not that he really could, anyway. The last couple of months had seen a shift in the balance of our relationship. While we had once been equals, the power now tipped in my direction. His whopping hang-ups, which had always ruled our world, had all but taken a backseat to mine.

I told Jake that the pain I felt on a daily basis was like a heavy fog that couldn't dissipate because there was no sunshine to scare it away. Babies were sunshine. I spoke of recovery and happiness, something that would come when I had my own child to dote on. And surprisingly, Jake hung on my every word, the hope in his eyes a telling sign of the weeks of struggle we'd experienced together.

Of course, I understood that was why he was being so pliable with my idea in the first place. He was ready to grab for any rope I dangled in front of him. My poor husband just wanted peace back and was willing to sacrifice his own well-being for the sake of it. If I was promising him a better, less stressful life, he was inclined to slurp up the Kool-Aid I was pouring.

"If that's what you think will make you happy, Casey, I'm willing to try. But you have to do something for me then… actually a couple of things."

"Okay what?"

"No more wandering. And you and I need to start talking again like we used to. We need to be the pair we've always been. If you can promise me that, I will do my best to give you a baby."

I wrapped my arms around him as tightly as I could. That was a deal I was more than willing to make.

Say what you will about my ill-conceived notion that a child was the answer to life's problems, but trying to conceive had started the healing process, even if it was only one tiny baby step at a time. My mind wasn't constantly consumed with death anymore, and I was able to venture back into the world. I returned to the sidelines of his concerts and took joy in his successes once again. And as my mood improved, Jake took notice, and our playful banter returned.

That didn't mean there wasn't any more crying, because there was, lots of it, but it seemed more manageable now, like there was a beginning and an end to the sadness. Things were still hard and the setbacks all-consuming, but now I knew I could survive this. I was stealthy enough to move through this world until my strength returned. And with Jake by my side, I couldn't fail.

CHAPTER FOURTEEN

JAKE

A Screeching Halt

I checked my phone. Dammit. I stepped up my pace. There was an ovulation chart to take into consideration, and I'd promised Casey I'd be back in three hours. Unfortunately, there'd been label bigwigs in attendance, and I was expected to kiss their asses for a reasonable amount of time after the concert, so by the time I was able to leave the venue, it was already pushing four hours, and Casey's window of opportunity was closing… according to her, not science.

Casey was probably already lying in bed waiting impatiently for me to deposit my seed. She'd expect me to be locked and loaded the minute I walked through the door. I sighed. There was nothing sexy about baby making, at least not the way we were doing it. But failure was not an option. I had to put a baby in her stomach, or all hell would break loose.

Cringing, I thought about our earlier encounter. I hated arguing with her. Usually I was able to hold my tongue, knowing she didn't really mean the things she said these days. But sometimes Casey just got to me, like when she tried to coerce me into making a baby an hour before I was set to perform. Snapping at her the way I did only made things worse, though. It brought on another one of her marathon crying sessions – which I hated even more than the arguing.

As much as I didn't want a baby, I hoped to god she got pregnant sooner rather than later because I knew she wasn't capable of withstanding the myriad emotions that went along with one failed conception after another. After all, this was the woman who'd begun an ovulation chart the same month we started trying. She was leaving nothing to chance, which meant if things didn't go her way, the progress we'd made in the last couple months would be all for naught.

Believe it or not, this was progress. After her brother died, Casey stayed behind with her family as I continued on with the tour. I was making plans to cancel the whole thing when Linda talked me out of it. There was no point in me sitting around miserable, she'd said, when I could be on the stage making other people happy. It was what both she and Casey wanted, so after a two-week hiatus, I returned to the tour.

Casey joined me a couple weeks later – a broken woman. She floundered for weeks before hitting upon her plan for a baby. Initially I'd been reluctant, but after we began trying, her mood improved, so I jumped onto the baby train feet first. No matter that I had a deep fear of being a father; my issues had long since taken a backseat to hers, and I gladly focused my energy on her recovery instead. Still, I hated that she was questioning my loyalty. I had never once given her any reason to doubt it. Giving up on her was not an option.

My phone buzzed in my pocket. I purposely ignored it at first because I assumed it was one of the crew with a problem, and I wasn't turning back around. But then I worried it might be Casey, so I pulled it out of my pocket and checked the screen. Luke. Fuck! Why was he calling me? He only dialed my number when things had gone to shit and he wanted me to relate the information.

I drew in a sharp, ragged breath before forcing myself to answer. "Hey, Luke."

"Hey. Is Casey with you?"

"No. I'm just walking back to the bus. Do you want me to get her?"

"No, that's why I called you."

I could hear the stress in his voice and instantly sensed trouble. Tension settled in my shoulders.

"Why? What's wrong?"

Luke hesitated.

"Luke, what's wrong?"

"Okay, so...Mom's in the hospital."

I felt like the wind had been knocked out of me. My thoughts shifted straight to Casey. She couldn't take much more. "Why? What happened?"

"Doctors think it might be a mild heart attack. With her high blood pressure and all the stress of the past few months, it's taken its toll on her."

"Jesus," I exhaled. "Is she going to be all right?"

"Yeah, she's doing okay. The doctors aren't even sure if it was actually a heart attack yet. It's possible she just had a panic attack. They're running more tests. But Jake, regardless of what they show, Mom's really run down. She needs a break, and I know that Casey's not doing great herself, and you guys are on tour and everything" – Luke's voice wavered – "but I think I'm really going to need her."

"Yeah, of course, but..." I hesitated, knowing Casey didn't want her family worrying about her. "She's pretty fragile herself."

"I know but she has to be more help than Dad. He has zero patience with Sydney."

"Okay, let me talk to Casey. I'll get her on a plane."

"Thanks, Jake. Sorry to keep dumping all this on you. It's more than you signed up for."

"No, it's not. I'll call you back soon."

"Thanks, man."

Casey took the news about as well as could be expected. Of course, she wanted to get to her mother right away, but she would have to wait a few hours for flights into Arizona. I'd been making plans to go with her when Luke called back to let us know Linda hadn't had a heart attack but was suffering with an acute case of heartburn that simulated chest pains. She was expected to remain in the hospital a few days to undergo further testing.

I held Casey as we waited for her to board the plane. I'd brought along a small army of bodyguards with me today because I wanted to protect Casey from any further stress, and to be honest, I was in no mood myself to deal with a fan encounter.

"Sorry I didn't get home sooner last night. We never had a chance to make a baby."

"I know. Bart will just have to wait another month."

"Bart will have to wait a lifetime because I'm never naming my kid that."

We laughed at our shared joke before her face took a turn for the serious.

"Jake, I don't know when I'm coming back. If my mom needs help, I might have to stay."

I nodded solemnly. I knew it was coming, but hearing it from her made it more real. It's not that I didn't want her to help out her family; it was that so much distance between us probably wasn't the best thing for our relationship right now.

"What's that look?" she asked, running her fingers along my face.

"Look?" I asked, adopting an air of innocence. "I don't have a look."

Casey touched the space between my brows. "Liar. I can always tell when something's bothering you by the crinkled ridge that forms here."

"You're scarily perceptive," I replied, with the hint of a grin.

Wrapping her arms around my neck, she gave my lips a lingering kiss. "I'm going to come back."

I placed my hands on her hips and stared deeply into her brown eyes. "I know you will." Though in the back of my mind, I wasn't so sure.

Chapter Fifteen

Casey

What Could Go Wrong?

The man waiting for me near baggage claim was nearly unrecognizable. In fact, at first, I'd ignored his efforts to get my attention until I took a closer look and nearly passed out from the shock.

"Luke?"

"Who else would I be?" He smiled, but there wasn't a drop of levity behind it. Even his eyes, always so expressive, gave off no warmth.

"I'm… I don't know. You look totally different."

Granted, it had been a couple of months since I'd seen him last, but Luke had made the transformation of all transformations.

"Did you dye your hair?" The mere uttering of the sentence seemed ridiculous, but here I was staring at my brother, whose normally dark close-cropped hair was now licking at his ears and highlighted with streaks of blond.

"No, I just woke up one day and it was this color."

"Really?" Somehow that made more sense than him dyeing it.

"No. Of course I dyed it. Or a friend of mine did. I take it you don't like it?"

"I just… I'm shocked, is all. It might take some getting used to."

The other thing that was tripping me up was his weight, or the lack thereof. He caught me eying him and answered my question before I asked it.

"I've lost some weight."

"Some? Are you okay? You're not sick, are you?"

"No, Casey. I just lost some weight. No big deal."

"It's not some weight, Luke. You've lost everything! I mean you look… you look…"

I'll tell you what he looked like: a completely different person. And it wasn't just his outward appearance that had me all weirded out, there was a change in his overall personality as well. No longer the jovial goofball, Luke had a strained exterior now, as if his light, which had always burned so bright inside him, had burned out. My god, I'd been wallowing in my own sadness for so long that I hadn't even stopped to consider what Luke was going through. Sure, Mom had said she was worried about him, but she didn't mention this full-body makeover.

"Would you please stop staring at me?"

"Sorry. You could have warned me. I mean, would a Facebook update have killed you?"

Instead of answering, he bent down and hugged me. "How are you doing, sis?"

I fell heavily into his arms, feeling sluggish and worn and in need of my big brother's comfort, even if he now looked like a beach bum.

"I'm okay," I sighed.

"That's not what Jake says."

I didn't answer. What was the point in defending myself when neither one of us would believe it anyway? "How's Mom? I talked to her just before the flight. She sounded pretty good."

"Yeah, but you know Mom. She's pretending everything's fine in order to get home."

"You don't think she should leave the hospital?"

"Not if, when she gets home, it'll be business as usual."

We exchanged a knowing glance. "Who's got them right now?"

"Aunt Cheri came over to watch them so Dad could stay at the hospital, but she won't be able to handle them tonight, so you and I will need to take over."

I nodded. "How are they?"

"Riley's doing okay, actually. We've been keeping him busy in sports. But Sydney…" Luke shook his head. "She's a handful, to say the least."

My eyes clouded over. It was no wonder. "She misses her mom and dad."

"We all do."

"I know, but it's not the same for us. We lost our brother and sister-in-law. Syd lost her mom and dad. I can't imagine how that feels."

"She keeps asking for you, Case. She's gotten worse since you left."

"I know. I talk to her everyday. I can hear a difference."

"Here's the thing. Mom needs rest. She's having a lot of trouble controlling Syd. And Dad… he's no help at all. He has a really short fuse with her. Mom is doing everything."

"Could we hire someone to come in during the days?"

"They're at school during the days; that's not the problem. It's the nights and weekends, and now that summer break is coming up for them in about a week, I seriously don't know how Mom and Dad are going to handle it."

"Maybe summer camps," I said, brainstorming. "And we'll get them a babysitter to come in a few hours a day."

"Or… I was thinking…" Luke stopped mid-sentence, running his fingers through his newly grown out hair.

"What?"

"Of getting them away completely for a few weeks… so Mom can heal."

"You're going to take them on vacation?" I asked, surprised he'd even consider such a thing. But then with his alter ego in charge now, maybe he was evolving.

"No, Casey, not me. I was thinking maybe you and Jake could take them. I mean, summer break starts next week. Jake's on tour. It might be fun for them to see what that's all about. And during tour stops, you can take them on little adventures maybe. I could even get a week off myself and come and help. I don't know, it probably won't work, but I'm just throwing things out there at this point."

I bit down on my lower lip, thinking over his proposal. "I'd have to ask Jake. It's not the worst idea, though."

"Right?" He brightened. "It would give Mom a chance to rest up, and I think it would be good for Sydney to have you around. She needs a mother figure right now, and our mother just ain't cuttin' it."

"Because she's exhausted," I said, defending her.

"I was kidding. Damn, my jokes aren't landing anymore. Maybe I was only funny when I was the fat best friend."

"Stop it," I said, punching him in the side. "Anyway, I don't think I'm much of a role model myself."

"None of us are right now. We're all doing the best we can."

The look in his eyes gave me pause. Things had gone downhill since I'd left three months ago; that much was obvious.

"I'll call Jake tonight and run it by him, but he should be fine with it."

Luke snorted. "Oh, he's going to love it. Nothing spells fun like two bratty kids."

My eyes sparkled in mischief. "We'll leave the bratty part out, shall we?"

"I think we shall."

My brother and I grinned at one another as I linked my arm in his and said, "Take me to Mom."

My mother was holding court when I arrived in her hospital room. A female nurse and male orderly were laughing politely at something she'd said. I marveled at her strength. After her son and daughter-in-law died, she'd allowed herself several days to grieve before wiping away the tears, rolling up her sleeves, and getting to work making a stable home for her grandchildren to live in. In fact, they left their own home of thirty years to move into Miles and Darcy's house so the kids would feel as comfortable as possible during this horrible time in their lives.

Her devotion was admirable, for sure, but my mother hadn't allowed herself enough time to heal from the trauma of losing her oldest son, and the stress of it all was dragging her down. And now she was here, entertaining the hospital staff, when what she needed was both physical and mental rest.

"Casey!" She became even more animated upon seeing me. "This is my daughter." Then, from behind her hand, she motioned with her thumb. "The one I told you about."

Surely Mom had given them the lowdown on my hot rock star husband, and the three of us exchanged awkward hellos as they looked me up and down. I mean, what were they expected to say – congratulations? I walked over and hugged my father before leaning down and kissing my mom's cheek. The words I'd intended to speak sank down into my chest as I fought to control my emotions. This incident proved she was only human and that realization scared me. I couldn't lose her too.

"None of that, Casey. I'm fine. Everyone's making a big deal out of nothing. It was just a little heartburn… embarrassing, really. I'm absolutely fine and ready to go home."

"You aren't fine, Mom. You need rest. This happened because you're over-stressed and not taking care of yourself."

"Everyone's making such a fuss. It's annoying."

"Because we need you. Mom, you've got to get healthy. None of us can survive without you." I sniffled through each painful word. "You're what's keeping us all intact."

"What do you want me to do? I can't be lying in this hospital bed. Those kids need me at home."

"Well, I'm here now, and I'll take care of them while you get the rest you need."

My father perked up right away, grabbing my hand and squeezing it.

"I hate that you have to come here and take time away from Jake and your life," she said. "I promise, just a few days and I'll be as good as new."

After spelling out for Jake the situation at home and the need to get the kids away for a while, I dropped the bomb.

"How long are we talking?" he asked, trying to disguise the doubt in his voice. Neither one of us was used to caring for kids twenty-four seven, so I got his hesitation. I was feeling the same way.

"Three or four weeks. I'll take them on outings at the different stops."

"The travel might be tough on them and the bus feels pretty confining after a while."

"We'll manage."

"And what about your work?"

"I'll take some time off as soon as I finish the clients I'm working on now. Jake, I know this isn't ideal but, under the circumstances, I don't see any other alternative. I could stay here for the next few weeks, but I know my Mom – she won't rest. This is the only way."

"Checking us all into a mental institution seems easier."

"No doubt." I laughed at the visual image of his coping strategy.

"But we'll make it work," he conceded.

"You're sure?"

"No." He chuckled. "I'm not sure at all, but I can always force Lassen to babysit for a few hours if they get to be too much to handle."

"Oh no." I cringed. "I didn't think about him."

"I mean, Lassen can't even deal with a single Kleenex in his trashcan," Jake said. "How will he handle two little germ magnets?"

"Casey!" Sydney screeched as she flung herself into my arms and buried her head in my stomach. She'd become so clingy, something so out of character for the precocious child she'd always been. "I missed you so much!"

I smothered my niece in kisses, letting her hang all over me. "I missed you too.

A dead weight smashed into my back, dislodging Sydney.

"Riley!" she shouted, punching her brother in the leg. "Go away."

"Syd, he wants to see me too. Be nice."

Although I could tell she was fuming, I needed to set a firm tone now, or she'd walk all over me later. Besides, Riley, with his big gap-toothed grin, was a sight for sore eyes. I grabbed him and tried to kiss him, but he squirmed away and took off running in the other direction.

"Don't you run away from me, little boy."

I gave chase but that only resulted in him running faster as he squealed with laughter.

"Oh, I'm going to get you at some point, Riley James, and when I do, I'm going to double…no I'm going to triple-kiss you!"

"Nooo," Riley screamed and hid behind the chair. "Never!"

"Casey, Casey!" Syd's whole body was hanging from my arm. "Are you going to stay now that Grams is sick?" Her eyes were filled with hope, and my heart broke for her. I hugged her again.

"Better. Riley? Come here, you'll want to hear this. I promise not to kiss you if you surrender in full."

My nephew crawled out from his hiding spot but still stayed a cootie-safe distance away from me.

"So I'm going to stay with you until you finish school next week."

"That's just what I figured. Then you're just gonna leave us again," Syd huffed, sending a pile of papers to the floor in one fell swoop.

"Sydney!" Shocked by her sudden burst of anger, I stood there staring at my niece. This was going to be harder than I'd anticipated. Would Jake be able to handle this? More importantly, would Lassen? "Pick that up."

She crossed her arms and adopted the sourest of sourpuss faces. We stood there like that at an impasse for so long that Riley actually came over to pick up the mess.

"Nope. Not you, Riley. I appreciate the effort, but that's Sydney's tantrum and she gets to be the one who cleans it up."

Still no compliance. "Okay, I guess I'll just take Riley outside and tell him alone."

"Do it. Riley can't keep his mouth shut. I'll know twenty seconds after you tell him, and the paper will still be on the ground."

Luke, who'd apparently been standing in the doorway for our entire hopeless deadlock, joked, "I see you've met Sydney."

A long, shrill scream inexplicably originated from somewhere deep within our niece's body and saturated the room with negativity.

"Syd, stop screaming." I tried to grab her but she pivoted and sprang down the hallway to her room. The door slammed shut. Luke and I stared at each other, frozen in place, our ears ringing off the hook.

"Was it something I said?" Luke asked, wisely keeping his voice low.

I rolled my eyes at him.

"She was quite wonderful for me."

Luke and I startled, both forgetting Aunt Cheri was at the house babysitting while Mom and Dad were at the hospital.

"A perfect angel, actually. Of course, I was never a permissive mother. My kids always had the best behavior."

"Yeah. They're awesome. Well, we really appreciate you babysitting," Luke said, as he grabbed her purse and escorted our aunt to the door. "We'll see you real soon, Aunt Cheri. Thanks again."

Once the door was shut, his eyebrow lifted skeptically, and he said, "Correct me if I'm wrong but she's the one who raised Doug, the adulterer who broke up three marriages and got his daughter's third grade teacher fired, right?"

I nodded.

"Wow. Mother of the Year."

Suddenly the door down the hall opened and Sydney yelled out, "I don't care about your stupid surprise anyway!"

We exchanged resigned expressions. She was going to need to be dealt with. The only question was who got the honors.

Luke sighed, getting his hands ready to duel. "Rock, paper, scissors?"

"No. I'll do it. I need to get my feet wet before I have her with me full time for a month."

"That's exactly what I was hoping you'd say."

"Sydney, it's Casey."

I pushed the door open to find my niece under her blanket. I reached for it, but she yanked back and we played tug-of-war for a few seconds before I got the upper hand and pulled the soft fleece off her.

"I don't want to fight with you, Syd. I just got here, and I want us to have fun together, like old times. All you have to do is come back out and pick up the mess, and then we can have fun and you can hear my surprise."

"I'm not coming out while Luke's there."

"Why?"

"Because he was making fun of me."

I wanted to argue that it was just Luke and that he was only kidding, but looking at it through her eyes, I guessed I could see her point.

"If I get Luke to say he's sorry, will you apologize to me and clean up the mess?"

Sydney considered my compromise for an extended period of time before finally nodding. It was a small victory, but not without significance. Now I knew she was a pliable opponent, if not a pleasant one.

Luke dutifully apologized, and after the paper and pens were picked up, both kids sat on the sofa, rapt with attention. Riley's cheeks were burning bright with excitement, and even Sydney, used to playing hard to get, seemed sufficiently curious.

"How would you two like to go on an adventure?"

"An adventure?" Sydney asked, with interest. "Like a jungle safari?"

"I want to go on a monster truck safari," Riley added.

"No," I said, deflating a bit. Their idea of adventure differed a bit from mine, for sure. Cramped in a tour bus, driving for hours on end… maybe it wasn't as exciting as I'd hoped it would be for the kids.

"No. None of those ideas, though they do sound fun. My adventure is a little different. How would you like to go on tour?"

Syd's face lit up. "Really? With Jake?"

"Well, yes, and me too."

"But Jake will be there the whole time, right?"

"Yes. The whole time."

"Yay!" Sydney jumped from her seat and cheered. "Did you hear that, Riley? Jake's going to be there!"

"And me too," I reiterated, but no one was listening to me. By now, Riley was on his feet too, jumping up and down.

"We're going on tour, baby!" she sang out, and Riley repeated her word for word. I doubted he even knew what 'going on tour' meant, but it didn't matter. Sydney's happiness was all it took to spread the joy.

"I'm going to go pack now," Sydney said, racing down the hall. "Come on, Riley."

He happily followed after her like the obedient little brother he was.

"We aren't leaving for another week," I called after them, but they were already gone. After so much heartache, these kids finally had something to look forward to. My worry was whether Jake and I would be able to live up to expectation.

Luke and I waved the kids off at school and then drove to a coffee shop. After parking, I sat in the car a few seconds longer than necessary.

"You weren't kidding about Sydney."

"No."

"She's exhausting," I admitted. "Mom can't handle that day in and day out."

"No."

"The counseling doesn't seem to be helping."

"No."

"Stop saying 'No.' Don't you have anything else to add?"

"What do you want me to say? I don't have an answer to this, other than to pawn them off on you and Jake for a few weeks."

"Yeah, I like how you sprang it on me before I had a chance to see them in action with my own two eyes. Thanks for that, by the way."

His brows furrowing in response, Luke said, with clear desperation in his voice, "You aren't backing out, are you?"

"Of course not. I'm just worried about Sydney. She's not the same girl."

"And she probably never will be again. I think the goal now is to just make her a functioning member of society."

"That's not enough. I want her to be happy."

"Surrounded by all of us sad-sacks? Unlikely. Are you getting out of the car? I need coffee."

Luke and I waited in a line eight people deep, feasting our eyes on the baked goods calling to us through the glass. While we waited for the person in front to pay for her order, a pretty young cashier smiled at Luke before gliding her eyes over me curiously.

"Mornin', Tess," he said, "How's it going?"

"Can't complain. I haven't seen you in here for a while. I thought maybe you didn't like the way I was preparing your coffee."

"No, nothing so scandalous. I've just been holed up lately."

"You haven't been sick, I hope." She scanned him covertly, and I could tell she hadn't seen him since his massive weight loss either. It was rather jarring.

"No, just, you know… hitting the gym." Luke flexed his arms in his attempt to be the douchebag he'd only seen in movies. He failed miserably. My brother was just too nice a guy to ever pull off a move like that.

"Well, you look great." Her eyes lingered on him longer than was required for a random barista, and I took note. Luke, on the other hand, seemed completely oblivious. No wonder he never had a damn date.

After sitting down with our coffee, I asked, "You know she likes you, right?"

"Who? Tess?" he asked, glancing over. "Extremely doubtful, if not downright delusional. She's dating some tool."

"Really? Because that's not how it looked to me. She seemed overly interested in you."

"Trust me, Casey. I'd have a better chance of winning the lottery than getting a girl like that. Can we talk about something else?"

"Like your weight loss?"

"Why is everyone making such a big deal out of it?"

"You really do look great, don't get me wrong. Are you actually going to the gym, or were you just trying to impress the girl?"

Luke looked up at me over his coffee cup and actually smiled. "What do you think?"

"If I had to guess, then no."

"I've gone a few times, but people are crazy at gyms. This one time I saw some idiot put a water bottle in the Pringles holder on the treadmill."

I laughed. Luke and his goofy personality were still in there. Still, I needed a little more from him to ease my mind. "I'm just worried that it wasn't a conscious choice of yours to get healthy."

"Well, it wasn't like I said, 'My brother just died, whoopee, sign me up for Nutrisystem for men.' I just don't feel like doing much of anything these days, and that includes eating. Right now, life just sucks."

"Don't I know it," I said, covering his hand with mine. "I've been pretty depressed myself. I *am* eating, though, but only to keep my strength up so I can continue to bully Jake into getting me pregnant."

"There you go, Casey. Projecting your misery onto others. Good for you."

"You know me… always putting others before myself."

His eyes focused on his coffee and he smiled, but it was heavy with strain. "I'm doing better. I really am. Stop worrying about me."

"Sure, I'll just cross your name off my list of angst."

"Thank you. So, are you pregnant?"

"No. We've only been trying for three months. It's probably for the best if we don't get pregnant, but it just doesn't feel like that. I want one so badly. A baby would bring joy back into our lives, don't you think?"

"A baby's just a Band-Aid, Sis. It might stop the bleeding, but the reason for the wound will still exist. My advice would be to fix yourself first."

"That might take a lifetime," I huffed, taking a swig of coffee. "And I don't have the patience."

Both our phones buzzed at the same time, and we glanced down at the screens like mirror images. "Mom's been discharged."

"Yep, let's get home."

Luke and I walked over to throw our cups away and the barista called out to him, "Have a great day, Luke."

And, without hesitation, my brother answered, as he always did, "Have a better one."

My mother arrived home later that afternoon, looking surprisingly strong and healthy. Her mood was upbeat as well. I didn't know what type of happy pills she was taking, but I wanted some. How could she have such a positive demeanor in these trying times? She couldn't. At least that's what I assumed. This whole thing had to be an act, and when she was alone, I was certain my mother was suffering in silence.

This calmness of hers had to be denial all wrapped up in a pretty box with a magnificent bow.

The first topic she wanted to discuss as she took her place on the couch with a glass of her favorite ice tea was the kids' impending departure. She didn't think it was necessary for them to leave and tried to pull rank by letting us know, in no uncertain terms, that she was their legal guardian and the decision was ultimately up to her.

"Well, then, when you tell Sydney she doesn't get to go on tour with Jake, I want to be in an adjacent state," Luke said.

"Me too," Dad agreed.

Mom's eyes shifted among the three of us. I could see her resolve fading. "Fine. They can go. It's not like you'll make it four weeks with them anyway."

The wheels touched down on the tarmac and my heart leapt in my chest. We'd only been apart for a week, but it felt much longer. Jake had flown in from Texas on a private plane just to pick us up. It would have been easier for him to stay put and for us to travel to him, but Sydney begged him to come to the play her class was performing on the last day of school.

Although we'd told her it wasn't possible, Jake secretly made plans to surprise her. He had exactly four hours in

Arizona before we needed to be on the flight back for the evening concert he was to perform.

Although it was just him getting off the flight, I pulled out a cardboard sign and held it over my head. It had become somewhat of a ritual for us, and Jake loved it every time. Sometimes it was just a flimsy piece of paper, and other times I went fancy with colored paint on thick paper stock, but regardless of the materials I used, the sign always had the same four letters on it: CAKE.

Jake smiled as he walked toward me and ducked under his paper greeting to give me a kiss.

"You look hot," he commented.

"Well, it is ninety-three degrees outside."

He grinned. "Not what I meant, but okay."

Tucking the sign between my knees, I grabbed his face and planted one on him. "I missed you."

"I missed you too. Are you ready to be parents for the next month?"

"No. Are you?"

"God, no. It's going to be a disaster."

"Or," I said, coyly. "We could totally surprise ourselves."

He and I stared at each other for a moment before laughing and saying, "Nah."

Sydney's class was preparing for the play, so Jake and I visited Riley's third grade classroom first. They'd just started the party, and the children were lined up like little toy soldiers waiting for their turn to select their finger foods off the beautifully decorated table.

"Did you make something?" Jake whispered in my ear.

"I did. You want to guess which one?"

He scanned the elaborate selection of items, all tailor-made for kids with fun little designs. There were deviled eggs sporting funny faces and pigs in a blanket shaped like actual pigs and rainbow fruit kabobs. And then there was mine.

Jake was diligently trying to determine my contribution to the kid table, when a smile spread out wide across his face. "You didn't?"

I shrugged. "They said to bring hors d'oeuvres."

"They're third graders."

Okay, so maybe my shrimp skewers weren't the best choice, but how was I to know what a third grade palate was like? At least the skewers were colorful little swords. That looked third gradish, didn't it?

"Jake McKallister!" A voice from behind called out. "Wow. I'm Tiffany. Welcome. I can't tell you how excited I am to meet you. I'm such a fan."

Tiffany was Miss Soriano, Riley's very young, and very hot, teacher. By the looks of things, she'd heard Jake was coming and had dressed accordingly in a body-hugging shirt that accentuated her bosom. Too bad the bulletin she received about his arrival didn't also include information on his marital status. However, because she was Riley's teacher, I was inclined to give her the benefit of the doubt. It was possible she'd been imprisoned in a foreign country or had tragically been stuck in a well around the time of our wedding. Whatever it was, no way was Miss Soriano trying to hijack my man. Or was she? Within seconds of her introducing herself, I was effectively boxed out of the conversation.

Annoyed, I stood off to the side as a group began to form around him. I was about to swoop back in and rescue my husband when a strange sight caught my eye: a group of boys, Riley being one of them, was gathered around one central location. Curious, I wandered over and my eyes doubled in size at what I saw – my shrimp lying limp on the floor, and boys everywhere trying to stab each other with the plastic skewers. I gasped and looked back toward the teacher. She and all the mommies had formed a circle around Jake, and none were aware of the fight club that had materialized out of thin air.

My hors d'oeuvres were to blame for this medieval swordplay, and I needed to get rid of the evidence before anyone noticed. Stomping my way into the circle, I went boy to boy with my palm laid flat. "Hand it over," I demanded. One by one, the little swords filled my hand, and the boys scattered off.

As I was about to pick up my discarded shrimp, I could hear Jake disengaging himself from the conversation to come find me. With no time left, I used my shoe to scoot the shrimp under Tiffany's desk. With any luck, they'd sit there all summer cooking up a nice stink just in time for the start of the new school year. Smiling, I tossed the skewers in the trash and rejoined my husband.

My mom and dad were saving us seats in the front row of the auditorium, and we arrived just in time to see Sydney's class file in to take the stage. She glanced over and gave us each a wave before her eyes settled on Jake. A squeal could be heard throughout the room as she broke ranks, ran to him, and flung herself into his arms.

"You came!" she said, her cheeks flushed with excitement. Syd yanked on his arms attempting to pull him from his chair. "Come on, I'll introduce you."

"Oh, no." Jake sat back. "I'm here to watch you on stage, not be on it myself. Besides, your play is starting."

"I don't care. It's stupid anyway. I'm playing a celery stick. I don't even like vegetables."

"Celery?" he laughed. "Dude, that sucks."

"I know." Syd rolled her eyes. "That's what I said. I wanted to be the strawberry, but the teacher gave it to Kimmy because she's such a suck up."

"Okay." Mom stood up and pulled Sydney off Jake. "Get up there and be the best celery stick you can be."

"Fine," she huffed, stomping her way back to stage before turning around and saying, loudly enough for the entire auditorium to hear, "I'm *so* over fifth grade."

CHAPTER SIXTEEN

CASEY

Parental Units

"Catch me, Jake. Catch me," Sydney said, as she hung precariously over the back of her airplane seat. One false move and she'd be in his lap. Without even the slightest display of emotion, he reached out a hand and pushed her back over. This little scenario had played out no fewer than twelve times now, and by the blank look on his face, he'd gone into survival mode. I couldn't help but laugh because otherwise, I'd be crying. We were officially in way over our heads. Jake shifted his eyes toward me, the only part of him apparently still functioning, then pretended to break down in tears. Right back at you, bud.

We'd managed to get Syd and Riley strapped in for take off, but once the flight leveled off, Jake and I had made the rookie mistake of letting them take their seatbelts off, essentially setting them free to wreak havoc on every unsuspecting adult on the flight. Thankfully this was a private jet, and besides the two pilots and a flight attendant, the only other ones with us were on Jake's payroll, so they had no choice but to grin and bear it.

"There are only two of them, right?" Jake asked. "I can't tell because they seem to have multiplied."

He was right. We were only an hour into the two-hour flight, and Sydney had already visited the pilots twice, been in the bathroom four times, and had sung the song from *Frozen*, oh, I'd say maybe fourteen times. Not to be outdone, Riley had pulled out every elementary school game at his disposal – right now he was playing *Duck, Duck, Goose* – and yet still, somehow, had managed to fit time into his busy schedule to eat a snack in every unoccupied seat on the plane. The worst of it was, neither one seemed remotely close to slowing down. As for Jake and me, the past hour spent chasing them down had used up every last bit of our reserves, and we were now slumped lethargically in our chairs.

"Yes. Only two," I confirmed for him.

"I think I can officially say we suck at parenting."

"Agreed." I nodded my head. "Thank god we didn't get pregnant."

"I wasn't going to say that, but it's exactly what I was thinking," he said, then added, "Maybe once we grow up."

"Yes, that seems like a smart plan. Let's grow up first."

He stuck his hand across the aisle and we linked pinkies. It was the most energy either of us could muster.

Sydney popped up from behind the seat like one of those terrifying jack-in-the-box toys. "Hey, Rock Star?"

That was what she'd taken to calling him once the flight began. Jake displayed a pathetic little pout before turning his attention back to her.

"Yes, Sydney? What can I do for you?"

"Are we going to your concert tonight?"

Before he could give her an answer, Riley burst forth from behind Jake's chair and walloped him on top of the head.

"Duck!" he yelled, a look of glee on his seven-year-old face as he jumped off the seat and took off running.

Jake's eyes followed Riley up the aisle. "Does he really think I'm going to chase after him when he gets to Goose?"

I turned my head toward my sweet hubby and smiled. We both knew he would.

"So, are we going to the concert or what?" Syd asked again, but this time she would not be ignored. Grasping Jake's chin in her fingers, she turned his face toward her.

"It depends. Are you going to be good?" he asked her.

"*Duck!*" Riley popped me on my shoulder, choosing that spot because, with Vadim, Jake's bodyguard, sitting directly behind me, he couldn't reach my head. Again my nephew took off running. So far, this was a game I could get behind because it hadn't required any extra movement on my part.

Sydney leaned all the way over until her forehead was nearly touching Jake's. "Define good."

"You want a definition, do you?" Jake asked, breaking out a smile. It was no secret he loved her spunk. Regardless of how shitty we were at parenting, Sydney needed him. At this difficult point in her life, he seemed the only person she respected enough to listen to. "Okay, good means that you do what Auntie Casey says, that you don't get in the way of the crew, and that you don't run out onto the stage and sing 'Let it Go' while I'm performing."

"That's it?" she said, actually wiping her brow with the back of her hand. "What a relief."

Sydney let go of his chin and disappeared over her chair again. Jake and I exchanged confused expressions. What did that mean? What exactly was *her* definition of good? But before we could get our answer, Riley skipped by us, stopping in front of Vadim.

"*Du...*" He was only halfway through the word when Vadim grabbed his hand mid-*duck*.

"Don't even think about it, kid," he said in a menacing growl while throwing in a lip curl to the threat.

"Vadim!" Jake shot up from his chair, hands balled into fists. His reaction was so swift that it startled everyone on the plane. "Get your hands off him, now!"

Vadim immediately let go, and Riley, frightened not only by Vadim's actions but also by Jake's sudden eruption, burst into tears, flinging himself into my arms.

"What do you think you're doing?" Jake asked, bristling.

"These kids are not my job," Vadim challenged, clearly incensed and not backing down. If it came to it, he had the size and training to take Jake out in less than two moves. It's what made him a great bodyguard, but also a feared human being.

"Your job is what I say it is. These kids are my family, and you'll treat them with respect or you can find yourself new employment."

The two glared at one another. Vadim had been with Jake for years, and in all the time I'd known him, I'd never seen them disagree. But then, he barely spoke to me in the first place. When he had something to say to Jake, he always pulled him aside for a private discussion, as if I could not be trusted with pertinent information. I'd never really cared for him, but at the same time, I always felt that both Jake and I were safer when he was around.

"Sorry," Vadim mumbled, breaking eye contact with Jake and leaning back in his seat. I could only imagine what it took for him to stand down when it was clear by his body language that was the last thing he wanted to do.

Jake stood there a moment, still fuming, so I grabbed his hand, forcing his attention away from Vadim. Both Sydney and Riley had been watching the exchange intently, and how he handled himself now would be etched in their memories for a long time. I motioned toward the kids with my eyes and then at his chair.

The situation diffused, he nodded, but before taking his seat, Jake got the last word in with Vadim. "Don't ever touch him again."

"You want to talk about what happened earlier?" I asked, as he was getting ready for the concert. We'd arrived at the venue a couple hours earlier, but with the kids occupying every second of that time, this was the first opportunity I'd had to talk to him. And if it weren't for Kyle wandering into the hornet's nest and unwittingly taking over the parenting duties, we wouldn't even have had this chance.

Seemingly bothered by the incident with Vadim, Jake didn't look my way when he said, "Not particularly."

"I get why you were angry. I was too. Vadim didn't have any right to grab him like that."

"No, he didn't," Jake said, edgy once more. "There was no excuse. He was trying to intimidate Riley, and I'm not going to put up with that shit."

I understood then that this wasn't just about Riley. Vadim's aggressive behavior had triggered something in him. I imagine he'd been in Riley's shoes more times than he could count – the difference being, he hadn't had anyone to stand up for him during those dark times. His protective instincts had kicked in the minute Vadim grabbed Riley, and I had no doubt he would have defended his nephew with his life. I respected the hell out of him for that.

"Hey." I slid my arms around his back. "Don't feel bad. You did the right thing."

"No. I lost my cool in front of them... in front of everyone."

"A little bit, maybe, but it didn't affect the kids in the way you think it did. They didn't see you as being aggressive. What they saw was their uncle standing up for them. For better or worse, they now know you have their back."

"I want Captain Crunch," Riley demanded of Kyle.

"Nope, I'm sorry. That's not a dinner cereal," he replied, taking the box out of my nephew's hands and putting it at the top of the cupboard.

"That's not a dinner cereal," Riley mimicked.

"That's not a dinner cereal," Kyle mimicked back.

"You can't tell me what to do," Riley whined.

"You can't tell me what to do," Kyle whined right back.

As we re-entered the room, Jake stepped between the two. This pre-adolescent pissing match could go on all day without proper intervention.

"Okay. Enough, Riley," he said. "And no cereal for dinner. We may be amateurs, but your Auntie Casey and I still have some common sense. Catering has food for us. Go get ready and we'll leave in a few minutes."

The kids just stood there staring up at him. Jake looked to me, perplexed, then back at the kids.

"What?" he asked.

"We're ready."

"You don't have to, like, brush your hair or change clothes or anything?"

"We're kids," Sydney said in a snooty tone, lifting her arms in exasperation. "I thought you said you had common sense."

Kyle burst out laughing until he caught sight of our disapproving glares. "Well, she has you on that one," he said under his breath.

Now I stepped into the fray. "You know what, Syd? I don't like that attitude. You might have been able to walk all over us on the plane, but that was only because we were just getting our sea legs. Now that Jake and I know how you operate, we're not going to let you take advantage of us anymore. Got it?"

Sydney glanced between the two of us, no doubt trying to determine how much control she could relinquish without selling her soul. Finally she folded her arms in front of her and said, "I'm sorry."

It wasn't exactly a sincere apology, but it was the most she'd offered since I'd been around her all week, so I was inclined to take it. I gave her a quick hug. "Now, go brush your hair."

Riley looked up at Kyle, his face scrunched in confusion. "Sea legs? Were we on a boat?"

Kyle just shrugged his shoulders as if he too were baffled by the analogy. Yeah, maybe he hadn't been the best choice in babysitters.

Riley didn't make it past the third song before he slid to the floor and fell asleep on my foot. No joke – I looked down, and he was out. Too bad sleep wasn't that easy for the rest of us. I had to get him back to the bus, and I knew instinctively Sydney would not go willingly. My stomach did a little 'punch in the gut' number at just the thought of the confrontation that was sure to follow. In fact, by the time it was over, Riley would probably be wide awake again and bouncing off the walls for the rest of the night.

For the umpteenth time that day, I felt wholly unqualified to be calling myself their caregiver. As evidenced by the flight this afternoon, I was no mother. I could barely be called an acceptable babysitter. Sydney and Riley deserved better; but unfortunately they weren't going to get it because when you draw the short end of the stick in life, you just had to learn to make do.

Stop procrastinating. It was time to deliver the news. My hands broke out in a sweat and I swallowed the lump in my throat. It was best just to get this over with. I looked to Syd and opened my mouth to speak, but something in her demeanor stopped me. It wasn't how engrossed she was in the concert, or the way she was watching Jake's every move with unblinking fascination. No, it was that peculiar little smile on her face. Wait a minute. I knew that look. That wasn't just pride in her uncle. Oh, no. Like millions of girls the world over, little Sydney Caldwell had a crush… on my husband.

Ten. She was ten years old. And when I say ten, I'm talking she just turned that number. A few months ago, she was still in the single digits! This was not good. Why hadn't I seen this before? Had I just not been paying attention, or was it a recent thing? I was going to have to tread lightly here. The last thing I wanted to do was squash her spirit, because if there was one thing I was certain of, it was that my niece couldn't take any more heartbreak.

"Casey?" Syd interrupted my mini panic attack by pulling on my hand. She looked up at me with tired brown eyes, and like I had been many times since the death of her mother and father, I was struck by the change in this little girl. She used to sparkle all the time, but now it seemed as if a filter had been put in place to dull and subdue her.

"Yeah, sweetie?"

"Riley needs to sleep." She pointed down to my feet.

"Ya think?" I grinned. The kid was now sprawled out on the floor, the noise-canceling earpieces doing their job beautifully.

"I know you're enjoying the show, but…"

She shook her head. "I want to go."

"You do?"

Tears pooled in her eyes. Syd frowned and wiped them away with her sleeve.

"Are you okay?" I asked, hugging her to me. "What's wrong?"

Then came the downward flow as she broke into sobs. I stood there unprepared and helpless. What had I been thinking, bringing her here? She clearly wasn't ready to leave the safety of her grandparents. Holding her to me tightly, I grabbed my phone and dialed. He answered on two rings.

"Kyle, I need you."

Kyle gently placed Riley in the bunk bed as I extracted the earplugs.

"You sure that's a good idea?" Kyle whispered, glancing over at Sydney, who was still sniffling and blowing her nose. "The earplugs seem like keepers."

"Honestly, I don't know. I'm not doing a good job with these kids. I think I made a mistake bringing them here," I said, tucking Riley in and covering him with a blanket.

"You're doing fine. Can I give you a suggestion?"

"Please."

"Don't dwell on her tears. Don't even mention them. Some people prefer to suffer alone. Sydney strikes me as one of them."

"But she's so young. Shouldn't I try to get her to talk to me? Find out why she's crying?"

"You already know why. Her parents are dead. Nothing you say or do is going to change that."

"Are you suggesting I just ignore it altogether?"

"No. Let her know she can come to you, but don't push her. She's proud. Crying pisses her off. If you highlight it or make a big deal out of it, you'll only alienate her more."

"Huh. Okay. Do you have a psychology degree or something?"

"No. I speak from experience." A quick snapshot of pain flashed across his face. It was a rare moment of raw honesty from him. Kyle preferred to hide behind his smile and a truckload of jokes, but under it all was a sensitive guy who had more skeletons in his closet than most. After what he'd just told me, I had to wonder how much suffering he'd done in silence.

Grabbing his hand, I squeezed. "Thank you."

"No problem. If you need help with them, I don't mind. I like having conversations with kids. Grownups never ask me what my third favorite dinosaur is. Besides, it'll get me out of the scut work. Vadim always puts me on the shittiest detail just because he can."

"You should tell Jake."

"Uh…no. And you won't either. I already have one strike against me with the other guys for being Jake's brother, but if they think I'm running home to tell my mommy every time they're mean to me… yeah, not good."

"Ooh," I winced. "I see your point. Never mind. Go back to scrubbing toilets."

"I will. Thank you."

"So?" I said, a sickly sweet smile forming on my face.

He picked up immediately on the tease and mimicked my lovesick grin and singsong voice. "So, what?"

"When is Kenzie coming?"

"You already know she's coming next Friday."

"I just want to hear you say it. You always get that goofy look on your face."

"That's just my face. I'm naturally goofy."

"Ah, see." I grabbed Kyle's jaw and shook it. "There it is. That smile. You love her, and don't try to deny it."

"I'm not trying to deny it. I tell her all the time."

"So?" I tried again. I had intel on a certain subject straight from the source, Kenzie, and I wanted confirmation.

Kyle raised his eyebrows. "So what?"

"I know you're going to propose," I blurted out.

He didn't even blink at my extortion attempt. "You don't know shit, Casey. I know how you operate. You're using fake news to get me to confess to something that doesn't exist."

"Okay, deny it. I don't care."

"Yes, you do. Look at you all a-quiver." He laughed. "You can barely contain yourself."

"Fine. Yes. I'm excited."

"What makes you think I'm going to propose?" he asked, more interested in my answer than he was trying to let on.

"Um… gee, Kyle. Maybe it's because you were asking my opinion on what her ring size might be? I just naturally deduced from there. Plus Kenzie keeps talking about it. Apparently you asked her the same question."

"And she took that to mean I was going to propose?" he asked, seemingly surprised that any girl would come to such a preposterous conclusion.

"Um, yeah. Of course. Why wouldn't she?"

Kyle appeared stumped by that one. I could almost see the wheels turning in his head. "What if I were just getting her a skull ring or something?"

"Then you might want to duck after giving it to her because that's not at all what she'll be expecting."

"Great," he mumbled, suddenly distracted by the wall.

"Wait – you didn't *actually* get her a skull ring, did you?"

Kyle didn't answer my question. Instead he headed for the door. "Goodnight, Casey."

I followed behind him right on his heels. "Because if you were actually thinking of proposing, you could always employ my services… which, I might add, are free of charge."

"Oh, I'm sure they are," he said. Thankfully he accepted my meddling ways with amusement. "Anyway, it's been fun, Casey, but I've got to get back, or Vadim will kill me in my sleep. Remember what I said about Sydney. You're going for 'I'm there for you' not 'Let me smother you in my love.'"

"Got it. Thank you, Kyle. I can always count on you. And, you know…" I winked in his direction. "You can always count on me." Wink. Wink.

He shook his head, smiling as he purposely avoided responding to my goading. Kyle grabbed a Kleenex out of the box on the kitchen counter before walking over to Sydney and dropping it in her lap.

"How do you make a tissue dance?" he asked.

"I don't know," she said, looking up at him.

"Put a little boogey in it!"

Sydney wiped the last of her tears away and laughed.

"See ya, Syd."

"Bye, weirdo."

He caught her insult in his hand and pressed it to his heart, as if it meant the world to him. Sydney and I both giggled.

"Goodnight, ladies." He stepped out of the bus but then popped his head back in and with a sly smile on his face said, "Oh, and by the way, Casey, your services may be requested somewhere down the line."

I threw my arms in the air and had them perform a silent little boogey of their own.

"What was that all about?" Sydney asked, once he'd left.

"Just a little inside joke."

"Oh. He's funny. I like him."

"Me too," I said, tucking a strand of hair behind her ear. "Are you ready for bed?"

Syd eyed me skeptically. "You're not going to ask me why I was crying?"

"Do you want me to?"

"Nope."

"Okay, then, let's get ready for bed."

She dragged her feet, but eventually I did convince her to put on pajamas and brush her teeth. Sydney climbed up into the top bunk. Earlier in the day, she and Riley had fought viciously over the coveted spot, but in the end, she'd pulled rank over her little brother and claimed it for herself. I felt for Riley. Being the youngest myself, I couldn't have even dreamed of getting the top bunk back in the day. When we went on family vacations, I was lucky if I got the cushions off the couch.

I spent extra time folding the blankets and sheets over my little niece, hoping to swaddle her in comfort. Her life was so hard now, anything I could do to lessen the blow was at least something. Sydney surprised me by reaching out and lightly running her finger over a strand of my hair.

"You're so pretty," she whispered. "I wish I was you."

A flood of emotion threatened to overtake me as I hugged her. "You are me... in so many ways. We both have similar personalities, sarcastic and brave, and you look like I did as a kid, only you're much prettier than I was."

"You think I'm pretty?"

"I think you're beautiful. But trust me when I say being attractive on the outside might get you places, but it doesn't make you special without having a good solid core." I held my hand to her chest. "Inside here. This is what makes you count."

"What if I don't have anything left inside here?" she asked, placing her hand over her heart as well. "Then what do I do?"

"Everything that makes you who you are is still there, but it's just under a layer of sadness. I see your light trying to shine through. I know you want to be happy again but I think maybe you feel guilty... like you aren't allowed to be happy because your mom and dad aren't here to enjoy it."

A tear slipped down her cheek as she nodded.

"But you know that's not what they would want, right? They'd want you to live and smile and be happy. They always only wanted the best for you and that's what Grams and Gramps are trying to give you, Syd. Nothing we can do will bring them back but there's a lot you can do to keep them alive inside here."

Sydney silently tapped her fingers on mine, seemingly contemplating my words before saying, "My mom was going to take me to one of Jake's concerts this summer. Just us girls. She said we'd fly to any city I wanted to go to. That should have been her with me tonight."

"Oh." I had no idea how to respond to her. Something soothing or maybe insightful would have been ideal, but that had never been me. I thought with my emotions, not my brain. "Your mom was so awesome."

Sydney immediately broke down, covering her face to silently weep. Crap, that was such a stupid thing to say. It only served to make her miss her mom more. Now it was me stroking her hair.

"I cry for your mom and dad everyday, too. Did you know that? I miss them so much that sometimes I can't breathe."

"That's how I feel too," Syd said. "And mad."

"Yep. Me too. So mad that they had to die… for what? A text? If that lady had just looked up from her damn phone, they'd all still be alive."

"I'm so mad I want to hurt people."

"Is that why you're so hard on Grams and Gramps?"

"I guess. Someday everyone is going to stop loving me because I'm so mean."

Tears splashed down her face faster than I could wipe them away. I pulled her head to my chest and held her tight.

"That's never going to happen. You're way too loved. But I'll admit, I feel the same way sometimes."

"You do?" Sydney sat up, wiping her face in her sheets. She was now fully vested in our conversation. I was aware that Riley was asleep in the bunk below and that, if he woke, I'd be in for a long night, but it would all be worth it if I could get this little girl to open up.

"I'm scared that my sadness is going to push Jake away. I don't want him to get tired of me and decide to leave."

To my surprise, Sydney reached out her hand and placed it on my cheek. She had temporarily forgotten her own misery to tend to mine, and that's when I knew my sweet niece was still in there, buried deep under all the rubble. "He won't leave you."

"Why do you think that?"

"Because he loves you."

"Like we love you?" I asked.

She nodded, but I sensed that she wasn't convinced.

"Nothing you do will ever stop us from loving you, Syd. We might get frustrated or angry with you, but that's not the same thing. We're family, girl. We stick together."

"Then why are you afraid Jake will leave? He's family too."

That was a damn good question. Why was I always doubting his loyalty when he'd done nothing to deserve it?

"You're right. I'm not giving him any credit. Just like you're not giving us any. We're a pair, aren't we?"

Sydney nodded her agreement.

"You and me, we need to stop acting like Eeyore and be more like Pooh."

"Huh?" she said, looking perplexed.

"Winnie the Pooh?"

Recognition dawned on her face. "Oh. I've never seen it."

Seriously? What were they teaching these kids nowadays? "Eeyore is all doomsday and Pooh is sunshine. Which one would you rather be?"

"Eeyore," she answered, suppressing a smile.

"The correct answer is Pooh." I tickled her, and we both giggled.

"So what do you say? Shall we both give positivity a try?"

She shrugged. "I don't really have anything else to do."

"True," I said, laughing at her apathy. "I know it feels weird to have fun when your mom and dad can't be part of it, but I know they would want you to smile again and be goofy. So let's make it our mission to be crazy fun at least once every day while you're here."

"Like this?" She rolled her eyes up in her head and sucked her cheeks in.

"Ah, yes, the fish face. Nice start, girl."

I high-fived my smiling niece and silently cheered my first victory.

Jake came in a couple hours later, and I placed my finger over my lips to let him know he needed to be quiet. He nodded as he slid into place beside me on the couch and draped his arm over my shoulder.

"What happened?" He whispered. "Kyle told me Sydney started crying. Is she okay?"

I tucked both knees under me and sat up straighter, excited to tell him about the breakthrough I'd had with Syd. As I rattled on and on, Jake listened intently, nodding and smiling at the right moments. Finally when I stopped to breathe, he leaned in and planted his lips on mine.

"That's awesome, Case. I haven't seen you this happy in a long time."

"I am. I just feel like I really connected with her… like maybe I can help her get to a place where she doesn't want to cry twenty-four hours a day."

"And maybe she'll do the same for you."

I nodded, although I was wondering whether she already had. I now had a mission more important than myself, and it felt good.

"Oh, and just a heads-up. I think Syd might have a crush on you, so keep the strolls through the bus in your underwear to a minimum."

"I'll do my best to refrain from public nudity."

"Thank you. And, I have to say, you don't seem all that surprised that she's crushing on you."

"Because I already knew that."

"You did?"

"Yeah. She's always mean to me. That's how crushes work at that age. You'd know that if you hadn't been a card-carrying tomboy growing up."

"Hey, this tomboy had crushes. Lucky for you I threw the athletic shorts and jerseys away long ago. I'm all woman now," I said pushing my bosom into him to prove my point. His hands went straight for my breasts like a moth to the flame.

"If I promise to be really quiet," he said, his voice so low I had to strain to hear, "do you think we can get it on?"

I stood up and held out my hand. "I think that can be arranged."

We tiptoed past the bunk bed and confirmed two sets of eyes were soundly closed before sneaking into the bedroom.

"Lock the door," I said as I crawled quietly onto the bed. "And Jake, I'm not just talking once – check that damn lock no less than three times, then tip-toe your ass over here… but don't forget to keep your mouth shut along the way."

"Jesus, that's a lot of instructions to remember."

"If you can't recall three simple steps, then you don't deserve to have sex."

"Easy, woman," he said, placating me with his hands, "I didn't say I couldn't remember them. I was just pointing out the excessive number of demands. And might I add, this is almost as hot as the sex talks we had prior to our baby-making sessions."

"I promise this will be hotter."

Jake formed his fingers into a V for victory and headed straight for the bed before stopping himself and turning back around to check the lock.

"Only checked it twice," he whispered.

"Get over here," I laughed, as Jake crawled onto the bed, grabbed my hips, and slid me along the bed until I was snugly wedged between his legs, his erection pressing firmly against me. I wiggled a little against him, watching for his reaction. His eyes blazed at he stared down at me with an insatiable longing. Unable to keep my hands off him, I ran my nails up his abdomen, causing the band of muscles in his stomach to swell and contract with a seductive shiver.

I thrust my hips into his hardness, frenzied with desire for him. Our clothes still in place, Jake pushed repeatedly against my dampening mound, sending darts of pleasure rushing through me and drawing a loud moan from my lips. Our eyes widened instantaneously as we remembered our houseguests on the other side of the wall. Jake dropped down over me and covered my mouth with his hand, and we both stared at each other in amusement.

"Shhh," he said, breathing roughly, as his free hand found its way between my legs and he began applying liberal pressure to the area. I bit down into his hand to suppress the moans that rattled in my throat as my thrusting hips made contact with his increasingly quick movements. And then suddenly he removed his enchanted hand, causing an intense throbbing right down to my core.

"Easy," he whispered, placing two fingers on my lips. "I want this to go on forever. I've missed you so much, Casey."

Before I could reply, his soft lips were over mine and our mouths moved in the most sensual dance. Jake's tongue pushed forward, teasing my lips apart. Grabbing his strong jawline, I held him steady as my own tongue pressed and stroked against his. When he drew back, we were both panting and our eyes were glazed over in lust.

Jake slowly trailed his fingers downward, past my jaw, gliding smoothly along my throat and into the crevice of my breasts. His mouth then pressed into the cloth, dampening it, as his tongue circled my pebbled nipples. I heaved my bosom, welcoming his tender lapping. Jake sat back up and, grasping my waist, pulled me into him once more. His hands were now on my stomach, riding my shirt up as he glided across my sensitive skin. After pulling my top up and over my head, Jake took both breasts in his appreciative hands. I was wearing a fairly standard issue bra, but he seemed unbelievably riveted by the sight of my full, upthrust breasts, although I suspect his excitement had more to do with the fact that I was heaving them upward due to all the heavy breathing I'd been doing.

Jake gently began massaging my hardened nipples through the silk, running his thumbs in little circles over them as he dipped his head down to my arched neck, slicking his tongue along its length and sending delicious heat radiating outward. My nails rode up his back, forcing a soft groan that reverberated through the hollows of his throat. Acutely aware of the amount of clothing we were still wearing, I pulled Jake's shirt over his back before sucking his lower lip into my mouth and continuing on with a duel of feverish kisses.

Our bodies writhed with a labored impatience. It had been a long time since either of us had felt such intense cravings. Jake placed his arms on either side of my head and he hovered over my body, staring at me with a hunger that raged through his cloudy eyes.

"You're the sexiest thing I've ever seen," Jake said, sounding gravelly with desire. He gripped the waistband of my jeans and unbuttoned me, and I lifted my rump to aid in the removal. His fingers tickled over my bare flesh, sending goosebumps across my skin. I couldn't get him close enough.

"I need you," I breathed out slowly, reached for his throbbing length. Jake lowered his jeans just enough to free himself from the fabric, and his hardness pressed forward. In one fluid motion, I opened to him, wrapping my legs around his waist as he sank into me.

The bed moved to the rhythm of his slow and methodical thrusts, my hands grasping his buttocks as I brought him down harder. Jake's fingers circled my nipples, tightening them to his touch. I curved my back upward, stretching my shoulders back, and thrust my chest against his constantly moving body.

Reaching behind me, under the flow of my hair, Jake deftly released the clasp of my bra and dipped his head to swirl his tongue in a tantalizing tease over my taut, prickled skin. I clutched his head with both hands, running my fingers through his damp brown hair. A warm, delicious feeling of pleasure began coiling deep inside me. We moved with more intensity now, both letting go of the tension that had gripped our lives for too long. Why had I deprived myself of his love? No more. Tightening my legs around him, I rode his storm all the way to the euphoric end.

There was a renewed closeness between Jake and me after that night. We were like newlyweds again, sneaking in butt pats, neck nibbles, and near consecutive late night romps after the kids fell asleep. There was no more talk about babies and ovulation. Having the kids with us changed my mindset. Of course I still wanted a baby, but I was no longer going to force it. I had plenty of time to be a mom; but right now, what I wanted to be was a committed aunt, a loving wife, and a ravenous lover.

Jake was fully on board with the change in my demeanor. There was a playfulness to him that I hadn't seen in a long while. For the first time, I really understood how much my sadness had been dragging him down. When the angst had been on the other foot and it was I who watched him suffer, I'd felt that heaviness too. But as we'd moved past the struggles, the sun began to shine again.

That's what I had to do now. This past week had convinced me that I needed to lift the layer of fog that was clouding my heart and begin the arduous task of living life without my brother and his wife. It wouldn't be easy. I missed Miles and Darcy every day, but just as I'd said to Sydney the first night she arrived, they wouldn't want us to waste our lives away crying for them. The only way to truly honor Miles and Darcy's memories was to keep moving forward, to keep living the life they'd want for us.

Contentedly watching Sydney and Riley laughing and splashing around in the hotel pool, I looked up to the sky. "Do you see?" I whispered. "They're okay."

I hoped Miles was looking down on his babies with a smile on his face, knowing that they were loved and cared for, that Mom and Dad were doing right by them, and that Jake, Luke, and I would make sure his kids were afforded every opportunity life had to offer. Sydney and Riley were the bright, beautiful legacies my brother and his wife had left behind, and as a collective group, we'd see to it that they shone just as brightly without them as they had with. It might take time and patience, but it would happen. These kids would live their lives to the fullest. That would be how we honored their memories. Not by crying or wasting our lives away, pining for what was no longer here. We would live big, laugh loud, and love hard.

As we rolled down another interstate, I longed for the comfort of the hotel. These extended stretches of driving were tough on the kids. They got bored easily, and without a play structure to swing on or a pool to swim in, their excess energy was directed at us. Even off the bus, I was constantly trying to come up with fun new experiences. Sometimes I scored, and other times I crashed and burned. It really was a learning curve, and only through trial and error had I figured out what was and was not fun for them. For instance, informational stops where there was no climbing involved – not fun. Parks – fun; but only if they didn't have 'baby' playground equipment. Nature reserves – not fun; at least not without a functioning bathroom nearby. I only needed to clean poop out of one pair of pants to figure that out.

The only surefire way of keeping the kids happy and entertained, I discovered, was if Jake or Kyle were around… or better yet, if they were both present at the same time. For whatever reason, the guys were always way more fun than I was. They were like the fun dads who swooped in after the work was done and sucked up all the glory.

It was with those awesome fellas that I'd left the kids while I was in the bedroom working out some numbers for a client. An hour later, I reemerged to find the 'fun dads' sprawled out on the brown leather sofas looking as if they'd just run a marathon instead of spending an hour in the confines of a bus with two little kids. The TV was on and a princess movie was playing. Clearly Sydney had won whatever battle had happened in my absence. And I was sure there had been one since Jake would never willingly submit himself to such torture. The one time I'd convinced him to watch a 'princess movie,' a live-action version of Cinderella, he'd grabbed a bottle of whiskey and took a pull every time someone said 'true love.' Needless to say, he was drunk by the end of the movie.

Since Riley appeared to have the anti-princess gene as well, he was entertaining himself by climbing all over the lethargic guys. He was currently straddling the top of Jake's head.

"Do you know what personal space means, Ri?" he asked, trying to dislodge my nephew.

"No." Riley giggled as he shifted positions, a Twizzler stick protruding from his mouth.

"I didn't think so. Let me explain the meaning to you. It's when you allow the person you are annoying a small buffer of space. In this case, I'd settle for six inches."

"I don't know what you said."

"Which part?"

"None of it," Riley said, poking his finger in Jake's ear. "How come your ear is so big?"

Jake swatted his hand away. "I don't know. I wasn't aware that it was. Hey, I have a good idea. Why don't you play with Kyle? He doesn't care about giving people personal space either. Do you, Kyle?"

"Nope," he said, grinning, as he chomped on his own Twizzler.

Jake extracted Riley and dumped him onto his brother. And like a flea clomping on to a new host, Riley immediately latched onto Kyle, refusing to let him go.

"Hey, you have big ears too," he said, poking his finger into Kyle's ear canal.

"Get your finger out of my earhole."

Now Riley was examining his face up close and personal.

"And don't even think about sticking that finger of yours in my nose hole."

Sydney broke from the movie to comment on Kyle's word choices. "Does everything have a hole with you?"

"Anything that's important does, yeah."

Grinning like a fool, Sydney observed Kyle with starry eyes. I was pretty sure her crush on Jake had jumped over to him. She absolutely loved having Kyle around, so he began accompanying us on any outings that required security. That arrangement not only made the kids happy, but Kyle as well.

Turning Kyle's face toward him once more, Riley said, "Your nose is big, too."

"Only because you're seven. If you were normal-sized, it would look smaller."

"Really, Kyle?" Jake questioned, his brows raised in amusement. "Is that how it works?"

"Do you see Riley questioning my explanation? No. Not like your whole personal space speech. You've got to get down on their level, bro."

Riley was now busy prying Kyle's mouth open when I noticed him holding something.

"What's that in your hand?" I asked.

"My tooth," Riley said, totally unconcerned.

Jake and Kyle both bolted upright as I hurried over to check his mouth. Sure enough, there was a big gaping hole where his tooth used to be, and droplets of blood on Kyle's shirt.

"You didn't even tell me one was loose," I said.

"It just got loose when I was eating the Twizzler, so I yanked it out."

Jake and I both startled at the information.

"Didn't it hurt?" I asked.

"Nope. They're just baby teeth. And I get money when the tooth fairy comes."

"I love this kid," Kyle said, nodding his approval. "He's a trippy little dude."

I stretched my hand out for the tooth and set it in a plastic bag. I wasn't sure what the protocol was for baby teeth, but I figured it was best to keep it until further notice.

Once I'd cleaned Riley up, I plopped down next to Jake, who had taken to watching the movie.

"Look at you all into the movie," I teased, patting his thigh.

Jake's eyes rolled up as his tongue lolled out. "You cannot tell me that there isn't another woman in the entire kingdom who has her same shoe size."

"*That's* what you have a problem with?" I laughed, poking him in the side like Riley had been doing earlier. "Not the mice who turn into horses or the pumpkin that turns into a carriage?"

"I'm just saying, Casey, if you were a slovenly maiden – which, let's be honest, you sometimes are" – he smiled mischievously, flinching away in anticipation of the smack he both expected and deserved – "and then suddenly you put on a ball gown and did your hair up all fancy and shit, I'd still be able to tell it was you."

"It's a fantasy, Jake. It isn't meant to be psychoanalyzed. And watch your language around the kids."

"Sorry, guys. I meant shucks."

I could already hear Riley mimicking Jake's *fancy and shit* in a faint whisper and knew it would be resurfacing sometime in the near future. Sydney was no longer focused on the movie but on Jake's lively retelling of it.

"My point is, that prince is totally shallow. If he loved her that much after one dance, he would've been able to pick her out of a crowd without a damn shoe."

"Jake," I reprimanded again.

"Dammit. I mean darn it. Not swearing is really hard." He sighed. "Anyway, listen up, Sydney. A guy like that is not worth your time."

"A cartoon prince?" she asked, confused.

"Well, no, not him specifically. I'm talking the living, breathing kind. Those kinds should like you even in a pair of Chucks."

"Wow, Jake," Kyle said sarcastically. "Such a beautiful sentiment."

"Can you do better?"

"Yeah, actually, I can. Sydney, don't ever date a douche. Six words. Bam!" He made his fist explode to complement his advice.

"Kyle!" I scolded. "Language."

"Sorry, I meant boom."

"That's not…" I began, before stopping myself. These guys were hopeless, and I refused to be their mom. "Oh, whatever."

"You're looking at swearing all wrong. Think of dirty words more like sentence enhancers," Kyle said.

"You two are twenty-four and twenty-five respectively. I feel like there are less offensive ways of getting your points across."

"Well, you'd think," Jake said, sounding every bit like the troublemaker he was, before grabbing me around the waist and knocking me sideways on the couch. He was on me in a second, blowing raspberries into my collarbone. I squealed, wriggling my way out of his hold, but just as I was about to right myself, the kids, having watched our display in anticipation, took the opportunity to dog pile on top of us. We were already screaming when Kyle dropped into our love circle. The noise level only escalated from that point on as we screeched with laughter.

From the front of the bus, Lassen opened the partition and hollered, "Shut the hell up!"

And without skipping a beat, we all yelled in unison, "Language!"

CHAPTER SEVENTEEN

JAKE

The Rookie

We woke up the next morning to uncontrollable crying. Riley. Casey and I shot out of bed just as he was entering the room with Sydney's arm draped over his shoulder.

"Sweetie, what's wrong?" Casey asked, dropping to her knees and checking his body for injuries.

Wiping at the tears with the palm of his hands, he sniffled, "She didn't come."

"Who didn't come?"

"The Tooth Fairy."

It felt like I'd taken a punch to the nuts. I forgot the fucking Tooth Fairy! I had one job last night, just one, and it was to not forget to put money under Riley's pillow. Epic, goddamn fail. Casey and I traded horrified glances, each trying to blame the other for dropping the ball. Her eyes were all accusation and mine all contempt. Sure, I forgot, but it was Casey's fault for trusting me with such an important job in the first place.

Trying to figure a way to make this right, I rumpled Riley's hair and said, "Dude. It's probably there. You just didn't look hard enough."

Casey flashed me her most hopeful face as if she thought maybe I hadn't just ruined this boy's faith in fictional fairies forever. Hell, I might as well just out Santa Claus while I'm at it. The grim shake of my head put an end to her optimism. Not only had I forgotten the Tooth Fairy, but I was also lying out my teeth to a seven-year-old boy.

"Nope," Syd said, her disappointment in us evident with every subsequent word she spoke. "We pulled the sheets off. No money. No note. No nothing."

"The Tooth Fairy hates me." Riley collapsed to the floor, sobbing.

"No. No, sweetheart. She loves you." The kindness Casey spoke was reserved exclusively for Riley. I got nothing but angry eyes and a scornful mouth miming the word 'Money.'

"It's still early," she explained to him. "Maybe the Tooth Fairy was just delayed. Why don't we go to the bathroom and get cleaned up? Then we'll look up her phone number, okay?"

Riley looked between us, his sad eyes devoid of trust, but because he had no other choice, he sucked up his snot and followed Casey to the bathroom.

Once the two had disappeared, I felt another scornful gaze burrowing into me. "Really, Rock Star?" Sydney said, planting her hand on her hip. "You can't spare a dollar bill?"

"That's not the issue. I just forgot."

"Who forgets the Tooth Fairy? You lose a tooth, you get the money. It's not difficult."

"Yeah, Syd. I get the concept," I said, grabbing for my wallet and hastily opening it up. Shit! I only had fifties and hundreds.

"Go snag me Casey's purse from the front room," I demanded of my niece, sweat now dampening my forehead. Sydney took off in the opposite direction as I searched the drawers for loose change. She came back panting. "I can't find it."

"You can't find the purse?" I blurted out a little more aggressively than I would have liked.

"Hey, don't shoot the messenger."

"Okay, sorry. Do you have any money?"

"I'm ten."

"Right. I've got to think." Then it hit me… Lassen. He'd have change. But just as I was about to run to the front of the bus, I heard Casey call out a warning loud enough for me to hear.

"Let's go see if the Tooth Fairy made it here yet."

"Shit!" I whisper-swore.

Sydney's eyes widened as she slapped her hands over her mouth and started jumping up and down. Damn, she dealt with stress worse than me. Out of options, I grabbed a fifty out of my wallet and slid it under his pillow just as the bathroom door swung open and Riley ran for his bed. Syd squeaked and buried her head in my stomach.

Gripped with anxiety, Casey rushed to my side. "Please tell me you took care of it?"

"Oh, he took care of it, all right," Sydney said, finding great amusement in our shared trials.

We heard Riley gasp and then a sudden whoop of happiness. "No way!" he yelled. "A fifty-dollar bill?"

Casey gaped at me. "You can't give him fifty dollars, Jake. The going rate for a tooth is *one*."

"Yeah, well, you could've given me a couple more minutes to secure the ransom."

Casey might not have been thrilled by the dollar amount, but one person sure was. Riley was thoroughly delighted by the generosity of the tour bus Tooth Fairy, and he let his happiness soar, shouting to the heavens as he kissed his fifty-dollar bill. "I love you, Tooth Fairy," he proclaimed. "And I'm sorry I called you a diarrhea head."

"See?" I said to Casey. "He's happy. Disaster averted."

Syd nodded her head in agreement. "I'm knocking my tooth out tonight."

Although I'd proven my lack of trustworthiness with the Tooth Fairy incident, people kept giving me more chances to screw up. And when I said people, I meant Casey. She seemed to have more faith in me than I was worth. The kids had been with us nearly three weeks, and during that time, Casey had taken on the vast majority of childcare. She'd been wearing thin from daily outings with Sydney and Riley, working her freelance job, and making sure the kids were emotionally secure, all while I continued on with my normal routine.

Occasionally I joined her and the kids, but more often than not, I had commitments that needed tending to. She understood that and it wasn't an issue… until I had a day off. Then I was fair game, and there was nowhere to hide.

Take today, for example. Casey had a deadline looming, and while I'd been hanging out with the kids – the three of us had been engaged in parallel play, me on my keyboard and them with their toys – apparently that wasn't enough.

"I have to finish this by tonight, and honestly, I need a little break."

"Yeah. Sure. We'll play some video games."

"No," she said abruptly, the word bursting from her mouth aggressively. My eyes expanded in response. Seeing my surprise, Casey tried for a calmer approach, but I'm not going to lie, it still came out like a youth football coach barking orders out to all his pint-sized players. "Video games are noisy and someone always gets mad – usually it's you. No, what I want is for you to take them away… FAR, FAR away… for just a few hours."

"Oh. Do you mean like…outside? By myself? Without you?"

"Yes, Jake, that's what I mean."

She wanted them, and me, gone. It was a fairly straightforward demand: take the kids away for a few hours or die a long and brutal death. Okay, so maybe it wasn't that dramatic, but I wasn't keen to find out just how far she'd go to secure a little freedom. After all, Casey was looking especially disheveled and fidgety. Just the fact that it was noon and she still hadn't changed out of her pajamas or brushed her hair was indication enough that, if I balked at her request, shit was going down.

When Casey had the whole Medusa thing going on, I listened. No sense in needlessly turning to stone. Besides, she'd committed me to the task before even asking. Refusing was not an option. The only question now was how much effort she'd require me to put in.

"Okay…um…," I said. "Where am I supposed to take them?"

"I don't know. I just Google 'fun things to do with kids in the area,'" she said, distracted. "You can do this, can't you?"

No. I was pretty sure I couldn't. In fact, I was fairly convinced that I was nowhere near competent enough to go out on my own with two kids, and I was about to confess that to Casey until I caught sight of her eyes. They were blazing hot, as if she were preparing for my stoning. Maybe messing with her right now would not be the best choice. No, I could most likely do this. It was just for a few hours. Besides, they were two little kids. How hard could they possibly be?

"Sure, babe, no problem," I said, as an idea, a really goddamn good idea, popped into my head. Kyle. "I'll get my brother to come with me, and we'll take them somewhere."

"Kyle can't go. He's picking up Kenzie at the airport today."

Ah, shit. I wanted to stomp my feet and complain, but I was entirely too old for that behavior to be cute anymore. There was no way around it. I was going out by myself with the kids. Today was going to suck balls. With no options left, it was time to be a man. Placing my hand on her shoulder, I bent down to kiss her cheek. "No worries. I'll take care of everything. You go get some work done, and I'll wrangle up the herd."

"Thank you. You're a lifesaver. Can you shut the door behind you?"

And then there was just me… and them… in the wide, open world. Did anyone else see a problem with that? If there was a guy less qualified to babysit kids than I was, I'd like to meet the hapless dude. I mean, I was a decent playmate to Sydney and Riley, and had become a reluctant slave to their every want and need, but that didn't mean I could be trusted to keep them safely by my side in a public place.

From my position plastered up against the bedroom door, I watched the two kids lying on their stomachs on the floor of the bus, happily watching YouTube videos together. They looked so sweet and innocent, but I knew better. These moments of peace were actually just them fully charging up their batteries so they could then use their stored energy against me later.

Sydney, sensing my presence, held up her empty plastic bowl and without even bothering to make eye contact, asked, "Can I get some more berries, please?"

Pushing away from the safety of my bedroom door, I walked over and grabbed her bowl. After filling it with some more berries, I handed it back to her. She thanked me, but again, no eye contact.

"Can I get some more berries too, please?" Riley asked, not taking his hands or eyes off the screen. Instead of hand-ing his bowl to me, he just kicked it over. I picked it up off the floor and filled it with berries too.

"Oh, and Jake?" Sydney called out. "Crackers too."

Irritated, I grasped the kitchen counter attempting to hold my tongue. Who did they think I was, their personal servant? I didn't see any obvious injuries that might prevent them from getting to their own feet and preparing something tasty. I walked back and handed the berries to Riley.

Sydney turned and raised a brow at me. "Did you forget my crackers?"

"Nope," I said, defiantly. "I'm just not going to get them for you."

"Really?" she asked, intrigued by my rebellion.

"Really, Syd. I'm not your snack bitch. Get them yourself."

I now had both kids' undivided attention, and once they saw the smile on my face, they understood I was kidding. The two dissolved into hysterical laughter. At least my swearing had their attention, and what Casey didn't know wouldn't hurt her. It was time to get this show on the road. With the clap of my hands and the boom of my voice, I announced, "Who wants to go on an adventure with me today?"

Riley jumped from the floor in an instant and flung himself at me. I caught him mid-flight. I took that as a yes. Sydney was more practical in her response.

"Just you?" she asked, sounding every bit as skeptical as I felt.

"It looks that way."

"You sure that's a good idea?"

"No." I laughed. "It's not a good idea at all, but I don't have a choice. So what do you say?"

A wide smile broke out across her face as she eyed me with a splash of mischief. "Heck, yeah, I want to go. This ought to be good."

"Yay. Yay. Triple yay!" Riley sang out, obsessively repeating the same phrase until Syd covered his mouth with her hand.

"I wouldn't get too excited, Ri, he's probably just taking us to some boring baby park."

It was obvious by her tone that Sydney had no faith in my abilities, but she underestimated me. I was no ordinary snack bitch. No. I was a goddamn rock star, and if I couldn't bring the fun, no one could.

"No, Syd, not a boring baby park," I mimicked her condescending attitude. "We'll go wherever you guys want to go."

So that was my first mistake.

I was such a rookie. Who let me off the bench in the first place? The only positive that came from my blunder was that I learned a valuable parenting lesson: never let kids be part of the decision making process when it came to outings. Because if you did, they'd choose Chuck E. Cheese every single time.

Mistake number two was requiring my niece and nephew to be clean and presentable. Unbeknownst to me, with kids this age, some assistance and assembly was required. Had I known what a production number it would become, I would've dragged two little snot monsters around all day and been happier for it.

Sydney refused my help, proclaiming she could manage the task on her own; but Riley – oh, Riley! – he was like three kids in one. The boy stood in the bathroom for five minutes just waiting for me to come in and turn the water on. He didn't even bother to call me. He just waited there in the bathroom naked, driving his matchbox car all over the basin. Had I not popped my head in to see if he was done, he might have stood there all day.

And once he did finally manage to shower, Riley needed help with everything. I had to towel dry his hair and brush his teeth and help him into his clothes and tie his shoes, all while he played. I had no idea what kids their ages should be capable of, but I was fairly convinced that Riley was just playing me so he didn't have to do any of the work.

My third mistake was inviting Lassen to come along.

I knocked on his partition. "Lassen?"

He opened immediately like he was engaged in a game of peekaboo and let out a quick, jolting growl.

"Oh, shit." I jumped back.

"Sorry, I thought you were the kids," he grumbled.

"That's how you greet them?" I asked in surprise.

"What do you want, Jake? I'm busy."

"Since we both have the day off, I was thinking we could hang out… go to lunch or something."

Instinctively I knew adding the kids into the equation would not go over well, so I chose to leave out that valuable piece of information. So too did I understand that any mention of Chuck E. Cheese's would be viewed like the petri dish of death for a germaphobe like Lassen, so I omitted that too. At this point, my information was given out strictly on a need-to-know basis.

"All right. Sure," he replied. "That sounds fun."

If he only knew just how much fun he was about to have…

I went back to check on the kids' progress. Sydney was wearing purple sweats and an orange t-shirt with the saying, "The cool kid just showed up." I had a good laugh at that before deeming her ready to go. Riley had switched the shirt I'd just dressed him in, and the neon yellow one he was now wearing was inside out, but once I corrected it, I was happy with my colorful troops.

Mistake number four was having the kids say goodbye to Casey.

"Are you serious?" she asked me, just the hint of a smile on her face.

"What?"

"Jake, they can't go out like that. Sydney doesn't even match."

"She doesn't?"

"No. You can't put purple and orange together, and look at her hair. She needs to comb it, at least. And Riley, is that your pajama top? Wait – does he have shampoo in his hair?"

"I don't know."

"What do you mean, you don't know? You didn't help him shower?"

"No. Was I supposed to?"

"Well, he has shampoo in his hair, so yeah, you probably needed to help him."

Casey got up from her table and shooed the kids back into the bathroom. A few minutes later they came back looking clean and color-coordinated. I wasn't sure what type of black magic she'd employed, but I wanted some of it.

With a sly smile, Casey grabbed my face in her hand and kissed my lips. "You're funny. It's a wonder you make it out the door everyday on your own."

"I know. It's a flippin' miracle," I agreed, happy to see her less stressed.

"Thank you for doing this for me. I really appreciate it." Casey then leaned in and whispered, "I'll make it up to you later."

I grinned. "I'm going to Chuck E. Cheese's for you, so yeah, you'd better."

"Chuck E. Cheese's?" She gasped as if I'd just told her I was taking them for a spin on an alien spacecraft. In hindsight, maybe that would have been easier. "By yourself?"

"No, I'm bringing Lassen and Vadim, just in case Chuck E. gets handsy."

Casey shook her head uncertainly. "When I said take them out for a few hours, I assumed you'd start small, like a park or something. Chuck E. Cheese's is like the big leagues, Jake. Are you sure you know what you're getting yourself into?"

I shrugged. How hard could it be? "I'll be fine. Get your work done and take a nap. We're going to have a great time."

I announced the last sentence loud enough for the kids to hear. They yelled their approval.

Moments later, Lassen crawled out of his hole. Since the kids' arrival, he'd been hiding out in the front of the bus as much as possible. He let me know every chance he got how unhappy he was with the current living arrangement. And I'd let him know that I didn't care what he thought. Lassen was spoiled. He'd had it good for too long. It was time for him to pay his dues.

My driver stopped dead in his tracks when he saw the kids' excited faces. Lassen's eyes immediately found mine and they narrowed to angry little slits. Just wait until he figured out where we were going. Those slits would be pointed missiles.

"You ready?" I asked, in a high-pitched and overly excited voice. The kids ate it up, running and screaming out of the bus.

Casually, I walked passed Lassen, purposely avoiding the eye daggers he was shooting at me. "You coming?"

With a loud, exaggerated huff, Lassen stomped off the bus.

I had hoped to surprise my disgruntled driver with our mystery destination, but Riley was enthusiastically belting out a song of his own creation, appropriately titled, "I can't wait to get to Chuck E. Cheese." Interestingly enough, he just repeated the chorus over and over. I was going to have to work with him a bit on his songwriting skills.

The scowl on Lassen's face had not eased one bit the entire car ride. Maybe I thought he'd gradually accept his fate, but by the looks of it, he was going to hate me for a very long time.

After pulling into the parking lot, he leaned over and whispered a threat for my ears only. "I won't forget this."

Walking into the establishment, I immediately understood what Casey meant by calling it the big leagues. This place was teeming not only with sugared-up kids but wildly frustrated adults as well. I glanced at Lassen, who was already holding his hands over his ears. I had to agree – the sound level in Chuck E. Cheese's was unlike anything I'd experienced before, and I was used to music blasting in my ears on a near daily basis. It was an odd mix of screaming kids, pop music, pinging and binging of hundreds of machines, and the sounds of "Happy Birthday" being sung every few minutes by Chuck E. and friends.

I grabbed Lassen by the arm to move him along. He'd gone into some freaky survival mode, complete with glazed over eyes and emotional detachment. It was like the lights were on but nobody was home.

"You all right there, bud?" I asked, patting his back. "I'm going to need you to snap out of this because you and I are about to divide and conquer. Which one do you want, Sydney or Riley?"

"I want to go home."

"That's not one of your options. If you don't choose, I'll pick one for you."

Sydney and Riley had two totally different approaches to enjoying their day. Syd wanted tickets, lots of tickets. Apparently her strategy was to hoard as many as possible so that she then could trade them in for a toy, which in the end would cost four times what it would have at Target.

Riley didn't give a rat's ass about the tickets. He was all about the games, and this particular place seemed to have hundreds of them to choose from. The minute I stepped foot in the establishment, I knew keeping both kids happy was not possible without a tag team approach, and that's why I was now giving Lassen the option.

"Sydney," he mumbled.

"That's the spirit," I said, grinning.

Lassen spent the next hour or so following Sydney around and mindlessly supplying her with endless amounts of tokens. It had been a wise choice, indeed, because there was no way my friend could have survived the more physically demanding activities Riley was choosing, like Dance Dance Revolution and the Human Hamster Wheel.

The one giant positive to being in a kid's joint like this was that no one, and I mean no one, was expecting me to be in such a place. With a baseball cap pulled down over my forehead, I could have been any other dad chasing his kids around.

Vadim stood off to the side watching the proceedings, all while keeping a healthy distance away so as not to draw attention to me. Unfortunately that strategy backfired, as my security guy was targeted by a suspicious group of moms. I could see their point; he was definitely giving off a pervy vibe standing there in the corner by himself looking out over the crowd of kids.

The situation grew out of control faster than a brush fire fanned by the Santa Ana winds, and soon Vadim, an ex-Russian mercenary, was at the center of the firestorm. Moms with pitchforks closed ranks around him, demanding an explanation for his whole creeper-in-a-corner act.

A pimply teenaged manager was called into action. He weighed all of a hundred and twenty pounds and shivered as he got his first look at Vadim in all his Terminator glory.

"S...S...Sir do you have a child here?"

Vadim didn't answer. Nor did he even turn his head to acknowledge the guy.

The rail-thin little manager reached his arm toward Vadim, possibly to lead him out of the establishment, but if he laid even one finger on my bodyguard, I was certain he'd be in a deadly chokehold in a matter of seconds.

Sending Riley over to Lassen, I broke through the group and introduced myself. As I pulled my cap off, several people actually gasped.

"Guys, it's okay. He's my bodyguard. Sorry if he startled you. He was just trying to protect me."

The manager's mouth dropped open. He couldn't have been older than nineteen. I wondered what life skills this kid possessed to have been made manager of a Chuck E. Cheese's, or to potentially handle a situation with a real pervert in the place.

"I'd appreciate it if we could keep this quiet, so I can stay here a little longer with my niece and nephew."

"Oh, yeah... Okay...uh...I... Sure, sorry."

"We're good, then?"

"Um...yes." The man-child manager turned to the mommy gang and asked, "Are you all okay with this now?"

There was a collective head nod from the mob, and as they dissipated, I replaced my cap and grabbed Vadim's arm, dragging him with me as I went back to the kids. Only I couldn't find them. Or Lassen.

"Shit, where are they?" I immediately felt a tightness in my chest. I knew better than anyone how quickly things could turn wicked.

Vadim went into mercenary mode. His body taut with purpose, he scanned the play area like it was a battlefield.

"Jake!" Sydney waved, calling out to me as she glided down the slide coming from the Sky Tubes. One kid, thank god.

"Where's Riley?" I asked, still trying to make sense of his disappearance.

"In the tubes, with Lassen."

All tension dissolved as I processed the words she'd spoken.

Gaping at her in surprise, I asked, "Lassen's in the tubes?"

"Uh-huh. I think he might be stuck, though," Sydney said, as if a man the size of Lassen stuck in a suspended hamster house was no big deal.

"Wait, Syd, are you sure he's stuck?"

"Well, he's crying, so…"

"Lassen's crying?" The shock of what I was hearing was causing my head to spin.

"Actually, it was more like moaning." She proceeded to mimic the sound he was making.

"Oh, god, where are they?"

She pointed up to the highest tube. "You want me to show you?"

"Yeah, that might be a good idea."

Mistake number five was inviting Lassen to come along. I realize that I already mentioned this mistake, but with the current situation we found ourselves in, I feel it's worth repeating.

Sydney scaled the rope walls like Spiderman. My journey up wasn't as effortless. I wasn't that old, but damn, I felt like I was, as kids as young as four whizzed passed me at lightning speed. How in the hell had Lassen gotten up here? Although he'd lost quite a few pounds as a result of a health scare last year, he was still a big man.

It didn't take long to figure out where Lassen was. There was a human traffic jam twelve kids long. Most of them were turning around and squeezing by me to use another tunnel by the entrance. I crawled toward Lassen who was lying on his stomach at a bend in the tubes. Riley was sitting behind him patting him on the back.

Sydney got to them first and impatiently demanded, "Move it, big man."

"Back off!" Lassen's growl echoed through the tubes.

"Dude, are you stuck?" I asked, finally reaching my friend.

"No. I'm claustrophobic."

"He was crying," Riley offered.

"I wasn't crying, I was panicking. There's a difference."

The situation was too funny not to laugh. So I did. Hysterically. Sydney and Riley joined me.

"When you're done, will you call the fire department, please?" Lassen panted. "They're going to need the jaws of life to cut me out of here."

"You don't need rescuing. I'll help you," I said, before addressing my niece. "Syd, I want you to take Riley back through the entrance and then wait with Vadim until I come out."

"Not a chance. I don't want to miss a second of this."

"Sydney," I scolded through barely controlled laughter, "if you do what I say, and you hold Riley's hand, and you stand next to Vadim until I get Lassen out, I will buy you a buttload of tickets so you can get any toy in the prize booth."

Syd eyeballed me. "Any toy?"

"That's right."

"I want the giant pastel slinky."

"Done."

I was pleasantly surprised by how easily Syd caved. Damn, bribery was a legit parenting tactic. I didn't care how much that giant slinky was going to cost me; my niece's cooperation would be worth every penny.

"Okay, come on, Riley."

"Hold his hand the whole time, Syd. That's the deal."

"I know. I know. See you on the other side, Rock Star."

"How old are you again?" I laughed, and then turned my attention back to Lassen as the kids scooted back out and climbed down through the entrance. "Okay, I think our best bet is to have you move forward and not back."

"I'm not going anywhere. Perhaps you didn't hear me. I can't fucking move," he spat, under his breath. "And I don't appreciate you laughing at me. This is all your fault in the first place."

"Hey, I just brought you here. You're the chump who decided to take a tour through the tubes."

"For you, Jake."

"Me?"

"You handed Riley off to me, and then the little shit took off into the tubes. I had no choice but to follow him in."

Now I felt somewhat bad for him… nah, not really. His predicament was what *America's Funniest Home Videos* was made for.

"Dude, I hate to say this in such crude terms, but you're like a giant butt plug…nothing's going in or out. Kids are piling up, and it's only going to get worse. So what I need you to do is to take a deep breath and start squirming your way out."

I felt a tug on my shirt.

"Excuse me, mister," a little voice said. I looked back to find the most adorable little golden-haired girl, no more than four, trying to climb over me. Her pigtails bobbed as she again repeated. "Excuse me."

"You're not going to be able to get through," I tried to explain to her. "It's best to go the other way."

"But I want to go down the slide," she pouted.

Coming up behind her was her dad. "What's the hold up? Is he all right?"

"He's just a little claustrophobic," I explained. "Give me a second, okay."

"Is he dead, daddy?" the girl asked.

"No, he's not dead. Hey, wait a minute, are you Jake McKallister?"

"Yeah, I am."

I pushed on Lassen with all my might, but he simply tilted to the right and did not move.

"No way! I mean, *no way!* This is crazy. What are you doing at a Chuck E. Cheese's? You don't have kids, do you?"

"I'm here with my niece and nephew."

"I can't believe this. Can I take a picture with you?"

"Oh, my god," I heard Lassen complain.

"I'm kind of busy right now," I explained, even though the situation seemed fairly self-explanatory. "But after I get him out… sure."

"Yeah, yeah, no problem. Can I help?"

Another child and adult came up behind the dad and his daughter.

"It's Jake McKallister," he filled in the newbies. They were sufficiently impressed. A camera flashed. And then another.

"Lassen, if you start inching forward, I'll buy you a pastel slinky from the prize booth."

"Shut up. I'm moving."

And much to my surprise, he had wriggled his big body past the bend and was slowly but surely slithering his way through the tubes. I crawled after him. Behind me was an ever-growing pile-up of bodies. After making another turn, I could see the slide directly ahead.

"That's it, buddy. Just follow the light."

Lassen didn't find me funny in the least. His panting was out of control, like a dog in some serious heat. Through the power of sheer will and terror, though, my driver mercifully arrived at the top of the slide; but instead of maneuvering his body around and taking the ramp on his ass, Lassen just inched his body forward and slid down head-first like a rag doll. When he got to the bottom, Lassen oozed his exhausted body off the slide and collapsed into a heap.

Sydney, still holding Riley's hand, walked over and nudged him with her shoe. "You okay there, big man?"

I didn't hear Lassen's reply but, by the look of surprise on Syd's face, he hadn't used a PG-13 word.

After rescuing Lassen from his living hell, we allowed him to lick his wounds in a far corner, while the kids and

I continued to play. True to my word, I began buying the place out of tickets so I could win my niece her coveted giant pastel slinky. Syd's bargain prize was understandably impressive. I should have known it wouldn't be your average everyday slinky. No, this one was the size of a large possum, and somehow we were going to have to make room for it in the confines of the tour bus. Riley went for a less remarkable yet still highly satisfying Nerf gun. They were happy.

Less happy was Vadim, who'd been forced to call in back-up when my presence at Chuck E. Cheese began making the rounds on social media. Crowds surged through the front doors as Vadim shuttled us into a private party room. While waiting for rescue, the kids and I used the left over *Frozen* party supplies to decorate Vadim. At six foot five and a solid wall of human steel, the man didn't flinch once; but then after the incident with Riley in the plane, he really didn't have room for dissent.

Once safely in the car on our way back to the venue, I struggled to keep my weary eyes open. Never had I needed a nap more than today. Casey was right. I should've started off small. From this day forward, it was T-ball all the way for me.

Chapter Eighteen

Casey

The Secret Keeper

Jake and I, along with Kyle and Kenzie, watched from a distance as Luke attempted to flirt with a woman at the open bar. It seemed to be going well at first, with him sliding in next to her and offering up some funny tidbit to break the ice. She smiled, tilting her head back. Definitely interested. This was good. Jake and Kyle clinked their beer bottles together, proudly cheering on their protégé. They'd spent the last hour giving him lady-wooing tips, and once they felt their baby bird was ready to fly, Luke was kicked out of the nest; or in this case, the luxury poolside cabana we were all sharing.

It was family week on the Outlast tour. True to his word, Luke had secured time off work and was staying with us for the last six days of the kids' visit. Kenzie had arrived in town a couple of days before him, but I hadn't seen much of her. She and Kyle had been holed up in a hotel room. I didn't blame them one bit, as the two hadn't been together for nearly three months due to work responsibilities.

Since moving to Los Angeles, Kenzie had become quite the social media darling after starting her own YouTube channel for small town girls living in the big city. Her fun personality combined with a talent for connecting with the average, everyday person had brought her millions of subscribers and started her on a path to a whole new career.

Initially she'd planned to take her show on the road and travel with the tour, as she'd been doing since getting together with Kyle. The two had even bought their own motorhome for the road. But then an opportunity presented itself that she couldn't pass up. Kenzie was tapped to fill in for a daytime talk show featuring a panel of women when one of the leads went on a three-month maternity leave after the birth of her child. Although she'd appeared on a reality show, Kenzie had never done live television so she was initially quite hesitant to accept the job. Kyle was the one who ultimately talked her into doing the show and so began their long-distance relationship.

Jake and Kyle, having the day off, joined us at the pool. The cabana was in a secured area, so Jake was able to relax without worrying about being bothered, and the kids were currently off having a blast at the hotel-provided child care facility. This was adult time, and we were sucking up the quiet moments.

My hand in Jake's, we sat side by side in our own individual lounge chairs watching the Luke show. Although there were ample chairs around them, Kyle and Kenzie had squeezed into one lounge chair, vying for butt space.

"Hey," Kyle said, wriggling around. "Hands to yourself. I don't appreciate it when you manhandle me like a piece of meat, Kenzie. I have feelings."

"We'll talk about your feelings when you get your hand off my ass."

"I only have it on your ass to keep you from crushing my balls."

Jake audibly groaned before getting up and dragging another lounge chair up next to them. "There. Problem solved."

Following Jake's entire spectacle with his eyes, Kyle turned back to Kenzie with a dopey grin on his face. "Geez, what's his problem?"

"I know," she agreed. "As if we want to be apart. I like squeezing in with you, sweetie."

"Me too, honey-pie."

"Oh, my god. Can you two take that cutesy shit someplace else?" Jake grumbled, but the upturn of his lips gave him away. "I can't hear what Luke's saying."

"He's across the pool, dipshit," Kyle explained. "You couldn't hear him anyway."

"I know, but I just want you to shut up. Oh, damn, look at that…a hand on the shoulder. That's a bold move," Jake said, assessing Luke's performance.

"Too bold," Kyle replied. "We told him no physical contact at the first meeting. Makes him appear desperate."

"But she looks interested, right?" I asked, a hopeful tone to my voice; but one look at the female in question and the way she leaned away from him answered my question. "Crap. She's not."

And just as predicted, the woman got off her stool and walked away.

We all let out an audible sigh. Another one bites the dust. Luke walked back with a dubious smile on his face as if to say, 'See, I told you.'

Obviously, baby bird was not yet prepared to fly, and after giving it his all, he had plummeted to the ground in a puff of feathers.

Luke dropped into an open chair, sprawling out every which way.

Kyle, who'd taken to being his wellness coach asked, "Did you ask to buy her a drink?"

"I did," Luke affirmed. "And she accepted."

"And you told her a joke to break the ice?"

"Yep. She was squirting some Germ-X on her hands when I walked up, so I told her hand sanitizer was a gateway drug for OCD."

"Nice," Kyle smirked. "Good one. And did you compliment something about her?"

Just by the look on Luke's face, this was where things had gone downhill. "I told her she had nice lips."

"Lips?" Kyle's brows shot to the roof. "Lips? That's just... Dude, come on, that's just creepy."

"What? You said nothing cliché like eyes or body."

"I know, but I also said to compliment her shoes or watch. Something she won't take offense to."

"And I would have – had she been wearing a watch or shoes," Luke said, sounding exasperated by the interrogation. "She was wearing a bikini! There was no safe thing to compliment. I panicked."

"Okay. Maybe I was being too ambitious with you. Clearly we need to take baby steps here. Start small... and with fully dressed females."

"Like you're such a closer, Kyle," Kenzie jumped in to the conversation. "I fell for you the first day we met. I followed you around with these honkin' lovesick eyes of mine, and you had no clue."

"Right, but in my defense, you smelled pretty bad."

Kenzie laughed, poking Kyle in the side. "You're such a dick."

"I guess that just leaves us with Jake," I said. "Do you have any swagger you'd like to share with my brother?"

"Yes, Jake," Luke leaned in, interested in his answer. "Please teach me how to objectify women."

"The only time in my entire life that I've ever pursued a woman was your sister. Would you like to hear how I objectified her?"

"No," Luke threw his hand up to stop Jake. "I'd rather die alone. But thank you anyway."

"Who wants to go for ice cream?" Luke called out.

His two intended targets, Sydney and Riley, shot up and ran for the door, screaming, "I do! I do!"

"Anyone?" he joked. Again the kids shrieked. "If only there was more enthusiasm. Hey, do you two want to come?"

"No, thanks," I answered, eyeing Jake with interest. He'd better say no. We hadn't been alone in nearly a month, and Luke had just opened up a window of opportunity.

Catching my vibe, Jake scanned me with a knowing smile before answering, "No, I'm good."

Luke glanced between us, no doubt sensing the smoldering tension, before his face dropped in disgust. "Ew. I'll be sure to get a double scoop."

Once the three had left, I snuck up to the door and peeked out the peephole.

"Are they gone?" Jake asked, his voice full of hope.

I turned around and, using the same high-pitched voice Luke had employed to entice the kids for ice cream, I asked, "Who wants to objectify his wife?"

Jake shot up and ran for the door. "I do!"

Tucked against Jake's sturdy frame, his arms tight around me, I smiled at the memory of our quick and feverish lovemaking session.

Before he'd even finished his sentence, I was in his arms, legs wrapped around his waist, and was pressing impassioned kisses onto his lips. Together we toured the room in a tangle of arms and legs before Jake dropped on top of me on the bed, and we were off. There was no foreplay or sexy banter, just the quick, frenzied sex that came from having no extended alone time together. And then it was over, and here I was, panting in his arms. I giggled at the absurdity of it all.

"What?" he asked, and I could feel his smile against my cheek.

"Nothing. I was just thinking that this is how sex will be once we have our own kids."

"You mean fast? Yeah, sorry. My bad."

"No," I said, turning around to face him. "Not fast. Frantic."

"Shit, I know. That was like a quickie on crack. I keep thinking the kids are going to walk in on us."

"And that's why I have you check the lock…"

"Three times, I know," Jake groaned, rolling onto his back. I turned too, propping myself on an elbow just to soak in his handsome face. "Is it weird that I'm going to miss them?" He added.

My chest burst with love for this man. Even though the whole babysitting thing had been pushed on him, he hadn't shied away. He'd gotten in there and done the job. Yes there were times he seemed way out of his league, but he'd surprised me on more occasions than not. Even with that potty mouth of his, or maybe because of it, Jake was a big hit with Syd and Ri. He might not realize it himself, but my husband was a natural at fatherhood.

Gliding my fingers over his face, I kissed him and whispered, "You're such a good man. Do you know that?"

The smile that forced its way across his lips was not lost on me. It was so subtle, but I knew what to look for.

"What was that?" I asked.

He played dumb. "Huh."

"That smile. Why are you fake-smiling?"

"I'm not faking anything," he protested. "That's the way I smile."

I stubbornly stared in his eyes, trying to get him to admit his deception. He stared back defiantly. At an impasse, I asked, "Why do you do that? Why do you doubt that you're a good person?"

Surprisingly, he let the tension roll off his shoulders and answered me truthfully. "Maybe because I'm not, Casey. Has that thought ever occurred to you?"

"Do you honestly believe that?"

Jake regarded me a moment, behind the hair that fell over his eyes before unexpectedly sitting up. "I don't want to do this right now. Please, just let it go."

I reached for him, but he stood up and moved away from the bed. I watched him grab for his boxers and slide them on.

"I mean, everyone has done something they're not proud of, right?"

"Casey." Jake shook his head. Clearly he was frustrated with me, and couldn't seem to decide what to add to his sentence, so he just stopped at my name.

And now I had a choice: keep pushing for an answer and watch him walk away, or give up on bedside counseling for the sake of peace. I chose the latter simply because I was cold.

"Hey," I said, patting the sheets. "Come on. Don't be pissed. Lie back down with me."

He contemplated his options, clearly hesitant to trust my intentions.

"I promise I won't bring it up. Just come back and warm me up."

Jake relented and crawled back under the covers with me. Pulling him into my arms, I gently placed a kiss on the tip of his nose. A moment passed while we looked intently into each other's eyes.

"Sorry," he mumbled. "I don't know why I did that."

I traced my fingers along his chest, contemplating how I wanted to reply. "Someday, Jake… someday you'll trust me with all your secrets."

He seemed to be considering my words as his body slowly relaxed under my touch.

"Maybe someday, Case. But not today."

Chapter Nineteen

Jake

Go Big

Kyle waited with me in the dressing room before the show. Pacing back and forth, he was making me nervous, and I wasn't even the one proposing.

"Dude, relax."

"Sorry. I feel like I'm going to hurl."

"Stop stressing. It's not like she'll say no."

"Really? Because I'm not so sure about that. I don't have a whole lot to offer her."

"How do you figure?"

Kyle motioned toward his entire self. "I think this speaks for itself."

Maybe a few years ago I would have agreed with his self-deprecating assessment, but Kyle was not the same lazy doofus he'd once been. Of course, what kind of brother would I be if I didn't bust his balls? And this really was the perfect opportunity. "No one said she had taste."

"No." He acknowledged with a chuckle. "Thankfully, Kenzie doesn't have a sophisticated palate."

"Yeah, well, you picked a girl who has her priorities straight. She's not after money and power."

"Thank god, or I'd be screwed."

"For sure. Anyway, as I was about to say… you give Kenzie something no one else can give her."

"Obviously," Kyle said, jokingly pointing towards his shaft and boys. "But I wasn't talking about sex."

"Neither was I." I laughed as well. "Shit, if that was the criteria, I'd be scared right now too."

Kyle flipped me off, the grin on his face dying off as he gave more thought to his impending proposal. I remembered the feeling well and had been as nervous as my brother was now. I imagine there would be nothing quite like getting turned down by the person you want to spend the rest of your life with. Still, Kyle had nothing to worry about. Kenzie was his Casey.

"What if I get out there and get so nervous that I crap my pants?"

I winced at the mental picture.

"You're not helping, Jake."

"You'll be fine," I placated him. "Just focus on her face… and breathe."

"Okay, yeah, you're right," he said, dipping down into a crouched position as he took long, ragged breaths. Looking up at me, he asked, "What can I give her?"

"Huh?"

"You said I could give her something no one else could. What is it?"

"You make her happy, idiot. And trust me when I tell you – that's all that matters."

The plot was in place, and Casey and I were its supporting characters. It actually came as a surprise to me when Kyle told me he was going with the grand romantic gesture for his proposal and not something more laid back, like laying an engagement ring in the middle of a pepperoni pizza and yelling, 'Surprise!' You know the whole rallying cry – 'Go Big or Go Home'? Well, Kyle was the guy that gladly went home… and took a nice, long nap once he got there.

Yet here he was ready to put himself out there in the biggest way possible – in front of a crowd of thousands. If she said no, there'd be no coming back from the humiliation. Not that it seemed likely Kenzie would refuse him, given the fact that she was fully expecting a proposal out of him. Two and a half years was a long time to date without some sort of long-term commitment. At some point, women get tired of waiting, as Keith could readily tell you.

Step one of the plan was to keep Kenzie away from the concert… or at least until I'd had time to prep the audience. Thankfully, talking someone's ear off was Casey's specialty, so I had complete faith in her abilities to stall Kenzie's arrival as well as to make up some excuse why Kenzie had to be looking camera ready. A fake party immediately after the concert had been the ploy.

Step two was getting the audience to do what I'd ask them to do at the exact time requested. I waited until the end of the second song to address the crowd. After going through the standard greeting, I filled them in on Kyle's proposal idea, and not only was the audience game to play along, but excitement buzzed from every corner of the stadium. After they'd participated on the television show Marooned together, Kyle and Kenzie's love story was fairly well known, so getting the crowd enthusiastic for their proposal was no issue at all.

And finally, step three was getting my little brother engaged. In my opinion, there was no one more deserving of a good woman and a great life than Kyle. He was loyal to a fault. If he deemed you deserving, even if sometimes you absolutely were not, there was nothing he wouldn't do for you. I'd been on the receiving end of that devotion my whole life, so I could attest to Kyle's exceptional character.

It made me happy to see that my brother had found someone who could finally turn the spotlight on him.

While performing, I kept an eye out for the cue from Casey. She loved being a part of this – not because she wanted her hand in everything but because Kenzie and Kyle meant so much to her and their love story was something we could both get behind. The go-ahead was delivered to me by way of a schoolyard chain of communication passed from one band member to the next until my guitarist leaned over and whispered, "It's time."

I glanced toward where I knew Kyle was hiding with Sean on the opposite side of the stage. Even though I couldn't see them, I trusted that my manager would get Kyle onto the stage even if he had to drag him out there himself, so I wrapped up the song I was performing and carried the microphone toward the front of the stage, clipping it in the stand before addressing the crowd.

"Lights!" I called out, and like magic, the stadium went black. Seconds later, the glow from thousands of cell phone lights illuminated the darkness and the theme song from *The Blue Lagoon*, a throwback to their reality show days, began to play through the speakers. A spotlight clicked on, showcasing Kyle as he made his way to the center of the stage. Cheering him on, the crowd was electric.

A second spotlight switched on, illuminating Kenzie, who appeared stunned as she stood on the sidelines with her hands clasped over her mouth and eyes opened wide.

It really was a beautiful moment… until Kyle ruined it.

"Kenzie, get your butt out here."

Oh, god, Dude! I'd had so much faith in him until then. You don't start a proposal that way. But then again, maybe you did if you were Kyle since Kenzie appeared to eat that shit up, laughing her way across the stage to meet her man.

Once she arrived, the song cut out, and Kyle said to his beloved possibly the most romantic thing I think I'd ever heard.

"Thanks for coming."

Again, I cringed, Kenzie laughed, and the audience responded with riotous applause. Okay, so apparently Kyle was doing things his way, and it appeared to be working.

Kenzie's smile lit up the already bright stage. "You're welcome."

Taking her hands in his, Kyle stared deeply into her eyes, and I knew this was the moment of truth. My stomach was tied up in knots for him. Kyle wasn't just my younger brother, he was my best friend, and I wanted this to be perfect for him. So I hung on his every word, hoping he didn't mess it up, until it occurred to me that Kyle wasn't aiming for perfection. Unlike me, he'd never required it. He recognized life for what it was and lived it well. He accepted people for who they were and withheld judgment. So it made sense that a proposal from an unpretentious guy like Kyle should be no different. It wasn't going to be polished, or even grammatically correct, but it was going to be heartfelt, loving, and full of humor. That was Kyle.

"On paper, Kenzie, you and I are an odd pairing. You being the pasty white, big Bambi-eyed Northern Californian who says 'Hella' way too often. And me being the sun-kissed, devastatingly handsome Southern California boy who speaks in proper slang. But sometimes, you know, when the stars align, a girl like you gets lucky."

Finding Kyle's opening insults wildly entertaining, Kenzie's face was alive with excitement as she shook her head in amusement.

"Who am I kidding? Of course I'm the lucky one. I'm actually not even sure how I managed to snag a woman like you but I can only assume it had something to do with starvation and disease carrying mosquitos. I'm convinced if we'd met anywhere other than a deserted island, you would've taken a pass on me. But we didn't, and you didn't, and here we are today. I keep waiting for you to come to your senses but thank god you never have because you're my dream girl, Kenz. The day I woke up and realized I was in love with you was the best day of my life. There's no one I'd rather grow old with than you… well, except Jake, but he's taken already. Anyway, you know I'm not a flashy guy and big gestures are something I leave to others, but tonight I make an exception – for you."

Kyle dropped to his knee to a chorus of oohs and aahs from the crowd. He flipped open the ring box. "Tonight,

I'm going big – Mackenzie Ann Williams, will you marry me?"

She said yes.

The time had come to say goodbye to the kids, and as much as I was happy to get back to normal, I was going to miss them; more than I thought I would. The thing about kids was, they didn't care who you were. In their eyes, adults were nothing more than snack bitches. And in my spoiled world, it was a refreshing change of pace.

"Where's your bag?" I asked. Both the kids' luggage had been sitting at the door moments ago, and now only Riley's remained.

Sydney crossed her arms. "I put it back. I'm not going."

My eyes widened. "You're not?"

"Nope. I'm staying with you guys."

I immediately sought out Casey, who appeared just as perplexed as I was.

"No, sweetie, you are going back," she said, stepping into the conversation. "You, me, Luke, and Riley are leaving for the airport in a few minutes. Go get your bag."

"You're not listening," she answered, stubbornly. "I'm not going."

"Me neither," Riley said, standing by his big sister, even though he had no idea why.

Casey, Luke, and I stared at one another. No one knew how to tackle the situation, as all of us were pathetic newbies with no life skills when it came to defiant children.

"Luke, would you take Riley for a short walk? I'll text you when the car gets here."

Looking immensely relieved, Luke ducked out of the bus with a protesting Riley.

Casey addressed Sydney. "Where's this coming from? Why don't you want to go home? You have so much to look forward to. You have horseback riding camp and swim lessons and play dates."

"I don't care about any of that." Sydney bowed her head, her shoulders trembling. "I don't want to go back to that house."

"Your house?" Casey asked, glancing back at me as if I had some explanation for Sydney's sudden emotion.

I shrugged, as in the dark as her.

"Mom and Dad's house," Sydney choked out the words. "I don't like living in it anymore."

Then I understood. The memories were too much for her. The house symbolized all she'd lost. Dropping down to her level, I pulled her into my arms. Sydney shook miserably, and I could feel her heart breaking as she clung to me.

I sought out Casey for help, but she too was overcome by emotion, leaning against the kitchen counter for support.

"I get it Sydney, I do," I said, speaking softly. "The house is filled with memories of your mom and dad. And everywhere you go inside reminds you of them."

She nodded into my shoulder, gripping me tighter, as she continued to cry. Although I'd never lost someone like she had, I knew what it felt like to go back to a home that was no longer mine. Everything looked the same, yet nothing felt familiar. I knew the lessons I'd learned from my own tragedy might be of comfort to her, but was there a way to reveal my past without scaring her?

Treading lightly, I said, "When I was a little older than you, something bad happened to me too."

"I know," she said, pushing back from my shoulders and wiping away her tears. "You were kidnapped."

Although we'd never discussed it with her, I wasn't surprised that she'd heard of the kidnapping. Even though I thought of it as a secret, no one else apparently did. "Did your parents tell you that?"

"No. Kids at school. They know you're my uncle. They've told me stuff."

My stomach knotted at just the thought of what this little girl might have heard about me. "You know, not everything people say about me is true."

"They said you killed someone," she answered, matter-of-factly.

Okay. Well, shit. That was true.

"I told them you'd never do that," Sydney continued. "But then they showed me some websites that also said you killed someone."

I purposely didn't seek out Casey's help this time, more out of shame than anything else. Sydney had been subjected to information she was entirely too young to know all because she was connected to me. I could only imagine the things Grace and Quinn had heard when my story was the only thing in the news in our town for a year. This was the moment I'd always feared, and one of the main reasons why I didn't want a child of my own. There would come a time, as it had now with Sydney, that I'd have to admit to the things I'd done.

Swallowing back my pride, I said, "It's true. I did kill someone. But I didn't want to. Do you know what self defense means?"

"No."

"It means if someone is trying to kill you, you have the right to fight back and defend yourself. That's what I did. I fought back."

"And you killed him instead."

"Yes. But if I hadn't fought him, Syd, I wouldn't be here with you now."

She nodded her understanding… or so I thought. "He would have killed you like that girl killed my parents."

"Well, yeah. But…"

"I wish I had been in the car with my mom and dad. I would have self-defensed like you and killed that girl… and then my parents would still be alive."

"No, Sydney, that's not what I meant. It's not the same thing. The girl who killed your parents, she made a terrible mistake. She wasn't *trying* to kill them, though. I don't want you to spend your life angry at her and avoiding places that remind you of your parents, because if you do that, you'll grow up into a bitter, unhappy person."

Tears trailed lines down her cheeks. "I don't want that."

"No, and your parents wouldn't want that either. They'd want you to forgive that girl and move on. Honor your parents by living the best life possible."

Sydney and I stood there staring at one another. I couldn't imagine what she was thinking. So much for the pep talk I'd hoped to have with her.

Finally she answered, "Okay. I'll go home."

"And you'll smile and have a good summer?"

"I said I'd go home. I didn't say I'd be happy about it."

I reacted to her sass with a quirked brow, and Syd actually laughed. I hugged her tightly to me, glancing at Casey for the first time since our conversation began. She was understandably emotional, but there was also mad respect in her loving gaze.

"Jake?" Sydney said, stepping out of our embrace.

"Yeah?"

"What about you? Did you forgive him?"

My heart began to beat forcefully from just the memory of that last day, our final confrontation. He'd mocked me, beaten me to within an inch of my life, and when I was flat on my back with no fight left, Ray had attempted to strangle the life out of me. I was only alive today because he'd failed. What had happened to me was no accident. It was cold and calculating, perpetrated by a man who thrived on the pain of others. A person like that didn't deserve forgiveness.

Sydney's rich brown eyes watched me intently, her innocence demanding a response. I could have lied – should have, probably – but for the sake of my tortured soul, I offered her the truth.

"No, Syd, I haven't. And I never will."

Chapter Twenty

Casey

Forgiven

After bringing the kids back to Arizona, I lingered a few days at home. Just like Sydney, there were memories I hoped to recall and a person I needed to forgive. The woman who killed Darcy and Miles was barely a woman at all. Eighteen years old at the time of the accident, she'd also lost her life. Her family, in the throes of their own grief, had reached out to us at the time of the accident. They'd wanted to apologize, but at the time, none of us were ready to hear what they had to say. Now we were.

So I made the difficult call and arranged to meet with the woman's family at a local park. Mom and Sydney had chosen to accompany me, and as we crossed the grass, the three of us locked arms in solidarity. We were in this together. Always. And what we found at the end of the path was not the family of a monster but grieving parents of a young woman who was missed just as fiercely by her family as Miles and Darcy were by ours.

Her name was Beth, and she'd only recently graduated high school. She'd been a student at the local community college at the time she'd made the decision to send the fateful text that killed not only my brother and his wife but herself as well. She was human and she was loved… far from the hideous beast I'd pictured in my mind. As they spoke lovingly of their daughter, I could feel the weight lifting from me as the anger began to fade.

Sydney had remained stoic throughout the short meeting. Even when Beth's parents specifically apologized to her, she hadn't uttered a word. It wasn't until we were in the car on the way home that she finally spoke.

"I forgive her."

I returned to Jake with only two weeks left before the end of the tour. He would have already been done by now had he not been forced to reschedule dates that had been canceled due to our family tragedy. I was ready to go home. It had been a year of such ups and downs that we both needed a chance to just chill.

After the emotional meeting in the park where I followed Sydney's example and forgave Beth, I felt stronger and more determined than ever to reclaim the Casey I'd once been. Yes, I had bad days, but they were fewer and farther between. I poured myself back into work and spent more time around Jake's crew, joking and hanging out. Even Lassen and I had mended our rift and were on good terms once more, even though I still took the opportunity to mess with him when the opportunity arose.

Most importantly, Jake and I had found our rhythm again. We were back to being a team. I hadn't realized how much I'd missed the playful banter and sexy innuendos until they returned to our marriage in full force. In a year of extremes, it was only natural to keep the trend going.

"You got a minute?" I asked, sliding onto the couch next to Jake and grabbing the pillow to cradle in my arms.

He muted the TV and turned his body toward me. "What's up?"

"So, you know how since Miles's death I've been pretty erratic with my period, and charting my ovulation was all over the place?"

"Yeah."

That one word of his was loaded. I could see by the look of concern on his face that he was guessing where this was going… and he'd be right.

"Well, I haven't had my period for a while, and I thought it was just normal variation but, the thing is, I wasn't really paying much attention to my cycle because all my focus was on the kids."

"Just tell me, Casey. Are you pregnant?"

Jake didn't seem thrilled, but he wasn't upset either. If I had to describe his mood at the moment, it was decidedly neutral.

"I don't know, but I thought all week I'd be starting and I didn't. When I actually counted back, I realized it's been eight weeks since my last period. I don't know if I've ever gone more than six or seven weeks without one."

"Do you feel different?"

"No, not at all. I don't *think* I'm pregnant, but I also don't know why I haven't started. Anyway, I was going to ask Dom if he'd drive me to the store so I can pick up a pregnancy test."

Jake pulled out his phone.

"Who are you calling?"

"Sean. We've got all day. I'm going to see if he can get you a doctor's appointment."

"I don't need to see a doctor, Jake. Women have been peeing on sticks for a long time."

"Right, but none of those women are my wife. We're getting you an appointment."

I relented to Jake's request, and later that afternoon, we were brought in through the back door of the doctor's office and escorted into an exam room. The first thing they had me do was pee in a cup. I eyed Jake. All this pomp and circumstance could easily have been avoided.

"I hate to say I told you so," I said, exiting the bathroom with my brimming cup of urine. "But I told you so. Going on a stick would have been so much easier, by the way. Do you have any idea how hard it is to pee within the parameters of the cup? I thought I knew where my urine stream was coming from but I was totally off. Peed all over my hand."

Although not known for biting his nails, Jake was nervously chowing down. Upon hearing of my toilet trials, the stress lines in his forehead softened, the finger was removed from his mouth, and my hubby broke out into a grin. "Maybe keep that fascinating story between the two of us, huh?"

The nurse stopped in briefly to take my blood pressure before exiting with my pee cup. While waiting for the doctor to arrive, I examined the stirrups on the side of the table.

"How much would you pay me to put my feet in the stirrups and greet the doctor like that when he arrives?" I teased.

"Nothing," he said, shaking his head in amusement. "I would pay you nothing."

"Yeah, he probably wouldn't blink an eye anyway. Do you think he gets bored looking at vaginas all day?"

"I don't know," Jake said, wrapping his hands behind his head and leaning back in his chair. "I wouldn't."

"All day, Jake. He looks at them all day. You can't tell me that wouldn't get old after a while."

"Sure, Casey, whatever you say. It would be such a bore."

I extended my leg out to playfully kick him with my bare foot, but his reactions were spot on and he managed to scoot his chair back in the nick of time.

"Why'd you have to get me a male gynecologist anyway?" I complained.

"He was the only one I could get on such short notice."

"Oh, wonderful. Male *and* the last gyno left on the shelf. Goody."

Jake grinned, shrugging his shoulders at my remark. "I honestly didn't think it mattered."

"Of course it matters. Would you want a female doctor sticking her fingers up your dick?"

"Nooo..." He laughed. "I wouldn't want *anyone* doing that, male or female. Would you please just sit quietly until he gets here?"

"Fine, but he'd better not be hot."

Jake's eyes widened in surprise, but before he could respond to my off-color statement, the doctor walked through the door... and thankfully he was aging and rather unattractive.

He also cut right to the chase. "Congratulations. You're pregnant."

CHAPTER TWENTY ONE

JAKE

The Ugly Truth

I let the words sink into my dense skull. Casey was pregnant… with my child. I was going to be a father. Was it hot in here? The tingling sensation that had started in my toes had worked its way through my body and was now lapping at my ears. What had I been expecting? We'd been actively trying to get pregnant, so this outcome was bound to happen at some point, yet still it was shocking. Sure, I could play dad all I wanted with my niece and nephew, but they were already fully formed human beings. Any damage that had been done could not be credited to me. But my own child? Oh, man, I was going to have to mold that baby from birth.

While Casey peppered the doctor with questions, I let my mind wander. Fading into a trance-like state, I stared pathetically at the poster on the wall, which showcased the female reproductive organs. At first pass, it seemed fairly straightforward. I'd seen it all, you know, from the outside; but when I really started studying the inner workings, I honestly couldn't tell you where my baby was currently chilling out inside Casey. On a side note, did anyone else think the diagram detailing the fallopian tubes looked like the Texas Longhorn's mascot?

Squinting to get a better look at the illustration, I was interrupted by the doctor. "Jake, do you have any questions for me?"

Um, yeah, I had a whole buttload of them, but none I actually wanted to ask out loud. I must have made some ambiguous gesture with my head because both Casey and the doctor exchanged amused grins. Now I had to come up with something tangible to save face.

"When?" I asked. "How?"

"How?" Casey giggled. "Did you need me to explain?"

I glanced back at the diagram. Yes, actually. That might be helpful.

"No," I shook my head. "I meant… how old?"

"Haven't you been listening at all?" she asked.

"Sorry. I'm a little shocked at the moment."

"No worries," the doctor came to my rescue. "We'll get a more accurate age assessment once your wife has the ultrasound, but from what Casey has been telling me, I suspect she might be about two months along."

...and all I heard was, *You've got seven months to get your shit together.*

Casey was beaming from ear to ear as her legs swung back and forth from the raised table like an excited child. The doctor was answering more of her questions, but like before, I wasn't listening. My focus now was solely on my wife and that look of absolute exuberance on her face. How could I not be happy... for her? I needed to get with the program, and quick. This was happening whether I was ready or not. By acting like some drugged-out lunatic, I was robbing her of this moment.

Plastering a smile on my face, I grabbed Casey's hand and squeezed. Her eyes lit up, sparkling as if they'd been created from diamonds. I loved seeing her this way and would do anything in my power, and pay any price, for that smile to never fade from her lips for as long as we lived.

I knew what had to be done. I needed to be the man she thought she'd married. The man who'd promised her his whole heart, but so far had only given her a sliver. If only I'd had the strength required to face my issues head-on, I wouldn't be standing here now, at the eleventh hour, wishing for a miracle.

After saying our goodbyes to the doctor, Casey hopped off the examining table, grabbed my face, and kissed me with a loud smack of her lips.

"I love you so much. I can tell by your crazy eyes that you're a little freaked out, but I promise you, this is a good thing. You'll see."

Casey stripped off her gown and stood before me in her underwear and bra, her hands caressing her flat stomach. "Isn't it just incredible, Jake? Can you believe our baby is growing inside me?"

There was just something so graceful about her standing there stroking the baby she had already fallen hopelessly in love with. She looked like an angel. My eyes clouded in love, I wrapped her up in my arms. "You're so beautiful, Casey."

We held each other for a long time before she pulled back a little and ran her fingers over the worry lines in my forehead. "You've got that face again. What's wrong?"

"You want the truth?"

Casey nodded, appearing distressed. She'd obviously learned to brace herself over the years when it came to morsels of honesty from me. She needn't have worried, though. I wasn't about to ruin this moment for her. I pointed to the diagram on the wall.

"Where the hell is the womb?"

Once we were back on the bus, Casey went straight to the computer to read up on all things baby while I took a couple of Tylenol and lay down. I needed more to take the edge off, like a bottle of vodka, but I didn't want to offend Casey. It's not that I was unhappy with the news. I was just ambivalent. The struggles that lay ahead for me were tremendous. Not only was I going to have to take a trip back down memory lane, but I was also going to have to face *them*… the ghosts that haunted my dreams.

"Can we talk?" She asked.

Casey stood in the doorway, and I blinked her in. She looked different than she did this morning before she told me the news. No, there was no baby pouch or telltale signs of pregnancy, but there was definitely a change to her. She was calm and serene, as if the baby she was carrying had brought her the confidence and happiness to alter her entire mindset. I envied her. Would I ever get to the same place?

"What's up?"

She sat on the edge of the bed and lay her hand on my leg. "I'm sorry."

"For what?"

"Not giving you a choice. I'm so happy about this baby, but I also feel guilty because I pushed you into being a father, and I knew you were only doing this to make me happy. And now I'm ecstatically happy, and you're not."

"I'm not unhappy about the baby, Case. I'm just worried about not having enough time to fix all the things I need to fix before it comes."

"There's no rush, hon. Just try to achieve perfection by Christmas."

"Oh, right." I laughed. "That'll totally be doable."

Casey climbed over me on the bed and straddled my waist. She batted her eyes at me and used her fingers to mold a huge smile on my face. "I want to see a real smile, Jake. You're going to be somebody's daddy. Isn't that the coolest thing you've ever heard?"

"It is pretty cool," I conceded, smiling for real like she'd asked.

Suddenly the flirty girl was gone and Casey was peering intensely into my eyes. "All jokes aside, Jake. Do what you have to do. For me. For baby. For you. Just get it done."

Casey took an impromptu nap shortly after our conversation, but sleep was impossible for me because I kept playing her words over and over again in my head. *Do what you have to do.* She was right. I had to pull it together. The time for excuses had expired.

Taking out my phone, I clicked on my contacts, scrolling through until I found the one I was looking for. He was the last person I wanted to talk to, but the only one I really could.

Staring at his number for an agonizingly long while and trying to decide what to do, I finally made my decision. The phone rang a couple of times, and I was planning on just leaving a message until he unexpectedly picked up.

"Hello?"

"Hey. This is Jake McKallister. I need to talk to you."

We arrived home in Los Angeles the following week and I went to see him the same day. He stayed late for me. It had been the same when I'd visited him in the past. And just as I had before, I arrived at the empty office shrouded in a dark hoodie and shifting my eyes for potential spies. Certainly my entrance more closely resembled a drug deal rather than the therapy session I'd actually come for. The reason for my secrecy was simple: I was embarrassed. Seeking help felt like a shameful sign of weakness, not to mention the stigma attached to it all. The fact that I was seeing a therapist wasn't something I was ready to share with anyone, and if the press caught wind of it, the choice would no longer be mine.

But getting caught wasn't the only reason for the discomfort I was feeling right now. The last time I'd been in this office, I'd stormed out in a fit of rage. Not only had I never gone back, but I'd also ceased all contact with the man, freezing him out completely. And now, a full year later, I was forced to return to him with my tail between my legs.

Sure, I could have scouted out a new therapist, but that would have required a complete rehashing of all I'd already discussed with this guy. And believe me when I say those were not memories I wanted to relive again. For two months we had painstakingly dissected both the physical and sexual abuse I'd suffered at the hands of my abductor. I'd worked through emotions I never thought possible, and even though those were the toughest conversations I'd ever had in my life, they weren't the reason for the freak out that had ended my therapy sessions.

"Jake," he said, dipping his head slightly in greeting as he reached out to shake my hand.

"Hey, James."

We exchanged an awkward glance, or at least I did. I'd acted like a fool during our last session, and just the fact that he was seeing me now spoke to his level of professionalism. It wasn't like he'd been purposely torturing me. The guy was a therapist. Getting me to open up about my past was his job. Was it his fault that he'd unintentionally stumbled upon a landmine? Was it mine for exploding?

I still remembered his shocked face when I'd shoved my chair across the room, taking out a standing lamp in the process, before storming out of the office in a state of fury.

"If you'd allow me, Jake, I'd like to apologize. I tried to contact you after the session to explain to you what happened, but you blocked my calls and I had no way to get in touch with you."

"Sorry about that. I…"

He held his hand up to stop me. "I'm not blaming you. What happened was my fault. I wasn't regulating our session like I should have. Your reaction was not unusual in the treatment for PTSD. When talking about traumatic memories, some individuals do experience symptom relief, but others can actually become retraumatized by the therapy they're seeking. It's my job to monitor your reactions and tailor the intensity of exposure to those traumatic events. I failed to do that in your case. I didn't read the signs correctly, and for that I apologize."

It was the last thing I'd expected to hear from him, and my surprised reaction was not lost on James.

"If you give me another chance to work with you, I'll be more mindful of the signs and slow it down if you become overwhelmed."

"I… that wasn't what I was expecting. Are you saying my freak-out was normal?"

"For trauma therapy, yes, although I would have preferred you didn't break my lamp."

"I'll pay for that," I said, failing to mask my smile.

James waved off my offer. "So what made you call me?"

There was no time for games. I was here for a reason and time was ticking. "Casey's pregnant."

Other than a slight arch in his right eyebrow, he barely reacted to the news. And why would he? Women had babies every day. Why would this one be any different?

James watched me with insightful eyes, causing me to shift uncomfortably in place. He was in his mid-fifties, with a tall, lanky frame and floppy brown hair more suited for a Beatles cover band than a head shrink. He had this calming way about him that seemed able to pull things out of me I hadn't thought I'd ever reveal. Within days of our first session over a year ago, I was describing to him some of the worst memories of my life. Would that happen again? And more importantly, could he really read the signs of an impending explosion? My hands suddenly turned clammy as the need to spill my guts to him became stronger.

"Well, I suppose congratulations are in order."

Although I hadn't meant to, my mouth morphed into a grimace.

James didn't need to be a behavioral specialist to pick up on my non-verbal cues. Any old Joe on the street could have done it. I was just that transparent.

"Or…uh…" James chose his words carefully. "Perhaps I should have said, sorry."

"No, it's good. I mean it's my kid, right? I'm happy…" I looked up to the skies, as if the act of searching my brain for the correct feeling required a glance to the heavens. "Or… I'm…" I stopped myself again. Was there a better word? Happy implied I was pleased with the news of my impending fatherhood, which, just by my hesitation alone, proved I wasn't. But not being excited about your own child when you're married to a wonderful woman who dreams of being a mother? That's shitty. *Congratulations, kid, you've got an ungrateful asshole for a father. Have a nice life.*

Remembering I was still having a conversation with an actual person, I said, "No, I'm happy."

James studied me intently, the slightest of smiles registering on his face at my obvious indecision. "I'm glad you're so... *happy*."

"Thank you." I settled back into my seat grinning. If I continued with this level of uncertainty, it would be a long night.

"You know, a baby's a big life changer. It's common to feel apprehensive even when you're excited about the new arrival."

Pointing to him, I said, "Yes, that's what I meant to say."

I wasn't sure why I was making light of the situation because in a few minutes this room would be a somber death chamber, sucking the life out of all who entered. Thankfully, James was blissfully unaware of his looming fate. He gave me a courtesy smile before switching to his 'therapy' face. It really was a genius expression. With one brow tipped upward, indicating interest, while the other drooped ever to slightly in order to convey concern, James had taken attentive apprehension to a whole new level.

"What about Casey's pregnancy is concerning you?"

The knot in my stomach instantly tightened. This was what I was here for. It was time to man up and face my issues. Catching his eye I said, "Everything."

"Okay. Can you narrow that down a bit? 'Everything' is harder to work with."

Dropping my gaze, I studied my boots, focusing on a muddy splotch on the right toe and wondering where I'd gotten it. But then, who cared? It was mud. Shaking the thought from my head, I walked over to the chair and sank down into it. James followed me over to the one opposite mine and took a seat as well.

Looking up to meet his eye, I noticed James still staring keenly at me. Shit. That's what I was talking about. He had that way about him. He made me want to spill my soul. I could almost feel the truth traveling up through my throat, preparing for a dramatic exit. Hopefully, the man was true to his word and would stop me this time *before* I went berserk on his power appliances.

"Before the wedding, I told Casey I didn't want kids. I said it was because I was afraid they'd be ashamed of me, and that I didn't know how to explain to them what happened to me as a kid. And while that was partially true, there's a bigger reason why I don't want kids."

James shifted in his chair, studying me. "Go on."

Here went nothing. "I'm afraid I'm going to hurt my kid."

There. I said it. The ugly truth was out. Becoming Ray, and all the horrible things he represented, was my biggest fear. Well, that and the fucking ghosts who haunted me, but that could wait for another day.

James nodded his head as if it were a totally common fear. Did he not understand the implications? There was a very real possibility that a part of Ray was living inside me, just waiting for the right opportunity to turn me into the monster he had been. The last thing I wanted was to be like him – a killer, abusing my children they way he'd abused me. I'd seen, heard, and experienced things no human ever should, and now, as a result, I was afraid of my own goddamn self.

"Have you ever hurt a child, Jake?"

"No, but I'm not around them very often. I did have my niece and nephew staying with me for a while, though."

"And how did that go?"

"Fine. I didn't hurt them, if that's what you're asking."

"Have you ever wanted to hurt a child?"

Heat lapped up my ears as anger seeped through my pores. "No," I growled. I wasn't sure why I was pissed at him when it was me who'd brought the subject up in the first place.

"What about Casey? Have you ever raised a hand to her?"

"No, but sometimes I feel like my whole life is one big act. I try so hard to be normal, but I know I'm not. I feel like there are forces inside me that are just waiting for the right trigger. I was thirteen when all this happened, so who's to say what influence Ray had on me, and when his evilness will present itself? Can I really be trusted? I mean, you saw what I did to your goddamn lamp. Obviously, based on my past, I have a propensity towards violence when I feel threatened or angry."

"Taking your anger out on an object is not the same as taking it out on a person."

"Right, but it's the escalation I'm worried about. There are no guarantees that I won't become progressively more violent down the road."

"I get what you're saying, and your concerns are valid, but statistics are on your side. Only a very small percentage of abused children become abusers themselves."

"That's not what I've heard."

"There's some research that suggests a higher causal link between the two, but there's very little evidence to support that theory."

"Research doesn't look at special circumstances."

"No, that's true. Nor does it take the individual person into consideration. If Ray had raised you, I'd be more worried about the impact he had on your ethics, but as it was, you endured one month with the man – not enough time, in my opinion, to change your moral codes."

"Oh, you'd be surprised what one month with Ray could do to a person. Typically it resulted in a shallow grave, so yeah, this was a special circumstance."

"Then I supposed we have a place to start."

"If you thought the library was impressive, feast your eyes on this," Carol, the real estate agent, said dramatically, as she swept her arms out in front of her like a fairy godmother conjuring up the space through her magical wand. "A designer kitchen with white titanium granite countertops and Wolf sub-zero appliances. Isn't it just to die for?"

"Wow," Casey said, her eyes nearly as wide and full of wonder as the agent's. "Look at that refrigerator… and those cabinets… oh, and that pot rack. Wait a minute! Is that a Teppanyaki grill?"

"Yes it is," Carol answered proudly, as if she herself had been responsible for its placement in the kitchen island. "As you can see, the owner spared no expense."

No. That much was obvious. The place was a trophy house, and it was the fifth one we'd looked at today. I was honestly having trouble telling them apart. These stately mansions were too big and too fancy for my liking. I preferred smaller spaces; but as Casey had pointed out, we needed room to grow.

"What do you think, Jake?" the agent asked, eagerly awaiting my approval.

"Yeah. I like it," I said with as much enthusiasm as I could muster. Unfortunately, it wasn't enough to fool either one of them.

"Is it the kitchen?" Carol pinched her lips in a sign of distress. "Do you prefer darker colors?"

Honestly? Like colors would be a deal breaker in a goddamn mansion. "No. Anything works for me. The only thing I require in my kitchen is a smoke alarm. I use that as my cooking timer."

The real estate agent humored me with a courtesy chuckle, but Casey looked anything but amused.

"Carol, can you excuse us for a minute?" She grabbed my arm and steered me out of the kitchen without waiting for a reply. I didn't time it but I'm pretty sure it was a seven-minute walk to the front door.

Once outside, she asked, "What's going on with you?"

"Nothing, I'm hungry."

"You're hungry?" she asked, placing her hand on her ever-expanding waistline and taking on the expression of a pouty toddler. "Would you like me to go see if they have a juice box for you?"

Although Casey appeared to be genuinely irritated with me, her sarcastic response struck a nerve and I couldn't hold back the laughter. "Actually, that would be great, thanks."

After a moment's hesitation, Casey recognized the humor in her words and joined me in a light-hearted chuckle.

Taking my hand, she led me to the top step and we both sat down.

"Talk to me. I can feel your frustration. What's going on?"

"I don't know. According to my therapist, I don't like change, and this feels like a big one."

"We don't have to get this place or any of the others we've seen today, but we do need to move. I love the townhouse, I really do, but security there is not great, and like it or not, you need more of it now than you did when you bought that place years ago. Since all the neighbors use the same manned entrance, it's fairly easy for outsiders, or just friends of the neighbors, to make unwelcome visits."

"That almost never happens," I said, defending my bachelor pad.

"But it has, and I'm not willing to risk our baby's security. Are you?"

Well, when she put it that way… "No."

"So, like I said, it doesn't have to be this house, but I need you to be an active participant in this. I don't want to make this decision on my own."

"I know. I'll be good."

"Thank you," she said, laying her head on my shoulder. We sat quietly for a moment, looking out over the expansive grounds.

"This isn't the worst place ever," I conceded.

"No." She laughed. "It's not."

"It's just… these places she's showing us are just showpieces. It doesn't feel like anyone actually lives in them. I guess I just pictured something more homey – you know, instead of a football field, just a lawn with a swing set. And, would it be too much to ask for a white picket fence? I mean, come on."

"In this neighborhood?" Casey asked, amusement clear in her voice. She turned toward me, taking my face in her hands, and peppered a half a dozen small kisses onto my lips. "What am I going to do with you?"

"If you haven't figured that out by now, I feel sorry for you."

She laughed and stood up, bringing me with her. "You know what? You're right. Let's go find us a home."

James and I had been meeting two times a week for the past few months, and although it was slow going, I had worked my way through some important issues, mainly about fatherhood. We talked at length about the type of man Ray was, and I began to see with my own eyes that I was nothing like him. I'd almost forgotten the manipulations and the mind-games he'd played on me, until James had brought those memories back to the surface.

To a thirteen-year-old kid, Ray loomed larger than life, powerful beyond measure, a giant among men. But looking back now, I could see him for who he was – a small-minded man who was only as strong as I was weak. Using pain and fear as his weapons of choice, Ray swiftly and brutally shut down rebellion before it could take hold. Ray knew I was strong. He knew I would fight. So he tore my wings off before I could ever take flight.

It took a person void of a conscience to callously and viciously destroy the lives of so many. Ray lacked the most basic of all human traits – empathy. No, I wasn't like him at all, because despite the extended period of time I'd spent with the man, he'd never managed to beat the compassion out of me. And despite the drastic measures I'd been forced to take in order to save my own life, I crawled out of Ray's hell with my humanity intact.

I knew then that I'd be okay, that my future children would be okay, and with those opening credits out of the way, James and I were able to return to the place we'd been the day I'd stormed out of his office the year before.

"Tell me what life was like for you in the basement."

On the surface, it didn't seem like a loaded question, but to this day, the secrets I kept and the burden I carried all went back to the answer to that question.

"It was a torture all its own."

James looked up from his legal pad, no doubt checking me for signs of stability, but also urging me with his eyes to continue. This was why I was here – to get it out of my head so I wasn't the only one carrying the weight. The memories poured from me then, as I told him about the dwindling food supply, the bugs, and the mattress I slept on that was covered in dried blood. I shared with him the fear I experienced every time the lights went out, shrouding me in darkness, and how Ray would sometimes throw me a bone in the form of a tea candle, which I would then watch obsessively until the flame eventually fizzled out and died, just like everything else in the tomb of death I was imprisoned in.

But it wasn't the darkness or the lack of food or the hopelessness that caused me to flee from that final conversation I'd had with James. No, it was the seemingly harmless dripping of water that triggered my dramatic exit… or more importantly, what those leaking and creaking pipes meant to me while I waited for the end to come.

"It was alive."

"What was alive?" James asked, appearing more than a little intrigued.

"The basement. The pipes were so loud, and they dripped and screeched. Sometimes they made these groaning noises that sounded humanlike. I started hearing things that weren't there… and seeing things, too."

"What were you seeing?"

"Ray's other victims."

James lifted his eyes, no doubt trying to determine whether I was messing with him. "You were seeing ghosts?"

I shrugged because answering his question seemed redundant. I was the only survivor, so anyone I was seeing in that basement of horrors was most definitely dead.

"Did Ray tell you others died there?"

He didn't have to. The minute I was dumped into the basement, I knew it was a death chamber and that I'd never make it out alive. Flashes of memory flooded my senses, and I could feel my blood pressure begin to rise. Yes, there had been others; and yes, he had told me plenty about them; but it didn't take more than opening my eyes to know the fate of those who had come before me. I could see it on the blood-streaked walls, on the tally marks made on the frame of the bed, and in the box of souvenirs he'd kept with the belongings of each of his victims. Mine was already there, waiting to be filled.

But it wasn't those victims that haunted me. As warped as it sounded, they were the lucky ones. When the nightmare ended for me, so did it end for them. Those were not the ones who haunted my dreams, nor were they the ones who appeared to me from the faulty plumbing.

My ghosts were the forgotten ones… the victims even the police knew nothing about. In their late teens or early twenties, most had led hard lives before colliding head on with Ray. Unlike me, they'd been tricked to their deaths, mostly through promises of drugs or money. They were Ray's first victims, the ones not killed in the basement or dug up around his home. There had been no justice for these guys, no closure, no funerals, and no tearful goodbyes. They were the forgotten ones – the ones left in unmarked graves never to be heard from again. These were the ghosts who haunted me in my sleep, the ones I'd been running from for half my life.

I tried my best to explain all this to James, and when I was done and he was staring at me like I was the apparition in this story, I articulated in a clear, even tone. "I know this is going to sound crazy, but they spoke to me, James. They still speak to me."

"What do they say?"

I leaned in, struggling to find the words. "They want me to set them free."

CHAPTER TWENTY TWO

CASEY

Nesting

My parents made the trip with Sydney and Riley. Although I was five months pregnant, my mother didn't trust me to take it easy during our move to the new house, and if I was being honest with myself, neither did I. After the extreme fatigue and the up and down emotions of the first couple of months of my pregnancy, I was now five months along and feeling incredibly energetic. I'd taken to calling the baby Red Bull for the extra spring I now had in my step. And with the move and all, having my mojo back had been a major step forward.

"How are you feeling?" my mother asked me for the hundredth time.

"Happy."

"That's what I like to hear." She beamed.

"And you?" I lowered the shirt I was fixing to the hanger and checked for her reaction. She seemed to be searching for an answer. Her well-being and that of the kids was always at the forefront of my mind, and I worried that she was hiding her true feelings behind a stoic exterior.

"I'm happy too," she replied.

"Are you?"

Mom took my hand. "The sadness will always be there, and I've accepted that, but I have to be thankful every day for the kids. When I think about how much worse it could have been…" her voice trailed off. "Did you know they'd originally planned to bring the kids with them to the restaurant that night?"

"Yes. I heard."

"So, you understand why I also feel grateful? They could all be gone, but instead I have these wonderful kids to watch grow, and they make your Dad and me feel young again. Riley's just such a joy. His energy and boyish exuberance is so much like Miles at the same age that sometimes I feel like I'm raising him all over again. And Sydney…" Mom's eyes filled with tears. "She's like a beautiful, wild, raging river… all that intensity and strength, but with so many obstacles in her way. How she handles the changing courses will determine the woman she will one day be. I've never felt more essential and needed. I have her future in my hands, and I won't fail her."

"I know you won't." I smiled warmly at my awesome mom. "You've never failed any of us. And if I'm even half the mother you've been to me, my child will be so lucky."

"I don't know, Casey. If you're only half the mother I am, then I might have to step in and whip you into shape. This is my grandchild we're talking about."

I tossed a shirt at her. "Okay, then, I'll be better than you."

"Well, now you're just making crazy talk," Mom said, grinning. "You know what I can't wait for? Seeing Jake as a daddy."

I stiffened a bit, knowing his reservations with fatherhood. "I know he'll be great… but he's not convinced yet."

"I can see that. Jake takes time to adjust to new situations. But he'll come around because that man will do anything for you."

"Including having a baby when he doesn't really want one."

Mom waved it off. "Sometimes men don't know what they want. It's up to us to gently guide them in the right direction."

"You mean the direction we want them to go?" I corrected.

"Yes, that's what I said… the right direction."

As the last of the moving trucks exited through the front gate, Jake and I walked out to the circular driveway and took a moment to appreciate our new home. Although no way near the small, quaint homestead Jake had imagined, it was a place we could both get behind. Fully enclosed behind a security fence and shrouded by full, majestic trees sat our fairy tale home, with a multi-colored slate roof and a stone tower with ivy growing up the side. The grounds weren't huge, at least not in Hollywood terms, but they provided for a nice amount of space for outdoor activities and included a pool, basketball court, and a little vegetable garden enclosed by – you guessed it – a white picket fence.

"Do you love it as much as I do?" I asked, wrapping my arms around his waist and laying my head against his chest.

"I do. It feels like home. You know what I love best?" he asked, a smirk lifting up the corners of his lips.

"Shut up." I laughed, playfully punching him in the gut. We both knew what he was going to say – the guest-house. The reason being that his mother-in-law would be in another building when she visited. That had been the running joke from the moment my parents had arrived, although it had been my mother, not Jake, who started the whole thing by insisting he'd bought the place specifically to keep her out of the main house. Jake had only run with the punch line.

His jovial mood was a welcome change. There'd been a heaviness to his step for the past couple of weeks, and although he wouldn't tell me why, it was clear the therapy sessions were to blame. Sometimes I wondered if they were making him worse, not better.

And it didn't help matters that he was so guarded. Jake was open and honest with me in all aspects of our marriage except one: the kidnapping. It was a topic that had always been off-limits to me. Although I'd learned to live with the secrets Jake carried from his past, that didn't mean I liked it.

"You seem a little happier today."

Jake caught my eye for a quick moment before tipping his head and kissing my forehead. "Things will be better "soon. I promise."

"Really?" Perhaps there was too much surprise in my voice, but it was the first time he'd articulated an end to his melancholy.

"Yes, really. I know I've been weird lately, but there are some things I'm working out right now. I can't say what they are yet, but as soon as I can talk about it, I promise to tell you."

"Maybe I can help," I said, perking up. Was there really an end in sight?

His body tightened against me. I could feel his hesitation. "No. It's something I have to do on my own."

"I just don't understand why I can't be a part of whatever it is you're doing."

"I know, but you will understand. Soon, everyone will."

There was a strange foreboding in his words, but just as I was about to ask for clarification, Riley came barreling out the front door and flung himself full speed into Jake's arms. "Can we go in the pool now? You promised!"

"Did you help Grams pick up?"

"Yep, she said I could come get you."

Jake rumpled his hair. "Well, a promise is a promise."

I was still watching Jake, analyzing his body language for clues to this latest mystery. I had to assume that *some things I'm working out right now* explained why he'd been disappearing every day for hours on end.

"Riley, can you give us a minute?" I asked.

My nephew groaned, clearly impatient for his promised playmate.

Jake leaned into me. "Not now, Case. There's nothing I can tell you yet. Give me a couple more days and then you'll have the answers. Will you do that?"

"Do I have a choice?"

Jake shook his head. "No."

Chapter Twenty Three

Jake

Where They Live

Casey?" I whispered, waking her from a dead sleep. "Hey, I was wondering if you wanted to go for a drive with me."

With her hair splayed out every which way and her eyes still sealed shut, Casey definitely didn't appear in any shape to keep me company. I nudged her again. "Babe, wake up. It's 7:30."

"Go away," she mumbled, her limp hand trying to push me away. "It hurts when someone you love says mean things like 'It's time to wake up.'"

Smiling, I traced a strand of her hair and tucked it behind her ear. "I'll buy you a coffee if you come with me."

One eye emerged from under the pillow she'd placed over her face. "Starbucks?"

"Sure. Wherever. But no meet and greets. Strictly drive thru."

"As if I want people seeing me like this. I look like I swallowed a blowfish."

"You look beautiful." I commented on this statement, or some variation of it, daily. That was my standard reply – the only reply.

She removed the pillow completely and raised her brow. "Why are you up so early? Can't sleep?"

"Something like that." In reality, I hadn't slept a wink, knowing what was coming. "And it's 7:30, which is not early for most people."

She pulled the sheet up over her head, hiding until I yanked it clear off her body. "Ugghh," Casey groaned.

"Let's go. I'll give you thirty minutes to get yourself ready."

"Thirty minutes?! I'm not a magician, Jake." Flinging the sheets off her body, Casey padded off to the bathroom grumbling, "But I'll do what I can to not look like a troll."

I grinned at her cranky response. "That's all I ask."

Waiting for Casey, I stood in the hallway, gripping my keys in one hand and, in the other, a twelve-year-old piece of paper featuring a list of cryptic directions pointing to a hidden location. Written from memory, it was a treasure map of sorts, but there would be no reward at this end of this path. I smoothed the worn paper with my fingers. The list was almost unreadable at this point and of no significant value to me. I certainly didn't need it to get where I was going. Each line on this tattered parchment was burned in my memory for life. Truth be told, I only carried it with me now for emotional support. It was a reminder that I wasn't crazy, and that where I was going was more than just a place that lived in my nightmares. It was real and as tangible as the paper in my hand. And after today, it would never be a secret again.

#1. From highway, take Poplin Rd.

"You're pulling in here?" Casey asked, scanning the surrounding area with a puzzled expression on her face. "Is this even a road?"

#2 At 3.24 miles, turn right onto a dirt path.

"Not officially. It's a back way onto the property."

"Whose property? Yours?"

"No. Not mine."

I expertly dodged the overgrown flowering bushes and the branches hanging so low off the trees that they smacked my windshield on multiple occasions. The dirt road I was driving along led to a sprawling farm about twenty miles north of Santa Barbara. This seemingly tranquil place was anything but, however. Its grounds held a terrible secret.

I pulled up to a locked gate, put my Jeep in park, and hopped out.

"What is this, Jake? Are we supposed to be here? Isn't this private property?"

#3. Enter 8652 into the master lock

I hadn't been here in years, and it was possible that the lock had changed. If that were the case, I had a chain cutter that would get me through the gate. But, to my surprise, there was no lock. All that was required was unclipping the gate and pushing it open. I walked back to my Jeep and continued driving.

#4 Left at fork in dirt road.

Casey's eyes were fixed on me now. She seemed to get that more was happening than just a leisurely afternoon drive. I pulled to a stop.

#5 Old barn with metal shingles

Exiting the vehicle, I walked around to help Casey out and then stood for a moment, staring at the old structure and gathering my courage. Dragging a deep breath in, I walked to the barn and, as I had in countless dreams, laid my hand against the tattered paneling. It was parched and unyielding, not like in my nightmares where the wood planks had a heartbeat and blood dripped from the cracks.

"Does this place mean something to you?" Casey asked, gripping my arm.

I heard her words but was too caught up in the moment to immediately answer.

"Jake? What is this place? Why have you brought me here?"

"You wanted to know my secrets."

Casey squinted, blinking out the sun, as she examined the barn.

"Do you remember on our honeymoon, when you asked what I was having a nightmare about?"

"Yes. I remember… you said ghosts."

"This place here," I said, gesturing over the farm, "this is where they live."

"Live?" she asked, shifting positions and rubbing her arms. I could see the goosebumps traveling up them as she spoke. "What exactly are you showing me here?"

"My nightmare, Casey. I'm showing you my nightmare."

She stared at me for the longest time, and I wasn't sure if I should continue or wait for her to catch up. Finally she took a step away from both the barn and me. That was when I knew my words had sunk in.

"Did he take you here?" Her voice shook as she spoke.

"No. Not me. Others… five others, to be exact, and this is where they died."

Again she took a step back, but now I could see real fear in her eyes. I grabbed Casey's arms to steady her. "Shit. This was stupid. I shouldn't have brought you here."

"No. I'm fine, just shocked. Give me a second to process, okay?"

I nodded, assuming the wait would be long, but Casey was a decisive woman and had a whole barrage of questions ready for me in a matter of seconds.

"How long have you known? Did Ray tell you about them? Are they buried in the barn?" The last question was whispered, as if she didn't want the ghosts to hear.

I reached into my pocket, pulled out the instructions, and placed them in her hand.

Casey unfolded the paper and I watched as she read the directions. "Is this what I think it is?"

I nodded, touching the wall of the barn. "A map to them. The boys who died here."

"Where did you get this?"

"I wrote it… from memory… so I wouldn't forget."

"So Ray told you about this place, then? About killing these boys?"

"Yes."

She pointed at the map. "How do you know he was telling you the truth? Maybe he lied to you. Maybe nothing is here at all."

"He wasn't lying, Casey. There was no reason for him to. As far as he was concerned, I was never leaving the basement alive. What did he care if I died holding his secrets?"

"But it doesn't make any sense. He killed all the others at the house. Why here?"

"These were his first victims. He didn't own that house when these guys were killed. Ray's father used to work on this ranch and brought him here as a kid. He knew every inch of this property and knew that the land was so vast that no one would ever hear screams coming from this barn."

She shook her head, either not yet willing to accept my explanation or just unable to fully process it. Studying the list of directions in her hand once more, something seemed to click into place for her, and she asked, "You've followed this map before, haven't you?"

Yes, I'd been here before, even sitting by their graves and apologizing for my cowardliness. Why couldn't I free them? What was this hold Ray had over me? Why did I insist on keeping his secrets? To lessen my guilt, I'd anonymously sent money to their families and prayed for their souls but I'd never had the courage to do the one thing they'd asked of me… until now. Today I took back control.

In that moment, a strange sensation crawled up my spine, raising bumps on my skin. They were here, crowding around, impatiently waiting. Had they known this was coming? Did they see me meeting with the FBI over the past few weeks and identifying them, not only by name, but also through their missing person reports? Had they watched as search warrants were secured and a recovery plan was put in place? Did they know about the memorial funds I'd set up in their names to help their families with burial costs or the interview I'd scheduled for the following day to publicly acknowledge the discovery of their bodies? Did they experience time the same way we did and if so, would they forgive me for taking so long to finally extract myself from Ray's iron grip? And most importantly, once I gave them their peace, would they finally grant me mine?

Not trusting myself to speak, I answered Casey's question with a nod.

Sensing my fragile state of being, she placed her hand on my chest and whispered, "Why? Why didn't you just… just…"

"Tell someone?" I finished her question, shame licking up my heated skin. "I don't know why."

We stood silently, her expression twisted in pain…for me. She deserved more but the words were stuck in my throat. There was so much I needed to say to her but that required a courage I wasn't sure I possessed.

"I'm sorry," I whispered.

Casey traced my face with her hands as a tear trailed down her cheek. "Why are you sorry? There's no reason."

"There is. So many reasons. I'm so ashamed of myself, Case. I did this. I kept them here all these years. All I had to do was just tell someone, anyone. They had lives. They had families… people who loved them… people who still don't know what happened to them. I was the only one who could save them, and I did nothing. I was such a fucking coward."

Casey stepped even closer, hands still touching my face. "No one knows what it was like being you… how much you hurt. You did the best you could, and I will never look at you as a coward. You didn't put them here, Jake. This… *isn't*… your… fault."

I clutched Casey to me, my throat holding back something between a howl and a roar. *Why me?* The two words I swore I'd never say threatened to escape through clenched teeth. They were weak words, pathetic, really, and didn't deserve to be allowed passage. Yet my whole life could be summed up by that simple question. Out of everybody he could have chosen, why had Ray picked me?

People speak of fate – the predetermined course of a person's life – but I'd always refused to believe I'd been placed on this earth solely to be the plaything for a demented killer. And so I worked to change my destiny, pouring my soul into music and making a name for myself outside of Ray's demented control. I reconnected with my family and made lifelong and lasting bonds. And, most importantly, I opened my heart up to a beautiful woman and allowed myself to love.

I did all those things to prove that fate didn't own me. But now I realized what a fool I'd been. I could change my destiny all I wanted, but I could never outrun my fate. Almost my whole life had been lived in his clutches. Ray's secrets were now my own, and his crimes had become my cross to bear.

As if it weren't bad enough that he'd taken away my freedom and my innocence, Ray had also taken any chance I might have had at a peaceful life by forcing his memories on me with his boastful claims of death and destruction. I couldn't even close my eyes at night without the fear that his victims would visit me in my sleep. Jack, Anton, Ren, Wilson, and Felix. I knew their names and had seen their faces, both dead and alive. I knew the towns they'd lived in before Ray destroyed them and who their families were and what they'd been like in life. But I also knew what their last words had been, how they died, and where they were buried. I knew all this because Ray had bound me to them for all eternity.

And when I'd come home, a tragic shell of myself, I'd tried to forget, blocking them from my memory for years until one day they found their way through the barriers of my mind and infiltrated my dreams. They weren't ghosts at all, but living memories forced upon me by the man to whose fate I'd been forever linked.

Yes, I should have told someone; but like Casey said, no one knew what it was like being me. There was no handbook for me to study or any tried and true path I could follow. I had to find my way through hell on my own, and the mistakes I made had brought me here into the loving embrace of the woman who was willing to forgive my sins for no other reason than because she loved me and trusted that my heart was good.

"I promised you answers, Casey, and I'm ready to lay myself bare for you, but first, there's something I have to do. I'm not going to keep his secrets anymore. This ends today."

I tipped my head in the direction of a row of SUVs driving toward us. They'd come in through the front gate at the main house, where they'd had to stop first to deliver the warrant. That's where I was supposed to meet them too, but my need to follow the map was too strong. This was the last time I'd ever come here. After today, I would burn those morbid directions and never feel guilt for them again.

In response to Casey's questioning stare, I replied. "They're with me."

Casey stayed behind for the rest of my journey, although she did put up a good fight. I understood she wanted to be there for me, but this was something I needed to finish on my own. James, who'd arrived in one of the vehicles, remained at the barn with Casey. I didn't need him because the closer I got to the end, the stronger I felt.

#6 Due South. A single boulder in the meadow with five marks carved in the base of the stone.

I led the agents to the place on the map where the bodies could be found, and then stepped back out of the way and watched them work. Although there was some doubt amongst the FBI agents that anything would be found, I knew better. They were there, waiting. Soon their purgatory would come to an end, and then they would be free.

It had taken me a long time to right the wrong, but now that I had, my hope was that there might just be a little bit of peace left over for me. My fate might have been tied to Ray's, but he didn't have any more rights to our story than I did. I could, and would, change the narrative. He didn't get to write the ending. I did.

About an hour into the dig, sudden activity caught my attention. I knew it then; I could feel it. They'd been found. The tightness in my chest instantly eased as I breathed out a sigh of relief. My voice low, I spoke to them for the last time. "Rest in peace, brothers."

They were finally going home.

Later that night, Casey and I were nestled under blankets by the fire and sipping hot chocolate. It was one of those rare nights in Los Angeles where the temperatures had dipped down into the 30s. And yes, while I was aware that such a temperature was considered downright balmy in some parts of the country, here in Southern California, we were a bunch of ridiculous cold weather wusses.

"My toes are frozen solid," Casey complained, before proceeding to prove it to me by running her ice-cubed digits along my leg.

"Stop it," I protested, flinching away from her. "You're going to give me frostbite."

"Speaking of frostbite, I'm worried about the orange trees out back. Do you think they're going to freeze over and die?"

I didn't have a lot of experience with Arctic temperatures, but it seemed logical to assume that tropical trees would be as pampered and fragile as we So Cal babies were. "Probably, yes."

"Maybe you should go out right now and pick the ripe oranges so they don't all die and go to waste."

"See, here's where I question your use of pronouns. It sounded like you wanted just *me* to go into the frigid outdoors… to pick oranges for *you*."

Casey laughed as she pulled the blanket higher. "Okay. You're right. Let the oranges die a glacial death. If it's a choice between juicy, colorful fruit and your ballsack, I'll pick the family jewels any day. No way is this baby going to be an only child."

"No way do I want it to be."

"Really?" she said, gazing up at me with stars in her eyes. "You want more?"

"Well, let's get this one out of you first, but yeah, why wouldn't I?"

"Well, you weren't real thrilled about this little one at first," Casey whispered as she pointed to her extended belly. "I don't want it to hear."

Reaching my hands out, I cradled her stomach before bending down and kissing my baby. "I'm ready now."

Casey ran her fingers through my hair, warming me with her loving gaze and gentle touch. "Ready for what, babe?"

"For him. My son. I'm ready to be a father."

Chapter Twenty-Four

Casey

Epilogue

Cold, bright, sterile. My hand was locked in Jake's, and fear and excitement kept my body in a constant state of shivers. In just a few minutes, this would all be over, and I would be holding my baby. I closed my eyes and made a silent plea for a healthy child and a safe surgery. It was a scheduled C-section, but that didn't rule out complications. Apparently, the baby was too big to pass through my average-sized pelvis. Damn the McKallisters and their perfectly robust babies.

"I'm just about to cut the bag," the doctor announced.

I glanced at Jake, who seemed a bit paler than normal.

"You're not going to pass out on me, are you?" I asked.

"No, I'm fine," he answered, making a show of standing up straighter. He was staying strong for me, but I could imagine that seeing my stomach opened up wouldn't be the most pleasant sight for him.

"You're a trouper," I complimented him.

"Me?" He chuckled, nervously shifting from side to side. "I'm not the one with hands in my stomach."

The doctor interrupted. "All right, Casey, you're going to feel some tugging now as I pull the baby out."

Looking to my husband for support, I found comfort in the intensity of his stare. Jake tightened the grip on my hand. He was my protector, and I felt safe with him by my side.

"We're almost there," he whispered.

I bit down on my lower lip and nodded. This was it. Every struggle we'd been through culminated here, in this room… with our baby. Jake broke eye contact with me the minute a hollow scream emanated from behind the sterile screen.

"Listen to that talker," the doctor marveled. "Already screaming and not even born yet."

"That doesn't surprise me," Jake said, his voice sounding full of both amusement and pride.

And then a real shriek, loud and insistent, echoed through the room.

Mesmerized by the birth of his child, Jake completely forgot about me, but I wasn't the least bit offended. In fact, nothing made me happier than to see my husband fully vested in our baby. Once fearful he wouldn't be a good father, Jake had bravely worked through his issues and, in the process, had come to embrace his new role as a daddy.

I studied his face for reaction. It was my only guide to what was happening on the sterile side of my body, and when I saw the smile light up his face, all my worries fell away.

"He's here," Jake said with nothing but awe in those simple words. "And he's perfect."

Tears of joy flooded my eyes as I waited for a glimpse of my new little man. Squeezing Jake's hand tighter, I felt the force of our connection. Every shared milestone became a memory we could look back on with love and pride – and this, the birth of our son, was a triumph that would last us a lifetime.

A nurse carried the baby to me, rubbing his cheek up against mine. With his red, swollen eyes, splotchy skin, and screams so loud they ricocheted off the walls, our baby boy was pissed off and he wanted the world to know. I could only assume his current mood was the result of being kicked out of his nice, warm apartment only to be man-handled by the landlord's hired help.

"It's okay, sweetie, you're all right," I soothed. He instantly reacted to the sound of my voice.

"He knows you," Jake said, marveling at the connection we'd already made. But I wasn't surprised at all. This wasn't our first meeting; not really. I'd been talking to him non-stop since the day I found out I was pregnant. And mine wasn't the only voice he'd been hearing.

"Sing the song for him," I urged. "He loves it."

And so Jake softly crooned the chorus of a ballad he'd written specifically for his son – a song that had instantly pacified the rising soccer star who'd lived and kicked in my belly for the last nine months. And just as he'd done countless times before, our baby listened. The screaming subsided, and both Jake and I gazed at his gorgeous face. He was a miracle created from our love, and the reason for the joy that filled our hearts on this momentous day.

"Okay, mom and dad, I'll bring him back soon. We just need to warm the little guy up." The nurse smiled affectionately, looking between us, before whisking our son away.

"Casey, you've got a little more work to do," the doctor said. "Jake will follow the baby to the warmer while I deliver the placenta."

"Okay." I nodded, feeling a sudden chill race over my skin.

Jake bent down and brushed his lips across my forehead. "I'll be right over there." He seemed just as hesitant to let go of my hand as I was with his.

"It's okay. I'll be fine. Keep an eye on our baby."

"You know I will."

And then Jake was gone. And the baby was gone. My only connection to either of them were the occasional updates Jake called out to me. I lay there for what seemed a very long time, alone on the cold table, dreaming of the moment I would be rejoined with the other half of my beating heart. I closed my eyes and waited.

"Casey," the doctor's voice boomed loud as he zapped me from my trance. "Everything went fine. We're going to transfer you to recovery, and then we'll get you all set up in a comfortable room. There's someone who wants to see you."

My droopy eyes snapped to attention when the nurse returned with Jake and our baby. Suddenly the sterile room erupted with color, and my body warmed as if it were basking in the sun's rays. The moment he was placed in my arms and those liquid blue eyes gazed upon me, it felt like the world had stopped spinning. He was mine. Ours. I wondered if my heart was big enough to hold all this new emotion.

"He's a big boy," she announced. "Eight pounds, eleven ounces, and twenty-two inches long."

I flicked my eyes at Jake, rolling them dramatically. He grinned. It was our running joke, and I couldn't help but point out his culpability in the size issue.

But I was only willing to spare a second away from the beauty that was in my arms. "Well hello there, handsome.

I'm your mom. I've been waiting a long time to finally meet you in person."

Jake cradled the back of the baby's neck and bent down to kiss his chubby little cheek. "Welcome to the world, little guy. It gets better, I promise."

I gazed adoringly at my loving husband and treasured son, feeling nothing but grateful for the life I'd been graced with. It wasn't that long ago my spirit had been broken in half by the loss of Miles, my beloved brother. At the time, I couldn't even imagine a moment as beautiful as this one would be waiting for me down the road. That was the truly wonderful part about life – it just kept moving along, bringing with it new and unexpected surprises for those willing to open their hearts and minds to love. I kissed the top of the baby's head and then reached my hand up to run it along Jake's stubbled jaw.

Bursting with happiness, I whispered to my men, "It doesn't get any better than this."

CHAPTER TWENTY-FIVE

JAKE

Epilogue

My heart pumping wildly, I pushed through the double doors and into the sitting area where both my family and Casey's were awaiting the news. Although everyone had been aware of the gender months before his birth, I still felt the need to announce it to our loved ones.

"It's a boy! Casey and baby are doing great."

"Oh, thank goodness," Linda said, blowing out a long, relieved breath. She and my mother exchanged a quick hug.

"How are you holding up?" my father asked, feigning concern.

"I was a little queasy, I'm not going to lie," I answered, a smile spreading across my face. "But I stayed upright, so you lose."

"Yes!" Kyle jumped from his chair. "Pay up, old man."

"Nope," my father shook his head, unwilling to accept defeat. "First I want confirmation from Casey."

"The lack of blood speaks for itself," Kyle protested. "You're just stalling."

Yep, they'd bet on whether I'd pass out in the operating room, and my own father had been hoping for a full-on smelling salts revival.

"Scott, you need help," my mother said, waving him off before asking about the baby. I went on to share his impressive measurements, his fiery disposition, and just his overall perfection.

Sydney flung her arms around my waist. "When can I see the baby?"

"As soon as they move Casey into her room and she's feeling up to visitors, I'll come get you."

Holding the baby in my arms, I rocked him back and forth, singing softly in his ear. Casey was on her way over from recovery and the first thing I wanted her to see when she came through the door was me being the father she always knew I could be. From the very start of our relationship, Casey's faith in me had been absolute and unwavering, and that, in turn, had given me the strength to face my demons and free the guilt that had slowly been chipping away at my battered soul. Casey had given me the one thing money could never buy: hope.

Now I could see the path ahead, and it was a beautiful one, filled with love and laughter and babies. There was a time where I wouldn't have dared dream of such a life. I couldn't imagine there would ever be a white picket fence or a beautiful wife or a team of kids running around. Not for me. But I'd been wrong. Through all the trials I'd faced in life, through all the spilled blood, and through all the hopeless tears, all it had taken to save me was the love of a patient woman.

The baby jerked in my arms as the peaceful little face I'd been gazing upon shifted without warning. Suddenly, my son was seized by a nightmare of his own making. I watched in fascination as his lips pouted and his forehead wrinkled in consternation. What perils could he possibly have faced in his very short existence? I could see maybe if he'd had a rough passage through the birth canal, or had a cord wrapped around his neck; but as it was, he'd had a fairly cushy entrance into the world.

"What do you have to be scared of, little guy?"

Running my fingers along his newborn skin and speaking in soft, soothing tones, I tried to lessen the frightening effects for him. No one asked for nightmares to invade their slumber, and it seemed especially unfair for one so young to suffer.

"You're safe. I won't ever let anything happen to you."

I wiggled my finger into his palm, and the baby gripped it tightly, as if he'd heard my solemn promise and was asking to shake on it. I wavered a moment, wondering how I could guarantee him safe passage in a world filled with dangers, both big and small. And did I really want to keep him safe from all harm? How would he grow into a strong, confident man if he never experienced real life? As tempting as it was to package him up in bubble wrap and send him on his way, I couldn't do that to my child. Just because my life had been filled with fright didn't mean he had to live his in fear. My son deserved the chance to make his own mistakes and earn his own scrapes and bruises. I wanted him to be a child free from worry, and for that to happen, I had to let him live.

"Within reason," I conceded.

My son opened his eyes at the sound of my voice, and for one magical moment, we connected. I was his dad, and if I played my cards right, he'd love me for the rest of my life. My fear of fatherhood had been misguided from the start. Kids didn't care what challenges you'd faced or what poor decisions you'd made. They were clean slates, open books ready and willing to be written in. All they needed was love and guidance, with a splash of fun, in order to grow into the people they would one day be; and those were things that without reservation I knew I could provide.

And, yes, one day we'd have that tough discussion and I would tell him my story because, just like with Sydney, if I didn't, someone else would. But I wasn't worried. This boy came from the sturdiest of stock. He was a Caldwell and a McKallister. It didn't get more resilient than that. Besides, I no longer felt the need to hide from my past. Every step I'd taken in my life had led me here – to this chair, cradling my newborn son in my arms.

Casey was rolled into the room a few minutes later, sitting up and looking strong and healthy, wearing a smile on her face that stretched from ear to ear.

"Gimme. Gimme. Gimme," she said, reaching for her baby.

"One more minute, mama," a nurse said, as she and another transferred Casey from the rolling bed into the plush bedding of her very own five-star baby birthing suite.

Once Casey was situated, I stood carefully and brought him to her side.

"He's so beautiful, Casey," I said, kissing his head, which was spattered with an impressive showing of dusty blond hair. "Can you believe he's ours?"

Gently I lay him in her arms. The moment they touched, I could feel their connection, and I watched in awe as the baby responded to her. He knew her, and my god, I think he already loved her. It was a powerful bond: mother and son. My own had given me life – more than once – but never had I been so grateful for her until just this moment when I witnessed my own son receiving the same gift I'd been given – that of a loving, protective mother.

"You don't know it yet," I said to my boy, still running my fingers over his wispy locks, "but you just won the mom lottery."

"And you don't know it yet," Casey cooed, "but your daddy's a famous rock star, and you're going to have the coolest damn life."

My voice was still in baby-talk mode when I added, "But only if you're not named Bart… which is what your mommy wants to name you. Doesn't that suck?"

"Jake, you know how I feel about the name," she said sounding entirely serious; but there was no hiding that smile of hers. "Besides, I already signed the birth certificate."

My eyes bugged out of their sockets before I came to my senses. I had yet to see this birth certificate she spoke of, so I was fairly certain she was just punking me.

Casey's nose crinkled up as she laughed at my reaction. "I'm kidding. How about this? I have a compromise for you. If I let you pick the boy names, can I name any future girls?"

I considered her treaty before responding. "Only if the names don't suck."

"Sucky names are in the eye of the beholder, Jake. Deal or no deal?"

I realized that I was most likely throwing my future daughters under the bus, but what could I do? I had to save my son. So – sorry Enid. I tried.

"Deal!"

Casey smiled and gazed upon our tiny son. "Well, then, hello Slater Scott McKallister. It's nice to finally meet you."

I contacted the visiting committee, inviting them to our birthing suite to meet baby Slater. There were rules on the number of people allowed to visit, but clearly they'd made an exception for us if only to get out of the path of the stampede that was now filing through our door.

As they filled every corner of the room, each wore the same dreamy, happy smile, and all were offering up a handshake, kiss, or hug. The cooing was nearly unbearable as everyone got his or her first look at our son. Casey took it all in stride, proudly offering our perfect specimen of a child up as proof of what superior genetic intermingling could create.

My father was the last one in, and he had to duck under the doorframe to keep from clipping the top of the head of the little blond passenger riding on his shoulders.

"Oh," he gasped, upon catching sight of his newest grandchild. "Look at that little beauty. Let the spoiling begin."

Those weren't just words, either. My father was a master spoiler and the worst possible example for growing minds. He did anything for a laugh, and that included gurgling water at the dinner table, spitting out food, and accidentally slipping out words that were decidedly not G-rated. So hysterically inappropriate was he that we'd been forced to assign a title to his behavior… Grampie Manners. His grandchildren knew they could only emulate his actions around him. Any outside Grampie Manners were strictly forbidden.

Touching Casey's arm gently, my mother asked, "Are you in a lot of pain?"

"I don't feel anything yet, but I'm figuring it'll be smarting real soon."

"Oh, please," Kyle scoffed. "I get so tired of women complaining about how childbirth is the most painful thing ever. Obviously they've never stepped on a Lego."

"Whoa, buddy," Kenzie said, laughing as she grabbed his hand and steered him away. "Sorry, Casey. I try but sometimes it's just a losing battle."

"Mommy," called the toddler currently residing on my father's shoulders, holding his arms out and wiggling to get down.

"Hold on, I'm getting you," my dad said, making an effort to remove the boy.

"I got him." Reaching up, I plucked the tow-headed tot off his perch. Arms immediately wrapped around my neck as he nestled against me.

"Were you a good boy while we were gone?" I asked, giving the fifteen-month-old child a kiss on his silky smooth cheek.

He nodded, his hair bobbing up and down, but he was no longer interested in me. His wide, curious eyes were trained on his mother and the newborn baby in her arms.

"Look what I have," Casey said, smiling up at him.

Setting the squirmy toddler on the bed beside her, I asked our firstborn, "What do you say, Miles? Are you ready to meet your little brother?"

The End

Made in the USA
Middletown, DE
14 March 2022